Jackie FRENCH

Legends
of the
Lost Lilies

Angus&Robertson
An imprint of HarperCollins*Publishers*

Angus&Robertson
An imprint of HarperCollins*Publishers*, Australia

HarperCollins*Publishers*
Australia • Brazil • Canada • France • Germany • Holland • Hungary
India • Italy • Japan • Mexico • New Zealand • Poland • Spain • Sweden
Switzerland • United Kingdom • United States of America

First published in Australia in 2021
This edition published in 2022
by HarperCollins*Publishers* Australia Pty Limited
ABN 36 009 913 517
harpercollins.com.au

A catalogue record for this book is available
from the National Library of Australia

ISBN 978 1 4607 5501 3 (paperback)
ISBN 978 1 4607 0938 2 (ebook)

Cover design by Lisa White
Cover images: Woman © Ildiko Neer / Trevillion Images; flowers
by istockphoto.com
Author photograph by Kelly Sturgiss
Typeset in Sabon LT Std by Kirby Jones

Printed and bound in the UK using 100%
Renewable Electricity at CPI Group (UK) Ltd

Chapter 1

I taught the arts of love for many years, so perhaps I am the only
person to be surprised never to have been asked, 'Have you ever
killed a man?' The answer is, 'Yes.'
   One of them was myself.

Miss Lily, 1942

THE ENGLISH CHANNEL, OCTOBER 1942

SOPHIE

She should have learned to knit. Or be sitting safely in her office, sipping tea weak enough for four cups a day till the next ration coupons were due, while deciding the ideal amount of salt gravy to add to each can of Higgs's 'bully beef' for the army.

Instead Sophie Greenman née Higgs, Countess of Shillings, buffeted by invisible air currents, clung to her seat in a grey plane in grey cloud, as if the war had sucked away all colour. Even the grey waves of the English Channel below them had vanished. Perhaps the entire world had disappeared into the impossibility that allowed another world war to happen.

More likely German fighter planes would flash through the cloud at any moment, spitting fire and death. Her first warning would be pain, and then unconsciousness (she hoped) as the plane dropped, flaming. She fought to keep a pleasant smile on her face in case the pilot next to her glanced in her direction. But he focused on his controls and the grains of grey beyond the cockpit.

What was she even doing there?

Once, in another world war, a much younger Sophie had risked her life each day. Now that life was owed to her husband, Daniel, his face clouded with loss he would not express aloud as he'd waved at the plane rising from the Thuringa landing strip; to her daughter, Rose, now sixteen, her life divided between boarding school, young men and the Red Cross; and to Danny, her son, resolutely insisting he would volunteer to join the forces in New Guinea as soon as he was eighteen and defend Australia from the enemy.

Instead his mother had flown across the world to join the battle. Mothers were supposed to step back in war, to be the helpmates, the comforters, to keep the home fires burning. They could be Rosie the Riveters in factories perhaps, but not vanish in a Lancaster aircraft. Rose and Danny would not even know yet that she had gone.

The pilot's eyes flickered again to his instruments, then back to the grey around them, fine as sifted flour.

'Hope you're a good shot,' said Sophie. Once she had discovered that the pilot knew nothing more than his orders to fetch her, she had spoken little to him, focused on paperwork, directions for the factories that must continue at maximum production in her absence.

The man smiled wryly. 'No idea. I've never fired a gun.'

'What? George, you're in the air force.'

'Why do you think that?'

'I assumed ...' When a telegram arrives from the head of one of Britain's most secret agencies, summoning you urgently to England, and two hours later a plane that has crossed a world at war to fetch you lands in your home paddock, it was natural to assume the pilot who insisted you must leave with him at once was in the RAF, even if he wore no uniform and the plane discreetly had no insignia.

'I'm a conchie, a pacifist. Mr Lorrimer pulled some strings to get me assigned to his organisation.' George stared ahead, waiting for her reaction.

Sophie tried to think what to say. Her own husband would probably have been a conscientious objector, if the need for his psychiatric services had not been so great. He would not kill again, but he could best serve humanity now as Captain Greenman. But Daniel had already fought in one world war. Anger spurted. How many would die in this war so that this man might — possibly — stay free?

'Be kind,' Miss Lily had taught, back in the months she'd trained Sophie and the other girls the arts of charm at Shillings, for a purpose Sophie's father had never suspected when he'd persuaded Miss Lily to introduce his daughter to the aristocracy. 'Kindness is the simplest act, and the most powerful. Kindness persuades when anger alienates.'

But how could your soul keep its kindness towards the enemy when so many young men — friends, neighbours, Higgs employees — had already died in Malaya, Singapore, New Guinea, or in Egypt with the British Army?

While they were flying now, Japanese planes would be making reconnaissance missions across the coast of her homeland. Japanese planes rained bombs on Darwin, Broome and Townsville, though few civilians knew the extent of the raids, nor the desperate loss of so many cargo ships sunk along the north and east coasts. Even Sydney had been attacked by submarines a few months earlier. Sydney housewives turned brooms and carving knives into bayonets to defend their homes; the government sent supplies to Alice Springs to prepare to possibly evacuate Australia's children there; air-raid shelters were ubiquitous and public buildings sandbagged; and everyone carried gas masks at all times.

And England? The London Blitz had been portrayed as stoic citizenry carrying on despite the devastation. Sophie knew better than to swallow brave headlines whole.

Yet here was this man, blithely talking of pacifism.

George glanced at her. 'I'm what you'd call a Quaker. The Society of Friends. I thought you knew. Violette didn't mention it in any of her letters?' he added tersely.

Sophie's informally adopted niece had mentioned many things about her lover in her letters to Sophie, until the

Occupation stopped all communication, including George's preferences for breakfast ('Porridge! Pah!'), his appreciation of pale mauve silk underwear, the dexterity of his fingers, and his general magnificence when nude, but not his religion, nor the consequences of his beliefs.

'I won't kill another human being,' said George quietly, his eyes back on the controls. 'You know Auntie Ethel's a Friend too.'

'Yes, but ...' Sophie hesitated. Ethel Carryman was one of the dearest women in Sophie's life, now a secretary at the Ministry of Food in London, the kind of secretary who worked sixteen-hour days to keep Britain from starvation and had other secretaries working for her, and who made most of the decisions for her boss while 'Chummy', a product of England's most exclusive schools and clubs (Eton, Balliol, White's), lunched, drank, dozed or committeed.

George gave a wry grin, his eyes back on his instruments. 'But any decent man would be prepared to kill for his country?'

'I know there are conscientious objectors.' Sophie tried to keep her tone light. Pacifist or not, George risked his life. 'I just didn't expect to find myself flying over occupied Europe with one.'

'Auntie Eth gets people fed. It's what she did in the last war too, only this time it's for the whole of Britain. I fly. I'm good at it. But this plane is unarmed.'

Sophie sat extremely still. 'So we've come all this way with no means of self-defence?'

'As you've seen, I have carefully avoided flying across anywhere occupied by enemy forces until now. And, in fact, we have the best means of self-defence.'

'Trust in God?' suggested Sophie.

George laughed. 'I was going to say "the human brain", plus two decades of flying experience, but I admit to a prayer or two. We've got this far, haven't we?'

Sophie peered into the grey, trying not to show nervousness. Or terror. Would James really have risked her life like this? 'Surely we should have weapons. There'll be German fighters here over the Channel, even over England.'

4

'Not many now in daylight. Let's hope it stays cloudy.' He gave what he obviously intended to be a reassuring smile. 'Trust me, Mrs Greenman, ducking and hiding is a lot safer than fighting an air battle.'

Which sounded sensible. But surely hiding among clouds *and* whatever weaponry planes now used would be even safer.

The plane dropped suddenly again, once, twice. Sophie wished planes would do what they were supposed to do: fly, and steadily too. If pigeons could keep a straight course, why couldn't planes? George manoeuvred the craft's nose upwards, and they rose into sunlight, pouring gold upon the clouds. The sky was an arc of perfect blue, the horizon visible around them. Just as they were now visible to any enemy in the vicinity.

'We can duck back and forth into the clouds, if necessary,' George assured her. 'I've been dodging German fighter planes for three years. I'm still here, so I must be doing something right.'

'Only for Lily,' muttered Sophie.

George glanced at her again. 'I beg your pardon, Mrs Greenman?'

Sophie thought of the telegram in her handbag, one that must have been sent days after George had been dispatched to fetch her. She knew James Lorrimer well enough to suspect that the short notice had been deliberate, to give her no time to reflect or others to persuade her not to come.

The telegram was carefully innocuous, having passed through innumerable post offices and telephone exchanges to reach her:

'*Lily needs you stop George will drop in stop love to all stop James stop*'

Sophie found that George was looking at her strangely. 'You don't mean … Miss Lily? Your …' He hesitated.

'Sister-in-law,' said Sophie evenly. That was the public face of their relationship. George was one of the few people who knew — or guessed — it had once been something entirely different.

'You're expecting to see her at Shillings?'

'Of course.' Lily had stayed at Shillings after the abdication in 1936, instead of returning to Australia with Sophie, to prepare the estate for the war they both accepted was inevitable.

George sat silent, his hands lightly on the controls. When he finally spoke it was with compassion. 'Mrs Greenman, didn't Mr Lorrimer tell you? Or even Auntie Eth?'

'Tell me what?' asked Sophie.

'Miss Lily is dead, Mrs Greenman,' said George gently.

The cold air outside seemed to consume her body, too. Was this why she'd been summoned? Lily, dying ...

But surely the telegram would have said if Lily was ill, or injured. 'How?' managed Sophie.

'Over a year ago, it seems, in France in the invasion. I'm sorry, I don't know any details. Just what I've heard.'

Sophie sat frozen, all words lost. But none it seemed were needed.

'Enemy to starboard,' said George calmly. 'Brace yourself.'

The plane soared towards the sun.

Chapter 2

Men rarely see women, only the roles they play in relation to them:
their wife, their daughter, their servant or mistress, or the friend,
perhaps, of any of these. That male blindness can be useful when a
woman does not want to be noticed.

Miss Lily, 1908

PARIS, OCTOBER 1942

VIOLETTE

The new client's bedroom wallpaper had vast pink roses —
Violette had discovered that a certain class of French woman
adored rose wallpaper. It also possessed a pink silk coverlet with
gold fringes, silk curtains with more fringes, a hovering maid
and a fire in its pink-tiled fireplace, despite the severe rationing
of coal and firewood and the relative warmth of the autumn day.
The stench of perfume was stifling.

Violette took the smallest breath possible and spoke quickly
as the room's owner stared at herself — and her new Maison
Violette creation — in the mirror. 'The dress is beautiful,
Madame. Exquisite! You look magnifique!'

Violette used the elegant French accent she had quickly
acquired six years before, when she had also procured the
accountant, chief cutter and two most talented embroiderers
from the fashion house where she had worked before opening
Maison Violette. Poaching staff had been easy when Aunt
Sophie's money flowed as freely as the river back at Thuringa.

The money no longer flowed from Australia, nor even dribbled, since the Boche occupied Paris the previous year and all communication had ceased. But by now Maison Violette was most prosperous indeed. And the Occupation provided other most excellent ... opportunities.

Violette stepped back to admire her design. It was indeed lovely, even if the middle-aged figure within it was not, despite the strength of the corset built into the dress as one could not always rely on clients to choose the correct undergarments.

True, one must obey the war-time fashion that dictated the least possible amount of cloth in every dress, even for such a person as Madame, wife of a monster in the Vichy collaborative government. But the almost-invisible pleating of the skirt! The quality of fabric! Ah, that was Violette's genius. For, while other Parisians had congratulated themselves that the Maginot Line made France impregnable, Violette had known the tide of war would flow this way again. There would be shortages, rationing — though even Violette had not expected Paris itself to be taken.

But war? Only fools had not prepared for it. Violette was no fool. She had been born in war, educated in war, and she'd grown wary and determined in its aftermath. Even in 1936 war had been sniffing and snarling in the shadows of Europe. And so, when the cellars of Maison Violette were restored in 1937, half the space had been carefully hidden behind a brick wall and a door concealed by a set of shelves that swung back. Several rooms also had new walls that left hidden storage rooms between them, all built by constructeurs anglais who could not betray the secret now.

For three years Violette had bought bolt after bolt of the fabric most perfect, as well as beading, furs, lace and feathers to give a chic shimmer to the plainest garment. Enough to see her house shine till the Boche were finally destroyed.

'It is marvellous. The way you display my bosom — it has always been my best feature.' Madame twisted, gazing at her reflection in the mirror.

'You are delighted. Good! You will outglow the moon tonight, Madame, and every other woman in the room.'

Which was not quite a lie. Madame was stout, as were most of the 'BOFs', those who could afford black-market foods like beurre, oeufs and fromage while others in France grew gaunt. Plumpness was a sign of power in Paris these days. As Miss Lily said, a beautiful woman needed the simplest of designs to complement her loveliness. Madame and those like her must have a dress so stunning that all looked at the garment, not at Madame.

Violette smiled at her customer graciously. 'I will see myself out, Madame. And next week, perhaps, something for Christmas? A red velvet, embossed with rosebuds and trimmed with fur?' Fur and leather was supposed to be kept for their German overlords, but there were exceptions. Violette bent to whisper. 'I have a secret store kept for customers such as you.'

'You are a genius, Violette!'

'There is no genius without those who have the panache, the elegance to wear what I create. You, Madame, have the genius!'

Violette accepted the kiss on both cheeks, as if they were friends, and the dozen eggs as 'a little gift'. Merde! Into the corridor, as the maid began to most carefully remove the treasured dress, then down the stairs. No servant appeared. Excellent. Violette quickly opened the door to the dining room, slipped inside, reached for the first decanter on the sideboard and emptied her vial into it. A moment more, and she walked innocently to the front door as the butler appeared, smelling of the fish he must have had for lunch.

Violette gave him her second-best smile as he opened the door for her.

A fulfilling day's work. And tonight, tomorrow or next week? Violette did not know who would drink from the decanter. Madame, her husband, his Vichy collaborators? Even perhaps, one of the Boche they worked for. It did not matter. All deserved to die. But they would die at a time when there could be no connection to Maison Violette, nor its proprietor, a woman who had access to nearly every house that mattered in occupied Paris, whether it was via wife or mistress.

9

That was important. Each death must be a different method, so that no pattern could be discerned and no one would look for an assassin.

It was not easy, devising fresh methods every time. A burglary gone wrong. She, Violette, was a most excellent burglar. A pin scratch that would turn septic — Violette had not known if the transfer of pus would work, but it had been so easy, and so effective, she wished she might use it again.

The suicide by cyanide of a collaborator industrialist, after his fiancée had given her affections to a German officer instead of her Vichy lover. The arsenic in the apple cake ...

The woman she had called Grandmère, the leader of the resistance cell in the organisation La Dame Blanche, would have been proud of her, had Grandmère not died after the last war, in which she had taught Violette not just how to hate, but how to kill.

This death might be the first to be investigated as murder, if several drank from the same decanter. But symptoms would not appear for twelve hours at least, and the essence of deadly mushroom might still be taken for food poisoning, or a simple mistake with a few deadly fungi among innocent ones. And, if not, who would suspect a dressmaker? More likely it would be Madame herself who would be accused, if she had found out about her husband's mistress. Or even the mistress, if she'd realised Monsieur le Politician was not about to leave his wife for her.

Violette breathed the autumn air, the smoke-thick fog, the whiff of chicory. The Boche may have forbidden dancing in the city, but the elegant still sipped their coffee in the pavement cafés.

They were not the same coffee drinkers as before the occupation, naturellement. These were collaborators, those who posted *Hier wird Deutsch gesprochen* on the door of their businesses and welcomed the Boche soldiers who flocked to Paris on leave. This was a city where all young men on the streets must be friends of the enemy, if not the Boche themselves. It was truly an 'occupation', where the best apartments, cafés and hotels were occupied by German soldiers or officials — the Ritz, the Hôtel Meurice, the Hôtel Lutetia, even picture theatres and brothels, from the most sordid to the One-Two-Two, were open only to the enemy or their most-favoured friends.

The City of Light was dark now and not just because of the curfew from nine pm to five am and the blackout. It was a strangely quiet city too: the building noise that somehow was always a part of every street — for no street was ever finished — had vanished. So had the street minstrels who in earlier times had performed on almost every corner. The hawkers had disappeared too. Fewer cars purred along the boulevards, and those cars were mostly military, or collaborators' limousines. One heard sirens instead of music now, or even the rare call of a bird.

For Violette this was still the most perfect city, and not just because a reverence for fashion had drawn her here. The world had heard of the invasion of Poland with outrage or even shock. Violette had felt relief — the waiting was at last over — and a shiver of excitement too.

She had been too young in the last war. But finally, she was what she had been taught to be since she was a child, following the path of her grandmère.

She stepped out gaily as the yellowing chestnut leaves fluttered above her, beautiful in a hat that was a wisp of violet net, twisted into a bow. Her silk stockings were from the hoard in the cellar, not from the black market. Her suit was cut so that even the slim-line skirt still swished across the stockings, a sound that whispered, 'Look at me. I can be seduced.' Her jacket bore wreaths of violets embroidered on each cuff and in soft sweeps under the bosom. And all, naturellement, in violet.

Every designer must have a recognisable style, a signature. Let the Boche-loving Chanel keep her trousers and pouff! to the omnipresent little black dress. Women in war-time wanted escape, a hint of the frivolous despite the restrictions. Men wanted femininity. Cloth might be rationed, but embroidery was not, and there were plenty of women desperate enough to spend their evenings using the sewing and beading skills they had learned from the nuns at school.

And she? Violette had the clothes she created, the elegance, the thrill, the comforts of the 'little gifts' her clients gave her, so she could ignore the rationing that slowly starved France not just of food, but also of its joy in eating and in sharing. She had everything she wanted.

Except a lover. Most simple to find, of course, but to her surprise she wanted no one but George. She felt both the pang of missing him and uneasiness, for George, of a certainty, would not agree with her activities. But why should he know? This was war, and in war one killed the enemy. All across the world now people died and people killed. She, Violette, merely happened to be extremely good and most discreet with it. War was a bubble floating out of time, and when it was over anything … inconvenient to remember … could be left behind.

And today she had adventure, challenge. Who knew what next opportunity war might bring? It would be most good when the war ended, of course, and the Boche were gone. There would be George again, and dancing, the scent of tripe à la mode and tarte Tatin from the cafés, and laughter from their customers on the pavements.

But now? Tomorrow the mistress of a man rumoured to be high in the Gestapo had a fitting at Maison Violette. The mistress herself was a nothing, of course, but might present most interesting opportunities for some small accident to happen to her lover, or even perhaps his colleagues.

Violette had eggs for an omelette tonight, as well as black-market cheese delivered by a boy on a bicycle, and a most excellent wine from her pre-war cellar. And she was young, and beautiful, and two men, no three, were staring at her admiringly …

Violette pressed a few francs into the hand of a legless beggar perched on a small cart with his hat upon the pavement and accepted his, 'Merci, mademoiselle,' with a smile.

Yes, life was good.

Chapter 3

The French chef chappie who invented Lord Woolton Pie never had to eat it for his supper after a hard day in the factory. Turnip, carrots, cauliflower boiled up with oatmeal to make a sauce and covered with a pastry of boiled potato and flour? 'You've got to be joking', I said, but he weren't. I had to break out my last tin of corned beef just to stop my stomach from weeping at the thought of it …

The Memoirs of Dame Ethel Carryman, MBE,
Volume 2: Misery at the Ministry

SOPHIE

'That's a German Junkers 88. Built for speed and low flying.' George's whole body seemed focused down as he eased the joystick back.

Sophie tried to sound calm. 'What's it doing over England in daylight? And by itself?'

'I'd say it's a lone intruder. Probably following the railway line to bomb a factory — you need daylight for that.'

Suddenly their craft whizzed forward, not into the clouds to hide as Sophie had expected, but directly towards the rear of the Junkers.

'What *are* you doing?'

'Stopping it,' said George calmly.

'You said we are unarmed!'

'We are.' The man's tone turned grim. 'But I'm not going to let those bombs land on England.'

The tiny Junkers was close enough to make out every detail now with the sun behind it. Their plane gave another surge towards the enemy plane's rear. The Junkers dropped down into the cloud.

Sophie closed her eyes for a moment in relief. 'Why didn't he shoot us?'

'The RAF have a saying "Beware the Hun in the sun". The tactic works for us Brits too. You can't see a plane approach you from the direction of the sun. The Junkers has a blind spot aft, as well. By the time the pilot saw us he knew we were in place to make a killing shot. He had to get his craft out of the way, fast.'

'Kill them with what? My fruit knife?' Or the pistol she carried in her handbag, which George need not know about, but that would have been no use if he did.

'The pilot doesn't know that.' Their own plane dropped too. 'Now *we're* chasing *him*.' Grey metal gleamed damply in grey cloud ahead of them, vanished, reappeared.

Sophie bit back the words, 'Isn't this dangerous?'

Of course it was dangerous. The only way she could help now was by keeping quiet, as the plane in front of them dropped, veered, lifted, with George seeming to know by instinct exactly where the Junkers would appear next.

'Need to stay far enough back so he doesn't wonder why I don't shoot,' George muttered. 'But not far enough back so that we lose him ... ah, there he is again. He's circling,' he added confirming Sophie's calculations. 'Trying to lose us while wasting as little fuel as he can. He won't have much to spare on a mission like this, not if he's carrying any weight in explosives, and he will be, to make the mission worthwhile. Eeh, got you, you wazzock!' The plane ahead dropped, as if the pilot had thrown out an anchor. George followed through the clouds.

All at once colour flashed into the world again, carved into neat fields of soft spring green, hedgerows, stone-ridged lanes. The England she had first seen and learned to love with Miss Lily, to love even more deeply with Nigel, the England she had left ...

But not sideways and then almost upside down. Sophie instinctively gripped the seat with both hands again, despite the belts keeping her secure. Part of her wanted to try to make sense of George's revelation. The other half simply wanted to survive.

A burst of gunfire. Sophie thought she could see the silver of each shot as it sped towards them. Their craft veered sharply upwards, back into the grey.

'Eeeh, now thee's got it, ye scunner. He's finally realised we aren't armed,' George translated for Sophie. 'He's chasing *us* now.'

'Oh, good,' Sophie muttered.

George flashed her a grin. 'Very good. He's having to move fast to keep up with us. That's using even more of his fuel.' He pulled the plane sharply to the right, up, then to the left and down, the cloud around them endless, the day endless …

… and if it did end it might be sudden, their fuel tanks exploding. It might be slow, the plane burning around them as they fell. Sophie waited for a flash of fire, or a green arrow as the ground below became their killer.

'Listen,' said George, an eternity of grey soup later.

'For what?'

'An engine.'

Sophie focused. 'To our left. Getting fainter.'

'I thought so, too. Got him, by gum!'

'What do you mean?'

'We stole an hour from him. He'll be pushing to get back to France now.'

'Not after us any longer?'

'No. He's realised how much he's wasted in the chase.'

'Can't he find another target?'

'He won't have enough fuel. Likely have to drop those bombs of his in the Channel pretty quick too, as he won't have enough to carry them back to land either. We've travelled back over the Channel again now, if my calculations are correct.'

How could they be, after that juddering, muttering chase within the clouds? Their plane dropped again and Sophie's stomach with it.

Cliffs, a grey sea, urgent demands for identification on the radio now that their plane was visible. George answered, more numbers it seemed than words, nothing she cared about. She was alive ...

And the Junkers would not kill anyone today. No factory would erupt in flames, no families be left bereft, no vital war effort maimed ...

But if George had failed in this insane exploit she would not have reached England. The urgent, unknown mission bringing her to England would not be fulfilled, because George Carryman had fought the enemy, using the only weapon he had — his own skill.

Had he done right? She could not judge. Had he risked himself, his plane, her and her mission to prove his bravery to himself, or simply to save those who'd have died as their factory exploded, a factory desperately needed for the war effort? Sophie could not judge that either, just as suddenly as she did not feel competent to judge his determination not to kill another person.

'And we'll land ourselves with at least five minutes of fuel to spare,' said George cheerfully. 'I'll buzz the Hall to give them a hint to put the kettle on.'

Shillings Hall without Lily, or Nigel. How can I bear Shillings now, so changed? she wondered. But one coped, of course, and carried on ...

Five minutes of fuel to spare before they crashed ...

The words finally registered. Sophie shut her eyes in silent prayer.

No, Sophie could not judge George's decisions, nor his bravery nor his morality.

Daniel, she thought. He had the wisdom to assess this man and what he'd done today. Now Lily was gone Daniel's wisdom was her only anchor in the world.

But Daniel was far away.

Chapter 4

*Where there is love, there is always grief, because if you did not
love you would never feel the grief. So is love worth it, knowing
that it brings pain as well? Always, my dears.*

Miss Lily, 1912

THURINGA, AUSTRALIA, OCTOBER 1942

DANIEL

Daniel Greenman woke among the tussocks by the river bank
and knew that last night he had been John.

He had been John for more than ten years a long time ago,
after the Great War, a simple man, living in a stringybark
hut by a farm gate, which he opened for sixpence or a loaf
of bread or simply if someone tooted the horn. He spent his
day trapping rabbits, collecting firewood or watercress and
carving a cross for every man he had seen die on the Western
Front, knowing that was a task that would last well beyond his
lifetime.

He had taken delight in the kookaburras' laughter, the march
of ants, not men, the gentle breath of a campfire, so unlike the
deadly flare of guns.

Gradually men had come to him: men broken but hiding
their pain, till their two am screams; men visited by visions
of blood just as he was. And he and the men had talked, and
slowly the men had healed, and word had spread of the man by
the gate who was good for a yarn and a cuppa from the billy
on the fire.

A gentle life, ripped open by Sophie Higgs. Sophie, who he had loved, comforted, slept with, who had deserted him in misunderstanding to marry Nigel Vaile, Earl of Shillings, leaving him Dr Daniel Greenman, psychiatrist, once again, but without her support beside him.

'John' had vanished the night he'd held Sophie in his arms. He had remained Dr Daniel Greenman — mostly. Dr Greenman remembered being John, but Daniel lived only in the present, away from the memory of every man he'd failed in France, every death, every scream of agony, every desperate face waiting as the life seeped out of it, waiting, waiting, waiting until they died before he could even begin to try to heal them.

Dr Daniel Greenman had established a life, even a psychiatric practice, now centred on the Bald Hill Repatriation Clinic an outpost of Sydney's Callan Park Mental Hospital, for those soldiers who needed more quiet and normal life around them than actual therapy. Dr Greenman could even cope, mostly, with his memories. When he could not he walked, and talked to Sophie, till slowly the feeling of ineffable failure faded and he could accept that Daniel Greenman, husband, father, doctor, friend, had a right to walk upon the earth.

There had only been one lapse before, when Sophie had been kept up north by floodwaters for three weeks, a morning like this when he found he had wandered from the homestead, with no memory of how he'd got there. A colleague, a close friend, had helped him then, six months of therapy he had carefully kept from Sophie. Sophie must be free to run her business, not feel bound to a husband who needed her to keep him in the present.

But the colleague was in the army now, vanished with so many Australian soldiers in Malaya, and last night, the past week, he had not held Sophie, and war had come again. John had crept over him once more in the darkness.

Daniel let himself watch a puffball of cloud, listen to the kookaburras' chortle, then stood up and brushed twigs from his suit, glad he didn't have to walk back in his pyjamas. He washed his face quickly in the river, thankful that the beard Sophie claimed he had grown to look like Dr Freud meant he did not need a daily shave.

He must be Dr Greenman now, for his patients, for the staff at Thuringa. He must be Pa for his two children, both due home from boarding school in a couple of months for the Christmas holidays. He had to tell Rose and Danny the cover story agreed on in those hurried two hours while Sophie packed and attended to the most urgent business matters. Sophie was ostensibly in Townsville — almost impossible to contact now with the Japanese bombing — sorting out a problem with one of the corned beef factories so vital for the war effort.

That tale would do for the time being, or even until Christmas. There'd been no hint about how long Sophie would be needed in that spare telegram. Possibly, hopefully, she was wanted merely as part of a team to discuss how the Empire could continue to feed Britain with increasingly limited shipping. But a request like that would almost certainly have gone through normal business channels, and not in a melodramatic summons from Lily Vaile.

He was not jealous of Lily. True, Sophie loved her — adored might even be a better term. But that love had never been the kind he and Sophie shared, and nor did Daniel Greenman subscribe to the fallacy that one love lessened another. Only selfish love was indulgent enough to shun the world and make a nation of two. Love for one person, on the contrary, should deepen one's ability to love others too.

Besides Lily Vaile was too good — the simple word was appropriate — for jealousy to be possible. Lily had genuinely wished for Sophie and Daniel's marriage. The happiness of others made her happy. Lily had taught that gift to Sophie, too.

Lily had also taught Sophie to put duty to others, including her country or the peace of the world, above all else. No, he did not think Sophie would be back for Christmas.

But he would manage, he told himself. Sophie's sudden departure had been a shock, but establishing routines without her would steady him. There would be a telegram soon, to say she had arrived; more telegrams, and letters, though letter arrivals were unreliable these days. Now he knew a relapse was possible he would be careful to avoid triggers, especially in the evening.

He had listened to the news on the wireless last night. From now on he'd avoid the news except for the morning broadcast and the newspaper. Midge and Harry had asked him to Sunday dinner, too — that would help. Midge was no fool, and she and Harry had known him first as John. Daniel suspected both would find excuses to invite him to dinner often once they knew Sophie was away for longer than a few days in Sydney.

Daniel adjusted his tic. Eventually he would need to explain to Rose and Danny why their mother had vanished to England at the behest of a mere telegram. It was an impossible job, one that Sophie could not do from England, and no one to do it but himself ...

He strolled through the garden as if he had merely gone for an early morning walk, as he and Sophie often did. The table on the verandah had been set for breakfast. He sat, carefully not looking at the chair that did not contain Sophie, as Mrs Taylor bustled through the French windows. War required a lot of bustling. Mrs Taylor was President of the Bald Hill Comforts for Soldiers Committee and Secretary of the local branch of Legacy, as well as their housekeeper. Besides, bustling made one feel as if one was really helping the war effort. Mr Taylor and their Johnnie were now Sergeant Taylor and Private Taylor, somewhere in the Middle East.

'Scrambled eggs this morning, Dr G. Hens are laying well.' Mrs Taylor put the plate in front of him. The days of a choice from the salvers on the sideboard had vanished, possibly forever, but apart from weak tea — long stewed on the edge of the stove to eke out the supply the coupons allowed each person — and a few other inevitable shortages, the privations of war had not hit them hard on a property where most of their food was home-grown. As a doctor and the woman responsible for organising so much bully beef, they were even allowed extra petrol coupons.

'And here's your toast too.' Mrs Taylor plonked the plate down in a way unthinkable before the war, when toast came in a silver rack, replaced with fresh slices every twenty minutes and the scraps thrown to the hens. Toast piled on a plate retained a bit of warmth for longer.

'Go easy on the strawberry jam,' she added. 'I'm saving the last pot for Master Danny and Miss Rose's holidays.'

'Thank you, Mrs Taylor,' he managed, his voice casual, glad she apparently had noticed nothing unusual about him. He obediently helped himself to only a teaspoonful of jam. His stepson's earldom was occasionally a burden to Danny's family. It appeared that an earl — even a sixteen-year-old schoolboy earl — could not be expected to go without jam on his toast.

'Morning, Dr Greenman. Mrs Greenman still not returned?' Rita, the older of the two land girls billeted in the homestead, laid a comforting, sun-browned hand on his for perhaps two seconds too long before sliding into her seat. Twenty-two, the daughter of the foreman in one of Sophie's factories, she had evidently decided that working with live cattle was preferable to packing their corned meat, especially if her father's association with his employer meant she lived in what she must regard as the luxury of the Thuringa homestead, the residence of a genuine earl. Her hair had turned blonde overnight.

Annie slipped into the chair on the other side of the table, accepting her scrambled eggs with a smile at Mrs Taylor. Nineteen, with brown hair as fine as rabbit fur, and as small-boned as a rabbit too, gave the glimpse of a smile that said she noticed the machinations of the Ritas of this world and was amused by them. She was the daughter of a country schoolteacher and his wife, and had actually done holiday farm work before enlisting in the Land Army when she left school. She had deferred her medical degree for war work.

'It may take Mrs Greenman some time to sort out the problems in Townsville,' said Daniel mildly. 'What do you have on today?'

'Fencing of course. Do you know how many miles of fences this place has?' Rita pulled a face, then tackled the scrambled eggs she would certainly not have had access to at home, slathering Mrs Taylor's home-churned butter on her toast. 'You should come out with us after lunch, Dr Greenman. Get into the sunlight for a while.'

Green shadows flickering through the trees on the tussocks. The afternoon river would mirror the slanting sun. The air would smell of bark and not of blood, the billy boiling ...

Daniel found that the young women were staring at him. He took toast, buttered it — essentially legal as it was made from the cream of Thuringa's cows, though all Australians were supposed to observe austerity no matter how many Jerseys grazed in their home paddocks — added jam sparingly, forced himself to bite, swallow, be Dr Greenman, damask napkin on his lap, not John, who'd once worn ragged shirt and shorts, the earth warm under his bare feet.

Sophie, I need you, he thought. I need the safety of your arms, the anchor of your voice. And in two months his children would be home. He did not know if he longed for or dreaded their arrival more.

Chapter 5

People look at the great houses of England and assume they are
timeless in their grandeur and gardens. But a cottage is more likely
to stay close to its original shape and purpose than the manor.
Shillings Hall has been a fort, briefly a convent when the sole heir,
a female, founded an order abolished twenty years later by Henry
VIII, a hospital, then a fort once again in the Civil War. It had
new wings added that now seem ancient, and was modernised
time after time over hundreds of years, few of which measures seem
modern now, except, you will be glad to know, its bathrooms.
Shillings has always been the centre of an agricultural community,
and a home, though the nature of both of those have changed too.

And now Shillings changes once again.

Miss Lily Vaile's welcome speech to the
new occupiers of Shillings Hall, 1940

SOPHIE

Sophie stared down at the paddock below them in horror.
'George, pull up! You can't land there!'

'Why not?'

She glanced at him incredulously as the plane headed
resolutely downwards. 'There are at least fifty sheep in that
field.' And no runway. She had last landed there with this same
man as her pilot, back in 1926, but in a far smaller aircraft.
An hour later the Prince of Wales had played his bagpipes to
rid Shillings of unwelcome guests, and Sophie had proposed to
Nigel ...

'Don't worry.' The reassuring voice broke through her memories. 'The sheep trust me. They know I'm a safe pilot. I bet you not one of them even bothers to move.'

'You are an insane pilot!'

'Well, possibly. But I haven't lost a plane or a passenger yet.' George pulled the joystick. The plane swooped, then levelled, still dropping.

The sheep didn't move. The aircraft was almost at the hawthorn hedge when Sophie realised each one was made of wood and the swathe of green 'grass' was painted tarmac. The plane bumped slightly as it landed, then ran smoothly across the field, as Sophie grinned at the pretend sheep. Every one of them was slightly different, some with lambs, some gazing up, most heads down as if eating the grass.

'Bob moves them every day. Wouldn't do for a passing Messerschmitt to guess there's any need for an airstrip here.'

'Isn't green paint a bit obvious when it's snowing?'

'Bob changes the colour with the season. Bob Green. General handyman.'

Sophie took a deep breath. Bob Green ...

'Looks like there's a whole committee to meet you,' said George.

Sophie stared out the windscreen as the plane drew to a halt. James, looking tired under his inevitable bowler hat, Mrs Goodenough, thinner and her apron temporarily discarded, Hereward still in most proper black with bright white cuffs, and he had lost weight too. But that was all. And why were the Shillings's cook–housekeeper and butler here in a field, instead of waiting to greet her at the front door, as was proper?

The one person who should be there was not. Lily, she thought. Lily's absence from her life in 1936 when she had decided to stay in England and at Shillings had cut like a knife. But at least Sophie had known that Miss Lily still carved love and grace somewhere in the world. She would have to walk down Shillings's passageways today knowing that no matter how many doors she opened, there would be no gentle smile, no faint perfume of oakmoss and roses.

24

She forced herself to smile, to show no sign of grief or loss as she scrambled out onto the wing, then took James's hand to steady her as she jumped down.

'Sophie! It is so good to see you.'

James looked too thin, too. 'It is always good to see you, James,' she said warmly, because the time for severe questioning had not arrived. 'No,' she added, as Mrs Goodenough began to curtsey. Sophie caught her hand and kissed the old woman's cheek instead. 'Curtseying is forbidden in war-time.'

'I don't think Britain has heard,' said James drily, as Mrs Goodenough flushed, clearly pleased.

'I have only just made the law. We must spread the word.'

Hereward began a bow, halted.

'Hereward, you are looking well. But I won't kiss you in case someone is looking and it ruins your reputation. My suitcase is in the plane,' she added. 'Along with some boxes of provisions to add to the rations. Could you have them taken up to the Hall for me, please?'

Higgs's Corned Beef had now added lines of boxes of mixed dried fruit and packaged dates for sale to the public. She'd had exactly two hours to pack, but Thuringa was always plentifully supplied with Higgs's produce, and Daniel and George had packed as much as George said the plane could safely carry. Sophie now wished she had demanded more time, a final night at home ...

If she'd had another night at home there would have been time to send a return telegram asking for more details before she left, coded of course, but less dramatic than the few words that had brought her here. She'd now had time to think of the questions she should have asked. Many questions, and for once James was going to have to answer them all, beginning with George's shocking pronouncement about Lily that had driven all words away.

'I thought it might be more discreet if you stayed in one of the cottages,' James was saying smoothly.

She bit back the words, 'But the Hall is my home!'

But it was not home; Sophie had made that clear when she left for Australia in 1936, leaving Lily in charge of the estate. Her title was a courtesy now, granted by King George at his wife's request in recognition of Sophie's role in the abdication of his fascist brother, now safely removed from any information that might help the enemy. And while Shillings Hall legally belonged to her son, even an owner had no right to stay in a house requisitioned by His Majesty's government for the war effort.

'I will see that everything is taken care of, your ladyship,' said Hereward.

Sophie presented him with a smile, despite the effort it took to manufacture it. 'You are a wonder, Hereward.' So she would not even have the reminders of Lily now, her parchment-lined small drawing room, her favourite seat with the dining room candles behind her — 'Always have the light behind you once you are over forty.' Nor would she now stay in the bedroom she had shared with Nigel, where the twins had been born, nor in the room she'd first stayed in and had occupied the last time she was here.

'And there's cherry cake for tea,' said Mrs Goodenough firmly. 'I saved the parcel of crystallised cherries and almonds you sent over. I knew your ladyship would be back again.'

'And you are a miracle, Mrs Goodenough. Cherry cake!'

'I'm billeted up at the house tonight. Too late to get back to Scotland now, but I'll be leaving at first light.' George grinned at her. 'Thank you for not screaming, fainting or bringing up your breakfast.'

'An eventful journey?' asked James.

'Only the last half hour of it,' said Sophie drily. James took her arm as they crossed the field, while the others headed towards the orchard and Shillings. For the first time she let her emotion show. 'James, George informed me an hour ago that Lily was dead!'

'Sophie, please wait till we're inside. Someone might notice us.'

'And wonder why I'm upset? I have been dragged from my home at a moment's notice with nothing more than an enigmatic telegram, told that the woman I love most in the world is dead, discovered that the man you sent to fetch me is a maniac conchie in an unarmed plane —'

'George is the safest pilot I know,' said James calmly. 'And you could have sent a telegram demanding more information and had an answer by the time George refuelled in Darwin. You came willingly.'

Sophie walked in momentary shocked silence. Yes, James knew her very well.

Had the woman who had created a chain of hospitals and refugee centres in World War I and helped remove a fascist king from England's throne been … just slightly — no, not bored — just *left out* of the dramas playing across the world while she debated the thickness of corned beef cans?

Sophie Higgs-Greenman would not abandon her husband, children and workforce except in desperate urgency. But, yes, she had been all too willing to believe that just the correct level of urgency had been thrust upon her. She shut her eyes briefly, as the world spun slightly. She felt adrift, not just in another country, but in part of herself she had never fully acknowledged before.

'But James, about Lily —'

James made a quick gesture to silence her. They had reached the cottages, a small cluster for the workers on the Home Farm, thatched, despite Sophie's offer of new tiled roofs when she married Nigel. The Shillings tenants were conservative, apart from their acceptance of flushing indoor toilets, bathrooms, a few telephones and electricity. But the flower-filled front gardens she had known before the war had now been replaced with cabbages and potatoes, though late roses and honeysuckle still climbed the walls.

'Everything will be clear soon.' James turned down the path to what had been the agent's house, larger than the rest and slightly away from the others. Nigel had given the house to Jones and Greenie, when it had seemed that he would die and his cousin inherit, a fate avoided by Nigel's marriage to Sophie and her producing Danny as the heir. As far as Sophie knew, Jones and Greenie had never used it but had always used Jones's usual apartments in the Hall.

She forced herself to speak normally. 'Are Jones and Greenie back?'

James shook his head.

One of Lily's letters at the beginning of the war had mentioned an assignment in Palestine or, rather, that *Autumn will turn summer's green to the tawny colours of Jerusalem stone. I fear their winter will be a long one*, from which Sophie had carefully pulled the other meaning.

'Who lives here now?' Sophie had no wish to stay with a stranger, or even a cottager she had known slightly from her years as lady of the manor. She felt odd, light-headed. Had she subconsciously expected that somehow everything would be the same?

'Bob Green's using the house now.'

Of course Bob Green would live here, as a relative of Greenie's. Most of the village was related to each other — and quite probably to Nigel's father, grandfather and other male ancestors as well — and the Green family was a prolific one. At times Greenie and Lily looked remarkably similar. Sophie felt her heart beat far too hard. The world suddenly seemed too clear, and yet as if it lurched just beyond her vision.

What would Bob Green look like?

The door opened as if the man who held it had heard his name. Of course he must have heard the plane land, and had, most probably, been waiting for their footsteps on the gravel path. And of course he would not have wanted this first meeting to be public.

Then there he was, framed by the door. A thin face. Was everyone in this country thin? Medium height. A fringe of short grey hair around an otherwise bald head, a luxuriant grey moustache to make up for the lack of hair elsewhere. Kind eyes, and the calloused hands and ingrained dirt of a handyman who gardened.

She knew the shape of those hands. She knew the eyes too. And yet Bob Green did not reach his hands towards her. He stayed in the dimness of the doorway, while she seemed unable to step inside.

'Sophie,' said Bob Green, as, for only the second time in her life, she fainted.

Chapter 6

SOPHIE

A faded chintz sofa beneath her. Embossed cream wallpaper, dark with age. The furniture had the look of two hundred years of discards from the main house. Even the square of carpet was Empire, but mended at the edges.

Bob Green sat on a small hard chair next to the sofa, watching her. A kettle's whistle in the next room informed her that James was making tea.

Sophie struggled to sit up as he brought in the tray: a silver teapot, slightly dented, with the Vaile crest; matching milk jug; the cherry cake proudly intact upon a cake stand; egg and watercress sandwiches unmistakably made with Mrs Goodenough's bread, though Sophie had never seen only one kind of sandwich ever served on the Shillings estate, whether it be at the tea stall at the church fête or in any of the tenants' kitchens. More than anything she had yet seen — even the Junkers, whose manoeuvres might have been an airman's college prank, for, after all, no shots had hit them — that single kind of sandwich spoke of war.

'How are you feeling?' James didn't sit. And only two cups, Sophie noticed.

'Embarrassed. I'm sorry — I haven't eaten since breakfast.' Corned-beef sandwiches, which in fact she hadn't eaten, as George had so clearly relished the treat. Australia might need to cut back its usual eight strong cuppas a day to four weak ones, but no one went hungry for lack of food in the shops. And she had been too tired to eat dinner in Lisbon.

'I'll leave you to your tea then.' James hesitated, then bent and kissed her cheek. 'I'm sorry, Sophie. There's a good reason for the urgency. I'll be back to answer questions later. I hope you'll forgive me when you understand.'

She nodded without replying, infinitely glad to hear the door close behind him, because she found she could not greet Bob Green with James watching, and James would know that too.

'Sophie,' said Bob Green again. He moved towards her, hesitated, then bent and kissed her gently on both cheeks. His lips were warm, and agonisingly familiar: Bob Green, who had once been her husband Nigel, but was her husband no longer, who had been Miss Lily, her teacher and mentor, and later her closest friend.

'Lily ...' said Sophie brokenly.

'Shhh. It's not safe to use that name. Someone might be passing the window.' Even Bob's accent was different: the soft burr of a villager, not the upper-class tones of both Nigel and Lily.

Sophie nodded numbly. 'George said Lily was dead. I had no idea what to say. For one horrible moment I thought it might even be true, till he told me you'd been trapped in France by the Occupation. I thought the story was that Lily Vaile is officially missing in France.'

'It's still the story. Lily even corresponds privately with a few people, like you and Rose and Danny, though you may have noticed a Swiss postmark since the Occupation.'

'I assumed that was because you are supposed to be in France.' He even speaks of Lily in the third person, thought Sophie with desolation.

'Exactly. It's to make sure no one links the Lily Vaile who is in France, either alive or dead, with Bob Green at Shillings. Neither Rose nor Danny have friends in England.' He smiled, slightly sadly. 'And those who have known Lily over the years are discreet about their connection.'

The 'Lovely Ladies' Miss Lily had trained at Shillings never spoke of her, except to each other. A finishing school in Switzerland or France for a 'gel' about to be presented at Court during her season was acceptable. Being more thoroughly trained in the arts of charm, both as debutante and wife, might potentially be scandalous.

'You mixed socially in Australia.'

'Lily mixed with the people of Bald Hill, none of whom have connections in Europe. There's obviously been gossip though,' Bob added. 'I suppose it's natural for people to think that Lily must be dead if there has been no news of her survival. Sophie darling, eat something before you keel over again.' He sat in the armchair opposite her sofa.

Sophie reached for the teapot. 'Will I pour?' she asked the man she knew, and didn't know, for this man was nothing like Nigel Vaile, and not only because of the balding hair and his shaggy moustache, and even further from Lily. 'As the only woman present?'

'This is hard for you,' said Bob gently.

'To see the woman I loved most in the world turn into Bob Green, just as in the past she would sometimes turn back into Nigel Vaile, whom I also loved?'

More than ten years ago, on their mission in Berlin, either Nigel or Lily had had to appear to die, to hide the truth that the Earl of Shillings and his illegitimate half-sister, the head of a female espionage network, were one person. Nigel had chosen that Lily should be the one to survive. Now she had been disposed of, too. 'Yes, it's hard.' Sophie acknowledged. 'I didn't realise how hard it would be. But Lily *will* come back after the war?'

'I'm hoping to be still very much alive at the end of the war,'

Bob Green said evenly, which did not answer her question. 'Are you going to pour that tea?'

Her hand did not shake as she handed him his cup, black, just as she took hers, too.

The teacup ascended. Even the way Bob drank his tea was different, but possibly that was caused by the moustache. 'Sophie, this hasn't been easy for me either. But there's no choice. This is war-time. If a bomb drops on us it would cause a scandal were Lily Vaile found to be a man, much less the deceased Earl of Shillings.'

She sipped her tea and managed to smile. Nigel … *Bob* … had lost most in this transformation: his home, his very identity. What was her loss compared to his? 'I'm sorry. I thought I did understand. But seeing you, hearing George talk about you … I don't think it had been real to me before.'

'It was so easy to be either Nigel or Lily as I chose for so long. Shillings used to be one of the most isolated estates in England, inbred, marrying their second cousins, deeply loyal to their earl and employer. I suspect the older tenants, at least, guessed that the earl at times became Miss Lily, and that Miss Lily became the earl.'

'And they loved them both,' said Sophie softly. She reached over and took his hand. 'As I did. And still do.'

Suddenly all that mattered was that he was alive. The shock of seeing him seeped away, leaving happiness so strong she wanted to cry.

He put his cup down to cover her hands with both of his. 'Sophie, darling, the estate is now full of strangers — not just those working at the Hall, but newcomers who have married people from the village and come to live here. What if I suddenly needed medical attention? If I collapsed there'd be a dozen capable strangers who'd offer me first aid, then have to be treated for shock themselves.'

She tried to smile. Nigel Vaile, Earl of Shillings, had only just survived surgery for a bladder tumour. The scars had pained him ever since. Almost an old man now …

... but not a bald one. 'You shave your head?'

'Yes. Baldness is an even more useful disguise than the moustache.'

'And Bob?'

He grinned. 'There's always a Bob, bobbing about somewhere. No one notices a Bob. Especially one who has a strong family resemblance to the Greens.'

'And there is the Greens' strong resemblance to your father.'

'Indeed. I have often wondered if Greenie is my half-sister. I sometimes imagine I might truly be Bob Green, living on the estate, working for James just as Greenie does. Have a sandwich. There is even butter on them. With Shillings officially part of the war effort the Home Farm is allowed to feed us all.'

'You spent the years before the war ensuring that it could.'

'As you did at Thuringa, and with Higgs's.'

She bit into a sandwich, felt the world steady. 'The telegram said that you needed me. So I came.'

'We do need you.'

'Ah, "we".' She slowly finished her sandwich. 'Your need is political, not personal.'

'The political is personal,' he said tersely. 'We are talking about the fate of your country, my country, millions of people. How could my personal needs possibly be more important?'

'Because Miss Lily taught me that we owe most to those we love. No one can substitute for a loved one. There are usually many who can perform a political duty.'

Bob smiled, a new smile created by the moustache, but familiar too. 'But who do you love? And with what sort of love?'

It had been one of the earliest lessons with Miss Lily, the four girls sitting on the hearth in her drawing room, toasting crumpets on the fire, spreading them with honey from the Shillings bees. There was Eros, sexual love, so embarrassingly but fascinatingly portrayed in the books of woodcuts in their bedrooms; Philia, or deep friendship, which Miss Lily hoped would bind Sophie, poor dead Mouse, Emily and Hannelore; Ludus, playful love; Pragma, long-standing love, which might eventually bind them all too;

Philautia, love of one self, which meant integrity, and dignity; and Agape, a love of everyone ...

The six were not enough. The love she felt for her children was none of those, nor was love of her country, for the bones of the land itself, felt by her for Thuringa and Lily-Nigel for Shillings, unless Agape covered those.

Miss Lily, Nigel, even James, worked not just for love of country, but for humankind. But what was their work in this new war?

'Is Shillings part of Military Intelligence now? I know James is in charge of it — your letters and his told me that much.'

'James is part of Military Intelligence — MI5 — but MI5 has no part in this organisation.'

'So what happens here?' And she realised. 'You're still at it, aren't you?'

'Of course,' said Bob Green. He smiled. 'Shillings is producing Lovely Ladies.'

Chapter 7

What is love?

I have loved many people in my long and varied life. I have loved as a friend, a comrade in arms, as a parent, a lover, a spouse. I can even say I have felt that vague but very real cliché: I have loved humanity.

So what is love that can encompass all these things? Love is, perhaps, simply the highest form of empathy: not just feeling for the one you love, but caring more for their wellbeing than your own.

Miss Lily, 1939

Sophie took another sandwich. Suddenly she was ravenous. 'Why train Lovely Ladies now?' The girls Sophie had trained with, in the magic summer before the Great War, had needed the skills Lily imparted to charm a husband, a lover, a dinner partner who might be a cabinet minister or a king.

True, those 'graduates' of Shillings had slowly been made aware they were part of a wider network of political connections and hopefully shared assistance, even to the extent of becoming agents of information, but they had not known that purpose then. They had certainly not been trained to be intelligence agents, or to liaise with resistance groups.

'For the same reason as always. Women may have more rights and opportunities than twenty years ago, but they are still powerless compared with men. The powerless are usually overlooked. A woman secretary, who chooses which files go onto the desk and which are buried, or who sees the minister. The secretary may write the speech or policy briefing even if it has a male's name on it. Women are the drivers in this war, as well as the nurses — both places where information can be discreetly obtained. Women serve tea and buns at railway canteens in occupied Europe as well as Britain, and can note the number of trains, their times, the number of troops and their directions.'

'The women men don't see.' Sophie sliced a generous hunk of cherry cake. No one made cherry cake like Mrs Goodenough, even when using the cook's carefully handwritten recipe, presented to each girl who left Shillings. 'Even after all these years running Higgs Industries, most of the mail I receive is addressed to Mr Higgs, not Mrs Greenman or even Miss Higgs. As soon as I train one supplier to work with a woman they retire or enlist and I have to deal with yet another who simply doesn't notice that the letterhead says *Mrs Greenman, Proprietor.*'

'Exactly. Have you heard of the SOE?'

'No.'

Bob gave a grim smile. 'It is not the kind of information included in a war-time letter. The SOE, Special Operations Executive, sends agents into occupied Europe. Its agents are superbly trained — a commando course in the Scottish Highlands, night-time parachute training, all the finest arts from how to kill silently using a knife or a garrotte, to picking locks, jumping out of moving vehicles or blowing up railway lines and bridges and, of course, sending codes in wireless messages. They have two problems. The first is that it is a male organisation, run by men and, until recently, they used only male agents.'

'I see,' said Sophie slowly.

'I thought you might. MI5 has had to lower its standards slightly and admit those who did not play cricket for either Eton or Harrow, but a pair of testicles is still essential for any senior position. None of them seemed to realise that male strangers are obvious in war-time. But a woman? She is someone's aunt whose home has been bombed, or a cousin come to help a family in illness, or to take the place in the shop of Uncle Pierre who has been taken as forced labour to Germany.' He gave a grim smile. 'There is also what might be called the Duke of Windsor problem.'

'That many in the British establishment have fascist sympathies?'

'Exactly.' Bob gazed out the window. 'It became obvious some months ago to all but the most stubborn in MI5 that every long-standing British agent has been either killed or imprisoned or their place has been taken by a German agent who continues to send coded messages. Fortunately, as good German officers, they send extremely well written fake messages. The women who decoded them became suspicious when the usual spelling mistakes and sending errors vanished. It took them some time, however, to get the men in charge to listen to their suspicions.'

'I can imagine,' said Sophie drily.

Bob nodded. Sophie still could not get used to the shine of his scalp, as if he'd polished it with the same pomade he used on the ends of his moustache. 'With the greatest reluctance, SOE has begun to send women agents instead. They have been far more successful, both in gaining information and in liaising with the French Resistance, but all our agents, at some stage, are betrayed.'

'By Nazi sympathisers within British intelligence?'

'Or collaborators who infiltrate the French Resistance. Which brings us here, to Shillings, which is not under the direct control of MI5 nor SOE, nor connected with Générale de Gaulle's forces or with the resistance groups.'

'And so free from betrayal to the enemy?'

'So far. We're just one of many small, semi-autonomous units set up since Dunkirk. It's the desperation gamble — there is even an official secret organisation of assorted fiction writers somewhere planning the kind of cunning plots that make their heroes so successful in their books, in the hope that at least one or two of their ideas might be useful in real life.'

'And at Shillings?'

'The trainees at Shillings Hall are taught how to blow up a bridge, if it should be necessary, and how to parachute into enemy territory at night. But their work is not to liaise with the local resistance groups nor engage in sabotage. Instead they become that amiable bombed-out sister-in-law who suddenly needs a home, or the charming old friend who needs a little flirtation to brighten her last few years of loss and heartbreak. SOE operatives may work for weeks or months till they are relieved or their mission is completed. The Shillings agents stay with women who are already part of the network, or who might resume their part in it with encouragement.'

'Your Lovely Ladies across occupied Europe?'

Bob nodded, and suddenly, in that movement she saw Nigel again, felt the world tilt almost back into place. 'Some continue to send information. Others have been quiet, either from loyalty to their country, or because they see no way to stand against the Nazis. But I know the women who studied here.' The soft voice was suddenly familiar, too. 'There isn't one of them who condones what the Nazis are doing in the lands they control. They may not spy for their country's enemies, but in every case so far they have accepted the women from here into their households, or found them a position where they can remain in occupied Europe indefinitely, slowly gaining trust and making contacts.'

'And sending information?'

'Yes. But their main task is to do what charming women have always done — persuade men to change their minds.'

'I can't see any woman changing Hitler's mind,' said Sophie mildly.

'No. But there are many in the German military, especially among the aristocrats, who believe Hitler has become unreliable, too extreme. Hitler came to power with a coup. He may lose power — or his life — in one, too. There are already mutterings. A little ... encouragement ... and the mutterings may mature into action.'

'Is that what Hannelore is doing?' How many years has it been since I mentioned Hannelore's name? thought Sophie. She had most carefully not asked about Hannelore in her letters, even in code.

Hannelore, Prinzessin von Arnenberg, had been the first true friend Sophie had ever made. It was a closer friendship than could have been expected between a German princess and the daughter of an Australian corned-beef king, meeting as Miss Lily's students in that final glorious season of 1913 and 1914. But Sophie had not written to Hannelore for over twelve years, since her attempt to lure Lily into supporting the political upstart Hitler had led to what almost everyone — including Hannelore — believed was Nigel's death.

'Does James still count Hannelore as one of his agents?' The last time Sophie had been in England and free to speak away from the eyes of those who might open letters or listen at telephone exchanges, James had told her that Hannelore had offered herself as a spy for England — which is what a double agent might do, of course.

'I don't know,' said Bob tightly.

Sophie put down her teacup, her hand trembling slightly. 'Nigel ...'

'I'm Bob.'

'Bob, then. What am I here for? Is it something to do with Hannelore?' she added warily. Messages from Hannelore had led her to plunge into danger in Europe three times now.

He tapped his napkin to his moustache, a gesture so obviously accustomed that she felt the shock of his transformation all over again. 'No, not directly.'

'What do you mean by that?'

'James says that Hannelore has given him good and, several times, vital information. She remained close to her uncle — Count von Hoffenhausen is now one of the highest-ranking Gestapo officers and holds an army rank of colonel as well. He's been in charge of hunting down any Hapsburgs and their supporters — Austrian and even many German royals are strongly anti-fascist. As a count, he is ideally situated to know who may be disaffected or could be blackmailed, or who could be seduced by the thought of a camp of handsome young men in black leather boots. Germany and Austria still take their royalty seriously. According to Hannelore, there are a growing number of aristocratic army officers who feel that Hitler and the Nazis have gone too far, who might even be planning their overthrow.'

Sophie absorbed this. She had assumed that the only way to victory was a military one. Yet the stalemate of the Great War had been ended when German troops began to desert, no longer following the Kaiser. Could the same thing happen to Herr Hitler? 'How has Hannelore been sending information?'

Nigel — Bob — took a sandwich, but made no move to eat it. 'You know better than to ask that question.'

She nodded, accepting she would have only the facts she needed. Hannelore had sent her a coded letter from Germany in the first war, via a friend in neutral Switzerland. Sophie imagined there were many ways a prinzessin might transmit useful information to England.

The realisation hit her so suddenly she would have spilled her tea if she had still been holding the cup. 'You said every long-term agent has been captured or killed. Hannelore too?' She could not bear it. That first year she had promised her friend kangaroos and sunlight, a respite from royalty and duty. Still, somewhere, she had a dream that one day, when the war was over, Hannelore might finally visit Australia. 'Ni— I mean, Bob, please. Is Hannelore safe?'

'I truly don't know. She has stopped sending information. Our last intelligence was that she is staying at the hunting lodge near Munich — it's too isolated for surveillance. Possibly — even probably — her uncle has suspected her activities and is making sure she can find out nothing more. But the lodge is as safe as any place can be in the war.'

'Then why am I here?' she asked quietly. 'And why so urgently?'

'Because a woman died in the south of France three weeks ago. An unimportant woman who lived in seclusion with her husband, who died three days before she did, of a particularly virulent strain of influenza. Her name was Amelie, Comtesse de Brabant.'

'But what has that to do with me?'

The familiar eyes met hers again. 'We need you to take her place.'

41

Chapter 8

When times are hard, hope costs nothing. Hope shared with friends can bring joy. Just possibly, hope may change the world.

Miss Lily, 1914

'You can't be serious.' Sophie took a slice of cherry cake, to show the impossibility of such a proposition, and also because she was still hungry and this was Mrs Goodenough's cherry cake, the best in the world.

'I am entirely serious. We have been looking for an opportunity like this for over seven months. The possibility that European aristocracy and disaffected army officers might lead a revolt against the Nazis is too important to ignore. Contacts in the resistance have ensured that the comtesse's death has been kept secret — she is said to be taking a long convalescence. But if she fails to appear for too many months there will be enquiries.'

'But why me?'

'Partly physical likeness. You are similar enough to be able to use her identity documents. Those can be forged, but genuine ones are far safer. But you were always our first choice for a mission like this, even if we had to supply false documents. The women trained at Shillings can't enter what is still a closed circle of society —'

'Rubbish. You always chose the best of English aristocracy, as well as European. I was the middle-class exception.'

'Exactly. Any English aristocrat already has too many European connections. They'd be recognised within a day.' The man in front of her smiled. 'But you were a small, defiant colonial fish swimming in strange waters, believing her only value lay in her father's corned-beef empire, totally unaware that she was both lovely and intensely lovable.'

'Sometimes I think that year was my only season of complete, uncomplicated happiness,' she whispered.

'But entirely complicated for me,' said her companion wryly. 'Offering you James as the most suitable companion for your future — and quickly, before Count von Hoffenhausen swept you off to a castle on the Rhine — when all I wanted to do was kneel before you at breakfast, and say "Miss Higgs, will you be mine?"'

'I seem to remember I proposed to you.'

'Almost a decade after I'd finally asked you to marry me.'

'You and Jones made a joint proposal, sitting together on the sofa, both of you in uniform. I wonder if any other woman has been proposed to by an earl, with his butler cum batman offering good reasons to accept him.'

'We've had quite a history, haven't we, my love?'

'You talk as if it's all over.'

'Is it?' he asked quietly. 'You are the one woman who can play this role, totally believable because you moved in those circles for years, and yet not widely enough to be recognised in Paris now.'

She looked at him with quiet horror. Yes, she had longed for something more challenging than paperwork. But this! 'It's impossible. Too many people know me and would recognise me in France. Even my mother is there, though we have only met once, and that was more than twenty years ago, so we could probably pass each other in the street and not notice.'

'The people you worked with in the last war aren't from the circles in which you will be moving.'

'It's not just old acquaintances from France or Belgium. People in Germany have met me too. Hannelore's Aunt Elizabat —'

'She remarried and moved to the United States in 1937.'

'And that horrible man at whose castle we stayed.'

'Who fled to Switzerland to avoid conscription into the army.'

'And Count von Hoffenhausen? I'd be mixing with exactly the kind of people Dolphie is hunting too. What do I say if I meet him? "I say, old thing, would you mind not mentioning I'm a British agent?"'

'He loves you.'

'He loved someone he had constructed in his imagination. He kidnapped me, drugged me —'

'And, yet, when he knew you would always remain faithful to your country, not his, he did not kill you, even though it would have been convenient to do so.'

'He didn't have time to, thanks to Jones and Greenie and then Violette. Anyway, he's married. I'm married. He would turn me in to the authorities within five minutes.'

'He is now a widower. Truthfully, I don't know if he would turn you in or not; nor can we risk it. But there is no reason for him to recognise you — you and the comtesse are similar in height and facial type, but when you become her your hair, dress and manner will be very different. If by any chance you see him you can even dash for the loo. But you will be based in Paris, and he is in Germany. There's little chance you'll meet.'

'What use am I in Paris, if I am to investigate the sentiments of German aristocrats?'

He looked at her patiently. 'Because Paris is where every German soldier spends his leave. The German army even gives each man a book on how best to enjoy it. Paris is being transformed with brothels for every class of soldier, nightclubs for every taste, and luxury hotels for officers and their French mistresses. Who better to flirt with than a beautiful young French comtesse?'

'I'm not young.'

He smiled. 'The comtesse was thirty-three. You look far younger than your age. And you are deeply, unalterably beautiful, and will be when you are ninety-four.'

She looked at him helplessly for a moment. 'I can't. I don't just mean I can't carry it off. The war may drag on for years. I have a husband, children, a business that provides vital supplies for

44

our armies.' And I might die, she thought, which would mean abandoning them all forever.

Her work with Higgs was essential, even if played out in boardrooms and factories, via long phone conversations and paperwork that seemed to reproduce itself faster than rabbits. England and its armies could not fight without food, and England did not even grow enough to feed its civilian population. Did her potential usefulness in Europe outweigh her undisputed achievements back at home, her loyalty to her family?

'Six months,' said the man she could almost think of as Bob. 'We're not asking you to sway the undecided, simply to evaluate current sentiment. Three months' training, while arrangements are settled — that is the fastest we can get you there — then three months in France.'

'You expect me to sniff out anti-Führer sentiments in three months? It might take me that long to find a good butcher.'

'Hannelore has sent us a list of names,' he said patiently. 'You may only need to get one or two of them to trust you to find out who might be further encouraged by contact from England.'

'So I just flutter my eyelashes seductively and say, "Guten Tag, Herr Kolonel, do you feel like strangling the Führer sometimes?"'

'You will know exactly what to do when the time comes.'

She sat silent. He was correct. Two decades of dealing with suppliers and factory managers and other men meant she was extremely good at tactfully extracting information they might wish to keep secret, from an inability to reach production targets to who was pilfering the petty — or not so petty — cash. She could even imagine giving a 'Heil Hitler' with a wink at an inappropriate time, and watching to see if the reaction was indignation, or male condescension for a mere woman who, of course, could not understand the significance of such a great man, to, just possibly, relief at being in company where Hitler was not revered. But knowing she could do it did not mean she should.

'You then return to England and make your report. Others can target those who might be persuaded, or support those who already want a change of regime. Your mission is simply to confirm Hannelore's information, and add to it. George will fly you home again.'

Sophie sat back, suddenly desperately weary. 'You can't ask this of me! I have children. *We* have children.'

She remembered too late Nigel had sacrificed a life with his children to protect a vital intelligence network.

He smiled at her, infinite sadness in his eyes. 'Our children will be adults soon and they have a stepfather who loves them. Armies are not composed solely of those who do not have children.'

She almost retorted, 'But soldiers *are* mostly men.'

If Nigel or Daniel had wanted to enlist, if they had been young enough, she would not have tried to stop them. Both had fought wars before. Danny planned to enlist on his eighteenth birthday, though it was hard to think of her gentle son as a soldier. She suspected he dreaded the thought of New Guinea, too. But within weeks of his birthday he would be in the blood and mud of the jungle island, with other young men as idealistic as he was, and with little more training than their school cadets and potting rabbits had provided. She had no legal power to stop him. She would not try to dissuade him either. It would be useless. Better he go knowing his family was proud of him, than having had to listen to her pleading.

If a boy would offer his life for his country, with so little of its sweetness tasted, shouldn't she? Lily-Nigel, even James, worked not just for love of country, but for Agape, that love of everyone.

She was not abandoning her children to be uncared for. She would even return before they left school, long before they turned eighteen and Danny could be sent to New Guinea with the Militia.

And there was that tiny whisper growing inside her: 'I can do this!'

She looked at the man in front of her. He would not have been a party to the plan if he thought she was betraying their children without the most overpowering of reasons.

'What do you think?' she asked. 'Honestly?'

She knew the look Lily and Nigel shared when they were suppressing anguish.

'I think,' he said slowly, 'that any chance, no matter how small, is worth taking if we can end this war. At the moment, we are losing, despite what the newspapers are saying. Britain is being ground down. If it wasn't for the colonies' raw materials we'd have lost a year ago. As it is,' he shrugged, 'we can't replace the ships that are sunk fast enough; nor can Australia, nor Canada. It takes less time to build a fighter plane, but they're not much use for carrying supplies for an entire population. With the lack of ships to transport food it's a toss-up which will happen first — that Britain will starve, or an invasion will be successful. Japan is perilously close to India and Australia — if they had moved less swiftly and paused to consolidate their positions as they went they would have been unstoppable.'

'But America has joined the Allies now.'

'They have only just begun to mobilise. Most of the fleet was destroyed by the attack on Pearl Harbor. Their main objective now is defeating the Japanese, though they'll be fighting in the war in Europe, too. If Hitler is eliminated, that leaves the USA free to focus on the war in the Pacific.'

'In other words, all faint hopes must be seized, even if this one means my possible imprisonment or death?'

'No!' he said sharply. 'Your new identity will be impeccable. And you will have Violette to help you.'

'Violette must be a major asset to your organisation.'

'It is now James's organisation, not mine; he refuses to have any contact with Violette.'

'Why on earth?' Violette had been separated from her mother, Greenie, at birth. Her early years had been spent with an elderly member of La Dame Blanche, the Belgian Resistance movement. Sophie believed that after the loss of her daughters the old woman had become viciously imbalanced, especially in the way she had accustomed the young Violette to exacting brutal revenge on any collaborator. But Violette had shown herself ingenious — and

47

ruthless — both in Berlin in 1927 and when Sophie had been kidnapped in 1936. 'Violette would be the perfect contact for agents in Paris.'

'I agree. James does not. James says Violette is truly loyal only to herself, enjoys risk, and is therefore unreliable.'

Sophie hesitated. Violette had never expressed love for Jones and Greenie, the parents she had so belatedly been reunited with; nor had Greenie been able to give her the love she'd had for the baby she'd been parted from, although she had tried. After her adoptive grandmother's death, Violette had, indeed, lived with no love in her life at all for several years. Yet Violette had been close to Jones, and even closer to Lily and to Sophie, who she admired, and who did not attempt to restrain her with too obvious parenting. But Daniel had expressed relief when Violette left their family circle.

'Daniel once called her a "possible psychopath",' Sophie admitted. 'Though he wouldn't tell me why. But Violette saved my life. James has to admit that.'

'James believes Violette saved you not for love, or loyalty, but because your gratitude, and money, would be useful. He said she also employed far more violence than was necessary and appeared to enjoy the bloodshed as well as the adventure.'

Sophie bit her lip, thinking back, then shook her head. 'She was much younger then. I would trust Violette with my life.'

'You might have to,' he said lightly. 'Violette's lack of connection with any British agency — and, as far as we know, any resistance organisation — will be an advantage. She is perfectly placed to vouch for your new identity.'

He reached out and took her hand in his. His was more calloused than she remembered, with a hint of ingrained dirt, but they were the hands she'd loved, small for a man, a little too large for a woman. 'Sophie, I love you. So does James. I don't think either of us would have conceived of this if we didn't think you would survive.'

'Despite the loss of every other agent?'

'Not quite every agent, now. And those were not from James's network. All of his agents are still alive.'

'So far.'

'As you say, maybe none of us will survive this war. But believe me when I say we are not sending you to certain death, or even probable death. You won't be caught in a truck with the resistance, trying to blow up a railway line, or discovered transmitting in a cellar with a two-way radio. We worked out your possible identity, and contacts who will help you, every detail, before I asked you here.'

'You said that Lily needed me.'

'She does.' Another wry smile. 'The fact that your country needs you, too, does not lessen that.'

He met her eyes. 'You are loved, and you are needed. But if this works,' Nigel lifted those graceful hands and Sophie, for only one second, saw Lily, 'then Hitler and his henchmen will be deposed. Rudolf Hess offered a negotiated peace when he parachuted into Scotland, even if Herr Hitler refused to acknowledge his mission when it failed. A negotiated peace on far better terms for the Allies is possible now.'

'The Japanese army will still be on Australia's doorstep if peace is negotiated with Germany.'

'The Japanese will also be facing the USA. If America only needs to fight in the Pacific and not in Europe too, the Japanese will be overcome.' He sat back in his chair. The sunlight from the window shone on his scalp and showed the wrinkles of his decades on his face and throat. Miss Lily had always automatically shielded her face from the harshness of direct sunlight. Yet there was still a glimpse of her as Bob said softly, 'You may end the war.'

Sophie stared at him. Sophie Higgs-Vaile-Greenman might be the lever that stopped the war? Unlikely. Remotely possible. Far better than a war dragging on for decades, or ending in the servitude of the lands she loved, certainly. Both possibilities were deeply tempting — as they were meant to be. Sophie Greenman had been using Miss Lily's arts for too long herself to be manipulated by them.

'What if I say no? Will George Carryman risk his life again to take me home?'

'If that's what you wish.'

Sophie wondered if that was true. Letting her think she had the freedom to choose might make her more likely to agree.

A chance to end the war. How could one say no to that? But such a small chance. The chance of a beam of sunlight in the unending black.

'I don't know,' she said at last.

'Good.'

'Good?'

'If you haven't recoiled immediately you will almost certainly agree.'

Sophie managed a smile. 'You let me announce the decision myself.'

'Things need to be hurried in war-time.'

'So I'll be training with your Lovely Ladies?'

Bob almost managed a smile. 'No. The less the others know of your mission and the less you know of theirs, the safer for all of you. Besides, you have already graduated as a lovely lady.'

Charm that had permeated her so deeply it was now an instinct? Walking, swan-like? Gazing with delighted intent into the eyes of whoever was talking to her, even if it was about the art of growing the largest marrow at the Thuringa Show? Pausing in a doorway for a few seconds before she entered a room, so everyone looked up at her? As she smiled for every one of them ...

She shut her eyes for a moment, remembering that magic winter and golden summer before the Great War. The shock of finding that European royalty actually liked her, this gauche colonial from an empire of corned beef. The laughter, the confidences, the loyalty as they left Shillings that last day, knowing they would always be alumni of that select academy, Miss Lily's Lovely Ladies ...

But now she was a member of a family, too. 'What about Daniel and the children? Will there be any way I can keep in touch with them once I get to Europe?'

She already knew the answer before he replied simply, 'No.'

Tea. She needed tea. She felt the pot under its cosy. Still warm. She poured herself a cup, sipped, found it stewed and bitter, then looked back at Nigel. He looked at her, that old, indefatigable love warming his gaze. She looked away.

She had risked her life before. Her hesitation now was for her family. But Bob — and Lily and Nigel — were right. Rose and Danny were strong and resilient, with a father and stepfather who loved and supported them, and friends and neighbours too. Daniel had his clinic. Midge and Harry Harrison and other friends and neighbours would always be there for him.

And Higgs Industries? She had taken on the chief executive role in 1937 to prepare for a coming war that few took seriously. But members of the board of directors could step in. She could only hope they could shuffle diverse data into patterns, find ways to transport goods as ships were sunk and railways commandeered, accept that they must make use of as many alternative methods of food storage as they could to reduce the amount of metal used — all while continuing to prioritise the welfare of her workers and their families.

She sipped her tea and tried for a normal tone. 'So, who trains these lovely ladies?'

'Two lovely ladies of past years. You were here with one of them.'

With Hannelore lost and poor Mouse dead there was only one possibility. 'Emily is here!'

'And doing a most excellent job. The other is Dorothy — I should warn you we only use assumed first names here. Dorothy was at Shillings three years before you. There are other instructors for skills like garrotting your opponent.'

'Dorothy and Emily haven't recognised you?'

'I stay away from the Hall. But to women of their class a handyman is as invisible as a woman is to a Colonel Blimp. I believe, of course, that you would have recognised me even if you had never known me as Nigel.'

He lifted her hand and kissed it.

Sophie flushed. It was the first intimate gesture between them since his supposed death, despite living as Lily at Thuringa for several years. He moved back slightly. 'James is nominally responsible for Shillings now, but he has a wide portfolio. Dorothy — referred to as Miss Dorothy — is in charge of the day-to-day running of the organisation. Emily teaches charm and the complexities of political connections.'

He stood. 'I'll show you to your room. It's not as luxurious as the Hall, but you'll be comfortable.' He smiled at her. 'Mrs Goodenough will bring us dinner. She doesn't trust me to give you a sufficient welcome home meal.'

'My home is Australia. And you, cooking?' She had never known Lily to cook — those lessons had always been with Mrs Goodenough.

'I place my week's meat ration in a pot with herbs and vegetables and a decent libation from the family wine cellar, much of which has been moved here, simmer on a low heat and eat portions each night with potatoes in their jackets or Mrs Goodenough's bread.'

'It sounds excellent.'

'It is. The vegetables vary with the season, as do the herbs. As for meat — I do draw the line at Spam or whale, but there is sometimes a spare rooster or hens too old to lay, or even a hare, and the estate provides firewood.'

He made his way across the living room and opened a door to a winding staircase that smelled of old wood panelling and fresh lavender polish, a familiar scent that almost made her cry again. 'Mrs Goodenough has promised us her special crumpets with honey for tea tomorrow. I was unable to tell her you would arrive today. Loose lips sink ships and all that. We are unlikely to have any Nazi agents at Shillings — James vets the staff here a lot more thoroughly than the other agencies do theirs — but we stay careful.'

He gestured up the stairs. 'Yours is the first room on the right. The bathroom is next door — plenty of hot water, as it's heated from the kitchen fire.'

The last fear — that he might expect her to share his room — vanished. Though the years of their marriage after Nigel's surgery had been characterised more by quiet comfort than by passion, and there had been no sign he might prefer that to change now, she was not comfortable sleeping in any man's bed but Daniel's.

He saw her relief; she saw it hurt him, and wished … No, she had no idea what to wish for at such a moment. Because this man was Nigel, despite the accent and moustache, but Lily had vanished, as surely as if she had indeed been killed in France.

Sophie was not sure she could bear it.

'I need to move the sheep from around the tarmac. A handyman's work is never done.' Bob smiled at her and vanished.

Chapter 9

Mrs Goodenough's Apple Jelly

2 pounds apples (any variety, but crabapples are best; red-skinned ones give a clear red jelly)
White sugar
Water

Slice but don't core or peel apples. Cover with water. Simmer till soft. Strain. I bung mine through a strainer, then pour that juice through a clean old stocking — the more finely you strain out the pulp, the clearer your jelly will be.

For every cup of juice add 1 cup of sugar. If sufficient sugar is not available, you may use half the amount, or even none, and the jelly will still set, but with less sugar the jelly must be eaten quickly as it will soon go mouldy. Simmer, stirring often, till a little dabbed on a cold saucer sets. Pour into clean jars at once and seal.

Blackberry and apple jelly: replace a third of the apples with blackberries, or loganberries, mulberries, raspberries etc.

Rose petal, lemon leaf, mint or other herb jellies: add mint leaves, rose petals, scented geranium leaves, a few dried cloves, chopped fresh ginger root etc to the final stage of jelly simmering. Use a slotted spoon to remove them before you pour the jam into jars. This technique will give you exquisite and very interesting jellies. The savoury ones are good with cold meat, the sweet ones excellent with scones or pikelets.

A small room, its bay window seat with a view across the hothouses and then to the orchard. A faded chintz-covered chair, a silk bedcover that had once been blue, but now showed only traces of colour, a Persian carpet so old one had to guess its original pattern, though the muted tones were still lovely. Pillows that smelled of sunlight and lavender.

Her bag was not just in her room, delivered presumably via the back door: her clothes had been unpacked and her dresses even ironed. Someone with a maid's skill still resided at Shillings and had been sent to ensure she felt cared for. A small apple-wood fire had warmed the room and scented it. It had been years since she had smelled apple wood ...

The bathroom did indeed have a plenitude of hot water, as well as pre-war gardenia bath salts. She bathed, wondering if Lily had stocked her cellar with bath salts and perfumed soap as her ancestors had stocked up on burgundy and port.

She hesitated before she dressed, eventually choosing a pre-war evening dress — burgundy silk, the one she would have chosen if this had been a dinner at the Hall, and long enough not to require the stockings she refused to buy on the black market. Her hair no longer needed a maid to arrange it, nor even a permanent wave for its curls — Thuringa was home to much comfort and beauty, but Bald Hill did not have a hairdresser she would trust with the chemicals needed.

The corridor and stairwell were cold as she walked back down to the living room, but the fire snickered contentedly there, too.

Bob Green, it seemed, changed only into clean moleskins and a jersey for dinner. He saw her look and grinned, the awkwardness of earlier apparently dispelled. 'It might be remarked upon, if anyone passed the window and saw me in evening dress, or if there were an air raid and the neighbours raced in to share the cellar.'

'You have air raids down here, too?'

'I don't think there is anywhere in Britain that doesn't. We make sure there are no vehicles that can be seen from the air, at least.'

'And wooden sheep on the landing strip.'

'We try not to have our people use the train — an unexpected increase in passengers at a local station is one of the best ways of deducing where there may be factories or troop movements. George mostly flies us in. We're on a training route to the RAF — or, rather, James had a training route diverted this way — so the number of flights above Shillings is not remarked on. If you go for a walk, a pilot may waggle his wings at you.'

'I'm too old to elicit wing waggles.'

'Nonsense. Do you mind if we eat in here? It saves trying to keep the dining room warm.'

Mrs Goodenough entered before Sophie had time to speak, carrying two bowls of soup.

Sophie stood to take them from her. 'You shouldn't have come all the way down from the Hall.'

'Goodness no, your ladyship. Not but what I would have, to see you home again. But I live next door now. I lend a hand up at the Hall, but in an advisory capacity.'

It was not a phrase that Sophie had ever expected to hear from the lips of Shillings's former cook–housekeeper. 'And I couldn't leave Mr Green to cope all on his own, could I?' Mrs Goodenough added. She smiled at Sophie and vanished.

Watercress soup, the soup Sophie had sipped the first night at Shillings; there was no first course in the austerity of wartime, even for a homecoming feast, but Mrs Goodenough had casseroled pheasant with cider and apples (pen reared, not shot, Bob assured her), roast potatoes, roast parsnips, Purée Crécy and fresh peas with mint, and after that a raspberry soufflé. Hazelnuts and quince paste followed, as Mrs Goodenough said goodnight.

Sophie took a hazelnut, undoubtedly picked from the hedgerows. She had never seen any grown in Australia. Quince paste ... quince trees and her first love, Angus, in the Great War. What was Angus doing now? The Home Guard, perhaps, with his artificial legs. Had Angus been happy?

Though Angus had not *quite* been her first love. It had been puppy love that brought her to England to acquire the polish to be the wife of a squatter's son. Then Dolphie, who she had loved, would have kept loving, if he had not been German and unable to reckon with such conflicting loyalties. She had met James at a Friday-to-Monday just before the 1914 war was declared, the same party where she had said farewell to Dolphie and Hannelore, the two of them and James so sure the war Sophie could not quite believe in was coming.

She and James had been — suitable. She would have married him if she had not met Angus and known passion, if she had not realised by the end of the Great War that she belonged in Australia, not at English political dinner parties. Had she loved Nigel because she had loved Lily, as teacher and friend, the mother she had never known? Or had she first loved Lily, intuiting that Nigel loved her, too ...

'Who knows about you?'

'That Lily is dead? Or that I'm not?'

'Either. Both.'

'Dorothy, Emily, and all newcomers only know Miss Lily is missing. Some of the old Shillings establishment and the village may guess that Bob Green is another incarnation.' Bob smiled as he added, 'Hereward and Mrs Goodenough certainly know, as do Jones and Greenie of course. Otherwise only James.'

She had not realised how alone Bob was. There had always been Jones and Greenie to support Lily or Nigel, a friendship so close she had sometimes been jealous of all they had shared. Hereward and Mrs Goodenough would always regard him as 'his lordship'. James was mostly in London.

Bob had endured this for three years.

'Are James and Ethel still ... friends?' she asked quickly. 'Ethel never mentions him in her letters, and I haven't liked to ask.'

James Lorrimer, dapper, impeccable and possibly the greatest epitome of a gentleman in England — his antecedents had been refusing peerages for centuries — and Ethel, six feet two in her size twelve shoes, who, as well as her work at the Ministry of Food, defiantly remained on the board of her father's Yorkshire cocoa empire and at times resembled one of the draught horses that pulled his wagons — were an unlikely pair. James had been destined to marry a lovely lady, if not Sophie. But when Sophie had last been in England he and Ethel were undeniably close. Ethel had even accepted Violette's help to achieve beauty, or rather, display the beauty that had always been there, all two hundred pounds of it.

'Ethel is a secretary to the Ministry of Food, which means in essence she runs a large portion of it.'

'I know what she does. That's not an answer.'

'It's the only one I have. Ethel's pacifism is as strong as her nephew's. James may not kill directly, but his actions lead to death. James hasn't mentioned her in three years.'

That was a tragedy. But there were so many tragedies in war ...

'May I see her before I leave?'

He shook his head. 'I'll try to arrange it, but it may not be possible. From tomorrow you become "Miss Jane" or the Comtesse de Brabant. No one else apart from George and Emily, who will be discreet, and Hereward and Mrs Goodenough will be allowed to know Sophie Greenman is in England. The Hall servants have orders to avoid the classroom areas from nine am till five pm. You won't have luncheon with the others. Even your teachers will only know you as "Miss Jane".'

She stared at him. 'I can't even write to Daniel while I'm here? To the children?'

'James sent a cable this afternoon. It will be sent to Daniel from Townsville, saying you've reached there safely, but that the problems at the factory are going to take a while to sort out. You can write to Daniel and the children care of James — he'll try to get any letters to them via air, rather than sea mail. They will appear to have come from Townsville too. I imagine Daniel will understand any oblique references. He is probably best placed to decide the right time to tell Rose and Danny that you're in England, not Townsville.'

'You're not afraid they might find that exciting enough to tell their best friends?'

'You're afraid they can't keep something so important a secret?'

She considered. 'No, not afraid at all.' Her voice was proud.

'I didn't think so,' said Bob Green, who in another life had been their father.

Chapter 10

*It is said that a good breakfast sets you up for the day. If you have
arranged to have the time for a good breakfast — porridge, at least,
or a chance to linger over toast and coffee or a pot of tea — you
have almost certainly also arranged your timetable to set you up
well for the day.*

Miss Lily, 1939

James was sitting neatly at the table in the drawing room when
Sophie came down, her sleep disturbed by the change in time
zones. It was now set with a breakfast cloth, with boiled eggs
in small cosies, excellent toast, a minute dish of butter, and a
lavish silver dish of marmalade. Mrs Goodenough presided with
a coffee pot, wearing her cook's apron — not a maid's, which
would have been well below her dignity.

Mrs Goodenough beamed at her. 'It's a joy to serve real coffee
again, your ladyship.'

'A friend of mine grows it for his own enjoyment in
Queensland, and sends boxes of the beans to us. I hope you have
had a cup too.'

'Truth to tell, your ladyship, I've never taken to it. But I do
like its smell. I hope you enjoy proper English marmalade again,
your ladyship. I had six girls making jams and fruit puddings
from the moment Mr Chamberlain came back from Berlin
waving that scrap of paper. Hereward made sure the cellar was
well stocked, too. If you have to announce peace, I said to him,
then it isn't going to happen. I laid down a few barrels of sugar
too, and don't you call me a hoarder, because there was a good
supply of sugar from the colonies still arriving back then.'

'I wasn't going to. I did the same.' Sophie sat opposite James. 'Thank you, Mrs Goodenough. This looks wonderful.'

'The tea is only Japanese, I'm afraid. His lordship had tea bushes sent here from Japan almost half a century ago, and they've been a godsend since the rationing. The Japanese is better drunk without milk, though you are welcome to it ...'

'I like it without. Thank you, Mrs Goodenough. It is so wonderful to be home, to see you.' Sophie smiled. 'The toast smells amazing. No one makes bread like you.'

'Well, I always did have a hand for it,' admitted Mrs Goodenough, pleased and flustered. She backed out of the door with only a hint of a curtsey.

'Good morning, James. Where is Bob?'

'Feeding pigs in galoshes and overalls. Good morning. Did you sleep well?'

'As well as could be expected.'

'Bob says you have agreed.'

'Actually, I simply didn't entirely refuse,' said Sophie drily. 'I suspect I would have agreed eventually. "Bob" knows me extremely well.'

'Sophie, I can't tell you how vital this is. Hannelore had access to the most influential members of the German military and government. More importantly, I trust her judgement. She believes there is a growing and influential movement among the high-echelon military against the Führer.'

And where is Hannelore now? thought Sophie. Simply being discreet for a while? Her means of communication lost? Or held against her will ...

But she would not think of that now. Instead she said, 'Royalty matters, even if they do not rule.'

'Of course they matter. Our king and queen do nothing practical, but by smiling and saying keep your chin up, and staying in London despite the Blitz, they engender real courage in their subjects. The perception of leadership, even where there is none, is extraordinary.'

Sophie beheaded an egg: impeccable, of course, the white set, the yolk perfect for dipping toast. She dipped, chewed, poured herself a cup of the fragrant tea. 'Ni— Bob gave me the outline. When do I began preparations?' She bent back to her egg.

James smiled, dabbing his lips with his napkin. 'Today. We may not have much notice of when you leave, though, as we'll need an opportunity to drop you into France.'

Sophie glanced up from her egg. 'When you say "drop" I presume you don't mean by parachute.'

'We may be able to get you to France in a fishing boat or submarine, or even by plane, but most likely, yes, by parachute.'

'James, I do not know how to parachute.'

'You will.'

'I see.' How Danny would have loved that part of it, and Rose, too. Unfair that her children must study irregular verbs while their mother leaped from an aircraft. Or did one simply tumble out the door? Undoubtedly, she would find out. 'And my other training? I presume I'll need more than learning how to pass myself off as this comtesse.'

'Far more. You're in for an intense few weeks. But Dorothy will arrange that. The trainees live up at the Hall, but unless you wish otherwise, you'll come back here each night.'

'Why? Security?'

His eyes were watchful. 'Partly, though none of the trainees know the real or assumed identity of anyone they meet here, in case they are captured. But Bob hoped ...'

'I'd prefer to be here,' said Sophie gently. She carefully changed the subject. 'Bob says you didn't wish Violette to be part of your organisation.' She found it easier to say the name Bob this morning.

James seemed to consider her words. 'I don't think Violette is suitable for an organisation or even occasional collaboration. She's unpredictable.'

'What do her parents think of her exclusion?'

'They don't know of it. But they don't expect to be told about other aspects of the network.' He shrugged. 'When the war is over they may well protest, or possibly agree with me. But in this one case …'

'You trust her loyalty to me?'

'Not entirely. You do realise that Violette enjoys killing people, Sophie? She did not have to kill the guards when you were kidnapped, and she arranged it to look as if they had fought each other extremely neatly for a girl who'd had no previous experience of murder.'

Sophie stared. 'She killed people to rescue me? Why didn't you tell me?'

'You were shattered enough,' said James gently. 'But I told Daniel. Lily knew as well.'

So that was what Daniel had kept from her. 'Did her parents know?'

'Not unless Lily told them. I don't think she did. What do you know of Violette's life before she met you?'

'Not much,' Sophie admitted. 'There were the early years with her grandmère, then an orphanage or … or billet of some kind, which she escaped. She admitted she was frightened there. That still leaves several years before she arrived in London to find her mother, to kill her for abandoning her. But she *didn't* kill Greenie, James.'

'Because Miss Green had not abandoned her, but had been told she had died. Violette doesn't kill people she regards as innocent,' agreed James. 'She doesn't kill people she likes, either. She is even loyal to them, to some extent. But trust her? Rely on her? No.'

Once again Sophie remembered Daniel's relief when Violette moved to Paris and would no longer be involved in the children's lives. What else had he been told, or guessed, about the young woman Sophie loved?

Yes, loved, thought Sophie. She loved Violette's passion, her determination, her laughter. Would a psychopath spend so much time playing with small children? There had been a night when Sophie had been up late working and had passed the nursery to see Violette cuddling Danny. 'He had another nightmare about the dragon,' Violette had explained, 'so I told him I cut off the dragon's head, and it fell *plop!* into the stockyard's dunny. Then we ate the rest of him for dinner, so the dragon can never leap into Danny's dreams again.'

Far too ferocious and totally inappropriate for a child, yet Danny's nightmares had indeed ceased. Psychopaths lacked empathy, Daniel had explained. Would a psychopath bother reassuring a small crying boy at midnight?

'You still agree I should ask for her help?' Sophie asked slowly.

'Only because I can see no other way this can be done. Ordinary agents must be inconspicuous — farm hands, factory workers. You will be hiding in plain sight in a world of wealth and privilege. None of our contacts can introduce you to the German military aristocracy without endangering their own roles. I gather Maison Violette is highly regarded among the wives and mistresses of high-ranking German officers,' he added with distaste.

'What did Violette say when you asked her to help me?'

'She hasn't been asked.'

'What? I just arrive? She might be ... taking a holiday.'

'Violette doesn't take holidays. She seems devoted to her fashion house.' He smiled. 'She uses only her first name now, and has discarded the very British Jones. We've kept her under observation, though not close observation. She does not take on new staff often, so we have no one in Maison Violette. Do you think she would help if you suddenly arrived?'

'Of course.'

'Then giving her notice of that would mean she had time to make her own plans and decisions about what you should do, which may very well not accord with ours.'

'What reason do I give Daniel for staying here once they know I am in England? I can write to him before I leave for the Continent, yes?'

'Of course. Leave letters for me to send to him and the children, too, typed perhaps, but with your signature, so I can add any necessary response to their letters. Tell Daniel there have been problems at Shillings, but you can't give details; then that it is proving impossible to find a way back home, but you will keep trying; you have been offered an interesting position and will tell them more when you see them. They — and everyone who reads it — will assume it is a classified position, for what other kind would the Countess of Shillings, the Miss Sophie Higgs of the Great War, have been offered?' He glanced at his watch. 'Dorothy is expecting you at ten am.'

There were many possible answers to that. Instead she chose, 'How is Ethel?'

'Well, as far as I know.'

'You don't still see her?'

'Her choice, not mine.'

'But you told her that Lily was dead? Presumably that's how George found out.'

'I'm sorry about that. She rang me up out of the blue, wanting Lily to support one of her causes. She'd had no answer when she wrote to Shillings. I told her there had been no word from Lily since the Occupation on impulse — a mistake, if she assumed Lily was dead, and told George.'

'She probably thought George already knew, as he works for you. I wouldn't worry about a security risk with either of them.'

James nodded, not looking at her.

'Ethel was good for you, James. You seemed more … alive … after a dinner with her. You were good for her, too.' Violette might have designed Ethel's new wardrobe and introduced her to the transformations of make-up and a flattering haircut, but Ethel had accepted she could be beautiful because of James.

James smiled faintly. 'I thought we were well matched too. Lily told me she most definitely approved, and not to take any nonsense from those who thought I should marry within my class. That's as close as Lily ever came to giving an outright order. But I am a second-hand killer, my crimes greater than if I wielded the weapon.'

'Ethel didn't say that?'

'I quote exactly.'

'I'm sorry, James. Ethel can be as stubborn as a seaside donkey.'

'It's not stubbornness. It's integrity. I love her for it. But you of all people know there is no choice but to fight this war, with whatever weapons we can find.'

'Including me? I'll try to see her before I leave. Could you make time for that?'

'Possibly. She can't come here for security reasons — she might recognise Bob, to begin with. Logistics are dicey at best. But if you do see her, don't mention me.'

Sophie had every intention of mentioning James and forcefully, too. She stood rather than reply. 'What should I wear to meet this Dorothy?'

'What you are wearing now. As a graduate lovely lady, as well as a countess and patron of a French fashion house, you are excused the charm and deportment lessons the women come here to receive. But that is all Dorothy's department ...' James stood, too. 'I must get back to London.'

He suddenly looked very alone. But that, surely, was an illusion. James had uncounted webs of agents at his fingertips, or rather, ones very carefully counted indeed, as well as colleagues and decades' worth of friends.

She leaned over and kissed him lightly on the lips. 'Take care, James.'

'I'll see you before you leave. Just let me know if there is anything you need done.'

'And you will always do it.' She smiled and went upstairs to change her shoes to ones with higher heels and add earrings and an ivory silk scarf to her grass-green woollen dress with its short matching jacket, the subtleties that a Dorothy would notice and respect.

Chapter 11

England is a land of social opposites ... the upper class own most of the nation's wealth ... the lower class ... have an astonishingly low material and intellectual standard of living ... some of this is poverty they do not deserve, but is due also to the low competence in domestic matters of the women.

A rough translation of the German Invasion Plans for the Invasion of the British Isles, 1940, published by the Military High Command, Department for War Maps and Communications, Berlin

SOPHIE

'Milk and sugar, Miss Jane?' Miss Dorothy's smile was warm as a tea cosy, and Sophie had no right to imagine herself pouring the brew over the woman's excellently cut grey hair, simply because this woman sat in Miss Lily's chair.

'Neither milk nor sugar, thank you.'

Miss Dorothy was slightly older than Miss Lily had been when Sophie had first met her in this room. Miss Dorothy even dressed similarly: a chiffon scarf flattering her neck, the light carefully behind her, a woollen dress of pale gold with a softly draped skirt, obviously pre-war, but the cut narrowed and the skirt shortened for the modern austerity look.

It was ... discombobulating to see someone else sitting where Miss Lily had so often sat, in the small drawing room with its parchment-papered walls. If she allowed it, Sophie might find it sad, tragic, *impossible* ...

But Miss Dorothy had not supplanted Miss Lily, Sophie reminded herself. She was staunchly taking on a role left vacant, transforming girls into the loveliest of ladies, so irresistible that they would gain the right attention, convince the right people to do the right things, and harvest the right information.

Sophie had expected Shillings to have gained at least a mildly institutional feel, if not green-painted walls and linoleum. But of course it was the same. That was the point: a small museum of the grace that all young women here must seem accustomed to, even if the most valuable and valued of the family's possessions had been sent to a Welsh mine for safety.

Not that Sophie had seen any young women yet. Days here were strictly timetabled so those in residence did not glimpse anyone they were not supposed to know. Sophie could hear vague chirping and laughter in the library, but could count only three voices, or possibly four.

'As I was saying, Miss Jane, you will do self-defence classes each morning from eight o'clock to eleven o'clock with the commander, then return to the agent's cottage, where it seems that Bob Green will go over other matters with you. Mr Lorrimer says that Mr Green worked for him for some years, but chose to retire here near his family. Return here at two o'clock each day for an hour of language with Fräulein or Madame, and an hour of the arts of disguise with Miss Portia. There will be other instruction too. Please don't wander about the estate — the tenants know you are here, of course, and may come to say hello, but we do try to obscure our exact inhabitants as much as we can. You will, of course, not disclose to anyone that you have been here ...'

'Except to all my family and close friends,' said Sophie sweetly, 'who would expect me to have at least visited the family home while in England.'

'Ah, yes, of course.' Miss Dorothy had clearly not considered that.

'Certainly. I gather my friend Emily is here as well?'

'*Miss Sophronia* has asked you to join her for dinner tonight, privately. Please do be careful with names. Would you mind arriving just after eight o'clock, when the other students will be already dining?'

Sophie laughed. 'Did "Miss Sophronia" really choose *my* name as her cover?' She stood. 'Thank you, Miss Dorothy. I promise I'll duck behind a tapestry if I see any of your young ladies approaching. I will attempt to look as Jane-like as I can.'

Miss Dorothy hesitated. 'You think our caution is excessive. But it's possible, even likely, that you will either be captured or have your cover exploited by someone you felt you could trust. The less you know the safer for all of us, but it's also safer for you. If you are captured you need to be able to confess as much as possible in the knowledge that none of it will help the enemy in any way.'

'To prevent the enemy torturing and killing me?'

Dorothy smiled. 'A slim hope. But we dangle on extremely slim hopes these days. If there are enough perhaps they will weave into a rope and we may survive.'

'Surely the knowledge that Shillings is your headquarters has value?'

'Not as much as you might think. We have air-raid warnings and deep cellars if the Hall is bombed. There can be other headquarters.'

Sophie repressed a stab of fury that Shillings might so easily be discarded. But Dorothy was correct. True value to the war effort came from the people, not the Hall.

'I will introduce you to Fräulein this afternoon. Hereward will show you the way out.'

Sophie turned. Hereward stood impassive in the doorway. She winked at him. 'I think Hereward has other duties. I will see myself out.'

Did Hereward return a flicker of a wink as he vanished? Sophie glanced at Dorothy, expecting an almost hidden frown. Instead she looked amused. 'I suspect the quondam Miss Sophie Higgs may prove to be more of a threat to Hitler than the RAF. One might almost feel sorry for him. But not quite.'

Half an hour later Sophie was again annoyed.

'Repeat,' ordered the commander.

Sophie lunged for the fifth time, plunging the carving knife once more into the dummy hanging on the post in the orchard, then upwards. It was proving extremely difficult to murder someone — even a dummy — in high heels.

'The heart is to the left, Miss Jane. Again.'

'This would be easier in flat heels or boots,' panted Sophie.

'Which none of you women are likely to be wearing,' said the commander grimly. Teaching persons who were not just female, but wore heels and in this case, jewellery, seemed to offend his military sense of propriety. 'Ah, that is ... acceptable,' he added grudgingly, as Sophie lunged again, hoping her shoes wouldn't be stained in this mud.

'Stand easy,' he told her.

Sophie perched on the fence railing. He glared at her but didn't comment. He had obviously been told that Sophie alone had the contacts for whatever mission she would be sent on. He did not have the power to give her a 'pass or fail' course and was simply to give her as many skills as possible in as short a time as possible.

'Now the problem with stab wounds to the heart or lungs is that, while they are effective, the victim may make considerable noise.'

'That does seem likely.' Sophie inspected her shoes and tried to catch her breath.

The commander frowned. It seemed he was not used to students' comments. He exchanged his frown for the small smile Sophie had observed in military men who would like to strangle you, but are not allowed. 'The next two methods, if done properly, should result in swift and silent death, without any bleeding.'

'No throat cutting, then? Excellent. I imagine a cut throat makes a terrible mess to clean up. And it is of course more difficult if you are a short woman, unless your target is sitting down, preferably with his back to you.'

'Indeed. Now for the next procedure I am about to demonstrate I advise you to wear an easily detachable silk or chiffon scarf at all times. A scarf has other uses, of course …'

Sophie suppressed the urge to comment that a scarf in shades of silver grey and ivory also matched almost any ensemble, in case the poor man exploded.

'Prepare the scarf like this, then drape like this, place over the enemy's neck and pull like this …'

Sophie slid off the rail, slipped off her scarf and repeated the procedure on the dummy.

'Quite well done, Miss Jane,' he condescended.

'No praise earned, I'm afraid. My maid showed me how to do that twenty years or so ago, as well as a most useful technique with a meat skewer in the kidneys. If you insert the skewer here,' she demonstrated, 'and in this direction, your victim will die instantly and silently. When the skewer is removed it can be used to truss a goose or turkey, a process which will remove all forensic evidence by the time the bird is to be served.'

'Your … maid.'

'She is otherwise engaged at the moment.'

The commander shut his eyes. She wondered if he was dreaming of being holed up at Tobruk or even in the Black Hole of Calcutta, rather than among the monstrous regiment of women at Shillings Hall.

'Commander, if it will make these sessions shorter: I can already theoretically kill or disable a man silently and have practised those techniques on dummies before. I am an excellent shot with assorted firearms — I can pot a rabbit at a hundred yards. In the last war I did not hesitate to shoot quickly and accurately when my target was human, not cunicular. I could show you two ways to eliminate an opponent with a high-heeled shoe, though I'm afraid I do not have any that would fit you.'

He glared at her. 'This course is not just about self-defence, but survival.'

'I survived the battle zones of one war for several years. I can dress a wound, splint a broken leg, trap, skin and cook rabbits, mice, pigeons, sparrows, and possibly hedgehogs, assuming that's the same technique as rabbits, and my father taught me how to disable a dog if it attacks me. I can find my way by sun and stars, ride bareback, side-saddle, or with any saddle or horse I am offered, and swim beneath a duck undetected to pull it under and have it for dinner.' An Australian stockman had taught the young Sophie that, though in fact she had been a woman. 'I can also install and command a field hospital. I had not practised stabbing a man in the heart, but as you said, as it is likely to be messy and noisy I may have wasted your time and mine learning to do so.'

He eyed her. 'Congratulations, Miss Jane. What *can't* you do that you might need?'

She considered. 'I need a refresher course in German. The more fluent I am the better, even if I pretend to know very little. But everyone subconsciously prefers those who speak their language well.'

'That will be attended to.'

'So I have been informed. I know the latest English fashions. I don't know what might be worn on the Continent. I presume you can't help me there?'

'That is Miss Dorothy's affair. What else?'

'How to parachute. Or, rather, how to survive a parachute jump. I suspect I can do the jumping part.'

'Which shows that you have never done it.' He allowed himself a small smile at the thought of her attempting it. 'That will be taught elsewhere.'

'Excellent. A sky flowering with parachutes above us every few weeks would make Shillings a little conspicuous. May I have lunch now, Commander?'

She didn't like the glint in his eyes. 'You believe we are finished, Miss Jane?'

'I believe you now intend to make me do fifty push-ups and various other exercises. However I live on a large property; I help with shearing, fencing and even chopping firewood since the war began. I find it relaxing after my other work is completed. I can bring down a stroppy fly-blown ram then dag it. I believe I can do without daily push-ups.'

'You will, however, follow my orders.'

'No, Commander. I am going to undertake a role where I will be the person who gives orders, rather than takes them. Learning to take orders might seriously damage the impression I must give. Would you like to join me at luncheon? No?' She had only offered because she was extremely sure he would not accept. 'Then I doubt I need another session with you, but I do hope we meet again, Commander.'

Sophie allowed her tone a touch of graciousness. She could almost hear the reply he did not utter: 'Not if I see you first, lady.' Though that was possibly not what he'd prefer to call her.

~ぬ~

'I was extremely badly behaved this morning.' Sophie served herself a large helping of green peas, a small helping of roast duck in orange sauce — the orange trees must still be doing well in the orangerie, as England's orange juice supplies were kept for children now, but even this attempt to recreate the glamorous life of the aristocracy for the trainees must be affected by meat rationing — and an enormous helping of potatoes baked in their jackets. They were dining in the Shillings library.

Emily's plate was more moderately filled, her impeccable burgundy velvet austerity dress adorned by two rows of perfect pearls, with subtle embroidery at the cuffs. One changed for dinner, naturally. 'What terrible faux pas have you made?'

'I did not even try to charm the commander. In fact I enjoyed making him furious, which of course the poor man was unable to show.' Sophie shrugged. 'I don't want to be here, but I can't be angry with James ...' Or Nigel, she thought. 'So I took it out on the commander. I should really have been practising "charm, effective on military personnel".'

'Not worth it. Minor public school,' remarked Emily. She neatly tucked her last small mouthful into the pouch of her cheek just as they had been shown by Miss Lily — the best way to continue a conversation during a meal without long gaps between mouthfuls, or even worse, displaying food in an open mouth. 'He's a bit of an oik really. From a decidedly second-rate regiment.'

'He does seem ... out of place. But he also seems to know his job.'

'He's capable. He doesn't want to be here either, but was wounded last year — he's off to Palestine soon enough. He assumes our girls and women are going to act as temporary liaisons with the resistance groups in occupied Europe, hence all the garrotting and daggers. I hope when he is redeployed James will find someone a little more suited to our establishment.'

'Who else is on the staff?'

'Darling, you make us sound like chambermaids. There's Madame and Fräulein for languages of course. Both have impeccable backgrounds, so don't worry about their accents.'

'I wasn't.'

'Of course, you deal with Continentals all the time, don't you?' The gentlest of digs at Sophie not just inheriting wealth from 'trade', somewhat more acceptable now than before the Great War, but also actually indulging in business herself. 'You'll have at least a half-hour with Miss Marcella tomorrow morning, instead of the commander. She was in a circus family before she caught the eye of her husband twenty years ago or so. I believe she was wearing a short pink skirt and spangles while standing on the back of a galloping stallion at the time. She is really quite delightful, despite her background. A half-hour will give her the time to judge whether you might be taught how to walk a tightrope between two buildings, or climb the ivy on a wall.'

'I don't think my role will need either.'

'But your escape might. You may seem to be succeeding then suddenly ...'

'Tightrope time?'

'Literally perhaps, as well as metaphorically.'

'Point taken. How is your spouse?'

'Visible. That is his job now. Gilbert is visible in the Home Guard, at regimental dinners, at war bonds rallies. Gilbert has always been superb at being visible.' Emily helped herself to another slice of duck. 'You were the great success of our year, darling. Poor Mouse, dead in childbirth, Hannelore's estates lost, and not even married, not to mention under Nazi rule, and here you are a countess and now married to a man who is ...' she considered '... effectual.'

Which was possibly the most damning comment possible about her own husband, Gilbert Sevenoaks. And Emily must not have been told that Hannelore had been a Nazi agent, and then a British one. 'You've been unhappy?'

'Strangely, no. Having a nonentity as a husband — one hardly notices he is at the breakfast table, as long as one makes approving noises after he speaks — has left me free. I've had my salons, the odd dalliance. I have my own network now. No, not like Lily's. Political. I intend to stand for parliament when the war is over and we have elections again. I will be the Conservative member for Little Worrington.' This was the district of her family seat. 'My future constituents will be horrified at voting for a woman, of course, but not as shocked as they would be at the idea of voting for anyone but a Conservative.'

'What does Gilbert think about that?'

'A trifle embarrassed, but he doesn't want to stand himself — it would interfere with the hunt and the shooting. He'll campaign for me. As I said, he is excellent at being visible. Ignore my waspish remarks. Miss Lily would gently reprove me. Gilbert and I are fond of each other, Sophie, when it occurs to us. Oh, an apple pie! Genuine pastry! Thank you for bringing our dinner all the way up to the Hall, Mrs Goodenough! Everyone else is getting tapioca pudding tonight.'

Emily waited till the cook had left. 'I keep seeing echoes of Miss Lily,' she said softly. 'It's hard. It must be worse to have lived here with Nigel, and to miss them both.'

Only a small number had ever known of Lily-Nigel's joint existence. Emily was not one of them. Sophie simply nodded.

'I miss her dreadfully,' confessed Emily. 'Dorothy too. We can teach grace, and manners. But Dorothy and I don't have Miss Lily's insight into others, the ability to feel as they do that Miss Lily said is the true heart of charm.' Emily smiled in memory. 'She was the most graceful woman I've ever seen. The most beautiful too, though I could never work out why, as her features weren't classically pretty at all. But when she smiled ... somehow all my memories of her are smiling. Oh dear,' she dabbed her eyes with an impeccable white handkerchief, 'this will never do.'

Sophie found her own eyes damp. 'She saw what was good and strong in us, and made us who we might be.'

To her surprise Emily rose. Sophie stood too, as Emily embraced her, then said, 'We may not have a chance to talk again. Your schedule is going to be full and we never know when there'll be the chance to get you across the Channel. You need to be ready fast, and my nose is kept to the grindstone. Just ... always have an escape route, darling, even if you can't manage a tightrope. You are my oldest friend.' To Sophie's slight shock Emily obviously meant that. 'I'd hate to lose you to a firing squad.'

'I have many reasons for staying alive,' said Sophie quietly.

'Good,' said the woman who was no longer merely Mrs Colonel Sevenoaks.

Chapter 12

Change never happens as quickly as people of good will hope. But look at the past; the children who slaved in coalmines last century because they were cheaper than ponies are now educated; women have the vote, and are even allowed to study mathematics, both seemingly impossible when I was a child. I have seen so much change in my lifetime. What will change in yours, or in your daughters'?

Miss Lily, 1937

VIOLETTE

The woman was young, blonde, endowed with a bosom that was perfection and a waist that was tiny, and strolled into Maison Violette's main salon with the aplomb of one who had spent two years using her attributes to hold the attention of men who would reward her with gifts and, just possibly, marriage, if one were free and she saw no better prospect.

This afternoon at Maison Violette was the occasion for arranging such a gift. It was, most probably in this case, a farewell one. Violette had enough experience to judge that from the young woman's face, smiling, but also evaluating which dress might not just cost the most but which looked expensive too, to make the most of the time she had invested. Ruby beading around the neck and cuffs and in two rows about the hem — most noticeable indeed, and by far the most costly of all the ensembles mademoiselle had been shown. The man, a Gestapo colonel, merely seemed amused as he gazed around the room, until he saw Violette.

77

His gaze stopped, as if he had found what he had been subtly searching for. He gave an almost imperceptible smile. She herself was this man's target, Violette realised, and the reason the gift was a Violette creation, rather than diamond earrings.

And she knew him. The Count von Hoffenhausen, the man Aunt Sophie called 'Dolphie', who had kidnapped Aunt Sophie and whose men she, Violette, herself, had killed. Pouff! They had deserved it. But this man had seen her then, though as far as she knew he had not known her name.

He knew it now. And not just as a couturier.

His young companion touched the colonel's hand and pointed at the model in the ruby-embossed dress, as she slowly turned for inspection. The dress's heavy silk was from a pre-war kimono, each a work of art in themselves, but turned into yet another work of art, which they deserved. Violette felt slight regret though each time she repurposed one of the kimonos. The Japanese treasured clothing for generations, its age as well as its beauty given respect. Sadly, this dress — though cut with such brilliance across the hip, its hem weighted with such perfection that it would hang straight no matter how its wearer moved or sat — would be discarded in a season if another admirer proved as generous, with only its rubies kept perhaps. But Violette had always accepted that for the ignorant, clothes were a transient art ...

'Mademoiselle Violette?' Yes, he knew her, and not for her designs.

'Yes, Kolonel ...?'

'I think you know who I am,' he said softly. Handsome, even if his hair was scattered grey. But this man was not just a Boche but a most committed Nazi who had worked to bring Herr Hitler to power.

'I think ...' Violette paused, considered, then smiled at him with almost full wattage. 'Yes, I think I do remember you. Will you have coffee in my office perhaps, Kolonel? Madame Fleurette can deal with ...' She let her fingers fly in a gesture that might have referred to the dress, the payment or his companion, giving equal unimportance to them all. 'Gisette!' she called to her assistant, 'two coffees, please, in my office.'

She considered the essence of a certain mushroom, as she led him to her office. She had brought it from Australia and used it only once. It was most useful, for the first symptoms of heart failure did not occur until a day later, and few would know what substance to search for even if they suspected the death was not natural.

It would be so easy to slip a teaspoonful of the clear, only slightly bitter liquid into his coffee, this man who had kept Aunt Sophie who Violette, yes, loved, in a dark cellar, too drugged to escape. This monster had fed the fires of hatred until now the world burned. But it would be best not to poison him, she decided, till she knew exactly what he wished from her. She doubted it was dresses.

Her smile did not waver as she led him in and sat with him in her office that was as much a drawing room as an office. Her desk, created for the Versailles of a king called Louis — Violette could never remember which number he was — looked elegantly not like a desk at all as Gisette placed the silver tray upon a side table, then poured the coffee exactly as Violette preferred it — strong, sweet and black. The colonel shook his head to cream and sugar. He waited till Gisette departed.

'Do you still correspond with the woman you call your Aunt Sophie?'

Ah, no pretence then. But no reason to give him more information than he had, either. Violette was glad now she had not drugged his coffee yet. This was … interesting. She smiled again, rather than reply.

He sipped his coffee, as relaxed as if discussing one of the Wagner concerts the Boche seemed to love so much. 'I have followed your aunt's life, you see.'

And Violette had met Aunt Sophie when a woman employed by this man's niece had pretended to be sympathique, to help her find her long-lost mother, not from kindness but so that Violette might endanger the Vailes somehow.

'You tried to use me as a weapon when I was a child.' She sipped her own coffee. 'Many have tried that. None succeeded.'

'I hope I do not underestimate you now.'

Another sip. Had he guessed she was not just calmly designing jewels of silk and chiffon for collaborators? Now he knew who she was, including what he might assume about her connection to Mr Lorrimer, it would not be a difficult deduction. But what could he prove, if he suspected murder?

But then the Gestapo did not have to prove. They had only to accuse. Those who confessed vanished, and so did those who did not.

The problem then was to find out if he had told anyone about her. He had come here, and alone, when he might have sent an agent to fetch her, to make her a little readier to talk.

Why?

He put his cup down and watched her over steepled hands. Long fingers, and soft. Even his coat would be unbuttoned by his valet. Violette thought of Aunt Sophie's hands, which washed up on Cookie's night off, held her horse's reins without bothering with gloves, built a campfire by the river and boiled a billy at a picnic …

'Mademoiselle, someone like yourself, who has English parents, must always be under slight suspicion. Unless of course you are known to be under my protection. Perhaps we may be useful to each other.'

Violette smiled at him again over her coffee cup. Sometimes men were enchanted by her smiles. Just sometimes, she chose to terrify. This smile had all the charm of a sunrise. 'Really, mon Kolonel? Please tell me more.'

Chapter 13

You would think that by having three disguises, I never would have had to pretend to be what I am not, merely select which aspects of myself to show to the world. But none of my public faces has been the entire truth.

Miss Lily, in a letter to Sophie, 1944, unsent

Dearest Daniel,

Townsville is hot, humid and strangely unchanged from when I last saw it. Much is changed of course, with the military presence, but I keep expecting that if I shut my eyes all will be as it was when I was here years ago.

As I mentioned in my cable, the problems here are not going to be easily solved, but it is vital that they are — corned beef is just too valuable to take chances with. I may also need to go inland to visit the suppliers — a factory can only be as effective as its materials. It will undoubtedly be difficult, uncomfortable and I very much wish I didn't have to go, as staring at the rear end of cattle is only really interesting when they are your own or, possibly, if you are a bull. But I don't have a choice or, rather, I do — to be where I most want to be on earth with you or heading into central Queensland to ensure that bully beef not just continues to be supplied, but that we can greatly exceed any production target we expected in the next twelve months.

I won't bore you with details and I probably won't be able to once I head into the outback. Communication has never been good there — one reason why I'm going — and it is probably far worse now. So you will be spared my adventures with bulldust, grass that either vanishes or grows to your knees overnight, and what is either drought or flood, because Queensland seems always to be in one state or another. So is Thuringa, of course, but it is different when it is your own drought or flood. The one person you might share some of this cattle misery with is Midge. I'd add Harry, but he wouldn't hear you, and Midge will tell him anyway after you have gone, in that odd sign language and lip-reading they have developed. Darling, please do see Midge if you want to moan about my cattle adventures. Midge will always understand.

I haven't mentioned to Rose and Danny in my letters to them at school that I might be in Townsville so long. That news might be better kept for the school holidays. What a time we live in, when even the number and timing of shipments of corned beef must be secret.

Darling Daniel, I cannot say how much I miss you, and love you, because I would shock the censor. Please remember all my previous statements on those subjects. PLEASE remember them and never forget. You are here in my heart, even if I cannot touch your hand.

Give my dearest love to Rose and Danny, and my anguish at not being there for Christmas. Perhaps only you can guess how much I wished this had not been necessary. But I promise that we will have Easter, at least, all together.

I love you more than I can say,
Sophie

'Please do take notes, Miss Jane.' Fräulein — no name given — spoke German in almost the same accent as Hannelore: *hoch Deutsch*, aristocratic and possibly even from the same region as Hannelore's northern estates, now all in Russian hands, apart from the Bavarian hunting lodge. Or had the estates been retaken by the Nazis? That might not necessarily mean her getting them back.

'The Civil Security Police are now as follows: the Gestapo,' continued Fräulein, for the German lessons combined information with language skills, 'the state political police and the Kripo, the state criminal police, now effectively working as one, under the umbrella, if you will, of the SS — the Gestapo owes greater allegiance to the Nazi Party than the Kripo, of course. They, and all SS officers, are not subject to the political or judicial system of any country and may work independently. They wear plain clothes and only their documents — which are with them at all times — identify them. If identification is essential then you need to find an opportunity to look for their documents — the identity disc of the Gestapo, the red identity card and the SS membership card.

'At times, however, both Gestapo and SS may do work of a paramilitary nature, in which case they wear a field-grey uniform, a peaked cap with a death's head, a tunic with back collar patches, rank on the left.'

Field-grey uniform, thought Sophie, imagining Dolphie in one. A peaked cap with a death's head …

'The Sicherheitsdienst, the SD, on the other hand, is the SS's information arm, and occupied mostly with civilian sedition, political espionage in neutral countries. Their agents are usually of a higher grade than the Gestapo's. Do not underestimate them, Miss Jane, though the Gestapo is more commonly feared. The Sicherheitsdienst tend to have more powerful connections. Often their identity is not known even to Gestapo agents and they may also act under cover as Gestapo agents. If a man of high military rank is not obviously attached to a regiment, suspect Sicherheitsdienst.'

Sicherheitsdienst, thought Sophie. Dolphie would almost certainly be Sicherheitsdienst …

'Fräulein.' Sophie spoke almost without thinking. 'Why are you here?'

'And not in Germany?' The Fräulein gazed at her hands, then looked up, not quite hiding her anguish. 'I had a niece,' she said quietly, no longer in the clipped tones of an instructress. 'My sister's child, a girl of joy, so loving, so intelligent, but born blind. An Untermensch,' she added bitterly, 'according to the Nazis. My sister's husband divorced her, for the crime of polluting the Aryan race. We … my sister and I, and my employer back then …

tried to find refuge with my employer in England. We were too late. The Nazis murdered my niece and every other child in the school for the blind.'

The Fräulein met Sophie's eyes. 'We must destroy the Nazis and the evil of their philosophy. Whatever your mission, Miss Jane, I cannot express how much I hope you succeed.'

~⊰⊱~

'Communication, of course, is the key.' The small grey-headed woman with a Belgian accent nodded at Sophie. 'You will know how we of La Dame Blanche used to knit our codes to be taken to Britain. That will not work for you, Miss Jane. Postcards sent to a collection point are useful — a postcard is so open and obvious it receives less censorship scrutiny than a letter, though if the person you have written to becomes a suspect, you will be too.

'For you, an advertisement is best. You will lose an earring and place a weekly advertisement offering a reward for its return. You may also advertise for staff, or whatever occurs to you. But the words you include will tell us what you want. The word "possibly" will mean you are ready to return to England. "Large" will mean you need to pass on more information. I will give you a list of words to memorise tonight.

'The key, however, will be another word, which you will memorise, a new one every week, which must be included. That will tell us it is indeed you who sends the message. Longer messages must be given to those who contact you. The code will be a simple substitution one — based on a poem is best, as it is easiest to remember under pressure.'

'So, we'll go no more a roving,

So late into the night,' murmured Sophie, suddenly thinking of her last night at Shillings with Nigel.

'Though the heart be still as loving,

And the moon be still as bright.'

'That will suit well. So, A now becomes N, and B becomes O ...'

Sophie nodded. 'I understand.'

'Excellent. If you ever need help urgently you must phone this number. It is for emergencies only, if, for example, you need immediate extraction or have information that must be passed on within a few hours.'

'I understand,' said Sophie again.

'Good. It is too dangerous to phone a contact directly — there are few private phones in France, so any call can be easily traced. Few in the resistance have access to a private phone anyway. This number will take you to a bistro that takes messages for any customer. But only use it if you have no other alternative — the owner will not volunteer information to the Germans, but he will probably cooperate with them if questioned and threatened. Once it has been used we cannot use it again.'

'I understand,' Sophie repeated.

'Here is a list of code phrases. "Tell Michelle there will be rabbit for dinner on Saturday" means you have information which is too urgent to wait for an advertisement. "Tell Michelle that Anna needs her bicycle returned" means you need a refuge or escape immediately. "Hugo won't be at Maman's for lunch" —'

'Pardon, Madame, but if I urgently need a refuge I might not have time to wait for a message to be delivered.'

'There will be an answer waiting for that one.'

'Wouldn't it be easier to tell me where the refuge might be now?'

'Much easier, but far less safe for those in France. Besides, the refuge could change. You are not the only one who may need a hiding place in Paris. Now "Hugo won't be at Maman's for lunch" will mean ...'

A woman with short grey hair, a face like an axe and eyes that refused to see Sophie as a person, perhaps because she had seen too many lost and one more would be more than memory could bear, appeared at Shillings only on Tuesday afternoons; her main work obviously elsewhere. She had no name here, for she did not stay for any meal. Hereward simply called her 'ma'am'.

'Interrogation initially will begin with alternating poor and good food, comfort and discomfort, a soft approach.' Her voice was matter-of-fact. 'The prisoner may be at one end of a long room while the officer at the other end works at his desk, apparently not aware the prisoner is there. You will be threatened with the firing squad.'

'Will the firing squad be just a threat?' asked Sophie quietly.

'Possibly. You may even hear rifles at dawn, a display purely to try to break you. But a firing squad is the penalty for any enemy who does not wear the uniform of a combatant. If they believe you will be of no more use, they may dispose of you. Or there may be mercy. It does exist, even in occupied Europe. Beware any guard, warder or fellow prisoner who befriends you and then asks questions. Have straightforward answers prepared and stick to them. Pretend to be more exhausted than you are — they may then ask the more important questions, so the questioning will be over sooner ...'

—❦—

Perhaps it was the air of Shillings, even though she did not sleep at the Hall, but every night she dreamed of her times there and woke surprised to find herself in the bed at the cottage.

Sometimes she, Hannelore, Emily and poor dead Mouse made a snowman, while Miss Lily gazed indulgently from the breakfast room, where the salvers steamed with food almost forgotten in England now — the bright yellow buttery rice and smoked fish of kedgeree, kidneys with bacon, finnan haddock, scrambled eggs with buttered mushrooms, poached eggs on their own small rafts of toast. More fresh toast to eat with lavish butter and a choice of jams and Mrs Goodenough's exquisite marmalade was brought in at regular intervals by Jones in his guise as butler: far more food than any of them would sample, but an education in how things should be done for the two girls in straitened circumstances, and for Sophie, wealthy but ignorant of aristocratic life.

Mostly she dreamed of sitting with Lily in the small drawing room where Dorothy now presided, while Lily talked of Balkan politics, or how to hide a sandwich snack in one's train for an extended and underfed formal evening at the palace, or the correct gifts for a maid, cook or footman who was leaving to get married.

The young Sophie Higgs had never been able to ask absolutely anything before, much less have it answered: what did High Church vicars wear under their black skirts? (Trousers, so disappointing.) And Scotsmen under their kilts? (A far more satisfactory answer, and a scandalous anecdote about Queen Victoria and a guardsman as well.) *Why* had the Germanic states federated, much like Australia, but somehow ended up with the Kaiser as king, instead of all the other royal contenders?

She often woke from those both smiling and in tears. It was deeply satisfying to be with Nigel again, even in his guise of Bob, and despite her longing for home. But Miss Lily was missing, both officially and in her heart, and while this could be borne at Thuringa with her family around her, it was unendurable here.

But this was war, when the unendurable happened every day, and you (mostly) managed to get through it.

The name she gave was Miss Portia. Sophie grinned. If one of England's greatest actresses had truly wanted to be anonymous, she would not have assumed the name of the role that had made her famous.

The delicate-featured woman before her had not followed that success, as many did, into film, possibly because by the time talkies had become popular she had been well past the age of most major roles for women. 'Miss Portia' must now be in her eighties, her white hair softly curled, her face carved with the laughter, kindness and fury of the hundred heroines whose lives she had briefly inhabited.

It occurred to Sophie that Miss Portia, too, might well have been a lovely lady at some stage of her life, one of the earliest perhaps. One day, after the war, if both she and Miss Portia survived it, she might ask.

Miss Portia was one of the few who knew the identity Sophie must assume. The actress looked at Sophie thoughtfully. 'You are the Comtesse de Brabant, which means you were once a chorus girl who called herself an actress.' She shrugged. 'If you had truly been an actress, you would not have given up the stage. Luckily your lack of any true interest in the dramatic arts means you don't know any of the luminaries in the profession. You lived in seclusion in the south of France — Vichy France — till your husband's death, for although he was fifty-two years older than you and in delicate health when you married fourteen years ago, he heartlessly lived to eighty-five.'

'Miss Portia, I'm not sure I can pass for thirty-three,' said Sophie frankly. 'I was taught that one can be beautiful at any age and have never tried to look younger than I am. I also suspect my skin has seen far too much sun.'

The actress smiled. 'Luckily the comtesse loved to sunbathe. Her husband's family refused to meet her and will certainly try not to meet her now, nor recognise her if they did. He refused to let her meet up with her former friends.'

'I feel rather sorry for her.'

Miss Portia nodded. 'A luxurious cage — not even shopping trips to Paris, it seemed. A local dressmaker copied the patterns from *Vogue*. Her maid described the comtesse dancing to record after record, by herself, in the ballroom. She drank a mix of Cointreau and champagne throughout the day, a hideous waste of both, but you need not follow her example in that. As for your age,' Miss Portia smiled, bringing a wave of affection and reassurance, 'you are fit — muscles do not sag as plump skin does. Your hair must be bleached, as the comtesse's is in her photograph. I am sorry to do that to such lovely hair as yours — I recommend an egg yolk conditioner each time you wash it, or comb with olive oil at night and have it washed the next morning, if eggs or olive oil are obtainable.'

Sophie imagined Daniel's response when she returned a bleached blonde. But perhaps a hair rinse might bring the colour back to her natural one.

'We will also give you hair pieces to make yours appear longer and thicker, and with a slightly fluffier curl. It doesn't matter if anyone discovers you use them — it would be seen as vanity, not disguise. Your make-up will also need to change. Would you mind moving over here into the direct light, Miss Jane?'

Sophie obediently moved to the brocade chair by the window. Winter sun gleamed in a thin honey trickle onto her face as Miss Portia moved a mirror over to her.

'Ah yes, a lighter shade of powder than you use now, I think, but use less of it.' She wiped Sophie's face gently with a wet cloth, then added half-a-dozen dabs of powder. 'Do this when your face is still damp, and your skin will seem softer. A brighter lipstick, and mascara — age does thin the eyelashes. You see what I am doing with the lipstick? A dab on the top of each cheekbone, then rub it in along here. Powdered rouge does age one, I'm afraid, but using whichever lipstick matches your dress on your cheeks will counteract the slight effects of gravity — the very, very slight effects, my dear. Now almond oil, just the merest dab on the points of your forehead and sides of your nose. See? They must not appear oily, but skin loses its natural oils as we age.

'Now, apply eyeliner. Perhaps try it yourself — a line just under the lower lashes, and another beginning a third of the way across the top of your lashes and extending just a little way beyond.'

Sophie stared at the image evolving in front of her. Even with her own hairstyle, she looked unfamiliar, and yes, younger. 'I'm a painted lady?'

'Well, the comtesse was on the stage, my dear, ever so briefly, and in the photograph on her papers is most definitely wearing mascara and eyeliner.' She picked up what looked like two crayons. 'This is theatrical make-up. Take the white and rub just a little below your eyebrow and upper eyelid, and two dabs on the skin between your nose and eyelids. Excellent. Now just the smallest amount below your eyes. Never powder anywhere around your eyes or mouth — if there is even a hint of a wrinkle it will accentuate it, but a little of this one around the mouth, and then a hint of the white on your nose — noses keep growing with age, and the white will counteract any shadow. Now the final effect — false eyelashes.'

Sophie stared at what looked like two strange caterpillars. 'What are they made of?'

'Mink, of course, short to thicken your lashes, longer hairs to lengthen them. There, what do you think?'

'That I would not ask the woman in the mirror to dinner,' said Sophie frankly. 'She would try to seduce my husband, sulk because he'd ignore her, and stub out her cigarette on the bread and butter plate.'

Miss Portia laughed. 'In other words, perfect. Now, these.' She held out two thin sponges.

Sophie eyed them dubiously. 'What do I do with them?'

'Place them between your top teeth and your cheeks. Exactly right. What do you think?'

'It's amazing,' said Sophie frankly. The face that looked back at her was suddenly, subtly, not hers at all.

'The face thins a little as we age, the cheeks sag, the faintest line forms between the outer nostrils and the mouth, and the mouth to the chin. The pads lift the cheeks, plump out the wrinkles and change your face shape, too, making it rounder. Wear them even in bed, but wash them well with soap and hot water twice a day.'

'My voice sounds different. It's hard to articulate.'

Miss Portia smiled. 'Excellent. It will soften your slightly clipped pronunciation, which I gather the comtesse never quite managed to achieve. Your smile needs to change, too. Show more teeth. I know this is not good manners, but you must be in character. Throw your head back when you laugh. No, more of a giggle.'

Sophie giggled, showing teeth, tossing back her hair.

'Very good. But all of this,' Miss Portia waved, 'is almost irrelevant. Age — and class, for that matter — is the way you walk, the way you hold yourself, regard yourself. Without that no make-up can be effective. Shut your eyes.'

Sophie obeyed. She heard the sound of curtains being pulled. 'Open them, please.'

A young woman strode towards her, smiling. She had changed so utterly that she was two yards away before Sophie recognised her instructress.

Miss Portia laughed, bounced into her seat, then relaxed into old age again.

'That was incredible,' said Sophie truthfully.

'Thank you. I played Juliet when I was forty-eight, though with very careful lighting, and not one single review mentioned my age. Now, walk for me, if you please. Ah yes, most swan-like.'

So Miss Portia *had* been one of Miss Lily's ladies, even if a mature one.

'But you have the walk of an older swan. You carry your children, the problems of your family and friends — all that is in your walk. Open your arms, please, as if you have wings. You are a young swan, ready to fly. Feel your wings open, the air under them.'

Sophie obeyed. It was silly, but suddenly she did feel lighter, could feel her face relaxing ...

'Tomorrow, or perhaps next week, you will soar towards the clouds. Who knows what you will find, only that it will be wonderful. Now imagine there is a light shining just above your breasts. What colour is it?'

'Gold,' whispered Sophie.

'No, gold is the colour of the harvest, of mature womanhood. You are the silver moon, the virgin huntress, and no, I do not mean literally virgin. Feel the silver light shine from you, like the moonlight lighting a path for you. Always imagine your arms are wings. Watch the light in front of you and you feel it glow inside. You may sit now — no, do not look around at the chair. That is the caution of age. Just sit! Excellent. We will practise again tomorrow. You may make a Juliet yet. Now, show me your knees.'

Sophie lifted her skirt. Miss Portia sighed. 'Your face could almost have passed for twenty-five, with no change at all, but not your knees. Knees always age with us. Luckily your role requires silk stockings, which will lift and shape your knees, as your hems must be at least two inches higher than they are now. You must begin to wear higher heels than you do now, too. Do not even change into low-heeled slippers. I don't know if you realise it, but there is a slight stride as you walk, even in the heels you have on now.'

Years in low heels and riding boots, thank goodness, thought Sophie.

'High heels will tilt your pelvis and make longer steps impossible. I want you to practise walking by placing one foot directly in from of the other, rather than slightly to one side, so your hips and upper body sway. We will also provide a corset that will nip your waist and hips as well as lift your buttocks,' the smile became a delightful grin, 'and make your breasts point upwards like an ack-ack gun about to assault the enemy, which sadly is the fashion these days in certain quarters. This will also eliminate any sag.'

Only as long as I am wearing it, thought Sophie regretfully. The downside of a bountiful bosom meant that gravity won a little sooner, especially when one had fed twins.

'Now, if you would unbutton your dress a little, Miss Jane.' Miss Portia peered at the portion of chest revealed. 'Excellent, not tanned at all.'

Sophie was suddenly glad she always wore high-buttoned shorts in the paddock, though that was more to keep off flies than protect her skin.

'A white bosom is far more seductive than a tanned one, especially if the face and arms are slightly darker. We must make sure your dresses are cut low at the back, too — the Japanese quite rightly find the nape of the neck extraordinarily attractive. Why do so many women cover theirs? Do not forget the perfume, a dab on each breast, your wrists, as well as behind your ears, a floral and civet one that breathes sex to you as well as others.'

'I am seductive?'

'Delightfully so, and with little subtlety. You will flutter your eyelashes, glance at men sideways, smile at men but not at women, unless you think they will be useful. You are also extremely wealthy and must use the black market if you are to sustain a pre-war lifestyle. Servants will be provided and a house has already been leased in your name. Your jewels will be the comtesse's, genuine and ostentatious. Wear at least two rings apart from your wedding band and engagement ring, as well as a necklace, bracelet, brooch, perhaps a jewelled hair clip — always too many. Diamonds, even during the day, no matter what you are wearing. Diamond drops in your ears even when you wear your pearls, which are the extremely long double strands you were given before your wedding, not the single strand you wear now.'

'Where will my clothes come from?' Sophie felt a strange revulsion at wearing a dead woman's garments.

'We are having several old Violette creations shipped over to the leased house — you will pretend that you slipped to Paris while your husband visited his brother in Monaco in 1940. This will be the reason you can claim acquaintance with Violette now. A few of the comtesse's favourites will be sent to Paris — it would be strange to abandon them all — and her usual dressmaker is making new clothes too. Don't worry — she has a dressmaker's shape for the comtesse, so fittings weren't needed before, and she will not think the lack of them strange now.' Miss Portia raised a perfectly shaped and coloured eyebrow. 'You will also have new underclothes: silk, naturally. But you long for haute couture and for parties, which is why you have come to Paris now you can finally spend your late husband's money. You may also possibly be hoping to lure a lover, but not a husband, as you enjoy your freedom.'

So a dalliance with German officers on leave would be logical for a woman of no scruples, thought Sophie, as most would be married, with no wish for a long-term liaison.

'What else do I need to know about my life?'

'Mr Green will give you a dossier with the basic facts, though it's unlikely anyone will ask you where you were born, or to whom. You have miscarried twice, which you might just once confess to a female acquaintance to form a bond between you. It is also possible the count wrote to his family about the pregnancies, even if they refused to meet you. Burn the dossier once you have memorised its information. If the wrong person finds it they may wonder why there is a dossier on the Comtesse de Brabant.'

Sophie had assumed there'd be no 'wrong hands' at Shillings. But even the 'right hands' might be dangerous, if the information could be obtained under torture.

Miss Portia gave a shrug that contained a smile. 'Your attitude will matter more than facts. You enjoy your title, but find French hereditary titles slightly amusing and far too recent. You will confess you find military rank more interesting, for it has been earned, and traditional German, Austrian or Hungarian titles impressive, even if they have ostensibly been abolished.'

'I suspect German military rank is given to men who were simply born into the right families and went to the correct schools, just like high English military rank,' said Sophie.

'Ah, but the comtesse does not know that. You are scrupulous in paying, over-paying and over-tipping. You delight, in fact, in spending as much as you can despite the austerity of war. You live for the day and wish others to enjoy the sunlight too. You order a bottle of champagne and drink a single glass; you procure the most delectable meals possible under rationing and manage a few mouthfuls of each course. You never abstain from caviar and will go to great lengths to attain all this luxury on the black market. You are charming and fun and extremely obvious —'

'And no one would expect so spectacular and obvious a charlatan to be a fraud?'

'We hope not, my dear,' said Miss Portia, patting her hand. 'Would you like to slip into these?' She produced shoes that were far more silver than grey, with heels almost as thin and high as chopsticks. 'Shall we try a walk across the room? You are a swan about to take wing, and you glow silver. Remember that from now on you will flaunt your body, your wealth and your availability.'

Sophie looked at her sharply. 'But I will not be available. I am prepared to flirt, to tease, even to promise. Small dinner parties, where the wine might be fortified with vodka to lessen inhibitions and make the conversation less discreet. Nothing more.'

'That is entirely up to you, comtesse,' said Miss Portia smoothly. She did not add, 'And to the exigencies of war.'

'I didn't expect to like the comtesse,' Sophie admitted, as she and Bob sat in armchairs by the fire in the cottage that afternoon, the dossier in her hand, a plate of Mrs Goodenough's buttered teacakes — though far less buttered than before the war — on the side table, as well as the familiar silver teapot with its Vaile crest, and small jug for hot water to add to the pot. 'I'm still not sure I do, but she had a rotten life. According to her maid's report, her husband expected a son and was prepared to almost keep her prisoner till she provided one.'

'Many men do consider themselves failures if they don't have sons. They transfer that resentment to their wives.'

Sophie thought of her own son, probably counting the days at school till he was back at his beloved Thuringa. And not long after the Christmas after this he might be on his way to New Guinea, or even fighting in northern Australia if the Japanese invasion had begun. She forced her mind to the present. 'What if some of the comtesse's former friends try to contact her now? A wealthy widowed comtesse might be useful.'

'Instruct your staff to say you are not at home. You are unlikely to meet any of her former friends at Maison Violette, or any clubs German officers might take you to.'

'The maid who provided all of this — she's trustworthy?'

'Totally.' He did not tell her how he knew. 'She will be in Spain by the time you reach Paris, however.'

Sophie nodded. The unnamed woman had already taken an enormous risk for this mission. 'What will happen when the comtesse disappears after I come back to England? Won't anyone I've been associated with be suspected?'

'The comtesse will die in a car crash. The flames will leave her body unrecognisable. Don't worry,' he added, 'no one will be sacrificed to take your place. A body will be taken from the morgue.'

She did not ask by whom. 'I'm not doing anyone out of an inheritance by spending her money, am I? No poor widowed mother?'

'Part of the count's estate was entailed and has already passed to his brother in Monaco. The bulk of his fortune was not entailed, so under French law it passes to his wife in the absence of children and as his parents are deceased. The comtesse's father died on the Somme, as did her uncles and two cousins, all in the one week. Another cousin and a remaining aunt died of the Spanish flu. Her mother died of consumption a year after her marriage — the count did provide well for his mother-in-law — and she has no siblings. Her will left gifts to a local orphanage and to her servants, which have already been dispensed as farewell presents, though they will probably inherit the same amount again when her death is officially recognised.'

'So French orphans will dine on turnips while I drink champagne?'

'They have recently received a generous anonymous donation,' he said gently. 'All beneficiaries will be slightly better off, not worse.'

'She really was alone, wasn't she? I'm glad she thought of the orphans. Should I arrange Christmas presents for them this year?'

'It would be out of character. She had no contact with the orphanage.'

'Except she was an orphan herself.' Sophie gazed at the flames in silence for a while, seeing the past, the possible future. 'Will we have a Christmas tree this year?' she asked at last.

'There'll be one at the Hall.'

'But one for us here, before I go?'

He reached over and took her hand. 'Yes, we will have a tree, and Christmas.'

'Thank you,' whispered Sophie.

The Parachute School at Ringwater, south of Manchester, had accepted that Miss Jane would train alone.

First the technique — falling with both legs together to the left or right, hands in pockets — then a series of progressively higher jumps while attached by a cable to a tower. The techniques were almost fun, reminding her of swinging on a rope tied to a branch above the river at home, then splashing down. This led to memories of swimming with Daniel, of teaching Rose and Danny to dog paddle, visions that wrenched the heart so much she had to firmly refuse the distraction.

James had somehow forwarded Rose's and Danny's letters to her from their boarding schools, not in their own handwriting, but via coded telegram, which was uncoded again by some unknown hand. Rose had dutifully knitted fifteen khaki socks, but doubted their shape would fit any known serviceman. Danny was glad cricket season had begun, and tactfully left out any details of the school cadet corps or weekend camps with the Militia which might disturb his mother.

She tried to tell herself she was no less their mother here, leaping on ropes, than she would be at Thuringa. But both obviously expected her to be home for the holidays. Christmas, without her children … without Daniel, whose letters were too full of local gossip, and too empty of himself.

She should not be here, and yet she irrevocably was.

The next stage involved three actual jumps from an aircraft, all at night, with a length of cable attached to the parachute so it opened automatically.

She had thought it would be terrifying, looking down. But all she saw was darkness and the faintest of lights to aim towards, the cold air sharp as tin against her face. The descent was peaceful, swaying, wind danced, a feeling of serene power as she tugged one cable and then another to direct herself. Was this what the eagle felt, or the powerful owl? She imagined parachuting above Thuringa, warm air currents sweeping her higher for a while, meeting the eagles face to face, after years of them soaring above her, but that brought desperate homesickness too: the smell of hot air and hotter rocks, the screaming of cicadas. Rose and Danny would be home by now ...

The second time she landed well, but on a stone. Her thigh swelled with an egg-sized lump. She didn't mention it.

'You're a natural, ma'am,' said the instructor, leaving the warmth of the hut to join her as she gathered up her parachute, exactly on target after the third jump in the pink and grey of dawn this time, seeing the birds' first flutters from the trees as she floated to earth.

The instructor was nameless, as indeed Ringwater was supposed to be, for she had come here by car, not train, and at night, but she had heard the name mentioned too often not to realise where she was. She wished she could tell him that her athletic skill came from being taught how to fall off a horse by the age of six — far more important than how to ride one — by the best stockwoman in New South Wales.

'There's a car waiting for you.'

Sophie laughed. 'How lovely. I didn't expect it till tonight. I must be needed to decorate the Christmas tree. I hope you have a merry one.' And that you don't spend it worrying about the safety of your family and your friends, she thought, and all the men and women you have trained. But who had the luxury of a carefree Christmas these days? 'I'll see you after Christmas, sir.'

'Nay, I'm told you won't be back again.'

'But I thought there were five practice jumps?'

'Your training has been cut short, it seems. But you'll do.' He held out his hand and shook hers. 'It's been a pleasure, ma'am, and it's not often I say that. And don't worry. They won't send you down if there's wind, or a storm. Good luck, ma'am.'

'Good luck to you, too,' she said. She hesitated. 'Do you have a daughter?'

He looked immediately wary. One did not ask such questions at Ringwater.

'Even if I confess to the Gestapo that my parachute instructor had a daughter, I doubt it would help identify you,' she said drily. If she informed them he had a false foot, which he hid well, they might have more success. She had noticed it merely because her father had hid well the fact he'd lost a limb, too, though, in his case, it had been his leg on the North West Frontier. So many wars since his ...

'I have a daughter,' the instructor admitted.

'If I were to arrange a Christmas gift to her, marked simply *To the Instructor's Daughter*, would it reach you?'

'Yes.'

'Then I may arrange it?'

'There is no need —'

'No, only a wish. If I survive the next week, it will be largely due to you.' Though any skill of hers would not prevent the plane that carried her from being shot down, nor a sniper killing her before she landed, or thirty seconds after. Both knew it and knew the other knew it, too.

But he had been kind, as well as professional, sharing Thermoses of tea and slices of his wife's boiled fruitcake with camaraderie, not flirtation, which she felt no need to practise till she reached France. Over twenty years ago she had left most of the jewellery she had brought from Australia as a gauche teenager — its flashily cut diamonds quite unsuitable for a pre-war debutante or, later, a countess — at Shillings. But there was a brooch of seed pearls, a stylised bird, that she would like this man's daughter to have.

'Thank you. My daughter will treasure it. Don't worry about your skill, ma'am. You've a knack for it.'

For a moment Sophie wanted to ask if she might meet his family after the war. But that would not be fair. Many, if not most, of the agents this man trained would not live to see the war's end. Let the instructor imagine every one of them celebrating the peace with friends and family and not wait, wondering who might finally be the survivors.

Chapter 14

I have never had an unhappy Christmas. Tragic ones, desperate ones, frightened, but even when I had to scrabble for it in the corners, I have found a crumb of happiness as well. There were a few years when I don't think I'd have endured life without it.

Miss Lily, Christmas, 1942

The car waited by a side gate. It was about ten years old, a well-kept Morris Minor, and Nigel was at the wheel, dressed as Bob in an elderly soft hat, a once-good tweed jacket sagging at the elbows and neatly darned at the cuffs, a shirt, faded tie and his usual 'best' moleskins.

She slipped into the seat next to him thinking, we must look like an old married couple, and nearly laughed for that was exactly what they were. She had changed into a yellow wool dress, its collar embroidered with green gum leaves, a pre-Occupation Christmas gift from Violette, the last she had received and her favourite, appropriate to wear in celebration today, under a waisted tweed coat in shades of gold to brown.

'Merry Christmas,' she said to him, leaning over to kiss his cheek. It was slightly rough with whiskers, which as Nigel he would never have allowed. 'You must have heard they let me out early for good behaviour.'

He did not kiss her back. 'A change of plans,' he said stiffly. 'You fly out tonight, if the weather holds up. Everything you need has been prepared for you.'

Her stomach clenched, but she kept her face impassive too. 'Ah. I see.'

So they would not have their Christmas, reading the cables and letters or presents from Australia Bob undoubtedly had to give her on Christmas morning. James had even promised to book a brief phone call to Thuringa. Just to hear their voices, to spend a day reminiscing with Nigel — for surely he might be Nigel again, not Bob, remembering Rose's first steps, determinedly tottering even though Danny crowed as he crawled faster than her towards the table that held cake, a treat for nursery tea. And when Rose's wet nappy had dampened the Vicar's lap ...

Wars sometimes had a truce for Christmas. This one did not.

There will be other Christmases, she told herself firmly. There would be Christmas in that magical place called 'after the war', too, when Lily would visit Thuringa, and help them choose the perfect tree to cut, usually a red gum that had sprouted a fresh straight trunk after being lopped for a half-dozen-years-ago Christmas. Home-made lemon cordial on the verandah — Lily loved the Thuringa cordial, though it was never served at Shillings, possibly because lemons in England were never as rich and pungent as the ones of home ...

'Christmas Eve makes a good cover,' said Nigel, starting the engine and still carefully showing no emotion. 'The curfew will still be in place from nine pm but there'll be celebrations, more people going from house to house. No one will be suspicious of a house with signs of activity at midnight.'

She nodded. Christmas Eve was a far more important event in France than here, or at home.

'The weather forecast is good, low cloud and little wind.'

'Good,' she said shortly.

'Sophie ...' His eyes held what might be anguish. 'It's not too late to pull out.'

'Of course it is.' So many had worked so long for this. She hoped that at the very least she was not shot while descending, unable to manoeuvre except by pulling on the strings of her parachute, nor in the first moment of vulnerability on the ground as she disentangled herself. Let her at least find enough information to have made her training worthwhile, some adequate recompense for the disappearance of Daniel's wife, and Rose and Danny's mother.

'You do think we can trust Violette?' she asked abruptly.

'You defended her to James.' He turned the car onto a minor road, then turned again into a lane, tufted with winter grass, the colour bleached by cold. Sophie suddenly longed for a glimpse of vividness again: the endless blue above Thuringa, a flock of king parrots in Christmas green and red, shrieking as they invaded the apple trees. She forced her mind back to the present.

'I know I defended her. But I've realised I only knew her in one incarnation. She's had so many lives, her childhood with that mad old murderess, her time in the orphanage, the years living on the streets. It's been six years since I've seen her.'

'Two things have never seemed to change through all those transformations. Her hatred of Germans and her loyalty to other women — those of whom she approves.'

'I'm not sure that's an answer.'

'Nor am I. At least she doesn't know you are coming. If you have the least suspicion of doubt when you meet her, vanish. It's better for this mission to fail than for the Nazis to know there is serious doubt among high-echelon officers. Put that advertisement in any newspaper on the list and we'll get you out of there, or phone the bistro. A contact will be with you within half an hour to hand you a small case with fresh identity papers, different clothes, scissors, hair dye and a place to wait until we can bring you safely back to England.'

Sophie nodded. Assuming there was still an England to safely come back to, or an Australia unconquered by the Japanese.

Impossible to tell how much danger her own country was in from the accounts in the newspapers, but James had told her that Australian troops had been holding their own against the Japanese in New Guinea, the first forces ever to hold them back, though James had added that was as much due to the exhaustion of starving Japanese troops and impossibly gruelling terrain and weather as Allied strategy or the Diggers' tenacity. The Japanese needed to capture Port Moresby to harry or even halt US forces.

They needed Australian iron and foundries, ship-building yards and coalmines to resupply their dwindling stocks. Australian agricultural produce was vital for starving troops and even the underfed civilians in their homeland. If the Japanese could be held back from those resources ...

Thuringa, she thought. I should be with my people, my family while we face this, not here in England. Mr Churchill had even refused to send Australian troops back from the Middle East to defend their own country. If Hitler goes, if there is peace with Germany, will England — battered, starved and deeply in debt to the USA — be prepared to help Australia against the Japanese? Or would they focus on India, the jewel in the Empire's crown?

'You look far away. Thuringa?'

'British foreign policy. I doubt Britain will ever recognise the debt they owe to their Empire.'

Bob carefully negotiated a rut in the country road. She wondered where he was taking her; she also realised that if she was leaving tonight it was best she did not even know the name of the aerodrome. 'Of course not. Britain will never admit how much they owe the colonies. Just as the general public will never acknowledge its debt to Welsh coalminers, Bermudan slaves or women who die in childbirth to create the next generation, or all the others to whom they owe their lives or prosperity. Shall we change the subject to something less gloomy? I have a treat for you.'

'Letters?' she asked eagerly. She would at least have her Christmas letters.

'And some gifts you would have been given tomorrow. I'll keep them safe for you till you get back, I promise. But there's another surprise, first.'

The car stopped by a hedge opposite a gate. He hauled a picnic basket from the back seat.

'A winter picnic in a paddock full of thistles? We'll freeze!'

'No, you won't. And this isn't for me. Come on.'

Sophie opened the door, breathed in the scent of cold stone walls and colder mud. Another car was parked behind the hedge, the motor running — only an official vehicle would have the luxury of so much petrol. The back door opened.

'Soapie lass! Don't stand there. Get in out of the wind.'

'Ethel!'

Ethel swept her into a gorilla hug, warm strong arms, smelling of cocoa and talcum powder. Sophie found she was crying, and Ethel was too. 'I didn't think I would have a chance to see you.'

'And you've told me far more than you realise in one sentence.' Ethel moved back, studied her. 'I'm not sure about the hairstyle, lass. And those high heels could take out a man's eye if you could manage a knees up in them.'

'I don't like my hair just now either. Peroxide smells. And my ankles, knees and back ache thanks to these wretched shoes.' At least she had not had to wear them at Ringwater. Even the Comtesse de Brabant could not parachute in high heels. Sophie slid into the back seat, already sagging under Ethel's weight.

Ethel still wore the make-up Violette had shown her how to use, her once shaggy eyebrows plucked and slightly defined, and some war-time substitute for rouge and lipstick to make her cheekbones more pronounced, and pinken her extremely pretty lips. Her suit was appropriate for the office, but the blouse was feminine, and the tailored jacket accentuated her figure instead of trying to disguise it.

'Twenty minutes,' said Bob briefly, and walked back to their own car.

Sophie watched him go. How much work must he have put into this meeting?

'He's scared for you,' said Ethel. 'He came up to London last Sunday. It were a shock to see him, I can tell you. When I heard there'd been no word from Lily I was sure she must have been killed. It must have took me five minutes to even believe I weren't seeing a ghost. But then when you've died once I suppose it's easier the second time. I'm that sorry for telling George she'd died. But it didn't occur to me he'd see you till long after the war was over.'

She rooted around in Bob's picnic basket. 'Scotch eggs! Oh my, how I have longed for a Scotch egg. And singin' hinnies. Mrs Goodenough is a fair treasure. I suppose it's all her doing?'

'Bob must have told her I was meeting you. Ethel, you and James —'

'Now that I don't want to talk about. Tell me about Midge and the boys. Tell me everything you couldn't let the censor see in your letters.'

'You and James suit,' said Sophie stubbornly.

'Nay, Soapie lass. James and I are such opposite bookends that when you put us together we make a half-decent whole. But I can't come at what he does.' Her mouth quirked. 'Our James has spent his life working with women. He's one of the few men I know who can take orders from one, too. But all the women he's worked with agree with what he's doing. He gets flapdoodled with one who doesn't.'

'Ethel, I hope I never have to kill anyone. My mission is different. But if I have to, I will kill. Maybe more than one.'

'Aye, and Anne and her husband are out in Mesopotamia again, and they're not digging up ruins in war-time, and one of my nephews is fighting in Africa, and a dozen others I know and love one way and another are fighting, too. But I don't have to share a breakfast table with them every morning, wondering who died because of them in the night.'

Sophie's words vanished.

Ethel raised an eyebrow at her. 'You're not going to argue?'

'That Hitler must be stopped, and the only way to do it is fight this war? No. You'd have heard better arguments than I can give and listened to them, too. Tell me about the Ministry of Food.'

'It's classified and that should tell you everything. Who'd bother classifying a recipe for eggless, sugarless steamed pud? Will knowing you add grated carrot for sweetness win the war for Mr Hitler if he finds out? The only thing in our carefully locked filing cabinets that might help him is to know where and when supplies come to England, and what our food reserves are. And the answer to that is about enough to last us till next Tuesday, which is the position Germany is in, too.'

'You're fed up with it?'

'Fed up to the back teeth. About ten per cent of what we do is worthwhile, Soapie, but without that ten per cent it's all over. Rationing means there's enough for everyone — or not quite enough, but enough to keep us going. It means the poor don't starve and the rich pay for their supplies on the black market and we sometimes even get to put them in gaol for it. It means orange juice for the kiddies and hot lunches for the workers. I've got one of Lily's last girls — 1939 — working for me, pretending to type, but really she charms visiting Americans into selling us more cans of Spam. I don't suppose you can say what you are doing?'

'No. Ethel, if ... if I don't come back, can you do three things for me?'

'Yes.'

'Find Hannelore, if you can. She may be dead, or a prisoner. She may be swanning around in a castle. But offer her a visit to Australia if it's possible, no matter where she is or what she's been doing. I promised her kangaroos once. I want to keep my promise.'

'The next?'

'Go to Australia, or wait till Daniel and the children come to England — they will have to at some stage, with Danny's position. When you see them tell them they are more important to me than the entire Empire, or the whole world, but because they are part of this world, will inherit this world, I have to do this. And the third — as soon as you hear I am dead go and see James. He'll need someone to hold his hand, and no one else will dare do that. Just for an hour. Please.'

A pause. At last Ethel nodded. 'I will.'

Chapter 15

**Baked Chips with Thyme and Garlic:
A War-time Recipe**

Oil, lard or vegetable shortening
2 large potatoes, washed but with skins left on, thickly sliced
Salt
Fresh or dried thyme
2 cloves garlic, halved

*Wipe oil or lard thinly over a baking tray, heat in a hot oven until
warm and the oil or fat thins. Add the potato and toss until covered
in oil/fat, sprinkle with salt and thyme. Add the garlic halves.
Bake in a moderate oven for 20 minutes or so until potato is crisp
and light brown.*

A French Recipe

VIOLETTE

Violette woke, smiling, on her perfumed sheets. She had been
dreaming. A strange dream, meandering it seemed for years. She
had worn a long skirt and small children clustered around while
she read them a story. Twenty children, perhaps, her children ...

Pah! Impossible. She could not imagine having one child and
most certainly not twenty. Violette lay back, looking at the grey
light dawning between the curtains. She had always loved this
time of the day, the opening of possibilities. Sometimes before
the curfew of the Boche she had walked through the night, here
in the streets of Paris, or even back under the strange twisted

limbs of the trees of Thuringa, just to see the first moment when black became not quite black, holding her breath for the first thread of light.

She and George had spent their last night together awake. He'd had a sudden twenty-four-hour leave almost a fortnight before Dunkirk.

They had not left the bedroom except to forage in the kitchen for a loaf, butter, cheese, a pot of caviar, smoked salmon and the cold roast lamb Violette liked more than either caviar or salmon. She had bought the caviar and salmon because it was proper to have such available when one's lover came to call, but George preferred his bread well buttered and with thick hunks of cold lamb too.

Violette had pulled the curtains half an hour before the dawn, turning off the bed lamp so no one might see in. She had lain in his arms, pillows behind them, waiting for the light.

'I love you, you know,' George said conversationally.

She turned to look at him and punched him lightly on the chest. 'That is not how you tell a woman you love her. This is not the place or time either!'

'Eh, that's true enough. But I might not get another chance to tell you for a while.'

'The Boche will not take Paris. They failed before and will again.'

'I think they will, you know,' said George quietly. 'Are you sure you won't leave for England?'

Violette shrugged. 'You do not abandon a friend in trouble. Paris is my friend.'

'What about not abandoning me?'

'You will be busy with your "not fighting".' They had discussed this, many times, or rather tried to, for each time they reached a place that Violette's mind could not imagine, where every life had equal value, when it so obviously did not. Violette's life began with her and radiated outwards, a few others circling like planets about her personal sun. George's, it seemed, took in all of humanity. Though, of course, most particularly her.

'Will you marry me, at least?' George reached over and took a small Cartier box from the pocket of his trousers on the chair. She opened it. A diamond winked up at her, large enough to hold the starlight. It was easy to forget that George Carryman was rich, like his Aunt Ethel, for both lived simply, using their wealth to buy planes and fund charities. And for a ring.

'C'est bon. I do not want to give it back,' she said honestly.

He laughed. 'Then don't.'

'But I do not want to marry you, either. I do not want to *not* marry you,' she added quickly, seeing the sudden pain in his eyes. 'I do not think this is a good time for marrying.'

'It's the best of times. The one certainty we would have would be each other.'

'But we would not be certain, not if the Boche take Paris. We will not see each other, not even know if the other is alive perhaps.'

'I know I love you. I know I always will.'

'How can you know that? You have not been to the future, like you have not been to the moon. You could say "the moon is made of green cheese" and no one could say different.'

'The moon is made of green cheese and I will love you forever.' He took her hand.

Something broke inside her. It would be stitched tomorrow — such small breaks always were. But just now she found herself saying, 'Then I will believe it with you. The moon is made of green cheese.'

'And you love me?'

'I will always love you. I will not marry you, not now. But I am not giving back this ring!'

'It is an engagement ring,' he said patiently. 'If you wear it we are engaged.'

'Not if I wear it on a gold chain about my neck. Always, and never take it off, until you put it on my finger.'

He had leaned towards her then …

'Mademoiselle?' Violette's mind stuttered out of the land of memory to the present day, where Gisette stood in her black dress and maid's cap at the door. 'Kolonel the Count von Hoffenhausen is here. He says he has come for breakfast. He has brought coffee!'

'Thank you, Gisette. Please tell the Kolonel I will be there directly. No, I will dress myself.'

Today's violet dress was already laid out in her dressing room, a heavy creamy-mauve silk embossed with deeper purple flowers, the sleeves left open like small capes, and pleats towards the hem of the tightly fitted skirt opening to show lilac lace, also pleated, in tiny waterfalls around her knees. A dress to make any woman imagine that when she wore it she was beautiful. She washed her face, ran a comb through her hair, two dabs of powder and lipstick, made sure the ring on its chain was hidden under the neckline of her dress, then walked steadily, careful not to seem to hurry in any way, to the dining room.

The scent of coffee greeted her: far better coffee than she had recently been able to buy from the dentist one of her customers had recommended. The colonel stood as she came in, the coffee cup in front of him. He bowed most correctly, clicking his heels. He knew better than to wait till she came close so he could kiss the air above her hand.

'Unless you have brought eggs too, Kolonel, you will have toast only, and no butter or jam.' Violette had both, of course, but it would be unwise to show such evidence of her black-market connections.

'I brought eggs and pork sausage and, as you can see, coffee.'

'Bon. Then you may eat them.' She took her place at the table, and poured herself coffee as he added, 'What have you for me?'

She sighed. 'Kolonel, we have an arrangement. I do not break arrangements. If I have anything for you I will send you a message, just as we agreed.'

'Messages may go astray,' he said tightly. 'I need to return to my work in Germany.'

'There has been no message to go astray. I have heard nothing.'

'You expect me to believe that?'

'No. But it is true.' She sipped the coffee. 'Kolonel, like yourself, I expected someone to contact me from England. No contact has come. Perhaps my parents persuaded those in power not to jeopardise my safety. Perhaps the Anglaise do not trust me for, after all, I am not one of them. Perhaps tomorrow I will find the French Resistance has housed itself in my cellar and is eating my camembert and sending code messages to London. But today?' She shrugged. 'I can tell you about the latest mistress of your colleagues, or who among the collaborators is getting rich extremely fast. But that was not the bargain we agreed on.'

'I have other sources for gossip like that. That is not my interest here.'

She sipped more coffee before she gave her words a carelessness she did not feel. The seamstresses, the embroiderers, the hundred women who worked in some capacity for Maison Violette would lose their jobs — perhaps their lives — if she were to be arrested as a spy or even interned as an English citizen, which thankfully she was not, although she was entitled to be one. 'You either trust me or you do not. As I must trust you.'

She poured the last of the coffee from the pot into her cup and smiled at him.

Chapter 16

Mock Brains

1 cup leftover porridge
1 tablespoon self-raising flour
1 small onion, peeled and very finely chopped
1 egg
½ teaspoon thyme
A leaf of sage, chopped
Salt and pepper
Plain flour

Mix and bind together with the beaten egg, form into flat rissoles,
roll in flour then fry in hot fat until brown.

A Ministry of Food Recipe

24 DECEMBER 1942

SOPHIE

The short mid-winter day was greying, though darkness was an
hour away, perhaps. Sophie stared at the winter-dull stone walls
on either side of them as Bob drove down the lane. It seemed
she was not even to take off from the landing strip at Shillings.
There would be no farewell dinner from Mrs Goodenough, no
few hours in the cottage to still be herself — not even a chance to
give the Christmas presents chosen from those of her possessions
still stored in the Shillings attics.

The lane grew narrower, topped with brambles. Bob stopped at a five-barred gate. Sophie automatically scrambled out to open it, then closed it once the car drove through it. She glanced around the field: winter-brown grass, high hedges on either side, sheep that were exactly as active as the ones in the field where George had landed at Shillings, and a hay shed. She slid back into the front seat. Bob drove to the shed and parked next to it.

The hay was real, exactly one bale deep on every side, with a door that led to a room with shabby armchairs, a carpet no one had swept since the war began and a bench with a kettle, teapot, tea caddy and a can of powdered milk.

Bob undid one of the two haversacks he carried. 'Cherry cake,' he announced. 'And a shooter's sandwich. Half the village gave up their meat ration to buy the steak.'

Sophie nodded, unbearably touched, then realised. 'They know I'm ...?'

'Heading off, like all the other women who pass through Shillings? Yes. But not where.' He moved to put the kettle on.

'Is my luggage in the boot?' She wanted to do a final check of the frocks she and Madame Portia had chosen for her role.

'It went to France last week.'

'Last week!'

'You'll find it unpacked and waiting for you, as if you have been driven up from the south of France. I've got a light brown hair dye for you. The peroxide blonde is distinctive, especially at night. The brown should wash out in a few rinses, so don't stand out in the rain too long. Your identity documents, ration cards, a few suggestive postcards and all the rest are waiting for you with those who'll meet you.'

It made sense.

If she had been going as a normal agent — if any agent's work could be considered normal — she'd now be heading for Beaulieu to learn how to survive interrogation and to learn maps off by heart, as well as how to be profoundly inconspicuous. But she knew nothing, except a little about parts of France and Germany, and her few visits to Paris. The comtesse had spent only a few months in Paris before her marriage fourteen years ago, as well as the one concocted visit, and it would seem odd if she knew Paris too well, did not stare at landmarks, or ask questions.

The comtesse had been so young. Sophie thought yet again about the woman she was going to impersonate. It would be so easy to assume she had been a gold digger, a self-centred opportunist. That would presumably be how she would be remembered, too, after Sophie's portrayal of her.

Amelie, Comtesse de Brabant, deserved better, but then so did everyone caught up in war.

Bob picked up the second haversack and handed it to her. 'There's your flying suit, clothes to wear under it as well as French underwear, whatever else you need. Better get ready before you open the letters and parcels, in case you need to leave earlier than planned. The lavatory is through that door there.'

She had been naked in front of him more times than she could count, though not for many years, and never as Daniel's wife. He seemed to guess her thoughts. 'Someone may come in.'

She took the haversack and slipped off to the lavatory, which smelled like every government lavatory she had ever been in. There must be a special disinfectant only available for government agencies, she thought as she unbuckled the haversack.

It contained slacks and a blouse of a subtly French cut, a headscarf, presumably to be discarded when she was united with what would soon be her possessions, socks and low-heeled, well-worn shoes. The flying suit itself was multi-pocketed, for knife, revolver, a shovel to bury her parachute, a small flask, emergency rations. A money belt to go under the flying suit contained five hundred thousand francs, not quite two and a half thousand English pounds, enough to buy a comfortable middle-class home: her ready money, although household and other bills would be paid with the comtesse's new chequing account — her husband had not permitted her that freedom. But black marketeers would require cash in large amounts, and cash must be withdrawn in person. It was just possible that the comtesse had been known by staff in their local bank, and one of those had moved to head office in Paris.

The haversack also contained the L pill. Sophie had been warned about this: a quick and lethal escape if she could endure the agony of torture no longer.

She would not swallow it. But it might, perhaps, be even more useful in her role than the revolver, which she must discard on landing, as well as all but the money. She wriggled the L pill through the minute hole into a pocket in her knicker elastic, brushed her hair with her fingers and scurried back to the hayshed room again.

Bob had been watching the door intently, though the hands resting on the arms of the chair were relaxed, the hands that had always seemed slightly large for a woman. Sophie felt he was capturing every second they were together.

Would this be 'the last'? There had been so many 'last minutes' in their varying relationships. She had expected never to return to England until the war eventuated and then was over, by which time she'd known one or both of them might be dead ...

I do not want to die, she thought. Even more, I do not want to die so far from those I love.

Bob poured the tea, English tea, strong enough to dissolve a spoon. Whoever stocked this room paid no attention to rations. She drank, nibbled the cherry cake, though she had no appetite. But it had been made with love. She would eat the shooter's sandwich on the plane, sharing it perhaps with the pilot. George? She hoped so.

'I left some Christmas presents at the cottage. Would you mind sending them up to the Hall for me? Perhaps you could give Mrs Goodenough's gift to her yourself.'

'What have you chosen for her?'

Sophie blinked. He spoke in Nigel's voice, not Bob's softer burr. His shoulders were subtly straightened, too, his gaze more direct.

She tried to keep her voice steady. 'Do you remember that diamond necklace I brought from Australia? A gift from my father and totally unsuitable for a debutante.' And too ostentatious for her to have worn since, too, but she could not bear to have something given with so much love reset.

'I remember everything.' He sat silent for a moment then added, 'She will protest wildly that it is too extravagant, and adore it forever. She can wear it with the hat with peacock feathers my great-aunt gave her the first year she came to work at Shillings. She was a kitchenmaid, but one day Cook was ill and Mrs Goodenough took over. She made that cherry cake — I believe the recipe was her grandmother's. My great-aunt relished it and Mrs Goodenough's career was set.'

'I'm glad. She has been a good friend to you. To us both. That's what I put on her card: *To my dear friend always, with love, Sophie.*' She managed a grin. 'The card will shock her even more than the diamonds.'

'What did you choose for me?' he asked lightly.

'You'll have to open it and see.'

He opened the first haversack again. There were envelopes in it carrying Daniel's writing, Rose's, Danny's, Midge's. Sophie picked out one of the small parcels and watched as Bob ... no, *Nigel* opened it. She had asked Daniel to send the gift in her second letter to him, so it might reach England by Christmas, though she suspected James had a hand in making sure the Thuringa mail reached her.

It was a two-sided photo frame. On one side Lily sat on the verandah reading to Rose as she careered about on her tricycle, while Danny sat neatly on a small chair at her feet. Daniel had taken the other photo, a lucky shot down by the river, Sophie laughing as Rose leaped to dive-bomb Danny, who was innocently smiling up at the camera.

She had expected him to smile. Instead he seemed to be thinking. 'Thank you,' he said at last.

'You don't like it?'

'I'll need to tell Mrs Goodenough to remove it quickly if anything happens to me, in case someone wonders why I have it.'

'Nonsense. The photograph is a gift from your war-time house guest, to show you her home. Put it on the mantelpiece.'

Nigel nodded, his face blank, as men affected when they did not want anyone to know they cried. Lily would have cried.

No, she could not think of Lily. Because every day she had repressed what felt like the deepest betrayal of all: she had come to England because Lily had needed her. She'd had Bob, and Nigel too. But Lily? Lily had been teacher, mentor, almost the mother she had only known in that one brief disastrous meeting at the end of the last war. Lily had shown her the world, and herself, and what she might be. Lily was her sister, her dearest friend.

And Lily had abandoned her.

She forced herself to smile. This was war. Her journey would be dangerous, but even to be in England was a risk now. These moments must be savoured.

'This is from me to you.' The gift was no larger than a tennis ball, wrapped in antique paper decorated with dragons. She opened it carefully, for the paper was a treasure too. 'It's beautiful. Perfect.' She gazed at the deep red antique Japanese pot, broken and repaired, with a loveliness that was felt, rather than described.

'I'll keep it for you until you get back. I'd like to imagine it at Thuringa. It's three hundred years old, perhaps. The Japanese have a special reverence for things that are broken, where you can touch and see their history in their repair. You don't mind having a Japanese gift?' He shook his head. 'They are one of the most civilised cultures in the world. This is military madness. When the generals are defeated sanity will return, and beauty.'

Sophie nodded. She found it hard to speak. Was this a gift from Nigel, or from Lily? For while it had been Nigel who had gone to Japan, who had met Misako there, it had been Lily who had returned.

She opened the next present, small enough to fit in the envelope with the card, which simply said *With all my love, forever, Daniel.* It was a ring, not costly but valuable: quartz with a thin vein of Thuringa granite, set in gold. Holding it, she could almost feel the sunlight of home.

She opened the next parcel, unevenly bundled and made secure with a vast amount of tape, wondering how much time they had before the plane arrived to carry her away. Knitted gloves from Rose, made from wool unpicked from a too-small jumper, and a triumph, with all four fingers and thumbs on each one suspiciously neater than the main body of the glove. She smiled as she held the gloves to her cheek, wondering which friend had helped her.

A kangaroo, lying exactly as the roos did in the shade of the red gums, Danny must have carved in woodwork at school. She marvelled that a young man had been able to recreate the grace and poise so perfectly. The wood looked like casuarina, brown-gold tinged with red, and may have been from home, too. She stroked it, finding it hard to put down, this link with her children. Cards that she read over and over, as Nigel watched her silently.

She would have loved to take the cards with her, the gifts, slip the ring upon her finger. But none fitted the life of the Comtesse de Brabant, and if she was caught all would be taken from her.

She had already told Nigel about the gifts Danny and Rose were getting, just as she always had tried to share news of the children who had been legally and quite possibly biologically his.

She glanced at him now, this man whose outward image changed so much, yet who was always the same person, even if he could not show all he was to the world. Did it really matter that she had not spent time with Lily these last months? She loved the person beside her still.

What would he do once the war was over, if it ever was, if somehow the Allies won? Would Lily Vaile reappear? He had never actually stated that she would. Lily Vaile had a claim on Shillings, as Nigel's sister, the earl's aunt and legal trustee. 'Bob Green' did not even own the cottage he lived in.

'You have lost everything, haven't you?' she said quietly.

'What do you mean?'

'Your title. The right to claim Rose and Danny as your own. Even your home.'

'I'm comfortable where I am. It's Shillings I love, not the Hall. I was never keen on being the earl.' He smiled at her. 'I somehow don't think our young man will turn me out when he turns twenty-one.'

'You can't be Lily again at Shillings, can you, even after the war?'

There would always be newcomers at Shillings now. Headlines in the newspapers, photographs, even the discovery of who Bob had been, a legal mess as well as a scandal, for if Nigel Vaile, Earl of Shillings, was alive Sophie's marriage was invalid and the money paid out by his estate illegal too, though that complication would be the least of it.

He stilled. 'You want her to return?'

'Of course. At least some of the time. Don't you? You told me when we last met that you were Lily-Nigel.' Surely that identity was too strongly forged to change.

He gazed at her, his expression impossible to read.

Time, she thought desperately. England's thinness extends to time, too. We have just minutes now, instead of the hours, days, years we need to talk. She chose the most pressing question. 'You didn't choose to be Lily so I could marry Daniel, did you?'

He smiled, an expression of love and infinite regret. 'No. Though the knowledge that there was a good man, and one I admired and trusted to help care for our children, helped me with the choice.'

Her heart cracked, just a little. 'There is a place where Lily would always be safe. Thuringa, especially once we tell the children. Daniel would be your doctor there. Bob could visit and become Lily between Sydney and Bald Hill.'

'This isn't the time or the place for decisions like that,' he said gently. 'When you get back, before you return home, let's talk. Fully and openly, as I have never been able to do. But no matter what happens, remember I love you, have loved you and always will.'

Why had he never been able to speak openly? All those years at Thuringa, even these past months too. Surely they had shared all that was possible between two people? But before she could ask, an engine growled above them and then came nearer, on the ground this time.

Sophie stood, knowing he would stand automatically too. A gentleman did not remain seated when a lady stood. She stepped towards him and put her arms around him.

It was the kiss of a wife for a husband, a husband for a wife. It was, she realised vaguely, infidelity, but Daniel had always known that Nigel — Lily — lived and that love remained too. A single kiss ...

They moved apart as footsteps headed to the door.

'Sophie, my love, I'm sorry ...' he whispered.

The door opened.

'Mrs Greenman?'

'George?' Her smile, her eyes reassuringly meeting his, were automatic. 'I hoped you'd be the pilot.'

Nigel gave a brief nod. Sophie realised he had moved to the shadows by the doorway. George was unlikely to see a resemblance to Lily, and if he did, might assume that Bob Green, too, owed some of his genes to the Vaile family.

'Our hearts will go with you,' was said in Bob's gruff vowels, as he slipped out the door. Darkness had thickened over the land while she had been inside. The Morris Minor engine started almost immediately, though its headlights stayed off till it reached the lane, and even then only the faint light permitted in the blackout shone above the stone walls as the car drove down the lane.

Our hearts, thought Sophie, watching that faint light vanish. George might think Bob meant those at Shillings or even those involved in this project, which must have a name, though she had not been told what it was nor any other detail that could help the enemy. Perhaps that was what Nigel had meant also. Or maybe not.

Chapter 17

Give a man a good idea to use, or a well-written argument or a decent speech, and two days later he will have forgotten you had any role except to type it.

Ethel Carryman, 1942

'It's a Lizzie again,' said George, patting the craft affectionately. 'A Lysander. She can land in thirty feet. Won't need your parachute tonight.' He did not say why he was landing in enemy-controlled territory.

'I had almost been looking forward to the parachute jump.' Those minutes floating in darkness, far from the world. But the world — and its guns — would still be below her. Landing at midnight by plane was surely safer.

Or was it? An aircraft was a larger and noisier target than a parachute. But it was not her choice to make.

She sat in the back behind him as he chatted, evidently reading her discomfort, though Sophie doubted he could have guessed the cause. 'She can't go fast, not more than two hundred miles per hour, but we'll cross the Channel at three thousand feet, above cloud level. There should be low cloud over the French coast, too. We'll drop to four hundred feet there, too low for German anti-aircraft guns to hit us.'

'Good plan,' said Sophie absently, her mind with Nigel — Bob — driving that absurdly anonymous little car back to Shillings. Then to Thuringa, Daniel, Danny and Rose, Christmas beetles and cicadas and the Boxing Day picnic by the river.

Had Daniel told them she had gone to England yet? Would he wait till after Christmas? Her twins might see every day the secret was kept from them as another betrayal.

The plane taxied across the field then abruptly ascended, dipping and bucking only slightly in the chill, still air. Above them stars shone like candlelight through holes in the black tin of the sky. The Lysander turned abruptly. Sophie gazed down, suddenly fully aware of what 'blackout' meant, for there were no lights below them, only the faint gleam of a river that George seemed to be following to the Channel.

'Messerschmitt to port,' said George suddenly.

Sophie looked around, and there it was, a black wasp against the stars. She could hear its engine now, too. 'Do we try dodging again?' She tried to keep her voice calm.

'Don't have the speed. They do.' Their plane dropped. Sophie heard the *chop*, *chop*, *chop*, as the Messerschmitt whizzed above them. Their plane made a tight circle.

'What are you doing?'

'Turning back. No other choice. There's scattered cloud over the Channel, but we can't hide in it while he has us in his sights. I'll aim for Scotland.' They dropped even lower.

Sophie shut her eyes. All the drama of the day for nothing. Suddenly she didn't want to face the Christmas she had already farewelled, trying to smile and eat whatever feast Mrs Goodenough had managed while waiting for another 'good' night to land in France.

'Well, who'd have thought it? The pilot is heading back himself. Must be at the end of a run and short on fuel.'

'Do we have enough?'

'It'll mean landing in a lane most likely on the way back, but we'll do.'

'I nearly forgot.' Sophie hauled the shooter's sandwich out of the haversack, pulled a small chunk off one end, then handed a larger hunk to him. He bit into it, his eyes widening. 'Steak! What's this with it?'

'It's a shooter's sandwich. Half hollow out a French loaf, sear a steak till it's still juicy inside, place it and its juices in the crust while still hot, add thinly sliced cucumber and tomato — hothouse at this time of year ...' and possibly a single pot of each plant in the Shillings's hothouses, for just such a gift as this '... then put the top on tightly and weigh it down with a skillet for at least two hours. Perfect food for pheasant hunting.'

'Meat you can get your teeth into,' George said reverently, and took another bite. 'Mrs Greenman, may I ask you a favour?'

'Of course.' She assumed he meant another chunk of shooter's sandwich.

'If you see Violette while you're in Paris, tell her the moon is still made of green cheese.'

'The moon is still made of green cheese. Got it.' She wondered what the code meant. James had been so definite that Violette was not part of any of his preparations.

'It's personal,' George added. 'Nothing to do with Lorrimer or the war. No need to hunt her out or anything, if that's not part of the job. Just if you happen to see her ...'

'I'll tell her.'

'Thank you.'

His flush gave her a fair idea of what the message meant. She wondered if she should warn him that Violette might have changed since the Occupation. But then she was trusting the woman with her life. Who was she to warn George not to trust her with his love? There had been little love in Violette's life. Even her parents' love when they had finally been reunited with her in her teens was balanced with puzzlement and wariness.

The moon bulged up from the horizon on their left, not the full moon that most pilots needed to land at night, but enough, it seemed, for George, as it had been for the pilot of the Messerschmitt before he turned for home. A hunter's moon, bright enough to see the target, its dapple shadows thick enough to hide in as their craft moved now from cloud to cloud.

George turned a knob. 'Ultra-shortwave radio, to get the landing signal,' he explained.

The craft dropped even further. Sophie strained to make out any detail. George must have the eyes of an owl. The land below them was still as black as the Channel, for France too observed the blackout. Suddenly Sophie could see four tiny stars below them. 'Is there enough light to land?'

'I've landed here before. As long as those torches are in the correct position and no one's let a cow wander into the field …' He turned the engine off. The plane glided silently down, bumped, then drew to a halt.

Dark figures immediately ran towards it. A hand helped Sophie out; two men and a woman scrambled in. In less than a minute the Lysander was climbing to the sky again.

Chapter 18

Shooting to Live
... the use of stationary targets should be abandoned in favour of
surprise targets of all kinds and in frequently varied positions. Such
targets would include charging, retreating, bobbing and traversing
figures of a man's size.

The Commando Pocket Manual
The British War Office, 15 August 1940

DANIEL

Rose had been home for three weeks, burrowing through the correspondence in Sophie's study — the girl ate business affairs like they were plums — choosing the most leaf-plump red gum sapling for a Christmas tree, decorating it, deciding on the menu for Christmas luncheon, conferring with the Bald Hill dressmaker about refurbishing her dresses for next year, and even standing her watch on the CWA stall, contributing twenty-four pots of apple and date spread to help raise money for new fighter planes, followed by two hours with the woman she had always called Aunt Midge making camouflage nets with the other volunteers at the Town Hall.

Rose had also knitted five and a half socks, slightly crooked at the heels, three face washers and a scarf.

Daniel was slightly in awe of his daughter. He had worried, when the twins were babies, that she might grow up to be outshone by her brother's title. But Rose glowed like the morning sun on the river. By the time she was thirty she would undoubtedly have made Higgs a global empire and would be gently urging her mother and stepfather to picnic on the hills and watch the kookaburras.

Danny Vaile, Earl of Shillings, returned from cadet camp grubby and hungry on Christmas Eve. He headed to the kitchen first, emerging with a doorstop of bread topped with cheese, lettuce, tomato and cucumber pickle and then more bread. 'Where's Mum?' he asked as he took an almost anatomically impossible bite.

Daniel hesitated. He would have to tell them soon. But not before Christmas Day, especially as James had arranged a wireless phone call from England for two o'clock, a whole half hour, extraordinary luxury, ten minutes for each of them. If he told them their mother was in England before Christmas lunch they might make unguarded comments or ask inconvenient questions during the phone call, with who knows how many exchanges listening in — a telephone exchange would be the perfect position for an enemy agent to learn their district's secrets. 'Still up in Queensland. I posted your gifts up to her.'

'Not home for Christmas? That's a rum do.'

'There is a war on,' said Daniel drily.

'I had noticed that, Pa.'

The word 'Pa' relaxed him slightly. Nigel had been 'Daddy' when the twins were small. Daniel had been Uncle Daniel, or Uncle Dada, as Rose pronounced it, which had slowly become Da then Pa, used one morning by both twins as if they had discussed the matter, as it was quite possible they had.

They were his children. Legally they were Nigel's. Biologically he suspected Rose had his genes, and Danny Nigel's. But it was he and Sophie who had guided them through childhood and now adolescence. He and Sophie ...

His mind twisted on the word. Sophie. Of course he managed without her. Perfectly well. After all, she had often been absent before on business, and it was not as if he was unoccupied between his patients and his hospital and the day-to-day decisions about the house and property.

He had not woken up on the river bank again, to find he had been John the night before. He treated himself as he would a patient: sufficient physical and intellectual exercise, a relaxed conversation with friends at least once a day, usually over dinner, so he didn't have to face an empty dining room or kitchen once Mrs Taylor had left for the day. And now he had his children again. The house echoed with laughter, feet running in the hallway in the eagerness of youth, leftovers evaporating from the larder, meat safe and refrigerator if Rose or Danny had walked past. It was just ...

She was away. Away in every possible sense, because once again she had stepped onto a plane to England and vanished from his life and back to Shillings and he had no idea what she was doing, as if their life together had never been ...

'Pa?' Danny looked at him curiously.

'Sorry, I was miles away. What were you saying?'

'Are the land girls still here?'

'Both have a week's holiday for Christmas.'

'Hope you and Mum gave them a jolly good present. They've been champs.'

'A dress each made from the old curtains up in the attic, and pearl earrings.'

'Jolly good.' He vanished towards the kitchen again.

Daniel woke on Christmas morning to find the bed empty. It had been empty for two months, of course, but somehow, subconsciously, he must still believe in Father Christmas, who would have spirited Sophie home and down the chimney in his sleigh.

But he would hear her voice this afternoon. Close his eyes and smell her perfume again, the warmth of her skin. Know that at that precise moment of the spinning galaxies, she was thinking of him and no other, of their children and their home ...

He arrived at the breakfast table to find juice from home-grown oranges in a cut-glass jug; home-grown fruit salad in a cut-glass dish; and Rose in an apron with an omelette in a frying pan. She kissed his cheek with 'Merry Christmas, Pa. I've given Mrs Taylor the day off.' She slid the omelette onto his plate, liberally flecked with herbs from the garden and a tiny scattering of cheese. 'Coffee is in the pot.'

It was perfect coffee too, not coffee essence, thought Daniel gratefully as he poured himself his first cup.

'Good morning, Pa.' Danny's face was proudly, freshly shaved. 'Merry Christmas! I say, is there any bacon?'

'I think Rose is doing omelettes.'

'Rose! Any chance of bacon?'

'Nitwit. There's a war on, haven't you noticed?'

'Mum brought bacon back from her last trip.'

'You'll have to wait till she gets back this time then, and hope she's been to a pig farm. I can do you grilled tomatoes.'

Daniel waited through breakfast. He even, at one level, treasured each moment of it, his happy children, the buttery taste of eggs, the scent of hot soil and gum leaves, the sheepdogs barking as they were fed their Christmas bones.

Gifts after breakfast, for the church service was not until late morning, a war-time necessity for shorthanded farmers, who must still tend to stock first. Thank goodness cattle didn't get fly-blown like sheep. Midge and Harry were probably already out with the clippers …

Danny had made them all most useful boxes in woodwork; Rose had knitted him a Fair Isle jumper, using multi-coloured wool rescued from older garments, duly admired.

He and Sophie (but not Sophie: he could not pretend to himself that Sophie had actually bought these, though she had engineered their purchase) had found them books, varied items of clothing and, as their main present, a crystal radio set each that they could take back to their respective schools. He felt their hugs, their sweet young breath and, just for a moment, the world felt right again.

Rose cooked luncheon, or, as she said, left it to cook itself while they went to church, the oven turned right down, stuffed with slow-burning ironbark wood and damper. Roast goose — Midge had been raising them for Christmas, the eggs hatched under her hens, the profits going to the war effort — and corned shoulder of mutton instead of ham. Roast potatoes, pumpkin, beans from the garden, extremely good gravy, the plum pudding Mrs Taylor had made, expertly reheated, custard, brandy butter, home-made crystallised fruit, simmered in honey and apple juice instead of sugar, and extremely sticky and needing an inordinate amount of chewing. They persevered. Crystallised fruit was part of Christmas.

Daniel glanced at his watch. 'I think we had better go to the study.'

'Why?' demanded Rose, passing Danny the custard for the third time.

Daniel felt the smile consume his face. 'Your mother has booked a phone call for two o'clock.'

'Mum!' Two totally different young people, but they both galloped in exactly the same way, along the hall and into the study. The phone rang. Daniel picked it up. 'Yes, Dr Greenman speaking.'

He did not understand the words at first after the operators had connected them, nor even who was speaking. James Lorrimer, he realised. 'Yes. No. Yes, quite. Yes, I will tell them.'

He should say something else to James, something about Christmas, weather, war, James's health. He could think of nothing, except that Sophie wasn't there.

He put the receiver down, to find two pairs of eyes — Sophie's eyes, even if neither had her hazel colouring — staring at him. 'Your ... your mother can't come to the phone right now. She sends her love.'

'All right, Pa,' said Rose quietly. 'What's happening? Mum's not in Queensland — I follow all the Higgs news and there's no problem that would take her away for so long. Where is she?'

'I don't know.'

'You must know!' There was a hint of anger in Danny's voice.

'Your mother flew to England two months ago. Your Aunt Lily needed her.'

'Why?'

'I don't know,' he repeated helplessly. What else could he tell them?

Rose took his hand and led him to the sofa. 'Tell us the truth, Pa.' She glanced at her brother. 'We've put two and two together over the years. Mum and Greenie and Jones, and Daddy and Aunt Lily did intelligence work, didn't they, in the Great War? Auntie Midge has said some things, and so did Violette — I know we were young then, but we remembered and they made sense later. I'm right, aren't I?'

'Pretty much,' he said quietly. 'Your mother did exactly what she has always told you in the last war — organised hospitals, first in England and then in France and Belgium. Jones was in the regular army with your father. But, yes, at some stage, all of them did intelligence work.'

'Is Mum doing something hush-hush now?'

'Yes.'

'What work?' The anger was still there in Danny's voice, as if his mother had no right to leave them without explanation or farewell. 'Where is she?'

'I don't know what she's doing, or where she is, except she isn't in England.' Or here, he thought. 'The ... the person I spoke to said we might not hear from her for six months.' He could not give them James's name. There was so much he could not tell them. Such as the truth about their possible parentage: he and Sophie and Lily had agreed that should not be until they were twenty-five, when Danny had already taken up the responsibilities of Shillings, and be less likely to impulsively say the earldom might not be his if he knew that Daniel might be his true father, and that the former Earl of Shillings was the woman he and Rose had known as their Aunt Lily. 'But I ... I know your mother wouldn't have left us unless she felt what she was doing was important,' he added, knowing it was inadequate, not just for them but for himself.

'More important than feeding people with Higgs?' demanded Rose.

'More important than us?' Danny's voice was hard. 'What's she going to do? Kill Hitler?'

'I don't *know*!' Daniel shut his eyes. The world shivered ... or was it him? Christmas heat turned to chilblain cold, the smell of cordite, the tinny smell of blood and the too-sweet stench of rotting flesh. A pile of half-frozen bodies outside the surgical tent. Another pile of arms and legs. Graves that stretched along the mud; someone was always digging graves. That was war and that was where Sophie was and she had chosen it and she had left him and he could not bear it ...

'What about Aunt Lily?' insisted Rose. 'Is she involved with whatever Mum is doing too?'

'I don't know.'

'I bet she is. Sometimes when Mum talks of Aunt Lily it's as if ...' Rose frowned. 'I don't know. Just that there's more than being sisters-in-law.'

So much more, thought Daniel desperately. Where could he begin? He could not do it. If he even began to talk of Lily he might spill it all.

Sixteen-year-olds should not have to deal with this! And yet he had to give them answers. Make them understand that Sophie ... Sophie ... Sophie ...

But he did not understand either. He did understand war, knew Danny was waiting till he turned eighteen to enlist, knew that his darling son did not know war, for no one could imagine it till they were in it, knew that Danny dreaded leaving for New Guinea, too, but would never say so, and he could not stand that either, not without Sophie at his side, could not stand that his son would see trenches, bloated bodies, men tearing out their eyes burned by gas. He could not help them, could not help his children, could not help those men, dying in agony untended ...

'Excuse me.'

Somehow he found himself in his and Sophie's bedroom. He curled up on their bed, trying to think. Perhaps if he slept it might all make sense. He could see what he had to say, he could comfort the twins, be wise for them just as a father should ...

It was still light when he woke, though the shadows reached to touch each other under the trees.

John sat up on the bed and stared around. What was he doing here? A too-large bed covered with a silk counterpane, not the blanket on the bed he'd made from fallen branches in his hut. This room — he had not been in a room since the hospital. Yet somehow he knew his hut was too far to reach tonight ...

Nor did John need it. There was a tree, three yards in diameter at least and hollowed at the base. A tree to show visitors, a red gum, its base burned or termite hollowed, that had grown its own scar tissue, strong enough for it to survive, just like he had been hollowed out by war but had survived.

But he was not hollow now. His name was John. He needed only a few blankets, a billy ...

The kitchen yielded two empty cans, perfect for billies, matches, two knives, a spoon, a mug, a loaf of bread. Ah, string. He'd need that to trap the rabbits. Another sharpening stone as his knives would soon be blunt from carving all the crosses, one for every man he couldn't save.

Footsteps. He hurried from the kitchen back to the bedroom, carrying his bundle.

A Fair Isle jumper lay on the bed. A jumper a girl named Rose had knitted.

John stared at the jumper, reality seeping in, as well as grief so strong he sank onto the bed.

He was not John. He was Daniel Greenman, who could not cope, but had to cope, for he had two children who needed him, a property to manage, a clinic to run, business decisions that somehow the board of Higgs thought he was competent to make, and he could not cope. He couldn't.

Nor could he be John. John had no children, but Daniel Greenman did, and Daniel Greenman could not leave his children.

But if he stayed as Dr Greenman people would still pester him, *need* him, when he did not have the strength to be needed.

He had failed ten thousand men, a hundred thousand men, uncounted men. The world would be better off without him …

He found his hands picking up the jumper, holding it to his face. Rose and Danny must have their father, for their mother had left them and their other father too, and there was only him. So he must stay Dr Greenman, but only for them, and he could not stay here, not where the wasps might buzz around him once again.

The footsteps had gone to the bathroom. Now they padded back to Rose's room. Dawn came early in midsummer. The children would sleep for another two hours, perhaps. A holiday.

He smiled suddenly, as everything grew clear. He could take a holiday. Daniel Greenman who was not John, but felt John waiting in the shadows, could take a few days' holiday, camping in the tree. It was not even far away.

Impossible to explain to them why a holiday was so essential in person. He was not even sure he could put it into words, no matter how clearly the decision was right inside his head.

No, he could not speak to them. If he talked to Rose and Danny the love between them would draw him back to this 'normal life' with which he could not cope. He left his horde on the bed then slipped into the study, found paper and a fountain pen, then hesitated. At last he wrote:

My dearest Rose and Danny,

I am tired and have gone camping for a few days in the big hollow tree. I love you.

Pa

He stared at the words. They did not seem enough, but what else was there he could say? That Mrs Taylor would care for the house, but they knew that already. At last he added:

PS I think you should phone your Aunt Midge now.

He looked at the words in relief. Midge would explain it far better than he was able to. And in a few days, a very few days of sunlight and the call of birds and no pressure from too many voices or walls that closed him in, he would be well again.

He tiptoed back to the bedroom and took the jumper for the tree might be cold at night. Now to the shed to find a box, to put his foodstuffs in, the flour and bread and cheese they'd give him for opening the gate. But there was no gate near the tree ...

He paused, then smiled. It didn't matter. God would provide. There was water in the river and other foods to harvest. There would be the song of leaves, a nightly orchestra of crickets, owls and frogs, the scratch of wombats and the thud of roos and wallabies. They were sounds a man could hear but still listen to God. And if he felt confused now all would straighten once he had slept in the great tree.

Once he had been healed under the trees. It would happen again, now.

Daniel tied his swag expertly with the string, lifted it across his shoulder and walked towards the trees.

Chapter 19

*Serenity can be found only in a single moment, the taste of a cup
of tea, the tap of bird beaks at a window, a child's smile. That
moment will break. There will be harder tasks than washing
the teacup. Every life holds tragedy, and sometimes triumph is
almost equally hard to bear. But look for that moment, and you
will find it.*

Miss Lily, 1939

SOPHIE

She journeyed to Paris blindfolded, as unaware of exactly where
she was as she had been in the cellar for the last fortnight. She
had been led to the cellar blindfolded; a tray with food and
a bucket of water left for her while she slept during what she
assumed was night, and her chamber pot taken away. It had
been curiously like her imprisonment six years earlier, except
here she was not drugged, had a lamp and matches, and was
even left French newspapers, magazines and a yellowed copy of
The Complete Works of William Shakespeare, complete with
photographs of famous actors circa 1900, to read.

She ate what was undoubtedly French bread, even if made
with a ration of chaff as well as flour, wrinkled apples, as well
as a Thermos of excellent stew, even if its tiny bones meant the
meat might be rabbit, squirrel or even sparrow, and walnuts with
their shells cracked but not removed, which reminded her that
even the sound of cracking walnut shells might bring dangerous
attention.

She had been blindfolded again when she was led out, dressed now in mauve silk, a 1939 Maison Violette. The dress — its wide skirt sadly out of date now — was accessorised with a mink coat in the fashion of the early 1930s, striped in shades of brown, a matching fur hat on her now peroxide blonde curls, a wedding ring, an enormous diamond engagement ring, another sapphire ring, and a sapphire necklace whose stones did not quite match either the ring or the dress.

She hoped the blindfold didn't smudge her eye make-up, or dislodge the fake lashes she had become used to wearing in her cellar. She allowed herself to be guided into what felt like a coffin, but smelled like a vegetable delivery cart and probably was for, as it moved, she could hear the clop of horse's hooves and the occasional plop of droppings.

The bird calls outside sounded like early morning, and the air as they led her out smelled of dawn, too. No one had given her any indication of how much time would pass, or even where she had landed. It had been a fortnight since she'd had a conversation, or even heard one. She wanted words. She was also soon hungry, thirsty and far too hot. The cart stopped four times, but no one came to let her out.

Slowly the noises around her changed: an engine, voices, other engines. The cart stopped again. She heard doors open. The cart moved, but not far. This time someone opened her ... cage? Litter? A woman's hand, calloused, extended, helped her out, still blindfolded. She could smell petrol, onions and horse.

'Do not turn around or look back.' The voice was unfamiliar. 'Walk forwards out the door, then to the right and walk down to the corner. The car will be waiting.'

'Lipstick,' said Sophie briefly. She opened her handbag, looked at nothing but its contents, applied lipstick and two dabs of powder without looking in the mirror of her compact, then obeyed the order to walk forwards.

I am a swan about to take flight, she told herself, and felt her body throw off the last kinks of her journey. I am young, and a silver beam of light leads me to the door. The door — a garage door — was slightly open. She waited for a minute to let her eyes adjust to the light, pulled on her gloves, adjusted her hat, placed her handbag under her arm, then walked out in small, slightly too sensual though elegant steps, her high heels clicking on concrete then pavement.

Paris. Bicycles, mostly ridden by young women, in socks, not stockings, a café opposite, a shoe store that advertised *German spoken here*. The smell of Paris, Gauloises cigarettes and chicory and far less scent of cat than during her last visit. Cats did not prosper in war-time. Nor were there any chic dogs being walked along the pavement.

She turned right. The limousine — hired in her name — was parked on the corner. She slipped into the back seat as if she already knew both car and driver, had merely left it to glance more closely at a shop window. Sophie Greenman would have thanked him for waiting. The Comtesse de Brabant carefully separated herself from the class she had once belonged to. 'Drive on,' she instructed.

The driver wordlessly pulled out into the traffic, conspicuous among the bicycle cabs that were more common than cars now on the Paris streets. Did he know who she was, or had he merely been asked not to speak to the woman he was to carry? She knew not to ask. Instead she smiled and gazed around with the expression of a woman who was delighted with Paris, herself and what the day might bring.

She had evidently been left on the outskirts of the city and on the opposite side of the city from where the house that had been leased for her was situated. Street after street, houses looking ridiculously normal with a scattering of German flags on cars or flagpoles, and an increasing number of German uniforms as they neared the city centre. She tried to peer eagerly, innocently, rather than look as if she was assimilating possibly useful information.

She had first known Paris dressed in war-time, though the uniforms had been French, English and American then, with a few Australians, New Zealanders and Canadians. Her next view had been the week she finally relinquished her empire of hospitals and had entered the quiet opulence of the Ritz, towels as thick as duvets and a tub of endless hot water where she had scrubbed away lice and ingrained disinfectant, then walked the streets each night marvelling at the small art galleries, still with paintings in their windows, greeting the cats who peered at her from laneway walls, and finally known they were at peace.

Wandering arm in arm with Nigel on a later visit, stopping to buy a single camellia, which he'd pinned on her shoulder, pottering among the bookstalls along the Seine, the scent of old pages and modern philosophy and scandalous works on cheap paper that would be illegal in England.

The scent changed to urinals, onion soup, but still the omnipresent chicory. More bicycle cabs, and bicycles, and still mostly ridden by young women, too, in their white socks. Those who sat at the tables outside the cafés were more likely to be stockinged, or at least use iodine to dye their legs and a fountain pen to draw the required seam up the back of their legs.

Sophie automatically checked the limousine for anything that might snag her own silk stockings — she had no idea how many had been sent with her, nor did she want to waste time hunting out a black-market supplier. The Comtesse de Brabant must always wear stockings. But surely Violette would know where they could be obtained.

Apartment houses, then mansions in a street lined with winter-bare trees, and lawns raked clear of any fallen leaf, with no cabbages, grapevines or onions growing in the front gardens, as if to advertise, 'I am owned by a rich person, probably a profiteer.'

They drew up at what must be 'her' house. Ostentatious, with a wrought-iron gate and posts topped with lions, rampant. The front garden on either side of the circular driveway was mostly roses, all bare thorny legs at this time of year, a camellia hedge on either side, still without blooms, and gravel paths.

She hoped the garden behind had been put into vegetables, for until she met with Violette she had no black-market contacts, and French rationing was not just severe, but cruel, for the customer must line up on the right day for onions, or for potatoes or cabbages, instead of buying all on a single market day, except for bread, of course, and pastry. But only Germans and collaborators ate pastry or meat or cake now, or those with inside knowledge and deep pockets, for a lamb chop cost as much as a third-hand car.

The driver — elderly, with a limp — opened the car door for her, accepted the tip she handed him and waited for the front door to open as Sophie, glad of the warmth of her fur coat, stepped through in the high heels she had become accustomed to but hated to the depths of her soul and hips. The maid who stood there wore the traditional black dress. She and the other staff had been hired from an agency only the week before. If Sophie was arrested, James had made sure none of the staff might be executed as accomplices.

The maid curtseyed. 'Good morning, your ladyship,' she said in French. 'Your luggage arrived yesterday. It has been unpacked and there is a fire in your bedroom. May I take your coat?'

Sophie relinquished it unwillingly for the hallway was chilly. But with fuel rationed — and scarce even if you had the ration cards — it would be unreasonable to expect the servants to have lit more than her bedroom and drawing-room fires, as well as the kitchen stove. Even that was a miracle of black marketing. The cook–housekeeper must have excellent connections, as well as the unlimited budget the comtesse's inheritance provided.

'Thank you. Luncheon in half an hour, please?' She had arranged for the car to pick her up again to take her to Maison Violette.

'Certainly, your ladyship. May I show your ladyship to her room?'

Far too much gold paint and golden alcoves — empty, as were the walls, of artwork. Whoever owned this house had either been canny enough to remove all valuables before the Occupation, or they had been 'requisitioned' by the Germans.

Pink silk covered her bedroom walls. What had probably been a pink silk canopy over the bed had been removed, to her relief —

terrible dust catchers. She resisted the urge to open drawers or visit the dressing room to see what wardrobe had been picked out for her. A fresh day dress had been laid out on the bed, suitable for a quiet few hours at home. She pulled the bell.

'Your ladyship?'

'Another dress, please. A good one. My green, perhaps.' If there was no green dress she could complain her maid had not packed it. 'I need to visit Maison Violette this afternoon. The lilies I ordered have arrived, I hope? They are a gift to her, to convince her I must, I simply must, have new dresses. My wardrobe is most scandalously out of date.'

The maid's eyes shone with sudden interest. 'Her clothes are magnifique, your ladyship. I saw you have several of her designs.'

'A long-ago visit to Paris.' Sophie stretched. 'But now I need something new. Do you know how many years it has been since I had any enjoyment at all ... I'm sorry, I do not know your name?'

'Isobel, your ladyship.'

'I have been in chains of marriage, Isobel. And, yes, I loved Henri, but I have been so bored.' Sophie winked at her. 'And so I left my blacks at home and came to Paris.'

'It ... it is not so gay in Paris since the Occupation, your ladyship. The curfew —'

'Pouff to the curfew! I am sure there are clubs which do not have to obey the curfew.'

Isobel was silent. Not a supporter of the Boche then, thought Sophie, for the only clubs allowed to open now were for German soldiers and officials, and their guests. She resolved to have as little as possible to do with the servants. It was not fair to cause them offence, when they needed the wage, even perhaps the place to stay.

'Will this dress be suitable, your ladyship?'

'Ah, perfect!' Another 1939 Violette, stiffened silk trimmed with darker embroidery, this skirt as well too long and wide for today's fashions, but beautiful. 'My emeralds, I think. The pendant and the pendant earrings, the small ring and the larger stone, and the gold hair clip too.'

'I will fetch them, your ladyship.'

'And I will bathe before lunch.'

'Yes, your ladyship. I will prepare it now, your ladyship. Will you lunch here, or in the drawing room?'

'Oh, here. Please tell me it isn't soup.'

A hesitation. Soup was most obviously on the menu. 'No, your ladyship. An omelette bavarois.'

Which could be made as a fast replacement. 'Excellent.' Eggs were also strictly rationed. Cook's contacts must be good. 'A glass of champagne?' she ventured.

'Alas, your ladyship, the cellar was emptied when we arrived.'

So Cook did not have the black-market contacts for wine. Sophie winked her heavy, mink-thickened eyelash. 'No matter. We will contrive.'

—⁂—

The bath was glorious: deep scented water in a tub brought up to her bedroom and placed before the fire, with a screen around it to prevent draughts. She allowed herself to be dressed in a garment that was mostly chiffon and feathers, and slipped into freshly ironed sheets topped with a mound of feather pillows, a glorious comfort after the pallet in the cellar.

Isobel brought in the tray, one that had legs that could be unfolded to make a small table on the bed, correctly divining that her mistress would eat there after her journey. The omelette was indeed excellent, the cheese that followed presumably from the black market, the salad leaves probably from the glasshouse and garden she could glimpse out the back from her bedroom window, the dressing piquant. The pastry for the tarte Tatin was delicately thin, possibly from the scarcity of butter as well as the skill of the cook. Gastronomically it would be no hardship to stay here.

She smiled at the maid as she came to collect the tray, realising that whatever face or frivolousness she showed outside this house, no one would ask the servants, 'Is your new mistress kind?' 'Thank you, Isobel. That was most excellent. Please give my compliments to the cook.'

The girl smiled with obvious relief. 'I will, your ladyship.' She hesitated. 'What would your ladyship like for dinner? There is chicken,' she added delicately.

Ah, a moment for tact. In pre-war days the comtesse could have demanded anything she wished for dinner. A footman or kitchen maid would have hurried immediately for the langoustes, the lobster, the noisette of lamb. But in these days even the chicken must have been procured with great trouble and enormous expense on the black market. Even a lamb chop could possibly not be obtained this afternoon, no matter how many francs were available to purchase it.

'A breast of chicken, poached,' Sophie announced, and saw Isobel's face lighten even more, for now there would be leftover chicken for the servants to share. 'A green salad, and after?' Sophie shrugged, which made the fur tickle her neck, which was already itching. Why did women condemn themselves to this kind of garment? 'Whatever else cook suggests after that.' She had seen winter lettuces in the back garden, so a green salad would be possible.

Isobel returned half an hour later to dress her. Sophie had already redone her make-up. She sat while the maid arranged her hair, not commenting on the hair pieces. She held her legs out one by one for stockings and more of those wretched mile-high heels, then stood for the dress to be carefully draped and fastened round her. Sophie found her skin was damp. She was more nervous now than on the journey. Then, the outcome had been clear: success or death. Now, she was about to enter a forest of maybes.

A girl she had known for fourteen years, as she became a young woman. Impulsive, self-centred, so lacking in empathy that even Lily accepted that only self-interest would motivate her.

And loyalty. Violette had that. But to whom was Violette loyal now? Surely, still, to Sophie, to Jones and Green and Lily, the only family she had. And yet ...

It had seemed so clear back in England. Violette would have all the connections needed. But Violette's actions were not always ... sensible? A little overdramatic, too. Violette would never be a lady's maid, like her mother, or a quiet dressmaker, but must head the only fashion house to rival Chanel ...

'The car is here, your ladyship.'

'Thank you, Isobel. May I have the lilies?'

A short journey, with the same quiet elderly driver as before, the vast bouquet of lilies beside her on the seat.

Tomorrow she must do the most obvious tasks for a comtesse newly arrived from the south, in a house stripped by its previous occupant: find a black-market source of champagne, of cognac, Burgundy, Bordeaux and moselle, perhaps, as well. Flowers, too, and chocolate and pre-war notepaper for the invitation list Violette would design for her, for those who liked wealth, fun, good food and most excellent wine, did not care particularly where they found them and wouldn't question a new acquaintance who could provide them.

The limousine drew up. 'When do you next require me, your ladyship?'

She smiled as he held his hand to help her out. 'I will walk back, I think.' And remember, perhaps, the ghosts of Nigel and Lily with her.

The driver glanced at the height of her heels, then quickly looked away. Damn — she had not thought how tiring the high heels would be. 'Or maybe four o'clock, perhaps. Thank you. But you may need to wait.'

'It is no matter, your ladyship.'

Nor would it be, for he was paid by the hour. But she smiled deeply at him. 'Thank you. You are so very kind.' Then gazed at the doorway in front of her.

Elegant. Discreet. Expensive. Marble pillars flecked with gold, and marble steps as well, three, leading to a polished door of bronze and glass. She pushed it open, once more a swan taking flight, the bouquet of lilies in her arms. I am young, I am young,

I am young, she told herself, for today's performance here would begin to establish her Parisian identity.

A woman approached: black clad, with a small violet embroidered on one lapel. Also elegant, discreet, expensive. And very expertly assessing. 'Good afternoon, Madame. How may I help you?'

'I am here to see Mademoiselle Violette.'

'But of course.' The slightest hesitation. 'You have an appointment?' She used the tone of one who knows with infinite regret that no appointment has been made. 'It does not matter. Even if Mademoiselle Violette cannot attend herself, I am sure we can provide all that Madame desires.'

'An evening dress,' said Sophie dreamily. 'And dresses for inordinate pleasure. Another coat, perhaps,' she gestured at her fur, 'as this is so sombre.'

Another assessment: rich enough to bypass the rationing then, and intelligent enough to accept that it would cost a lot to bypass.

'I will tell Mademoiselle Violette you are here.' This tone indicated it was a gesture only to a promising customer, and that Violette herself would not appear. 'Meanwhile if Madame will come this way?' She gestured to an assistant, another woman clad in black, younger, not as elegant nor as expensive. 'Please tell Mademoiselle Violette that ...'

'... the Comtesse de Brabant is here,' said Sophie, and watched the expressions of both women flicker into deeper interest at her title.

'That the Comtesse de Brabant is in the lilac salon,' said the first woman, with even more warmth in her voice.

'Yes, Madame Ilcy, your ladyship.'

'And would you give her these, too?' Sophie handed the girl the lilies.

'Certainement, your ladyship.' A slight curtsey from the girl, a buttery deference now from Madame Ilcy. Sophie let them take her coat, appreciate that the dress was a Violette, and the emeralds extremely large.

The lilac salon was exactly that, a comfortable room lined in lilac silk, two armchairs and a small table on a Persian carpet, the rest of the floor parquet. A plain room, expensive and elegant, where nothing would detract from the beauty of the garments to be displayed.

'Coffee, your ladyship? A tisane? Or champagne?'

'Champagne,' said Sophie, adding an absent-minded flick of her fingers. Champagne so early in the afternoon was extremely nouveau riche, and perfect for her role ...

An ornate silver tray, etched with violets, a champagne coupe, a frosted silver casing for a bottle of Veuve Clicquot, it's neck draped in a white linen napkin, a plate of macarons, another of small cheese gougères, steaming from the oven. Sophie took one and felt it dissolve in her mouth. Superb. Madame Ilcy poured a half glass of champagne, fizzing delightfully. Sophie sipped, then casually left the glass to lose its bubble on the table beside her. She hoped that the rest of the bottle — and the contents of her glass — would be enjoyed by the staff.

The door opposite opened. A model strutted in, the white tulle frothing at her feet. Sophie shrugged. 'Pretty, but I think not. I would like something a little more ... exciting.'

The girl pirouetted, retreated, no doubt to pass on the assessment to whoever chose the garments to be sent out.

'The ration coupons ...' asked Sophie delicately. No civilian in France would have enough coupons for a dress with so much material, unless they had an exemption from the authorities.

'Do not discompose yourself, your ladyship. It will be no problem.'

A walking dress next, spring green with flowers embroidered on the hem, the fashionably slim lines breaking as the model strode and turned, a slit in the skirt showing her long stockinged legs.

'Perhaps.' Sophie leaned back comfortably and took another gougère.

The next evening dress was black. Sophie shook her head immediately. The girl turned at once at the gesture.

The door opened once more. 'Ah,' said Sophie, leaning forwards. That fabric! Green satin shot with gold, a fabric no one had sold since the war began, perhaps, with gold embroidery in a subtle pattern across one side.

The dress was floor length, its lines slim and sweeping to the floor, the collar buttoned high but the neckline open in a series of scallops which showed a daring amount of bosom without flagrant indecency, and cut deeply but narrowly almost to the waist at the back. The skirt was slit like the walking dress, but on either side rather than the middle, though each cut was overlapped with pleated chiffon so the model's legs were tantalisingly glimpsed, rather than displayed.

'This. It is divine! How soon can it be made? I must have it this week, earlier if possible.' There was no need to pretend eagerness. It was far from her usual style, but Sophie found herself longing to wear it. Violette truly had genius to know that in war-time women yearned for a dress like this ...

'My dear Comtesse!'

The woman who entered was not the waif of more than ten years earlier, nor the rebel of Thuringa. Violette had absorbed Paris, from the perfection of her short curls to the heels as high as Sophie's, the violet dress that was a narrow sheath until she moved, once again showing the miracle of pleating.

The scent of lilies. Sophie stood for an embrace and six kisses, three on each cheek. Violette stood back. 'But you look younger every year, ma chérie!' She leaned forwards and whispered, 'Your hair colour! Magnifique!'

'My darling Violette, that dress! It could have been made for me!'

'I must have dreamed that you'd be here, Comtesse. There is another, too, that you must have, the softest froth of purple. Madame, the purple empire line for the comtesse and she must, must have the walking dress edged in gold. Few have the legs for a gold hem, or the poitrine for the empire line, but your figure — parfaite, always!' Violette kissed her fingers and the air. 'Now, my dear Comtesse, I must leave you for a little while to

Madame Ilcy, who will take your orders and, oh, the boredom of the measurements, for I think perhaps you are slimmer than you were?'

Sophie acquired the look of a woman who had desired slimness. 'I believe I am.'

'And then, Madame, you must show the comtesse to my drawing room. You are free for an apéritif, Comtesse? Please? It has been so long!'

Sophie inclined her head most graciously.

─◈─

An hour later, measurements discreetly taken in a comfortable warm room, nodding condescendingly as she passed a gaggle of women. Two of them were French and three had American accents. All of them over fifty, all rigidly corseted and rouged far too heavily. All were obviously envious of a much younger woman accompanied now by three Madames, not the single one they shared, ushering the newcomer to a corridor they obviously knew led to the fabulous Violette's own drawing room.

The first Madame knocked; the second opened the door to the 'Entrez!'; all three Madames inclined their heads and shoulders in what was almost a curtsey as they left Violette and the comtesse to their embraces.

Violette waited four seconds after the door closed, her hands still lightly on Sophie's shoulders, then gave a cry, hugging her, crying just a little. 'Aunt Sophie! I hoped when I saw the flowers, and then I saw you! But Aunt Lily has not sent you to liaise with the resistance, surely? It is not right! That is for ...' she hesitated on the word younger '... those who do not do important work, like you.'

'Is it safe to talk here?'

'Always. The walls are thick. No one will interrupt.'

'I am not with the resistance. But I need your help.'

Violette grinned, the grin of the urchin singing on street corners. 'I would have been most angry if you had not said that. Two years and Mr Lorrimer does not send a message.' She shrugged. 'So I have helped my country myself, me, moi.'

'How?' asked Sophie wryly.

'Oh, removing those who should not exist, of course. They all come here, their wives, their mistresses. They arrange that I have whatever I need. And then one day, pouff! They are gone.'

Murder? Oh my word. And this is exactly why James has never used you, thought Sophie. And what if Violette's ... activities... were discovered while Sophie was still in Paris or, for that matter, if the comtesse was known to be her friend? 'Violette, what if —?'

'You think I can be caught? I will not be. I make most certain of it. No method twice, no suspicion ever it is not a death most naturelle.' She looked at Sophie seriously. 'You think I just make dresses, me? But these are my family now, the cutters, the embroiderers, the girls who cook or clean, who make deliveries. I have over a hundred employees now and all can feed their families. You think I would risk them?'

Sophie thought of Jones and Greenie. Violette had not even asked after her parents. Family indeed.

'I do not think you would,' she said slowly.

'Good. Now you must tell me how I can help you.'

'I need to be visible so I am invisible. I must become the comtesse so I may ask favours, meet people ...'

'A spy? There is information I can give you, information from those Vichy rats I would have given Mr Lorrimer but he does not ask, and if he does not ask I cannot send, not without contacting the resistance and that is too great a risk, for they might ask me for favours and the Boche might hear.'

'Information about the Vichy government would be useful.' She could put any useful information in the advertisements in the *Paris Monde*. 'But I need information from Germany too. I want to meet high-ranking German officers, from the old military families, ones with aristocratic connections ...'

'The prinzessin has engineered this,' said Violette flatly.

Sophie hesitated. 'Not directly.'

'She would find a way back into your life, that one. She says she will spy for the English, no? But that is a show for Sophie.'

'She doesn't know I'm here.'

Violette shrugged. 'No? And yet you are here, where her countrymen are in power. She spies for Germany, she spies for England. Has she not shown she cannot be trusted?'

'It wasn't like that.' How could she make Violette understand how each of Lily's girls had been chosen, trained, to put the good of humanity even above that of their own nation? Lily was a far better judge of character than Sophie could ever be, for Lily had been right. As soon as Hannelore had seen the evil of Hitler and his regime she had turned to the country that would eventually need to defeat him ...

Suddenly she longed to see Hannelore again. After the war there *would* be sunlight, and kangaroos, time to rekindle friendship, which had been more than friendship, till the enmity of their countries eroded it.

Violette regarded her with raised eyebrows. 'You know her uncle is a widower now? His rich American wife, she died in an air raid.'

'I'm sorry.'

'He is not.'

'You have met him? He's in Paris?' Sophie tried to keep the alarm from her voice. James had seemed so sure Dolphie was in Germany.

A hesitation. 'He is not here now. He visits Paris sometimes, and buys his mistress dresses here. Not a mistress that he loves, of course, but a mistress for his arm, his bed. All Boche in Paris must keep a mistress. It is compulsory, even if they will not let us dance. But he does not love her.'

'Violette, I am not interested in the Count von Hoffenhausen.' Or not like that, she thought. 'I have a husband I love ...'

'Ah, of course. How is your Daniel?' Violette asked politely. 'And Aunt Lily and Rose and Danny and my parents?'

'All well,' she lied. Violette did not need to know that Lily was supposed to be missing in France. Nor did Sophie know how or even exactly where Violette's parents were. 'They send their love.'

'Sophie, please go home,' said Violette bluntly. 'You and the prinzessin — no and no and no. Even if she means good she will bring you harm.'

'I did not say I will meet her,' Sophie pointed out.

'You did not say that you will not.'

'Then I will say it now. As far as I know Hannelore is in Germany. I am based in Paris. I promise I have no intention of contacting her, nor any reason to think she knows I am here. But I can't tell you more than that. Violette, if I am caught I will not mention your name, but that will be because I have met you here, once only — all the help you can give me must be by messages — and so they will not ask. And if you are caught, there will be little you can tell, except who I am and where.'

'You think I would betray you?'

'No.' Sophie suddenly realised she meant it. Violette would be one of the few who torture could not terrify. She had grown up with violence, had endured it and had taken revenge.

'Good. So, what do you wish first?'

Sophie smiled. 'The names of the best black marketeers in Paris. The names of five possible dinner party guests who would be likely to pretend they remember meeting the Comtesse de Brabant in the south of France in exchange for extremely good food and wine. But no one who has lived in the south of France, in case they ever met the real one. They must be the kind of people who will ask me to dine with high-ranking German officers, or to visit nightclubs where I might meet German officers, ones who do not bring their wives to Paris ...'

'Ha. Wives are not invited to Paris. Paris is where one finds a mistress.' She made a fly-away gesture with her fingers. 'There were more German wives when the Americans still flocked to Paris before they joined the war. But Boche-loving butterflies? Pah! I can name you all too many. But let us think who would be the most use ...'

Half an hour later, Sophie's list temporarily complete, she stood. 'Thank you. If I come to the salon again it's best we don't meet. Perhaps you could send an employee for my next fitting?'

'Of course. It is done most often. I will think more, tonight, and ask, most discreetly, what Boche officers might soon be in Paris.'

'Perhaps put the next suggestions in a gift of pastries? Use the old lemon juice or vinegar invisible ink trick, and I will send you chocolates, with the writing on the inside of the box. Violette, my very dear Violette, please stay safe ...'

Violette gave a small cry and fell into her arms. Sophie realised the young woman was crying.

'You gave me a home,' said Violette. 'You were the first person, ever, perhaps, to care for me. My maman and papa, they cared about their daughter, but the daughter they longed for was never me. They did their duty, tried so hard to love me, but all they saw was what I was not. You did not have to give me a home, or give me a family, and yet you tried to, even though Australia was not where I belonged. You gave me all this ...' She waved her hand. She stepped back and smiled tearfully. 'You liked me. Me, truly. Even loved me, perhaps.'

'Yes, I loved you,' said Sophie gently. 'I still do.'

'Bon. For I love you too. I wish ... I wish you had been my mother. And one day we will kick the Boche back to his kennel and you and I will go dancing and drink champagne, and the next day you may go home to your Daniel.'

'Take care, Violette. You are precious to many people. To me, too.'

'But not to Mr Lorrimer.'

'One day, perhaps. He trusts as few as he can these days.'

Another hug. Sophie had a strange feeling this self-possessed woman was close to sobbing.

'I ... I have a message for you. From George Carryman.'

'You've seen him? He is safe?' The expression on Violette's face seemed to come from far away, beyond the world of Maison Violette, or even the strangely vulnerable but amoral girl Sophie had accepted into her family. No, not amoral, thought Sophie. It was just that the morals of others did not impinge.

'He said to tell you the moon is made of green cheese,' said Sophie.

'Ah.' Violette sat entirely still. 'What is he doing?'

'Flying planes.' Sophie considered, then added, 'He flew me here.' This surely could not be dangerous information, for the Germans must know planes landed and the identity of pilots was not kept secret.

'Still? The Anglais have not made him fight?'

'I think he is too useful. He is an extraordinarily good pilot,' said Sophie, with feeling.

'He is well?'

'Very well. No injuries, no illness. He was extremely anxious I give you the message.'

'Will you tell him that I, too, think the moon is made of green cheese?' It was a plea, and a declaration.

'I don't think I will see him for a long time,' said Sophie quietly. 'Not till the war is over perhaps or, possibly, not even then.' Violette and George? No, no and no. They were too different. She glanced at the young woman's face again. Or did George, just possibly, see what she had just glimpsed, the girl Violette might have been?

Violette composed her face, ignoring the tears on her cheeks. 'Usually I go to my most favoured customers. But if you want to meet people most useful, then I will arrange that they will be here when you come for your fittings. And I will most discreetly not be here to introduce you.'

'You are wonderful,' said Sophie.

Violette finally acknowledged she must blow her nose. The handkerchief was violet, too, edged with fine scallops of hand-made lace. 'Every life perhaps has an angel. And mine was my Aunt Sophie.'

Chapter 20

To Remove Blood Stains

These may be your own, or another's, but the same method works
for both. Immerse at once in cold water, as cold as possible, and
leave at least three hours and the blood will rinse out cleanly. Hot
water will set the stains, as will time, and then anything that might
remove the stain will also leach all colour from the fabric.

Miss Lily, 1912

Several older customers lingered in the foyer, watching enviously as Sophie was escorted once again by three Madames, though different from the first. One even stepped towards her, as if to object to an unknown and younger woman being given so much attention.

The Comtesse de Brabant again ignored her, as did the Madames attending her. One held her coat, another smoothed its drape, while the third opened the door. The car hired for her waited outside, the driver watching for her. He limped forwards to open the car door, so that the Comtesse de Brabant need only be exposed to a few seconds of winter air.

The customer who had stepped forwards gave a muffled exclamation. Sophie was vaguely aware of her hurrying up the corridor, undoubtedly to complain to Madame Ilcy that regular customers were neglected while this newcomer was fawned upon. Should she have smiled at the group, as potential dining acquaintances? The comtesse would probably seek out company closer to her own age, but Sophie was aware that discontented members of the old Junker German military class were likely to be older. If the women there today were included on Violette's list, they would likely accept her invitation from curiosity, even if not tempted by a formal meal, which must include meats and wines increasingly difficult to obtain, despite one's wealth. Even ancestral wine cellars were carefully closed to acquaintances now, lest they tempt one of the occupying powers to find a pretext to acquire it.

'Home, your ladyship?'

'To this address first, please,' she handed him the note scribbled in Violette's hand, 'and then home.' It might not be truly home, but it had a soft bed, copious pillows and a meal served on a tray while she rested her back and ankles abused by such high heels. It had been an extremely long day.

The address belonged to a café that smelled of tripe and onions, where Violette had told her cognac and sometimes champagne could be obtained. Sophie entered, gave her order — a table for six for lunch next Monday — scribbled her address on yet another scrap of paper, then folded it over the requisite extremely large bundle of francs, enough to buy a car in England.

She managed to sway gracefully back to the car instead of tottering, or, better yet, throwing the wretched green shoes into the gutter. She let her head rest back on the seat and shut her eyes for a moment. More black marketeering tomorrow, her first fitting and meeting whoever Violette arranged the day after. She must have a long talk with the cook, for she, too, almost certainly knew black-market sources.

A strange day. She was stirred, drained by emotion rather than exertion. She had not, in fact, realised how much she cared for Violette or, rather, that she cared, but had regarded her as immensely capable with little vulnerability.

The woman she had met this afternoon had been vulnerable indeed. No, she had never showed love for her parents, but she was correct: the relationship had been one of strained duty on both sides. Sophie had assumed that Violette's love for her was cupboard love: Sophie's wealth and connections providing the path to anything Violette might briefly desire.

But in choosing her profession Violette had defied Sophie's and her parents' expectations. She had not returned with a demand for a yacht or flying lessons. Her talent for design had ripened into genius — that green and gold dress was one of the most perfect garments Sophie had seen, its cut fashionable but also uniquely Violette, and beautiful — it recalled the first day of wattle blossom at Thuringa before any sprays had faded to brown. There had been matter-of-fact sincerity, and pride too, in the young woman's references to her 'Maison Violette' family. Sophie suspected Violette's employees were in awe of her and very slightly feared her, but loved her, too.

Sophie was suddenly glad that her masquerade was based in Paris. She could not invite Violette to the house — if there was indeed any anti-Nazi conspiracy it might be discovered at any time, and the Comtesse de Brabant implicated if her name was linked to the participants, or if they offered her name under torture. Hopefully James's agents in Paris would know of any arrests, and Sophie could make her phone call and vanish. Violette could not.

But Sophie might still be able to meet her discreetly at the salon. Violette, of all people, would make sure her private rooms were exactly that. Sophie felt a strange longing to know the woman Violette had become. George Carryman, like his Aunt Ethel, had integrity to his backbone. He loved Violette. It seemed, too, Violette had remained faithful to him, despite the years that had parted them, and more years still to come, unless the revolt James hoped for eventuated. Had George seen a deeper integrity in Violette that the traumas of her early life and the uncertainties of living with strangers in unfamiliar lands had hidden?

Sophie smiled, as the car turned into yet another tree-lined street. Violette's mother was ... unconventional ... as well, made respectable only by the close friendship with Lily-Nigel, and membership in James's and Lily's networks.

What would Lily make of Violette? Once again Sophie wished she'd had at least an evening to talk about the plans with her. Nigel and Lily were one, but the aspect of personality displayed was different, even, sometimes, it seemed, their way of looking at the world. Or perhaps her relationship with Lily simply had the freedom of one woman talking to another.

The car slowed.

'Madame.' For the first time the limousine driver did not use her title. 'There is a black car outside your house.'

Sophie opened her eyes.

'I am afraid it may be the Gestapo. If I drive past we will be followed, caught and your guilt assumed. I suggest I leave you at this corner here, where you might move back out of sight. I will then continue to the house and say you have been detained at the salon, and I have come to fetch … another pair of shoes, perhaps. I will find you to let you know if it is safe to return.'

'Or I can hope the Gestapo have merely come to check on a stranger.'

'That is possible, Madame, but not likely. As a newcomer you may not know the Gestapo. I think you should not risk …'

Was he the contact who had been arranged? Unlikely, as he would be too easily traced to her — nor had he used the code phrase. Simply a good man. 'The risk is greater for you if you arrive without me, monsieur. Drive to the house.'

He did not hesitate. Already the slowing car might have been remarked upon.

He parked behind the car. A driver in civilian clothes sat in its front seat. He did not turn to look at them, but Sophie glimpsed his watching eyes in the car's mirror.

She waited for her own driver to open the door, then gave him a rich smile. 'You have been perfection.' She handed him a pile of francs. 'This is for you. You need not tell the agency, heh? And I will ask for you to drive me again tomorrow.'

She managed to glance with unwary curiosity at the car as she stepped up to the front door, relaxing as the limousine drove off unhindered. Yes, that car did look like officials trying for anonymity — or possibly a threatening lack of anonymity despite the plain clothes. But, also quite possibly, any stranger in Paris might be questioned, especially one who had come from the part of the country till recently nominally under French control.

The door opened. The figure that greeted her was not any of her maids', nor even likely to be one of the gardeners', not in a suit so sombre and of such a subtle cut. 'You will come with us, Lady Shillings.'

Her title was still the courtesy Lady Nigel, despite his presumed death, given to her for life for her services to the nation in 1936. She did not correct him. Nor did she dispute the title.

Had one of the women in Maison Violette's foyer recognised her? Possibly. But they could not have found her address so quickly. She had not even given it to Madame Ilcy, only to Violette. Nor did anyone on the French side of this operation — and few even on the English — know her title.

Violette?

Impossible.

Tomorrow, if she had a tomorrow, she would work out who had betrayed her. Someone listening at the door perhaps ... but Violette had said that nothing could be overheard.

Violette. Violette.

'Ja wohl, mein Herr,' she said politely, turning obediently before she had even crossed the threshold. She glimpsed his look of surprise that she had not argued or tried to plead, as she stepped towards the car.

Then she ran.

Around the side of the house, shedding high heels and then her coat. Over the back fence, hoping there was no 'chien méchant' to bark and guard the grounds, through next door's canny bed of leeks and cabbages then under a box hedge.

The hedge was thick. She paused under its foliage, listening. Shouts, and men tramping, but they were looking for a woman running, not one lying under a hedge. Trousered legs passed within a yard of her, pausing, voices calling. She stilled even her breathing.

Eventually the legs moved on.

She could not risk moving now. She must hope that no one from the houses nearby had seen her crawl in.

What now?

She had no shoes; no coat; a bedraggled dress; torn stockings. The identity papers in her handbag were useless, if the Comtesse de Brabant was known to be the Countess of Shillings. She could not go far without fresh ones. Even on the street she might be asked for them at any time, especially if she looked conspicuous. And she would be. A peasant might be barefoot, but her haircut, her silk dress, even the handbag, proclaimed she was not a peasant, and by now the dress would be suspiciously torn and stained.

She did have the money belt around her waist, under her chemise, but all it contained was money. The Comtesse de Brabant would not carry a pistol or identity papers made out in another name, though both were presumably hidden in the false lining of a hatbox waiting back at the house, a hatbox she had not even had an opportunity to ask for. Her handbag only contained comb, lipstick, handkerchief and more money.

Wait and knock on a neighbour's door and claim she had been attacked? Hope they might lend her shoes, let her sit in the warmth, and most importantly, let her make the phone call that would bring rescue ...

But the inhabitants of a prosperous neighbourhood must all have made their peace, to some extent, with the invaders. If they were even slightly suspicious, they would call the police. If not suspicious, they might call the police anyway to apprehend a poor old woman's attacker. And the Gestapo might even now be sending officers from door to door to ask if she'd been seen.

Find an empty house? By now at least a third of wealthy Parisians had left for the provinces in the exode de 1940. Most of the middle and working class had returned, but not those who could afford a country house, rich in orchards, vegetable gardens, even hens or half a black-market pig. But any empty house near here, too, would be watched.

Think.

It would be dark soon. Curfew lasted from nine pm to five am, not even dusk to dawn at this time of year. She would wait till the lights went off in the houses around her, then keep to the shadows, creeping from garden to garden, avoiding all those with dogs if possible, and high stone walls, peering out till she found a public telephone. But this was unlikely to be found in a suburban district. Unlike England, where middle-class households often had a telephone, and there were public call boxes even in the slums, relatively few French families bothered with a telephone. Why pay a large deposit for such a device when shopping and social life were mostly local? A phone in France was usually for business use. James's escape plan had assumed she would have access to the phone in the house, or even Maison Violette.

She would need to find a street of shops, preferably with businesses above them. She did, at least, have a supply of jeton de téléphone, the tokens needed to make a call.

In any case, she could not make that call tonight. The Gestapo would still be hunting her, as well as the French police. She would be all too visible looking for a telephone now, and even more so after curfew. If only she'd had one more day, the next agent would have contacted her, given her information that would undoubtedly have included convenient telephones as well as possible places of refuge. But she would need to find shelter if she was to spend the night hiding, or she would freeze. She suspected her fingers under their gloves, her toes in the laddered stockings, were already turning blue.

Or try to reach Violette ... Logic slammed the door on that. She would undoubtedly be arrested if she travelled the streets after curfew. And if Violette had betrayed her, the Gestapo would be waiting. If Violette had not informed on her, then the Gestapo would be watching the first place 'la comtesse' had visited after her arrival. Violette and her 'famille' were in even more desperate danger if the Gestapo knew of her past connection with the Countess of Shillings, but it was already too late to warn her.

I'm sorry, Violette, she thought, trying to huddle into a small, heat-conserving ball. Was there a traitor at Shillings? But Bob had said none of James's agents had been arrested. Or had James simply not told Bob to ensure Sophie's cooperation ...

Hot soup, she thought. Silk long-johns, woollen blankets, the summer sun glowing on the sand along the Thuringa river ...

'Madame?' The voice was a whisper, not a Gestapo command. A face looked down: three days of grey stubble, a fringe of grey hair. 'Please, come, before they see us.'

She scrambled out. Her rescuer had already melted into shadow. But then one shadow moved towards a garden hut. She bent till she was no longer a human shape and crept slowly into the same shadows and towards the hut after him. He paused, looked around, opened the door and ushered her into its earthy darkness. He entered too, then shut the door and bolted it.

But not complete blackness, Sophie realised. Coals glowed dully from a fireplace made from an old drum with what might have been a drainpipe for a chimney. The floor under her feet was hard-packed dirt, but it felt swept. She could make out a wire bedstead with blankets and pillow, a battered table and old cupboard, as well as a wheelbarrow, spades and shovels and other garden implements.

'Madame.' Her rescuer gestured to a wooden fruit box by the fire, evidently a seat. He was sixty perhaps, his thin body bent from heavy work. She held her hands out to the fire, then turned and warmed her back, while he lifted a kettle and poured water into a pot.

She longed for coffee or strong tea. This was only a tisane, linden flowers perhaps and rosehips, but it was hot. She sipped, then exchanged the mug for a tin can and a spoon placed on another box, his table.

The tin held carrot, leek and potato soup and was totally wonderful. She ate it all, scraping at the sides, before whispering, 'Monsieur, the Boche are hunting me.'

'I know. I saw,' he said softly. 'They came to this house in case the Madame had seen you. But the Gestapo do not know I am here and Madame —' he spat '— her monsieur runs a nightclub for the Boche, but they are too fine to remember, to tell the Gestapo, "Old Jacques, he lives down in the potting shed." Or maybe they think that if the Boche saw me they would send me, too, to Germany to work there in the factories. Then who would grow their leeks and asparagus?'

Sophie nodded. Almost all able-bodied men had now been sent to labour for the German war effort.

'I cannot hide you for long,' he added apologetically. 'Someone might come at any time for the secateurs or a bucket. Nor do I have much food.'

And she had just eaten what must have been his dinner.

'You are kindness itself, monsieur. But I must leave when curfew ends.'

He looked relieved. 'If you would like the bed, I have many times slept with just a blanket, in the army.'

'I would not sleep. Do you perhaps have water? And a mirror? And, by some miracle, a needle and some thread?'

It was indeed a miracle, for he had them all, though the mirror was a cracked shard. But these, and the light of the fire, were enough for Sophie to rip her petticoat to hide her conspicuously peroxided hair up in a scarf, to dampen the expensive silk so it no longer fell in shapely lines, but sagged a little, like nylon made to look like silk.

'Monsieur, another miracle — shoes?'

'They are not much, Madame.'

They were perfect: wooden pattens, held in place with strips of faded cloth. 'Monsieur, please sleep. I do not wish to deprive you, for I am sure they work you hard.'

He nodded, once more looking relieved. At his age, a full day's labour must be exhausting. He added another handful of prunings to the fire, then gave her two of his blankets, both ragged but clean. She wrapped them round her shoulders and waited till he snored.

She looked in the mirror again, taking out a bright pink lipstick that would clash with her green dress. She plastered it on her lips, smudging it slightly, added streaks of a red lipstick to her cheeks then rubbed them in as an excess rouge. The eyebrow pencil made the line down the back of her legs — deliberately unsteady — to denote an attempt at stockings. She would have liked a full-length mirror, but hopefully she looked both different and sufficiently slatternly.

She glanced at the man on the bed. She suspected he would normally be up at dawn and asleep at dark, for lack of lantern or candles. A good man, who had risked his life, his livelihood, his few scraps of sustenance, for a stranger. She leaned against the shed wall on the floor by the fire and allowed herself to doze, waking each time she began to slip down. At last she peered at her wristwatch, gold and patterned with two tiny diamonds.

A watch was useful, but this one was conspicuous and if — or more likely when — she was taken it would be confiscated. She would have liked to leave her rescuer the vast diamond engagement ring, as well as the necklace and earrings, but they were too valuable, and too conspicuous. He might be suspected of theft. But a pawn broker would take the watch, for no one would have reported it stolen.

She shoved the jewels into her handbag, leaving the gold wedding ring and a pile of francs with the watch in the enamel mug on the 'table', large denominations enough for ...

... she had no idea what this man would want. Cognac, the train fare to go and see his daughter, a decent suit? She hoped in the depressed war economy this much cash as well as the watch might cover the price of a cottage and the land it stood on, for his own. His choice. She would have little further use for money, for without identity papers she could not rent a room or take a train, nor even last more than a few days without being subject to a random inspection.

She padded her brassiere with rolled-up squares of bird netting that had the effect of both giving her a most improbable poitrine as well as spoiling the elegant line of her dress and shortening it too.

I am going home, she thought. I have achieved nothing, except expense and risk for others, a possible betrayal of Violette and all who worked for her, heartache for myself, for Daniel, Rose and Danny, and who knows what problems for Higgs. She had not even met Lily, for whom she had left her family and crossed the world. But perhaps on her return to England she might talk to her. No, she *would* talk to her, and make it extremely clear to 'Bob' that she deserved it, as well as the revelations Nigel had hinted at before she left.

Because this failure was not hers. If she had been in Paris for a month, even a week, she might wonder where or how she had let her disguise slip. But the Gestapo had come for her too soon, and known too much, for this mess to have been caused by her. Someone in James's network, or even at Shillings, had betrayed her.

She hoped they would find them. She hoped James would tell her what had happened to the traitors too. She hoped that Violette, resourceful Violette, would find a way to convince the Gestapo she had been about to call them, or even to escape when the dark-suited figures first arrived at the salon, though it would mean abandoning all she had worked for, and her 'famille' as well.

She glanced at the sleeping man. She was glad goodness existed even in this twisted Occupation.

'Bonne chance, monsieur,' she said softly, and slipped from the door, one of the blankets around her shoulders, before he could endanger himself further.

Chapter 21

Kindness is contagious. One kind act will lead to another. An act of cruelty makes it more likely that the recipient will lash out in turn. It is simplistic to say, 'Do good and good will follow.' But simplistic can be true, as well.

Miss Lily, 1912

She kept to the gardens until the increasing light told her that it was past five am and the curfew had ended. Then she quickly let herself out of a front gate, sauntering down the road, the blanket still around her shoulders. A car muttered behind her. She let the blanket fall to her feet and gazed at the driver seductively, waggling her fingers and hips in invitation. He ignored her.

Excellent. She must look sufficiently like a tart who had spent a hard night. She walked on, still swinging her hips, but otherwise allowing herself to look as weary as she felt. A hard night indeed.

A huddle of shops, a bakery, a café, the proprietor putting out chairs and, yes, a public phone. She fumbled with cold fingers for the jetons, and dialled. A local number — Paris automatic exchanges covered only small areas.

'Bistro Tante Louise.' A man's voice.

'Excuse me, monsieur, I have a message for Michelle. Please tell her that Anna called. I need the bicycle she borrowed back again.'

'Ah, Anna!' The voice became friendlier. 'Michelle told me you might call here. She said to tell you she has left the bicycle two days ago at …' a pause while a note was read '… the Boucherie at Rue Didot.'

Sophie took a deep breath of relief. 'Thank you, monsieur.'

'A pleasure, Madame.'

Sophie moved back into the café to consider directions. The code phrase 'The Boucherie at Rue Didot' should be translated to a butcher's shop only two streets from here, where she would join the undoubtedly long line of customers waiting for their weekly ration. Her contact would wave from across the street and she would join them.

'Half an hour,' Bob had said. If she went there now she would need to wait twenty-five minutes, which so early in the day might actually take her into the butcher's shop, where she would be expected to have ration cards and identity papers as well as being registered there. Best to wait here, and in addition she was fiercely hungry, and the next meal might be another long vegetable cart–journey away.

She glanced at the proprietor, an elderly woman with unlikely red hair and a cleavage as wrinkled as two cabbage leaves, who nodded towards an empty table, obviously used to seeing a woman of the streets using the telephone, for after all, there was a war on, and one must eat and contact clients somehow.

Sophie sat and was glad of it. The pattens were as uncomfortable to walk in as the high heels. She tried not to imagine Violette being questioned, tortured perhaps, to tell all that she knew of 'Countess Shillings'. There was no reason why the Gestapo in France would have any records of the Countess of Shillings, though there would presumably be more available in Berlin. But as a prominent member of Paris society with access to important homes, Violette must have been investigated on her own account.

I should not have gone to her, she thought, should never have considered it. Yet Violette had always seemed so indestructible. She had not realised the vulnerability till yesterday.

The proprietor brought strong black chicory coffee without comment, and fresh bread to dunk in it, adulterated by who knew what grains and possibly sawdust too, waited for her payment, then brought change, just as a black car slid past, slowly enough for its passengers to peer into café windows. It slowed even more at the café. Sophie looked straight at it, smiling, eyebrows raised, as if hopeful it might be a client, then looked back to her coffee. The car moved on.

They were still looking for her.

She nibbled the bread quickly, then sipped the coffee. It was reasonable for the Gestapo to assume she was still nearby. They could easily have searched any road traffic in such a quiet area. The Ritz or some other hotel would have been harder to police, but the Germans had taken over all the grand hotels in Paris; nor could Sophie have discreetly entertained there.

What now? If she moved into the full light of the footpath she would be recognised. Her contact knew it was an emergency. They would wait. So should she. In a couple of hours the road and pavement would be more crowded. She could even ask the proprietor to find her a bicycle taxi — she'd be less visible inside its cabin — in return for a large tip. Paris taxis had carried reinforcements to the Battle of the Marne in the Great War. They could carry an allied agent in this one.

An hour later she bought more coffee. This time the bread was accompanied by an almost transparent slice of sausage, possibly made from horse, pigeon or even rat. It seemed this was one of the days when French cafés were allowed to serve meat. Sophie ate it and was grateful. Another hour, and the black car had passed twice. Another coffee, the bread covered with a faint spread of stewed berries pretending to be jam.

Lunchtime approached. The café grew more crowded.

'Soup, Madame?' the proprietor asked. She shrugged. 'It is onion. Always onion.'

'Merci, Madame. You are very kind.'

'The Boche have not yet worked out how to ration kindness.'

The soup was thick with the not-quite bread, and hot and good. Sophie paid once more. A workman in dusty overalls asked if he might be permitted to share her table. Sophie smiled a flirtatious acceptance, glad when he did not meet her eyes. He was only after sustenance, it seemed. He ordered soup and ate it quickly, sopped in bread.

The streets were now as crowded as they were likely to be. Sophie gestured to the proprietor. 'Madame, a taxi, if you would be so kind?' She held out francs.

The proprietor looked startled at their number, but pushed them into her décolletage. A few minutes later she returned. 'Your taxi is here, Madame.'

'You have been most kind, Madame.' Sophie stood, then found an iron hand around her wrist.

'I think not, Lady Shillings.' The workman smiled at her.

The index and middle fingers of Sophie's right hand plunged towards his eyes, missed, but left two scratches bleeding with the profusion of all scalp wounds. He reared back, startled.

She ran again.

They must have recognised her this morning, had been waiting to see if they could arrest her contact too. Thank goodness she had not gone to the butcher's shop. Those on the pavement stood back as she ran, the man in overalls pounding after her. She stopped, so suddenly he almost ran into her, punched him hard straight on the nose, then kicked high and hard with the wooden patten, and heard him grunt as he doubled over in pain.

She ran again, desperately hoping the contact might have come to look for her, that a hand might discreetly say, 'In here, Madame,' and draw her to safety, or at least temporary obscurity. She hoped the proprietor had taken her handbag and could make good use of its contents and that the jewels would not enrich the Gestapo. She hoped that George might suddenly descend onto the broad street in his Lancaster and carry her away. She simply hoped ...

People stood back in front of her now, staring. If only she could run to England ...

She glanced across the street, hoping for an alley she could duck into, a place to hide, a fire escape to climb, and saw the car, the same black car, blocking the bicycle traffic as it slowly kept pace with her. And suddenly there was a man in front of her, suited, but his task obvious as he barred her way.

She feinted left, ducked right and under his arm, then met the black car as it surged onto the pavement. Women screamed. A dark-suited arm circled her neck. She ducked, but he grabbed her hair and held it fast. If only she had kept her hair pieces ...

A man emerged from the car. Sophie recognised him from the day before. But this time he grabbed both her arms and quickly and efficiently handcuffed them. His companion released her hair, then grabbed her right arm and the other her left.

She did not struggle now. Why bother, when escape was impossible? Instead she walked to the car as sedately as possible in handcuffs, pattens and two men on either arm.

'Well caught,' she told them in German, smiling. The captor on her right shrugged, pushing her head down and her waist too as he shoved her into the back of the car. He fastened the handcuffs onto the doorhandle, then sat on one side of her, the other agent on the left.

Houdini might have escaped, though possibly not in pattens and after so long without sleep.

'How did you find me?' she asked, still speaking in German, with carefully pleasant curiosity. Had the café proprietor called the police, or, surely not, the gardener ...

At first she assumed he was not going to answer. Then he, too, smiled, with genuine enjoyment. 'We had alerted the telephone exchange, Lady Shillings. You would either have a refuge with a sympathiser nearby, or need to make a phone call.'

She should have waited until midday to call, or at least till office hours, when there would have been many calls to sift through.

She had been in France for a fortnight and operating on her own for just a little over twenty-four hours and had already failed completely.

Her training meant she knew what came next. Questioning, including torture, imprisonment and hard labour if she was lucky, for as long as her body survived it, but more likely a firing squad as an English spy, unless, perhaps, the local Gestapo believed her important enough to be used for a prisoner exchange.

Would she be that lucky? What exactly did they know of her? Just her name — or their version of it. Unless Dolphie or a German agent in England had entered her details into Gestapo records — and those records were available in Paris — her captors would not know the Countess of Shillings's connections included the gratitude of the House of Windsor, Lily's network across Europe and America, plus the extent of the Higgs fortune and her knowledge of world food resources and merchant shipping.

It might not occur to the Gestapo here that one mere countess, a failed agent, was worth any exchange at all. If she told them, she would also be giving the enemy information they might use in many ways, including blackmail of those who valued her.

Interrogation, torture, death. The only uncertainty was the timetable, not the ending.

Chapter 22

I have never directly asked any of my young women to venture into danger. Others did that afterwards, as I knew they would, and I encouraged my students at Shillings to do right, no matter what the personal costs. It is my responsibility, and always will be, for everything that happened to them after that.

Miss Lily, in a letter written in 1943

The car turned down an avenue of trees, bare branches supplicating the sky. Shillings in winter, she thought. She wanted to shut her eyes, to remember apple wood in the fireplace, the scent of crumpets. But if there was any remote chance of escape in the time to come she must know exactly where she was. The dark-suited men looked amused as she gazed out the window.

A set of iron gates, a second, then a third, all locked. The car stopped. The building beyond, tall, grim and stained by age, could only be a prison.

'I would say "Auf Wiedersehen",' the man on her right said lightly, unfastening the handcuffs, 'but I doubt we will meet again, Lady Shillings.'

She wondered again who her betrayer was — not the exchange operator this morning, but whoever had notified the Gestapo yesterday.

The thought crept back: Violette. The perfume of roses and civet stronger than the lilies' perfume as Violette kissed her cheek.

She thrust the memory away as a man in a Gestapo uniform opened the door, pushing her head down as he pulled her out by the shoulder, with the negligent ease of a man who did this a hundred times a day. Another man in uniform seized her other arm and her handbag, then they marched her across the cobbles of a yard, as she stumbled slightly on the unfamiliar pattens. She heard the car behind her vanish back up the driveway.

She glanced at her captors: in their sixties, she thought, both with bellies that Daniel would describe as goodly shelves above the toolbox. She was suddenly desperately glad that Daniel did not know she was here, must never be told, nor Rose nor Danny either, about the degradation and pain of what would happen next. James would make sure the details were kept from those who loved her. But James would know, and Nigel. They might already know she had been taken. Please, she thought, let Jones and Greenie return to Shillings soon. Nigel should not be alone.

A door, an office off the corridor where her name — her correct name — was entered. A silent wardress in grey, like a slightly overfed greyhound, searched Sophie briefly, removed her belt, gestured to her to take off her suspender belt and leave it in a small pile with her pattens. Then she was led along a corridor with the damp-earth air of below ground, then up an iron staircase, cold on her scratched feet, passing floors with iron-barred gates. The wardress stopped at the fourth floor. She unlocked the gate and waited, almost politely, for Sophie to precede her. Just as silently she unlocked a cell. Sophie entered and the door was locked behind her.

The room was small, scarcely longer than she was and perhaps twice as wide. The window was frosted glass, heavily barred on the outside. Painted plaster from the peeling walls littered the floor.

A rusty iron bed; a roll of thin mattress; a blanket; a stained lavatory seat with a tap in a collar of rust above it. A small window in the cell door, with a rusty basin resting on a ledge below it. The walls exuded the smell of urine, mould, long-unwashed bodies and a hint of mice.

Sophie unrolled the mattress, then examined the walls, scratched with unknown implements, a hairpin perhaps, or even a fingernail, maybe a harder piece of plaster. The scratches were mostly dates, names, all French and none she recognised, a few curses and an advertisement for services the inmate was unlikely to ever render to her clientele again. But in one corner a prayer had been carefully inscribed, in English, *Hail Mary, full of grace* ...

Sophie wondered where the writer was now. Heaven, probably, for she doubted many English agents left here alive. Had her predecessor been an agent of SOE? Who had betrayed the woman who had written those words?

Who had betrayed her?

Sophie sat and tried to think. She was cold, and the day's meagre food had only touched the edges of her hunger. Body, brain, emotions were drained. She was scared to even entertain conclusions in case she could not bear them.

Wheels outside. The window in the cell door opened briefly. Something splashed into the basin. She inspected it: water that smelled of cabbage and even contained a few shreds of it, along with three beans. She shut her eyes and drank it, swiftly, for what little nourishment it might offer, then replaced the basin, in case there might be another offering.

There was not.

Darkness outside dimmed the frosted window, though the light through the crack in the door's window showed the prison's lights were still burning brightly. The cold seeped into her bones. A woman's voice began *La Marseillaise*. Others joined in what was evidently a nightly ritual. Finally, the floor echoed with cries of 'Vive de Gaulle!'

Another song was taken up, a French folk song Sophie had heard back in the Great War, and then another. She wondered whether to try a song in English, to see if any other British agents might be here or, just possibly, to add a small piece to a jigsaw of information: there was an Englishwoman in the cells.

She began *God Save the King*. Voices hushed respectfully, but no one sang with her, so she stopped at the end of the first verse, heartened by the cries of 'Vive Churchill!'

To her surprise she slept, despite the cold that had become pain, the wildlife in the mattress and the bodily fluid stains on the stinking blanket — partly from exhaustion, perhaps, but also because for the first night since childhood she had no useful thoughts to occupy her: no plans for tomorrow or next year. She was now a package to be delivered to her fate, at least till she reached a place where volition might be possible.

The frosted glass announced it was early morning; slightly more frosted this morning, the ice melting as the day passed. She sat, stiffly, stood even more stiffly, and began to move her arms and then her legs to try to warm herself. Faintly, down the corridor, two prisoners were conversing in Morse, each contributing a line of a rude song about Hitler's, Goering's, Himmler's and Goebbels's personal endowments. She wondered if anyone else in the building, apart from herself, had actually met the Führer. Was there someone of high enough rank here to have done so?

The wheels again. This time a lump of bread — it could not be called a slice — dropped into the basin, along with a green shred of what, after examination, she decided had once been cheese. She ate the bread, consigned the greenery to the lavatory, then wished she had thought to wash her underwear so it would dry overnight, or at least be damp but cleanish. It was unlikely she would be issued with fresh clothes.

A day. She exercised just enough for warmth, so she didn't feed her hunger. She washed her underwear, meticulously wringing it out as dry as possible, for what else was there to do? A night, which seemed colder, and sleep more impossible, perhaps because she was less tired but her hunger was edging towards starvation. Another day. A night. Identical, tracked only by the changing light outside, the twice daily creak of wheels followed by the slither of a pretence of food, the only variation the songs, yells of encouragement, and sometimes sobs or screams, the booted tread of guards. She tried to hear Violette's voice among the cries and songs, for surely Violette would have yelled in defiance if she was here. Each evening when she did not hear her, she hoped a little more that the connection between them had been overlooked.

She wondered if she would be left here, shut out from life, till the war ended, or the world; she realised she was being left till she wondered exactly that.

She tried hope, but it was hard to hope when you did not know the mechanics of any miracle that might help. The resistance might storm the prison. So might the tooth fairy. A whirlwind could blow her back to Australia; or Lily, who had masterminded miracles before, might walk through the door, immaculate in ... What was the correct dress for rescuing prisoners? A demure pink and grey tweed suit perhaps, with dusty pink high heels? A pink chiffon scarf? A picnic basket certainly, with cherry cake, lamb and chutney sandwiches, or even Rose's hilarious first attempt at scones, when she had used salt instead of sugar, and they had each solemnly eaten one while Rose watched on proudly ...

The next day they came for her.

The wardress grasped her arm so hard there would be bruises. She did not speak when Sophie wished her good morning in French and then in German, nor as they stepped along the metal corridor, down flights of stairs and along the underground passage, nor even when Sophie smiled as they emerged into daylight. 'Ah, the sparrows of Paris! Always so cheeky!' She spoke in French again this time. Perhaps Polish or Lithuanian would have been more appropriate, but she knew neither ...

A single car stood in the courtyard, its Nazi flag limp in the mid-winter chill. The pavement felt frozen under her bare feet. The wardress opened the back door, shoved her in before Sophie could do more than turn, then marched away without looking back.

I am a non-person, Sophie realised. This woman had children, perhaps, nieces or nephews maybe, or even a dog. At times, almost certainly, she is kind. But she cannot afford to be kind to me. To her I am simply an object on the conveyor belt of life.

She did not attempt to speak to the driver, who wore the uniform of a German army private.

The car started with an efficient rumble; it was driven, quietly and competently, turning once, twice, three times. Sophie realised she was being driven around the same block, not once, but several times. Why? To confuse her? Surely even an infant would not be confused. To give her hope that she was being taken somewhere better? But any reasonable person would know that what came next must be worse. The car turned once again into the prison courtyard.

This time she managed to step out of the car before the wardress reached her, though she waited for the woman to take her arm.

A different doorway. A corridor, stairs. The wardress knocked.

'Komm herein!'

The wardress opened the door and stood back to let Sophie enter.

The man at the desk was in his mid-thirties perhaps, in uniform, hair shiny with pomade, chin also shining from recent shaving. He stood, clicked his heels — more shine upon his boots — and bowed. Sophie crossed to the chair in front of the desk, upholstered in brown leather and comfortable-looking, and took her seat.

'My dear Countess!' he said in the French of a native Frenchman. 'I have only just heard that you were here. A thousand apologies.'

Sophie quickly sorted through her responses, then gave him an indulgent look she might give her son. 'It is war-time, Colonel. One expects ... hostilities.'

'One must always expect good manners, Countess. Please, call me Henri. A cigarette?'

'You are most kind but, no, I do not smoke.' Sophie wondered at the name. Was it his real name? Or was this a subtle power game, using the name of her supposedly dead husband.

He put the silver cigarette case and the silver lighter back into his pocket, just as the door opened again. Sophie smelled it before she saw it. Coffee, in a tall pot on a tray, and two small cups. Such small cups.

'Coffee, Countess?'

'That would be delightful. I wonder, could we perhaps have a little bread and butter with it? Or even cake?' Sophie smiled again. 'Cake is impossible, of course, but you seem to be a man who can produce miracles.'

'I hope I can today. Of course we shall have cake.' He raised his eyebrows at the wardress. The wardress left. Sophie wondered if the signal had been to truly bring something edible, or merely meant, 'Ignore her.'

'Will you pour?'

'Of course, Henri.' She made sure her hand did not tremble as she first poured for him, then herself, adding cream to hers and sugar, purely for their nourishment. She managed not to gulp, then deliberately poured herself another as he regarded her over the lip of his own cup.

The wardress entered again. To Sophie's amazement she pushed a trolley, this one of polished wood, not metal. A plate of madeleines, another of tartines already spread with butter, croissants.

'Please help yourself, Countess.'

She took a madeleine, took the smallest bite, tucking it under her tongue in case the colonel wished to speak and she had to answer, hearing Lily's voice a war ago, explaining the art of eating and conversing simultaneously. She imagined herself, almost a child in her too-expensive, too-indulgent dress, sitting in Lily's silk-lined drawing room, the fire flickering, the crumpets toasting, Lily slightly in shadow, the chiffon scarf at her throat, gazing at her with what Sophie had assumed was indulgence and which probably had been. But there had been other emotions too, which Sophie had not guessed at the time.

Miss Lily, she asked mentally, when offered a feast and you are starving and are reasonably sure that charm will not affect the outcome, should I focus on the man or on the food?

She laughed, the answer obvious. Henri gazed at her, startled. Sophie finished the madeleine in two bites, took a croissant, ate it neatly but swiftly, and took another before she explained. 'Please excuse my manners, Henri. I doubt I will see another croissant for a long time. Perhaps never.'

'My dear Countess, you are mistaken.' He met her eyes, held them. She felt like saying, 'My dear boy, you are far too young and far too stupid.' But she would play the game, at least till she had eaten everything on the trolley.

She crossed her legs, glad they were still excellent and that she had managed to wash, laborious as it had been with so little water. But what else had she to do to pass the time, except to wash and to remember?

'Henri, you are handsome and far, far too charming. And this feast is a treat.' She began on the tartines.

'Dinner at the Ritz, tonight?' he suggested.

'My dear man, you aren't serious?'

'Of course I am. How could one resist the temptation to dine with such a companion?'

She glanced regretfully at her putrid dress. 'Women always say, "I have nothing to wear." But you too must admit this is not suitable for the Ritz.'

'That can be remedied. You might even have your own personal couturier, from Maison Violette.'

She responded with careful casualness. 'If only there were dresses like Violette's in London.'

He kissed his fingers to her. 'Only say the word and a dinner dress will appear.'

'And shoes? Stockings?'

'Naturally.'

Sophie looked at him from under her eyelashes, nibbling the last tartine. She felt nauseated — too much food, too fast, after too little. She hoped her complexion had not turned lime. 'I would adore to dine with you at the Ritz. And a dress from Violette would be divine.'

She caught a hint of his surprise. She was supposed to be defiant, courageous, tell him frankly that she would never betray her country no matter the torture or the bribe.

'I will ask them to call Violette now. I am sure she will attend to you herself, as she did four days ago. Just a few questions first.'

'Of course, Henri.' So they knew Violette had spoken to her. She hoped she would not be sick.

'You came here as the Comtesse de Brabant.'

'That is correct,' she said composedly.

Another flicker of surprise. He had not expected any capitulation, Sophie not even disagreeing with what they evidently already knew.

'You came to spy?'

'Yes. Terribly bad mannered, I know, but there is a war on.'

'Who were you to meet?'

'I don't know. There were to be contacts, but you did not give me time to meet them.' She managed a smile. 'If you had waited, I might have led you to members of the resistance. I was to establish my identity in Paris and cultivate contacts in whatever aristocracy I found here, both French and German.'

He blinked, hearing truth in her voice. 'What was your ultimate aim?'

'To find information, of course, but primarily to encourage an anti-Hitler sentiment among the class of people I would meet as a comtesse.' She kept the smile through growing nausea. 'So much more effective than a resistance worker on a bicycle throwing hand grenades. But sadly, I hadn't had time to even buy a suitable dress for my endeavours, much less peddle propaganda.'

'Your contact was Mademoiselle Violette? She once lived with your family, did she not?'

At all costs she must try to keep further suspicion from Violette. 'You know she can't have been, as Mademoiselle Violette must be the one who contacted the authorities. The people who brought me to Paris did not know my address here, and no one else in Paris knew my true identity. Even Mademoiselle Violette did not know I planned to come to Paris. I suspect she would have told you at once if anyone from England contacted her. I should never have trusted her,' she added, letting a small tinge of resigned bitterness enter her voice.

'But you hoped Mademoiselle Violette would help you?'

'Yes. I was mistaken.' A shrug, a rueful smile. 'She is, like you, French. She accepts the conqueror, as long as she does well.'

And ten thousand French women are quietly resisting you, she thought, though you do not see them.

He looked at her, amused. 'We French are perhaps more formidable than you think. We will become partners with the Germans. It seems you underestimated Violette, too. She phoned us as soon as you had left.'

She shrank, as if from a physical blow. It was impossible. And yet, all along, she realised, she had subconsciously known it was the only explanation that fit the facts. If the Germans had been waiting for her, had been told of her true mission from England, they would have waited to see who among their number she contacted. But Violette saw only a spy from England, and that is who the Gestapo arrested, a woman who must be removed before she could do damage.

Had Sophie once again failed to see Violette, except as an extension of her parents? Why should Violette be loyal to an England she hardly knew, simply because her parents were English? She finally had a life she loved, a home, a 'famille', even her own revenge campaign. Why risk it to further an English plot, when the English plotters had failed to contact her for years?

And yet Violette had seemed loyal to Sophie. Or had she merely played a game, till she had acquired the life she wanted using Sophie's funds as its foundation? No, Sophie had seen love, too. Or thought she had.

'What organisation sent you here, your ladyship?'

He had seen her shock. She met his eyes, held them as she smiled again. 'You don't know that? Shameful!'

He smiled back. 'Mr Lorrimer's work, I presume.'

'Of course.' So Violette had told him that, too.

Henri sat back, relaxing cat-like. 'It is a pleasure to talk with someone so ... civilised ... about these matters.'

'A pleasure to talk to you too, Henri. And of course to eat your pastries.' She hoped he could not hear them churning in her shrunken stomach.

'And Miss Lily is organising it all?'

She did not flinch, as she was prepared for him to know the name. 'No. The woman in charge of this operation is not called Dorothy, but that is the name she uses. I'm sorry — I know no more about her identity. I could probably have found out, but I thought it best to know as little as possible.'

She crinkled her eyes at him. 'An interview like this was always possible. You are now going to ask me where I prepared to come here, and I will tell you the truth there, too — several places, one almost certainly in Northern England judging from the local accents — though they may have been concocted to discombobulate me. No one told me the names of the places, and nor did I ask. I had the impression that the major decisions were made in an office in London.' She gazed at him innocently. 'I hope that is helpful, Henri?'

'A facility in Northern England, an office in London? I think you are playing with me, Countess.'

'I think I am, too,' she said demurely. 'You should not be so charming, Henri.'

'Perhaps you would find my colleagues ... not so charming?'

She met his eyes. 'I suspect they will not be. Henri, I was urged to come to France by James Lorrimer. My contact in Paris was going to use the phrase "Don't you long for the first daffodils of spring?" Until someone spoke those words to me — and so far no one has — I have no contacts in France to give you.'

'But you made a call the morning we arrested you?'

'To a café where they take messages for customers. I am sure you know that already, from the telephone exchange. But that café was to be the intermediary only once, if I was in immediate danger. They passed a message back to me. A contact — I don't know if they were French or English — was to meet me in the line outside the butcher, where they'd take me somewhere safe, with new identity papers and a disguise till I could be fetched back to England, either directly or even via Spain. I carefully did not ask, and they carefully did not tell me how I was to return. The phrase I used was something like "Tell Michelle Anna needs the bicycle back again",' she added helpfully. 'If I'd had another escape route, I would have taken it.'

'You had a blanket and pattens that you most certainly did not have when first apprehended.'

'I found them in a back garden, probably discarded. I hid in the gardens near the house that had been rented for me till curfew ended, then attempted to use the first public phone box I found. That is the truth.'

He smiled. 'I almost believe you. Perhaps I do believe you. But sadly I think there are ... details ... you may decide to give with other methods.'

She kept her smile steady. 'Henri, whatever happens next — and I have a fairly good idea of what it might be — please believe that you have gained more information this morning than any of your colleagues will, no matter what methods they use.'

'I almost believe that too. Let me trade honesty for honesty then. I cannot promise you freedom, but I can offer comfort in return for more-useful information. A small manor house outside Paris, servants who will of course be your gaolers, but as long as you do not attempt to escape or contact anyone beyond the social life that will be offered to you, you may forget the war exists for a while.' His own smile was suddenly grim. 'It is a luxury enjoyed by very few in Europe.'

'And not one I could accept,' she said quietly, 'even if I had the information to give in exchange for it.'

He stood. 'I am sorry. Truly, I am most sorry.'

She stood as well and offered him her hand. The room swayed slightly. Her nausea grew.

He bowed again and kissed her fingers. 'Goodbye, your ladyship. I wish I could say "farewell". Let me at least show you to the door.'

'Thank you, Henri.' She managed to make it almost to the doorway before vomiting the tartines and the pastries neatly upon his shoes.

Chapter 23

At the harshest moments of my life I have found lasting friendship, even love. Those times were grim, indeed, but if I could write the story of my life again, I would not erase those chapters if it meant sacrificing what I gained from them.

Miss Lily, 1939

The same wardress came for her that afternoon, silent, though her grip was not as punishing as before. Women's voices yelled 'Bonne chance', 'Good luck' and 'Vive de Gaulle!' as Sophie's bare feet paced along the corridor beside the wardress's boots.

But this time, as they stood at the prison's front door, the wardress hesitated. 'I'm sorry,' she said quietly in French, not looking at Sophie, her lips hardly moving.

'It is not your fault.'

'I have children, Madame. My husband is a prisoner in Germany. I must work ...'

'I understand. We do what we must.'

'God go with you, Madame, and see you safe.'

'Thank you,' said Sophie quietly. They moved towards the waiting vehicle — not a car this time, but a police wagon.

She climbed into the back herself. The door clanged behind her. It had a small grille high up, through which she could peer. The other metal walls were blank, except where someone had attempted graffiti that was illegible. They drove through quiet Paris streets, past pavement cafés, where brightly dressed women sat with men in German uniforms or complacent civilians; women on bicycles; old men tending gardens. It seemed to Sophie that the bicyclists all carefully did not look at the black van, self-satisfied and purring along the conquered streets.

The car turned into a street Sophie recognised from photos she had seen back at Shillings, some of the very few shown to her, not so she would recognise the place, but to make real the threat of what she might face so she might either prepare for it or retreat from the mission before even more resources were wasted on her. As they have been entirely wasted, thought Sophie.

This was Avenue Foch, now nicknamed Avenue Boche by the French, for almost all the nineteenth-century mansions behind its now-wintry leafless chestnut trees housed German agencies. The van turned as guards swung open high metal gates, accelerated a short way then stopped, as she expected, in the courtyard of number 84, the headquarters of the Sicherheitsdienst, the intelligence service of the SS.

Through a doorway, into a vestibule with a wide staircase, the kind of entrance she had been used to as a debutante, a lovely lady. These stairs should lead to a drawing room, with tea, perhaps, or cocktails, or the intimacy of crumpets and honey.

Instead the room was bare, except for a desk, one upholstered chair behind it, a wooden chair, slightly battered, on the other side. The man at the desk did not look up from his papers for several minutes while Sophie sat and waited. He wore a grey uniform, impeccably pressed, his hair brushed back as if he were not concerned over his receding hairline.

At last he scribbled his name and smiled. His teeth were immaculate, but too narrow: a fish's teeth, not a tiger's. 'Pardon me, your ladyship,' he said in German. 'The most unexpected aspect of war is the increase in paperwork.'

'I know,' she said with feeling, in the same language.

'Ah yes, you operated an Australian business. You are wealthy and so feel privileged and secure.'

'Not invariably, but usually.' She smiled at him. 'You are perceptive.'

'That is why I have this job.' His lips, but not his eyes, smiled back at her.

'So I imagine. Mein Herr, you have not given me your name.'

'No, I have not, have I? Your ladyship, we wish to know the name of your contact in France.'

'I have already explained that I do not know it. I was on my way to meet them when you arrested me.'

'How did you get to France?'

'By plane. I had trained to land by parachute, but the pilot had passengers to pick up in France. Men, who kept their heads down, so I could not describe their faces. Young, one tall, one medium height,' she added helpfully.

'Where was that?'

'I don't know. Two women met me, their faces covered in scarves. They blindfolded me. I balanced behind one on a bicycle — it is unexpectedly difficult to balance blindfolded on a bicycle.'

'Where did they take you?'

'A house, I think. I could smell soup cooking and then they fed me some — leek and potato. There was a church nearby, perhaps. I could hear hymns — it was Christmas Eve. After that, a cellar, in the same house, if it was a house. I didn't know how long I stayed there until they took me out — I found out later it had been a fortnight. It was a full day's journey to Paris in a horse and cart, but I was blindfolded and under what felt and smelled like sacks. We may not have come to Paris directly. Someone helped me from the cart, still blindfolded, and asked me not to look behind me and told me that a limousine had been booked for me under my assumed name. What else can I tell you? I have been to Paris before, though never for long and believed no one would recognise me under another name.' She shrugged and smiled again. 'So, I wore make-up to look younger, and my hair has been dyed. The car arrived, ordered in my assumed name through an agency. Whoever ordered the car had also paid for it, but I tipped the driver. I used the same agency the next day — it was convenient. The bicycle taxis are a trifle undignified and look chilly.'

'What was your eventual target?'

'To meet and charm influential Germans or members of the Vichy government and gather information. There was no specific target, as it was impossible to know what chances I might have to make friends in Paris. I expected my former ward, Violette, to help me, though I had not seen her since 1936.' Sophie shrugged. 'I did not know if she would help or not, but I did not expect her to betray me. I understand though why her loyalties have changed. Her home is France now, after all.'

She waited in case he would say Violette was being questioned; Henri and the French authorities had been mistaken and that someone else had called the Gestapo; that they wished to know Violette's associates too. Instead he said, 'Go on.'

'But there was to be another contact here, as I explained to your colleague, who would announce himself with a password, but no one has made contact.' She smiled at him sympathetically. 'If you had left me alone for a few more days you might have more names. Of course, possibly only red herrings.'

'Red herrings?' He frowned. 'Communists?'

'No. I apologise — it is an English saying. Herrings are not red, so a red herring is something that misleads you. My purpose in Paris was to meet as many influential people as possible, to influence them in turn and to gather information about the loyalty of well-born French men and women. If I had done my work properly I would have met many people in the next few days and you would have had to check them all. All would probably have been innocent, though I hope I would have found some who do not welcome the Occupation. I might also have gained useful information from German officers on leave,' she added, as Violette (Violette!) presumably had told them she wanted German contacts too.

To her relief he seemed to accept that her target was Paris and to gather information, rather than acting on information already received in England. 'I still believe there is more you are not telling us, your ladyship.'

'There is, but none that is important. I can tell you the sandwich I ate on the flight here. It is called a shooter's sandwich, so appropriate for war, but really it was invented for gentlemen to eat while hunting, so not at all suitable for me. I was too nervous to eat. Mein Herr, those who sent me assumed that at some stage I would be in a room like this, with a man like you. They were very careful indeed to make sure I knew no more than the facts I would need. My mission was open ended and depended on Mademoiselle Violette's help, or those who would be influenced by black-market food, champagne and an assumed countess. It is ironic, of course, that I really am a countess, though not a French one. A British agent who had been sent to liaise with the resistance would need to know much more than I do. But the woman I was to impersonate did not know Paris well, so I did not need to either.'

'It seems the true Comtesse de Brabant is dead.'

'Yes. The Frenchman, Henri, did not ask me about that. Her maid must have been a member of the resistance, because the English authorities were told that her identity would be suitable for an English agent who wanted to meet well-born French people.'

'Who helped conceal the body and the death?'

'I have no idea. I was told the maid has escaped to Spain, but now I think about it, that might have been a lie, so I would mislead you in a conversation like this. Possibly there was a butler, not a maid, or not even someone in the comtesse's service, but an undertaker or even an attendant at the morgue. It was made very clear to me that I should not ask unnecessary questions.'

'That is a pity,' he said slowly.

'Because you must use ... other methods ... to find out what else I know?'

He nodded.

Sophie looked at him with compassion. 'It would be easier if I screamed defiance at you, wouldn't it? Behaved as your enemy should. I'm sorry, I am not defiant. I came prepared to tell you everything I know that might be of use to you. But, mein Herr, if I did have any other information, torture would not make me betray my country. The only effective weapon would be to threaten those I love. You have none of those at your disposal.'

'There is Mademoiselle Violette,' he said musingly. 'But, I presume, as she betrayed you, you do not feel any love for her.'

'You are wrong,' said Sophie quietly. 'Yes, I trusted her. That was my mistake. I had been warned not to contact her, that her allegiance is to the present government or, in truth, to whatever government is in power. I also did not realise how vulnerable she must be. Her past connections with England are too well known. She could not afford to offend the country she has chosen as her home. She chose her career, her employees, her life here, over someone she knew for a few years and who had given her such a lot of money. Of course, it was not very much money for me, but a gift I could well afford. And an investment in her talent, of course, which ultimately also benefited me. I still feel affection for her, even love — but, mein Herr, I would sacrifice Violette, as she sacrificed me.'

'And your mother?'

'What?' The exclamation might have come from the sixteen-year-old Sophie who had never met Miss Lily. 'My *mother*?'

He looked pleased. 'Yes, your mother. She lives in Paris. You have perhaps contacted her already? I have arranged to have her brought here.'

Sophie began to laugh. 'That will be an interesting reunion for both of us. I have met my mother only once, for perhaps an hour, since she abandoned me when I was six weeks old. Yes, I continued her allowance till this war made it impossible, but only because a clause in my father's will stipulated it. I didn't like her. I think she quite liked me but did not want it known I was her daughter, as she had shaved at least a decade from her age, and a then twenty-four-year-old offspring would have been embarrassing.'

'Ah. I see. That does ... fit ... with what we have discovered. You would not be upset if we tortured her?'

'I would be upset if you tortured anyone. But I would feel no more emotion over her pain than I would for anyone you picked up off the street — possibly less, for I did not think her a kind woman that time we met, and anyone else probably would be far more of a loss to those who love them. But, as I said, I have nothing more of value to tell you, so the question is academic.'

He smiled at her, his first smile. 'It is conventional to say I am sorry to do this. But I am, in fact, well suited to my work.'

'I thought you might be.'

'Would you care to spit in my face? Yell "God save the King"?'

'Neither,' she said evenly. There was a limit to how much pleasure one could give to others. She had reached it. Not that it mattered, for he would take his pleasure with her now.

He pulled the cord that had perhaps once rung for coffee, or linden tea and madeleines.

189

Chapter 24

Sugarless Apple and Date Spread

Take 3 dozen cooking apples, such as Granny Smiths or Bramley Seedlings. Peel and core. Cover with water immediately, and add 1 cup chopped dates. Simmer till very thick, stirring often so it does not burn on the bottom. Bottle while hot and seal. Excellent instead of jam, or to replace custard over a steaming pudding.

Mrs Taylor, 1943

SHILLINGS ESTATE, ENGLAND, JANUARY 1943

NIGEL

He knew when James's car drew up. If the news had been good James would have telephoned, discreetly talking of his Aunt Bertha who had evacuated to Scotland and was enjoying hillside rambles.

Nigel answered the door, glad once again that he could open it himself now, instead of waiting for butler or maid to answer the bell, to take the hat and coat, to announce the visitor and leave while he sat politely waiting for the ritual to unfold. He let James follow him wordlessly to the kitchen, the one room a wood stove kept warm — all he allowed himself now Sophie had left. He and Mrs Goodenough and Hereward had used most of their hoarded luxuries for Sophie.

He sat at the kitchen table, to let James have the warmer seat. 'How bad is it?' he asked quietly.

'She has been arrested.'

'As the comtesse?'

'As herself. She's in Fresnes Prison.'

He did not ask how James knew. There would be watchers, even if not communication. The watchers were also supposed to protect.

He forced himself not to yell. 'How?'

'Violette. The Gestapo arrived at the house before Sophie had even returned from meeting her. There was no time to intercept her. She fled and seemed to vanish — the watchers did try to find her. She was arrested the next morning before we could rescue her.' James did not say, 'I told you not to trust Violette.' Nor was there need.

A sea ran through him, then its tide retreated, leaving him colder than he'd ever been. He had been lonely before but always, since 1913, there had been Sophie. Knowing she was alive, happy or at least fulfilled, had been the small glow that had warmed him each chilly night.

James stood. For a moment Nigel thought he might embrace him. Instead he turned, lifted the cover on the stove and put the kettle on.

'Don't bother. I've used up my month's ration and haven't bothered to dry any alternatives.'

'I brought some from London.'

'Black market?'

'Of course not. I filched it from the Home Office canteen. And sugar too.'

Nigel's lips twisted in what was not a smile. 'You are treating me for shock? I don't think a cup of tea will do it.'

'Whisky?'

He shook his head. 'What chance of rescue now?'

'None, in Paris. But if she is transferred it will probably be to Ravensbrück, by train. The prison and the train station will be watched to see which carriage she is placed in. The train can be derailed ...'

'She might be killed!'

James said nothing.

'Can't you offer an exchange of prisoners?'

'We could try. But that would immediately rouse suspicion — her known aristocratic connections are not enough to warrant that kind of intervention. The Gestapo would suspect she knew more than they think she does now. They would continue to ... interrogate ... her.'

James turned his back to pour the hot water into the teapot. 'She may know more than the Gestapo have probably considered. Shipping timetables from Australia, supply routes and destinations, the cargo capacity of the merchant marine fleet. The Germans with their Kaiser, Küche, Kinder simply do not see a woman as an industrialist. Sophie has possibly a better idea of the Empire's trade than anyone in existence.'

'And yet you risked her.'

'As did you.'

Nigel nodded. 'Me, more than you. If I had told her she owed her duty to her family, to her business, she would not have gone. I had to be persuasive. Lily ... I ... used to be skilled at that.'

'I'm sorry,' said James softly. 'We may yet get her out. Or she might survive as a prisoner till the war ends. Ravensbrück is bad, but not the worst.'

'*If* they send her to Ravensbrück.' They both knew that, as a spy, she might be shot at Fresnes instead of sent to indefinite imprisonment at Ravensbrück. Her aristocracy might even make an early death more likely. A countess who survived and recounted torture would be ... embarrassing.

James poured the tea. As he lifted the teapot over the second cup Nigel said, 'I would prefer to be alone. If you don't mind.'

'Are you sure?'

'Very sure.'

They both knew he would not, could not cry with James, with anyone. Except, perhaps, with Sophie.

'You won't ...'

'Do myself harm? I have an estate, tenants and two children, even if legally none of those still belong to me. While there remains a chance I might be of use I must be ready to take it. So will you please go? Now.'

James left. He had just shut the front door after him when he heard the howl. He sat behind the wheel of his own car and bent his head. Now he could weep as well.

Chapter 25

A French Onion Soup, 1943

So — you must first queue for the bread, with the correct coupons, and then on another day for the onions, and on yet another — do not forget the coupons — for a small amount of oil or lard. You will queue for cheese too, but even with the right coupons and francs you probably will not find it. No matter. Take the stale bread, cut it into croutons and brown them by the fire till gold but no more. It would be difficult to find enough coal or wood to char them. Now chop the onions finely, the same quantity as bread, and sauté them in the oil or lard slowly. This will take at least an hour and again they must be gold, no blackened piece to make them bitter, and almost dissolved. Add water and leave by the fire overnight or simmer for an hour if you have the fuel, then add the bread. Leave to cool and then reheat, scattered with the cheese, if perhaps you have it.

This is not the best onion soup the world has seen, but it is excellent and far more gratifying than stale bread, water and some onions deserves to be.

SOPHIE

The SS Korporal lit the brazier while she watched: the better to build anticipation, she assumed. The poker was heated till the tip was red hot, then white. Her interlocutor ripped the dress from her shoulders — his strength impressed her as well as his ability to shock.

Then she stopped thinking and endured. The poker's tip touched one breast, then the other. She smelled the flesh burning before she was aware of pain. She did not attempt to stifle her screams, nor her instinctive attempts to leave the chair, to crawl across the room. There was no need to pretend now, not before these two men.

The assistant looped a rope around her waist to tie her to the chair.

'Will you speak now, your ladyship?'

'Anything,' she gasped. 'But I know nothing you can use.' She tried to keep her mind empty of all they could use, but did not know she had, from the long history of Miss Lily and Shillings and her network, to Hannelore (please, let her simply be staying discreetly silent for a while in Germany) or the tactics of La Dame Blanche, and most especially, the routes ships took as they carried corned beef to England, Egypt or Malta. Even Violette's assassinations ...

She arched backwards, trying to find the least agonising position, dimly aware of the poker in the brazier again. Hands pushed her roughly forwards. The poker pressed, slowly, dot by dot, upon each of her vertebrae. Screaming did not help, but there was nothing she could do but scream. The man who had wielded the poker seemed content.

'There is worse to come,' he commented.

'Please ... I will tell you anything. Anything! But there is nothing I know to tell ...'

She sat slightly forwards as the corporal held one foot, and then the other, but another rope pressed her back on the burns on her vertebrae. She had known the next was coming, each toenail ripped from its bed. She did not even have the breath now to scream, or even the strength to breathe. She vanished ...

... she woke, drowning, gasped for air, found agony as well, then breathed water, floundering, till her head was raised. She lay on her side on the floor, choking, heaving, realising her body had reached its maximum comprehension of pain.

It seemed her torturer accepted this as well. He peered down at her, puzzled and vaguely disappointed. 'I did hope you had information. You are — interesting — your ladyship.'

Sophie wondered in the frayed thread that was left of her mind what Miss Lily, circa 1914, might have offered as a charming response to this. He obviously enjoyed defiance. Perhaps she should have offered him a little. But she could not care.

'If you have nothing to give, then it must be the firing squad.'

She found to her horror that her body craved death. Her mind, too, wanted to sleep, to cease ...

To cease upon the midnight with no pain. A man had written that. It seemed that she, at least, would not achieve his goal. It would not be midnight, and there would be pain.

'Take her away.'

Footsteps. Then more footsteps, two more corporals. Each draped one of her arms over their shoulders, then dragged her, bloody toes dragging on the floor, screaming, as they went down the stairs.

She could not walk. The men threw her into the back of the van as if she were a dead sheep. They must have ridden in the front of the police van, for they were the ones who grabbed her hair to haul her out when the van reached Fresnes again, a journey that might have been five minutes or four days, for she floated in and out of consciousness and pain.

The two men hauled her back to the cell from which she'd come that morning. She was vaguely aware of the wardress watching, expressionless, of women banging their fists against cell doors, yelling encouragement. Sophie bit her lips, so the only sound she made was 'Mmmmmm'.

They dropped her on the floor. She managed, finally, to crawl to the bed, then pull herself up on it, to lie curled in a foetal position on one side. She tried a humming that was not a scream. It helped. She could focus on the humming. She could not scream now, for that would terrify the other women on this floor.

A voice emerged, from the usual cries of 'Vive la France!' and 'Vive de Gaulle!' that accompanied any passage along the corridor. A woman's voice, young. *'Ave Maria ...'*

The other women quietened, till the hymn was over. *'Pray for us sinners, now and at the hour of our death.'*

Sophie found she wept.

'Madame? Shhh, please do not speak.' It was the wardress.

Sophie could not have spoken. She no longer had the strength even to hum.

Her dress was pushed down again. Sophie felt the coolness of a lotion on her breasts, her back, what must be dressings on her wounds and then a strange garment being pulled over her, like a multi-layered silk chemise. She felt her dress pulled up again, and fastened somehow at the top. Then two tablets on her tongue, water in a glass held to her lips, which she swallowed.

The wardress vanished. At last agony ebbed to mere pain. And then the impossible. She slept.

And woke and yet still felt as if she dreamed. Two SS privates hoisted her up with no more emotion than if she had been a sack of potatoes, or possibly less, for a sack of potatoes had more value in war-time than a captured Australian countess. But if she shut her eyes again she was sure she would sleep again. She resolutely kept them open.

The wardress was absent.

The cries from the other cells this morning were different.

'Go with God, chérie!'

'We will not forget!'

'May angels guard your rest.'

They know, thought Sophie vaguely, lost, a strange feeling this body was not hers, because *her* body would be in agony. To leave at dawn must be to go to death. Efficient. Get execution over early so the place can be tidied up for the day.

Her bare toes scraped down the corridor, the metal stairs. Agony did come then. She tried to think of love instead of pain, of Daniel, Rose, Danny, Nigel, Lily, Bob, crumpets and honey and the golden pre-war winter. Or that Jones and Green might suddenly appear, machine guns in their hands, to shoot her way out of this, as George swooped back to take her to Thuringa.

Thuringa. If she fixed her thoughts upon the river perhaps she might be granted a short afterlife there, to glimpse those she loved again, to whisper, 'Goodbye, I love you,' in the warm breath of sunlight that might be warmer, just for a moment.

Would those she loved ever know what had happened to her? Were records kept? No other prisoner even knew her name. She should have told them, screamed it out, so if any of the other women survived the war they might say, 'Yes, she died by firing squad,' and, if they were kind — and surely they would be kind — they would not add, 'I think she had been tortured.'

Too late.

You should stand proud before the firing squad, who should be a squad, too, not just two old men who had not shaved, one with a stub of a cigarette he did not bother to remove. Instead she felt dizzy, as if she was about to faint. How ironic, to lose the last moments of life in a faint.

The men who held her shoved her onto a chair polished with dried blood and the sweat of those going to their deaths. From here she knew her body would be cremated.

She did not know if there were watchers. She did not care. Her world was pain. She wanted only to sleep, where pain would vanish.

Someone muttered an order, and then another. Shots and then more pain.

She fell.

She ... thought.

Realised that she thought.

Realised she still felt pain too, that the pills must be dulling it, and her reactions too.

So she was not dead. Shot, yes. She could see blood covering the front of her dress, which had not been bloody yesterday as the poker had cauterised the wounds it made. Should she call out, or mutter at least, to let them know they had to shoot her again?

Someone shoved her into wood ... a wheelbarrow. She should move, at least, for otherwise she would be thrust into the oven alive. She had heard they did not care if those who were cremated were still living after they'd been shot. No — this way she had a few seconds to focus on her first night with Daniel, diamond stars piercing the sky and love encompassing her as well as the heat of his body; the first glimpse of Rose, then Danny, the first red-faced and furious at being thrust into the world, the second pale and helpless; the moment she had informed Nigel she was marrying him, the love, the shock, the gratitude, the love. Daniel, lighting a swaggie's fire for her after they had crept out one night to make illicit love naked among the stars, some above and some around them, floating in the river, and then billy tea, and laughter, at how shocked the children would be if they had seen them. Rose, practising her first 'running writing' at the desk in Sophie's study; Danny training a sheepdog to 'get away back', turning to smile with pride at her when the dog obeyed. So much love ...

A door clanged open. She felt the oven's heat. And then another tablet, shoved into her mouth. She swallowed automatically. The door swung shut again. Someone held up her head, her shoulders, shoved what felt like a massive hessian sack down to her waist, then roughly pulled it down over the rest of her and tied it loosely below her feet, which for some reason had lost their pain.

The resistance? Had they rescued her?

The wheelbarrow moved. She made herself stay still, despite her skin trying to shriek at the scrape of hessian on her injuries. Then blackness fell like a shutter and she fell into dreams.

If you dream, you are alive. If you are alive, you can be aware you are dreaming. If you are asleep, you should not feel pain and yet she did: a dingo gnawing off her feet and then tearing at her breasts, and then her back, leaving only her face free to scream.

But I like dingoes, she thought, even when they take the lambs. She had never been afraid of dingoes. This dream is not correct, she thought. The dingoes vanished and a fire took its place, the campfire by the river, swaggies' wood and transparent flames just snickering while the billy boiled until the flames grew red and sucked her down.

She woke to dark. She moved and found wood above her and below and on either side. A coffin then. For some reason, they had decided not to burn her so they had buried her alive.

The world lurched. Were they lowering the coffin? No, it didn't feel like downwards movement. Was a coffin airtight? Would she suffocate before or after they had buried her?

It seemed a long way indeed to find a cemetery. And finally, she slept again.

Chapter 26

In this practice, which we have called 'The Pursuit', the shooter is started off at a run ... on an obstacle course consisting of jumping a ditch, running across a plank over water, crawling through a suspended barrel, climbing a rope, a ladder and over a wall, finishing up with a one hundred yard dash ... without warning or waiting, two surprise targets are pulled, one after the other, and at each he fires a 'burst' of three shots. The targets are exposed for no longer than it takes to fire three shots at the fastest possible speed.

The British Commando Pocket Manual, 1940

THURINGA, AUSTRALIA, JANUARY 1943

DANNY AND ROSE

Their mother was somewhere in Europe. Their father was camped in a hollow tree, and Aunt Midge had gently explained he was suffering from a form of shell shock from the war before they were born, and that he had behaved like this ever since that war until shortly before their birth. Their telegrams to their Aunt Lily saying *Mum urgently needed stop Pa ill stop* had brought only a return telegram suggesting they seek help from Aunt Midge, which they had already done, a promise of a doctor from Sydney, and Aunt Lily's *love always my darlings*, but no explanations.

They sat on the verandah, two young people who had suddenly become adult in the past three weeks. Mrs Taylor fussed, bringing lemonade sweetened with honey from Mr Reynaldo's bees, and scones with strawberry jam which neither of them wanted, but ate, because Mrs Taylor needed to help, and food was all she had to give.

Cicadas shrilled. The air smelled of gum leaves and cattle droppings and rosemary from the mutton being roasted for a lunch they would not want to eat, all that meat in war-time, though of course it could be eaten cold. Cockatoos screamed down by the river, the normal summer sounds and smells when nothing was normal at all.

'I'm not going back to school,' said Danny at last. 'Thuringa needs a manager. I know Pa doesn't work the cattle, but he made decisions. Besides, someone in the family needs to be here till Mum gets back.' He did not add, 'Or till Pa regains his senses.'

He glanced at Rose, wondering if she would point out that this would mean not only failing to do his Leaving Certificate, but abandoning school cadets, the Militia, as well as being drafted to fight in New Guinea. Farming was a reserved occupation. Although men and women in many farming families volunteered, they couldn't be conscripted for the Militia, or ordered by Manpower to work at factories and other jobs essential for the war effort. Apart from producing armaments and uniforms, food for the armies and the Empire was the most valuable war work of all.

Strangely, he would have felt more comfortable with needing to stay here if he had really wanted to fight, as some of his friends at school truly seemed to want to do. But it had been hard enough being away from Thuringa at boarding school. He had never admitted to anyone how much he shrank from the thought of leaving for New Guinea, to be lost in mud and jungle, hatred and destruction, for years, or perhaps forever.

But Rose had her own focus. 'I'm not going back either. Mum's desk is piled with letters that should have been answered weeks ago. It's not like the old days, when there was a general manager and Mum just oversaw things. Preparing for the war, all that's happened since — she's taken over more and more control since that last trip to England.'

'You don't know how to run a business.'

'I know enough to understand that someone needs to be at the head of one, especially now. Someone who can make decisions quickly and know they'll be carried out. I know how to ask for advice, and I know how to take it, too. Higgs doesn't need radical changes just now, but there are problems that need to be sorted out.'

Danny snorted. 'You're just going to march into the board meeting and say, "I'm taking my mother's place"?'

'Exactly,' said Sophie Higgs-Vaile-Greenman's daughter.

'They'll laugh.'

'Then I'll fire them. I'll get Pa to sign a power of attorney. I'll type out letters for him to sign about school, too.'

'I think you need to be twenty-one to have power of attorney.'

Rose shrugged. 'Then Aunt Midge can have power of attorney and she can appoint me to deal with Higgs.'

'Do you have enough experience running a business?'

She looked at him patiently. 'I don't have *any* experience. But there are others at Higgs who do, in their various areas. What I do know is how the various parts of Higgs support each other — how when hail destroys a bean crop in New South Wales a bit of imagination means we can look for peas in Victoria. I've sat at Mum's desk watching her work or discussed plans with her since I was three years old. I know how she *leads*, Danny. If there were others who could do this there wouldn't be so many urgent requests for help on Mum's desk.'

Danny was silent. He knew how to manage a property. He also knew how to love it. Cattle, fences, water troughs and windmills were reasonably simple and mostly ran to a timetable. The Higgs business empire did not.

'I can do it,' said Rose calmly.

'Yes, I think you probably can. But they won't.'

'I've seen how Mum handles them. I'll be right.' Her voice was just slightly too confident, her hand on the lemonade glass slightly too tight. 'I rang Dr Patrick this morning.' Dr Patrick was the doctor the telegram had promised, sent from Sydney by Dr Edwards, the Superintendent of Callan Park Mental Hospital, to take over the Bald Hill Clinic. 'I asked Dr Patrick about Pa, too —'

'You talked to a stranger about Pa!'

'He's a psychiatrist. It's his job to help people like Pa! It turns out he knew all about him being John after the First World War.' Her voice shook slightly. Another part of the family history that had been kept from them — the years when their father had been a man called John.

'Does Dr Patrick know how Pa was cured back then?'

'He said he thought it was probably just time and quiet in the bush. He said not to argue with Pa or plead with him to come back.'

They had tried this repeatedly, with no success. Pa had just smiled at them and offered them native sarsaparilla tea boiled in an old baked bean can, and promised he would be home 'in a day or two', which he had been promising for a fortnight now. 'Dr Patrick said Pa might be doing what he knew would make him better.'

'We just leave him there?' asked Danny incredulously.

'Dr Patrick will go out and talk to him often. But he said we need to go there every day, too, so he doesn't forget there's a life here to come back to — just talk to him about what we're doing, but not try to get him to come back.'

'Of course we need to keep going out there. He needs food to begin with.'

Rose was silent. This morning Pa had offered them leftover rabbit stew, thickened with watercress and some kind of sweetish tuber. The bed of piled-up bracken and tussock inside the tree had been neatly covered with a blanket, and the ground swept with a broom made from young wattle branches. There had even been logs pulled up around the fire as if he expected company. He had seemed happy, pointing to where the first star would shine tonight and the tree it would shine directly above. He had even asked if she and Danny were happy, and seemed relieved when they both assured him they were, because their first tears and incredulity had distressed him, though they had not brought him home.

'Rosie, things will be all right, won't they?' It was the question Danny had asked when they were four years old and shadows threatened in the nursery.

She answered just as she had back then. 'Don't worry. Tomorrow the sun will shine ...' She stopped, for tomorrow Mum would still be away and probably still not have sent any sensible answer to their telegrams, and Pa would still be living in a tree. She held out her hand. Danny gripped it hard.

They had each other.

Chapter 27

The Führer's Leberknödel

Although an avowed vegetarian from 1937 onwards, Herr Hitler consumes his favourite liver dumplings in a vegetable broth, as well as sausages, though the latter are delivered to his mistress, Eva Braun, and only after midnight, to be discreet. Nonetheless he vows that when he rules the world, all shall eschew the eating of any flesh at all, except, perhaps, liver dumplings. A cup of finely minced liver is blended with a cup of breadcrumbs and two eggs, chopped parsley, a little nutmeg. The small balls are then boiled in a broth of celery and onions and served as soup.

From Notes on a Lecture by James Lorrimer, MBE, 1943

SOPHIE

'Sophie?'

She knew the voice. If she kept her eyes shut she might imagine the last week had been a dream. Her mission was still to come and now she lay on linen sheets at the house that had been rented for her, and the pain in her feet was from high heels and the pain in her back and breasts would be forgotten if she could just slide back into the lovely dark waters of deep sleep …

'Sophie, you must wake up.' The words were spoken in English.

She opened her eyes. Dolphie did not smile at her. He looked, instead, unbearably weary, eyes sunken, the jacket of his grey uniform removed.

This was not the house in Paris, nor any place she had ever seen. It was a hotel room that smelled strongly of turnips, decorated in a combination of clashing florals that could only be French. A zinc bathtub steamed next to the bed, which was indeed covered in linen, its quilt rolled to the end of the bed, for which she was thankful, as even the weight of the sheet was almost unbearable. But only almost. She realised she had been drugged with whatever she had been given back in 1936 to keep her sleeping through her kidnap. Tonight it had not just brought sleep, but some relief from pain.

'I need to clean your injuries while the water is still warm, and I need you to promise you won't make a noise. If anyone suspects you are here we will both be shot. Do you understand? No word, no cry.'

She wanted to say she had already been shot. She managed a minute nod.

'Good.' He pulled the dress down — it had been torn so much he hardly had to move her to remove it. The strange chemise was more difficult, as the many layers of blood-soaked silk were embedded in the wound in her chest. Sophie gazed down, vaguely curious. She had been shot in the chest, but she was not dead.

'This will hurt. I'm sorry. But I am glad their aim was good, and they did not hit you in the neck or lower stomach.' He picked up tweezers and began to extract layer after layer of the silk.

'What?' she whispered.

'The bullet-proof tunic — or nearly bullet-proof — was my great-grandfather's. He wore it in case of assassins. Genghis Khan is said to have invented it — layer after layer of silk. Ah, yes — the bullet hasn't penetrated far.'

Sophie glanced down, moving her eyes, not her neck, which seared with pain even with a tiny movement. A shallow wound and much purple bruising. She shut her eyes again.

She felt hands carefully slide down her knickers, heard the dip of a washcloth in water. He began to wipe, beginning with her face and then her hair, or rather with her scalp, for she could feel no pull at all. For some reason, her head had been shaved clean while she slept.

Neck, breasts, avoiding the scabs, stomach, legs, some prolonged scrubbing of her feet, the merest wipe of her pudenda, then gently turning her to lie on her front and washing her back and buttocks as well.

It felt wonderful and hurt like knives piercing every nerve.

'You need to drink. You've lost a lot of blood. I will put towels under you in case you want to urinate. Please, again, do not speak.'

She felt vaguely irritated. Men demanding that she speak, insisting she was quiet. But nothing felt quite real, including the soup he held to her lips, a chicken broth, perhaps with honey added.

She sipped, kept sipping, stopped when he removed the cup and placed a tablet on her tongue.

'Sulpha,' he said. 'Hopefully there will be no infection, but your feet were filthy and injured toes are susceptible to bacteria. I will give you morphine before we leave in the morning, but no more till then unless the pain becomes unbearable. If it does, tap the spoon against the glass.'

She moved her eyes a fraction; saw the glass on the bedside table and the spoon; again gave a tiny nod. He offered her another spoonful of soup.

This could not be a dream. If it were, he would be saying, 'I always dreamed of stroking your naked body, but not like this.' And yet his touch was more than kind.

'I will try to explain what has happened, but I'm not sure how much you will remember of this by tomorrow night — tomorrow's dose of morphine needs to be large enough to make sure you don't cry out in your sleep as we travel, though, as you will be strapped to the back of the car in one of my trunks, so hopefully Georg won't hear you. Georg is my driver at the moment.'

Not a coffin then. A trunk.

'Violette telephoned me. I had ... convinced ... her it was in her interests and her salon's to do so if you ever contacted her.

Unfortunately, she called the Gestapo first,' he sounded angry, 'which was not our arrangement at all. I was not even in Paris, but if I had been I doubt I could have prevented what happened once you were in custody. The only way to remove you from Fresnes was by bribery, and even then the guard had to be able to tell himself he was only passing me a dead body, though why he thought I should want it I'm not sure.'

He hesitated. 'It must be painful to know Violette betrayed you.'

She blinked twice at him, to indicate a query. He understood. Dolphie had always understood. Or almost always.

'I suspected you might come. An SOE agent admitted under torture she had heard of another organisation that was sending "stuck up tarts to suck up to officers" into Europe.' He gave a grim smile. 'She saved her life with that, though I expect when the story of her war is told she will have given away no information. Somehow no agent who survives has ever given information under torture. The agent also said it had something to do with lilies. Miss Lily's network operating still, and not just Hannelore.'

A cascade of blinks.

He nodded. 'Yes, Hannelore is safe, and yes, I discovered her ... communications, though she will not tell me how long she has been betraying her country, nor what information she has given. I have managed to keep it discreet. She is confined to the Lodge for her health, a consumption of the lungs.'

Sophie shut her eyes in relief, then opened them again when even that seemed about to lure her back into sleep. She knew the Lodge, had been there for a few deeply romantic hours after the Great War, when it seemed that she and Dolphie and Hannelore would find lifelong happiness together there and in Australia, before realising that both expected that she — and the Higgs fortune — would stay in Germany to help rebuild its power.

Her escape with Greenie and Jones's help had not been romantic at all, but she still remembered the beauty of the Lodge, dilapidated as it had been after the war. It was set in the woods of the estate, with its own home farm, and by a lake, where swans sailed.

At least she no longer had to pretend to be a young swan. Just now she felt like one that had lost its feathers and possibly the use of its wings.

'Hannelore has to remember to cough into a bloodied handkerchief when anyone visits, though few do,' Dolphie was continuing. 'And, of course, the phone has been disconnected, and I have her supervised, so she can't send messages. I'm taking you there, assuming we can make it that far without discovery.'

The Lodge was certainly preferable to Fresnes. It would be a joy to see Hannelore. But the woods near Munich were a long way from Paris, and the Lodge presumably staffed by servants loyal to the Third Reich. She raised her eyebrows slightly.

'How will we prevent you being discovered? You will need to travel in the trunk — I have told my driver that it contains classified papers, which is why it is so heavy, and must be guarded at all times, and taken to my room immediately when we arrive at the destinations on the way. If you are discovered in my room, we must pretend you are a prisoner from a labour camp sent to work for one of my properties, and that I decided to ... make use of you. If you are discovered in the trunk I will complain angrily that I have been sent a worker who cannot work, and I am returning you as an example of the quality of labour we have been sent, and you are confined in the trunk to punish you.'

He shrugged. 'We can only hope that whoever I spin that last story to is extremely gullible, but I can think of no better explanation for your presence. I will then relent and say that I will take you back. I shaved your head to make you resemble a prisoner ...' he grimaced '... as well as to remove the conspicuous peroxided hair and the lice. And no, I cannot pass you off as my mistress, as one look in the mirror would make that obvious. You would also need papers, even with me, and I have no way to procure forgeries. But I believe I can get you to the Lodge safely, and once there, you won't have to stay hidden for long.'

Two blinks. He smiled at her wryly. 'Why? Because, Miss Mata Hari, in a few weeks Hitler will be assassinated.'

Chapter 28

Sometimes the wisest speech you can make is to say, 'I don't know.' The world is vast, and even the best informed can only know a fragment of a speck that you think was once a cake crumb. Add another speck and you may suddenly see it was once part of toast with honey, and that the world is completely different from what you thought it.

Miss Lily, 1939

They were not travelling straight to Munich. Dolphie stated it would be suspicious if he not only suddenly appeared in Paris on the day of Sophie's execution, but then went immediately to his sister, a known associate of Sophie's, even if that had been long ago, and Hannelore was presumed to be a loyal supporter of Adolf Hitler. Instead they would detour to Austria.

'I am the head of my own section in Vienna,' he explained a few nights later. 'So luckily I rarely have to report to superiors. We should be at the Lodge in about a fortnight.'

But she was sure that before she had lost consciousness that first night, he had told her Hitler was to be assassinated in 'a few weeks'. How many weeks was a few? And how, and why, and by whom?

Sophie was still unable to move or even comprehend much — a combination of pain, her injuries, exhaustion from the day cramped in the trunk, as well as the effects of the drug. But she could speak tonight, even if she had little breath.

'You are Sicherheitsdienst?' she whispered. 'Is that how you know what ... what will happen to the Führer?'

He smiled at her from his seat at the table where he was dining on pale sausages boiled with cabbage. This room was larger than the one the night before, with a sofa that thankfully he could stretch out on to sleep. It smelled of boiled cabbage instead of turnip. Her meal was slices of the same sausage in a vegetable soup, with bread made perhaps almost entirely from wheat. He had fed her spoonfuls slowly and meticulously, insisting she eat it all before he began his own meal, the second course of the three he had ordered, suitable for a German officer of his rank.

'Did they teach you about the Sicherheitsdienst in England, or do you have a particular interest in German organisations?'

'England,' said Sophie hoarsely, knowing she wasn't giving him information of value. 'You didn't answer my question.'

'No, I did not,' he agreed pleasantly.

'Dolphie, please.' Every word was an effort. 'Why did you rescue me?'

His blackmailing Violette to inform him that a potential Allied spy had arrived was understandable. He might believe, too, that she had far more information to reveal, including about his niece. But he had not interrogated her, nor even subtly questioned her, much less handed her over to more experienced inquisitors.

That, perhaps, was to come. She had no way of knowing even where they were, much less where they were truly headed. It could easily be Berlin. Just now she had no choice. She couldn't even stand, much less plan her escape. But if he truly was taking her to the Lodge then somehow she might manage a phone call, or even send a postcard or an advertisement that James's agents would see.

'Because unfortunately there are few people I trust, and none who could be spared simply on the possibility that you might come to France. If Violette had kept to our agreement, you would not have needed to be rescued.' He ate a bite of the now cold sausage.

'Not ... an ... answer,' she managed. The drug that had kept her sleeping in the car was wearing off, the pain encompassing her again.

He put down his knife and fork. 'Very well. In the beginning my arresting you would simply have been a propaganda coup. Those fools in Paris have no idea of your true value: not just a dowager countess, but known and trusted by those in power, including their Royal Highnesses and Churchill. Once you were known to be in Germany — comfortably in Germany, not tortured by some little nameless sadist — the prime minister and the king would have had no choice but to agree to a high-level prisoner exchange.'

'Not Hess!' The Nazi third-in-command had parachuted into Scotland more than a year before, ostensibly at the request of Hitler himself, to offer peace terms to what he believed were high-placed Britons with fascist sympathies: England could keep her Empire in return for giving Germany freedom in Europe, and joining forces against the Soviets. But Hitler had repudiated the offer; and so had the man Rudolf Hess believed would help him make a treaty with Churchill.

'Does Hitler want Hess back?' whispered Sophie slowly.

'Not particularly, though his confinement in England is embarrassing. Perhaps you would be exchanged for many prisoners, not just one. That would be up to others. I would simply be the one who had ... acquired you. But now ...' He sat silent, as if wondering how much to tell her.

'Now what?' she whispered at last.

'Now things have changed. It is ironic. My job is to hunt Hapsburg loyalists who remain opposed to the Third Reich and wish to reinstate the Austro-Hungarian monarchy, with its policy of "live and let live" for ethnic groups, religions, even Jews.'

Sophie carefully kept her face blank, so that he did not guess she already knew his occupation, information that presumably came from Hannelore.

'They are mad, of course, but there are a surprising number of them. We've already sent about four thousand Hapsburg loyalists to Dachau.' He considered his plate, sighed, then picked up his fork again for the last piece of sausage. Even for a Gestapo colonel, it seemed, congealed sausage was the body's fuel and should not be left on a plate.

Sophie watched him, this man who could speak so easily of sending people to Dachau, some, at least, to torture like hers, and to their deaths. He looked back at her and smiled, seemingly knowing what she was thinking. 'It is war,' he reminded her softly. 'Every one of them would have killed me, if they could.'

'Dolphie ...'

'You wish me to get to the point? Very well.' He lowered his voice even further. 'There are many of us, experienced men of good family, who are loyal to our country, but who believe Hitler is leading us to destruction. The Russian front! Why did he not keep Russia as an ally until we had conquered England? Which we would have if we had only one front to fight. Madness, perhaps literally. He grows more unpredictable, more dangerous to our country every day.'

'So you and your friends will ... stop him.'

'Exactly,' he said, still smiling.

How could he seem so calm about a plan to assassinate the most powerful man in the world? A man he had once been devoted to?

Once again, he seemed to guess her thoughts. Perhaps he read her face. 'I love my country,' he said simply.

And it was simple for Dolphie, she realised. Everything he had ever done, or been, had been for love of Germany, except, perhaps, for protecting his niece.

'And me?'

'Removing one man is just the beginning. We will need to act fast so that our supporters can show there is a real chance of achieving a just peace agreement with England and its allies, or we will lose control. Churchill will listen to you. America will listen to Churchill. With Hitler gone we can negotiate properly — not the desperate delusions of the demented Hess, with Germany reigning over all of Europe, and England keeping only its independence and its colonies.'

This was what she had been sent to do. This was what she had failed to do. Yet this was exactly what was going to happen, though nothing she had done had caused it. Nor had James Lorrimer: English arrogance, she thought, underestimating Germany and the German military yet again. If we find Hitler's

rantings ridiculous, the men like Dolphie in Germany must find
them both humiliating and dangerous.

Would Churchill listen to her? Of course. She had proved both
intelligent and discreet during and after the abdication. That
did not mean he would accept her advice, or even ask for it, but
she could be exactly what Dolphie hoped, a liaison between two
governments. She might even phone James from the Reichstag.
She smiled. Or call Shillings first, so Lily might know before the
rest of Britain.

But Lily would not be there.

She brought herself back to reality, trying to focus. 'What
terms will Germany accept?'

'I do not know what compromises will be agreed to. Germany
must keep Austria, Hungary, Poland, the Slavic nations, the
Sudetenland and be returned our colonies. There can be no peace
with Russia, but England and America are natural enemies of
Stalin too, so I think that will not be a problem. Neither will
want to see Russia control Poland. Do France and Belgium get
their independence?' Dolphie shrugged. 'I do not know. Nor do I
much care. France beggared and betrayed us after the ceasefire.
We never would have disarmed if we had known about their
additional terms. It is only right that they should pay for that.
But they *have* paid. We will concede far more than poor Hess
tried to offer.'

'But what of Japan, and Australia?'

'Japan will not be able to hold out for long without allies,' he
said, using almost the same words as Nigel. Had it only been a
little over two months ago? 'Britain and America will be able
to focus their resources on regaining the territories Japan has
taken. The war will be over, Sophie. We will all be free.'

It was strange to have hope again, not just for her own life and the
possibility she might see her family again, but for an end to the
war. She focused now on regaining strength and movement —

a haggard invalid, hardly able to speak, would be little use in negotiations.

After a week, she was able to bear the cramped darkness of the trunk with less sedation, enough to dull the pain but not remove her from the world. Mostly she slept as the car travelled, for she carefully did not sleep at night, wakeful for the knock on the door that meant she must silently hide.

At each place they stopped Dolphie chose a refuge for her before she emerged from the case, under the bed usually, or behind a curtain, or back in the trunk: hiding places that he could help her to quickly, but that would not stand up to a search. But as Dolphie pointed out, if anyone suspected enough to initiate a search, they would both be dead anyway … eventually.

The rooms almost invariably had a single bed, in which she slept, while he slept on sofa pillows with a quilt on the floor, for few sofas were long enough for him. He claimed he had a soldier's toughness. She suspected he had in fact spent few nights away from a comfortable lodging and his batman — his usual man, who also drove for him — had been given leave.

'Your batman wasn't surprised?' she asked Dolphie one night. She was able to talk more now.

Dolphie shrugged. 'He suspects. I have been careful not to involve him, and he knows it and does not enquire too much. He also knows he will be safer if he has not seen me for a few months. His family has a farm, so with the food shortages it is common to give leave for harvests or plantings. Less so in winter, of course, but not unknown. No one would expect an officer to share a plot with his batman, but they would expect any batman to share his suspicions with the authorities.'

'He won't?'

'He hasn't. As for the future …' Dolphie shrugged again.

'What's your future, Dolphie? Your "after the war" future?'

He smiled at her. 'So very Sophie Higgs, so sure there is a future.'

'There has to be. I know mine exactly.' Sitting in the thin gum-tree shade on the river bank, forever echoing with children's laughter, although both Rose and Danny would be grown up by then, ducking and splashing in the water, with friends perhaps, Daniel stretched out beside her, his hat over his eyes, Lily sitting in a squatter's chair, her gauze-shaded hat keeping off both sun and flies. 'After the war' there would be time for that. 'There must be a good peace, and happiness ahead. What else do we work for?'

He laughed at that. 'Our Führer would say "For the Glory of the Fatherland". But I've never wanted glory for my country, just security and pride.'

'But you? Would you stay in the army?' She knew he had no need of money now, with the inheritance from his late wife.

'I hope there can be a peace with no need for a large army,' he said slowly. 'Let the factions fight elections, not in the streets. I will live at the Lodge, walk in the woods, inspect the pigs at the farm each day and send old Franz insane with all my questions. And perhaps I will make schnapps. I have always wanted to make schnapps, not just small amounts now and then, but vats full.'

'Schnapps?' she echoed incredulously. 'But it's just alcohol, no flavour, just the burn as it goes down.'

'Ah, you have not had good schnapps! Schnapps should be made from the best fruit, with no sugar added, just yeast, and then distilled and drunk fresh. I make mine from our cherries, and then another batch from the plums. Or I did before the war. The secret is to discard the first of the distillation, and the last. You want only the middle, with the heart of the fruit. Then you get the flame, but the fruit too. A good schnapps will leave fire in your veins for the whole night, but you will still taste it, too.'

She laughed softly. 'I believe you.'

'No, you do not. But you will.' He stretched out his legs, as relaxed as she had ever seen him. 'I will sit in my chair under the oak, watch the swans on the lake and beautiful women with long blonde hair will bring my schnapps up from the cellar.'

She touched her own bald head instinctively.

'It will grow again,' he told her softly. 'And one day it will be "after the war" and our dreams will come true.'

They talked for longer each night as she regained her strength, always in German. Dolphie chose rooms that were either isolated, or easily accessible, the ones where an occasional woman's voice in an officer's room would not be remarkable — though her appearance would be. Her hair had regrown to a velvet fuzz, but Dolphie would not let her see herself in a mirror. She suspected she looked like a spectre: hollow-eyed, white-faced, dappled with bruises.

It was strangely good to talk to him again. She had liked him from the moment they first met. He was interesting, with a capacity to love and be loyal to the niece he regarded as a sister, even if the sense of fun she had enjoyed before the last war seemed to have vanished in the tragedies since.

And he was kind. She had suspected that, long ago. Now she knew it. She needed care, if she was to be of use — and certainly needed to look as if she was a willing, well-treated negotiator, not a tortured captive — but there was gentleness in his touch, consideration in the way he gave her every chance of modesty, pulling up her sheets or towels. At times the daily blankness of the trunk seemed to suck away her entire world. The nightly talks with Dolphie restored her to herself again.

Each night he ordered a meal — as large as possible, three courses or four, to which his military rank entitled him. This food provided her a feast after they arrived, with some kept aside for a smaller meal, eaten while he slept, and a final one to last her through the day when she slept or dozed in the trunk, in pain, lurching and, at times, trying to fathom why they had stopped or where, and if it was voluntary or meant capture, though, if possible, Dolphie told her of the appointments or meetings scheduled for the next day.

They talked of the villages they passed through; of bomb damage in the towns; of crops that would be planted; how Japan should not have attacked America a little over a year earlier, but consolidated its territories before forcing war with such a major enemy.

But Dolphie did not give her details of the plan to kill Hitler. Having recently seen all too well the danger of knowledge, Sophie did not press him. She did, however, ask when his views had changed since his fervent support in 1936.

It was the eighth night, the first when the reduced dose of morphine gave her a semblance of alertness and the ebbing pain allowed her to focus on more than suppressing agony. She managed to feed herself tonight, though she had still let him bathe her, a strange, asexual yet almost devotional ritual — the scabs could not be soaked in a bath, even had she had the strength to get in and out of one.

Cabbage soup, mostly, with rye bread — even being an aristocratic colonel, it seemed, could not always guarantee white bread or chicken broth. The soup was usually followed by a stew that was mostly potato with shreds of smoked meat that might have been ham, or even Higgs's Corned Beef liberated from a captured ship, followed almost invariably by baked apples, with a small square of cheese and hazelnuts. The bread could be kept for midnight; the apples, cheese and nuts for breakfast.

Dolphie shook his head each time she offered to share the food. He breakfasted well in the dining rooms, and lunched, he claimed, magnificently. He drank wine, if it looked acceptable, beer if it did not. Tonight it was beer, a huge stein with a lid, from which he sipped and watched her.

She spooned her soup carefully. Dolphie had washed her dress, but there was no way to obtain needle and thread to mend it. He had, however, bought two silk nightdresses in Paris, a purchase that could legitimately be made for his mistress, though he claimed he did not currently have one. 'My last one was French, when I was on leave. My work doesn't often take me to Paris, though often enough, luckily, that a visit there is not necessarily suspicious — and, of course, every German soldier wants to spend his leave in Paris.'

She looked up from her soup. 'When did you begin to ... focus on Hapsburg supporters?'

'Soon after Sophie Higgs-Vaile-Greenman helped prevent our plan to keep a Nazi supporter on the British throne, and I was moved to other work,' he said drily.

'I can't say I am sorry for that.'

'King Edward VIII's Nazi sympathies might have prevented war for England and its Empire.'

'But not for Europe. Would Hitler really have been satisfied to leave Britain and its colonies free?'

'As an ally of Germany, yes, I think so, back then at least. Now? I have no idea. Perhaps Hitler will conquer the moon next. He has another madman, von Braun, who is designing rockets to take us there — don't laugh, I am quite serious — though they will take explosives to Britain first. But me? I spy on aristocrats. What else is a count good for?'

'A good many things. You served in the Great War. I assumed you were in military intelligence.'

'That was before the war, and not military. Nor, in fact, very intelligent. Intelligence agencies rarely are, but then your enemy's will not be, either.'

'Why?'

'Why did I say that, or why aren't they intelligent?'

'The latter.'

'I think,' Dolphie said slowly, 'it is because to be an intelligence agent you must believe in the rightness of your cause. Question it too much — question the methods — and you are no longer effective. But the very act of not questioning places your mind behind a wall you cannot see over and do not dare to tunnel through.'

'But you tunnelled?'

'I don't understand.'

'You are part of a plan to kill Adolf Hitler,' she said drily. 'Yet for at least a decade you were one of his most enthusiastic supporters. Did he change, or did you?'

'Both, of course. Who does not change? But mostly, Germany has changed under Hitler. It is a place where children denounce their parents, where parents carefully do not hear their neighbours' screams. Did you know that Hannelore's maid had a child who was blind? They killed her for being an Untermensch soon after the law changed in thirty-six.'

'Was that why …?'

'Why Hannelore became a spy for Britain? Yes, I think so. That and my participation in your kidnapping. She thought I loved you. She was right. But I loved my country more. I still do,' he said quietly.

Still loved Germany more than her? Still loved her? Sophie said nothing, spooning soup.

'What was your mission, Sophie? Simply to spy?'

For a moment she suddenly wondered if all of this — from the torture to the faking of her death, even the talk of assassinating Hitler — had been to extract this one piece of information. But if so, it no longer mattered. 'Yes, simply that. And to find and encourage disaffected German officers to do exactly what you are planning now.'

'And here we sit, and you are encouraging me nicely.' He hesitated. 'Hannelore did not tell the British I am involved in a plot? I have not told her, but she may have found out.'

'Nobody mentioned anything like it during my briefings. I think they would have told me if she had, as we know each other.'

'Good. There are too many fascists in British intelligence. If MI5 knew, I might be arrested tomorrow.'

'Why didn't you ask her yourself?'

He grinned. 'Because if I did that, Miss British Agent, it would mean telling her that I was, indeed, part of a conspiracy, and from that she could deduce who else might be in the plot. I could not risk that back then, in case she had ways I hadn't thought of to get information to England. Sophie, my friends and I aren't the only ones who know our leadership must change. There may be a hundred similar plots, or there may simply be mutterings. There are also those like the Hapsburg loyalists, resistance movements in every country we have conquered. Our Führer is scarcely universally beloved.'

'Are you going to tell her? Because if you don't, she is going to wonder why you have delivered me to the Lodge.'

'She might leap to an obvious conclusion,' he offered lightly.

She replied with equal carelessness. 'That you are madly in love with me?'

'No. Not madly.' His eyes were serious now.

She hesitated, suddenly unsure what he wanted. 'Lily claimed you went to a lot of trouble not to have me killed in 1936.'

'And that was proof I loved you? You are Hannelore's friend, one whom she has always loved. I would have done that for her.'

'I think I believed in your love because I felt it, too,' she said slowly. 'No, please, don't misunderstand. I love my husband deeply, fully. I am not trying to seduce you, even if I could, like this. But there has been a ... connection between us.'

'A might-have-been,' he said quietly.

'Just that. If there had been no war we would have kept on dancing, you and I. It was the war that made me feel so passionately that I belonged in Australia. If the war had never happened, I might well have married you, lived part of the year in Germany.'

'And part of the year in Australia to help your so-valuable Higgs empire, with its so useful riches.'

'I think you would have come to love Australia, too.'

'Perhaps. Hannelore has always longed to go there, though I don't know if the Australia she dreams of exists. Do you think we would have been happy?'

'If there had been no war? Yes. Because Germany and England were so precariously balanced that you and I and Hannelore would have had to work together to ensure a continuing peace. It would have been a full and good partnership. Did you love your wife, Dolphie?'

'I quite liked her, for a while. She had no political interests. Sadly, she accepted mine. She was half in love with the Führer, as many women were — I say the Führer, not Adolf Hitler, for few people know the man.'

'You admired him too.'

'I did, but not for years now. He has no sense of honour. People of our class —'

'Your class. I was born bourgeois, remember.'

'You were still brought up with a sense of duty, culpability.'

'As are many factory workers and farmers I know, Dolphie.'

He smiled indulgently. 'It may be as you say. In any case, Adolf Hitler has none of that. He is so sure he is right, no matter what others say, able to achieve a vision others could only see dimly. And for a long while he *was* right. So much so that he began to feel anything was justified to gain power and to keep it. He achieved so much he thought he could win anything. He ...' a pause '... has required high doses of certain drugs for some years, not drugs known to increase the user's good sense. He hesitated when he should have invaded England, after Dunkirk. Oh, a thousand stupid decisions ...'

'And the Untermensch?'

'The cruelty to Hannelore's maid's child, a girl who was intelligent and capable? Yes, that was madness also. There is no Teutonic race. I am related to almost every royal house in Europe.'

'I meant the Jewish people.'

'Ah, the Jews.' He smiled at her. 'Sub-races, mental defectives and deviants cannot be allowed to breed, or undermine society. We might not have agreed on everything, my Sophie.'

Could he really be condoning the murders and destruction of Kristallnacht, the horrors that refugees spoke of? Hannelore's aunt, whose crime had merely been to love her Jewish husband, had emigrated to America in 1937, rather than face the growing violence.

They were the same views as held by England's previous king, opinions held by many people, including the Eugenics movement in England, the United States, even Australia, with its native peoples uncounted in any census, deprived of wages, the right to vote, even the freedom to marry, live, raise their children as they chose. But she could not believe she had even entertained a 'might have been' where she and this man could have married.

'Sophie?'

She did not look at him. Could not look at him. Had to force herself to look at him, as he was her only chance of life now, too crippled to survive, much less to escape.

She forced herself to smile, to nod. 'What happens after Hitler is dead? I remember what you said about seeking peace terms. I agree — it will probably unfold like that. I will help if I can. It's what I was sent to do, after all.' She glanced up at him. 'But immediately?'

'There are men who will step into command, high-ranking men.'

'I don't want their names,' she said quickly.

'*Gut*. I was not going to give them. They will take control. I will be part of the takeover in Munich first, where I am well known. Then I will go to Berlin, while you stay safe with Hannelore.'

'You don't want me to go to Berlin?'

'No. Hitler's position has eroded enough for us to take control, but not easily and not at once. It would not be safe to make your presence public, especially as you have been officially executed. There are some who might be ... concerned ... about what you might say.'

'I will tell the truth,' she said evenly. 'But I don't know the names of any of those who tortured me. The men who arrested me behaved reasonably under the circumstances. Apart, of course, from being complicit in the torture that followed. As for my execution — spies are executed in Britain, too. I won't ask for an investigation or even help with one. I, too, want peace, not the destruction of either of our countries. There is one condition, though.'

'Yes?'

'I do not want to stay in Germany longer than is necessary to arrange a peace conference. Once that is in place I am no more use in Europe. I want to go home. I want my husband, my children, my real life.'

He seemed now to have accepted her marriage, her life in Australia. 'I suspect it will be simple to effect your exchange to England even before peace terms are arranged, or at least passage to Switzerland. From there you can make your way back to Australia.'

She nodded, though even that movement hurt her back. 'Good.' She wondered vaguely if she would ever live without pain again.

'And you? Why risk your life to come to Europe at all? Is Miss Lily still so impossible for you to resist?'

She did not tell him she had not seen Lily since 1936, or even that she was officially missing. That might still be dangerous information. 'That was part of it,' she acknowledged. 'A telegram arrived that said, *Lily needs you*. And so I left. Lily is my sister-in-law, as well as my friend. But I have resisted her requests in the past.'

Or had she? She had refused Nigel's first proposal. But had she ever refused a request phrased by Lily?

'Miss Lily was the first person to love me,' she said slowly. 'To even like me. My father loved his daughter. Miss Thwaites loved me as her pupil — a close relationship, but still one she was eventually content to leave behind to live her own life. I was too intelligent, even if I learned to hide it, and spoiled and self-absorbed, too. Lily accepted me — she had intended to send me to a finishing school and then have a friend oversee my debut, not include me in her network. But she liked me — exactly me. The only changes on which she insisted were the ones that were socially necessary. And yet she did change me. She changed all of us.'

She thought of Emily, once so competitive, now a friend; of Mouse, given the confidence to marry and have a child in her tragically brief life; of herself. Would she have had the courage to take on the Higgs empire, and the charm needed to persuade men to cooperate in her running it, without Lily?

Lily had taught her love, the many, many kinds of love. And Hannelore? Who was Hannelore now? But Dolphie was waiting for her answer. 'So, yes, I went to England because Lily asked me to. But also I knew she would not have called if there hadn't been something only I could do. Like you, I love my country.'

'And so we finally are working for the same cause.' For a moment she thought he might say something else. But then he said, 'I need sleep, Sophie, if I am to look like a loyal, hardworking Gestapo agent tomorrow. Good night.'

Chapter 29

In the past months you have learned charm, seduction and how to keep an excellent table and cellar. I hope you have also learned friendship, the most powerful and underrated force in the whole world.

Miss Lily, 1914

SOPHIE

It was the strangest journey Sophie had ever had, and in a way the most peaceful, despite physical pain that still edged on agony, and despite desperate worry: from personal concerns — Daniel's reaction to her damaged breasts — to his entire wellbeing, and that of Rose and Danny, and Nigel — as well as for every country caught up in this war.

For the first time in her life she was entirely helpless. Even when she was not in the trunk she could not walk unaided. Though she could speak German fluently she could never be taken for a native speaker, nor could her wounds be taken for anything but what they were — an SS attempt to extract information, thus marking her as someone who had information that might be extracted, and a botched execution.

She had managed with reduced doses of morphine in the past few days, so she was conscious as the car lurched up the still bumpy road to the Lodge — or perhaps in the hardships of war it had become neglected again.

The car stopped. She heard the driver's voice and then a woman's, a stranger's, the tone welcoming, but also officious. This, then, was one of those who ensured that Hannelore was not able to engage in any activities that might hurt the Reich. Even now, Sophie realised, she was not safe. Those who watched Hannelore would surely be suspicious of her, too. Was Hannelore even expecting her? Surely Dolphie would have mentioned that he had phoned her, or even written to her, but any hint might be seen or overheard.

Hannelore's voice, laughing. Sophie suddenly found that she was crying, from happiness, not pain. Hannelore safe and happy enough to laugh.

The trunk lurched as hands untied it. Sophie bit her lips to ensure she made no sound. Jolting and then an agonising thud. She heard a door shut.

Silence.

She waited, curled in the trunk. Somehow, she had assumed that as soon as she arrived she would be helped out, tended, treated as a guest. But Dolphie had never promised that. Instead he had shaved her head and talked of her masquerading as a servant from a concentration camp. But she could not work. She could not even walk.

The door opened. Footsteps, the clank perhaps of a stove door, one of the ornate tiled room heaters she had seen in Germany before, perhaps, being set and lit. More footsteps. The door opened and shut once more.

She waited.

This had been the longest time she had ever stayed in the trunk, and the roughest journey. Suddenly, unexpectedly, claustrophobia washed through her. The trunk's air holes must somehow have been blocked. She could not breathe! The sides were shrinking, slowly squashing her.

She wanted to scream, no matter what the consequences, simply to breathe fresh air again, to let her limbs stretch, to move, to feel that she existed outside this tiny space.

Footsteps again. The door. The trunk unlatched.

She could not see. The light burned her eyes. But she knew Hannelore's hands, even as they gently helped her move, felt her tears as she embraced her. 'Sophie. My Sophie. You are here.'

The room was Hannelore's bedroom, a larger room than the semi-cupboard Hannelore had inhabited here after the Great War, when firewood was scarce. Firewood was scarce again, but not, it seemed, on the estate of Kolonel Graf von Hoffenhausen. The room breathed warmth from the enamel stove. Water warmed on the stove. A curtained bed where Sophie could lie, carefully not screaming as her limbs uncramped, as Hannelore took the dressings off her wounds, exclaimed, put on fresh lotion and bandages.

Sophie glanced at her, in between shutting her eyes in pain. The gold of Hannelore's hair had darkened. She wore it long, tied by a silk scarf at her back. Sophie supposed she no longer had access to a hairdresser, nor a lady's maid. The blue eyes had faded. Her skin looked weathered, with lines of tiredness and pain. She wore a dress which had once been good, but the green wool had not only turned drab but felted with poor washing, something a lady's maid would not have permitted. No jewellery.

Her hands were the greatest shock — rough, ingrained with soil, the nails trimmed as short as possible, unevenly. Her poise was unshakable, her beauty inevitable, given her bone structure, her bearing, her smile. But she did not look like a prinzessin, merely another war-weary woman.

A knock. Hannelore pulled the bed curtains shut, then opened the door. Her voice was kind. 'Danke schön, Fräulein Kunster. No, thank you, I need nothing more tonight.'

Hannelore carried a tray in her battered hands to the uncurtained side of the bed furthest from the door and put it on the side table. 'Can you sit and eat if I help prop you up on pillows?'

'Yes. Please.' It hurt to move. She longed to move. Knew that only moving could ease the day's cramping. Hannelore placed the tray across her legs. 'Potato soup with sausage. The bread is rye, but we have butter, even some cheese. The farm supplies us. The potatoes we grow here.'

Sophie managed a minute spoonful of soup.

'Fräulein Kunster is the housekeeper here. Dolphie put her here to spy on me, but now there is no need and even danger if she sees you here. Dolphie will take her with him tomorrow morning.' She met Sophie's eyes. 'Yes, he has told me what he plans. He brought me the best news I have ever heard, and you as well.'

'Won't they be suspicious if there is no one here to watch you?'

'There is no "they". Fräulein Kunster is loyal to Dolphie, not to the Nazi Party. Now he wants her away. He must stay away from here too, in case the plot is discovered before they can strike.'

'When —?' Sophie began.

Hannelore shook her head. 'I don't know what, or when. It is best we know nothing.'

Sophie was becoming tired of knowing nothing. This was war, but knowing nothing was the worst of business practices. 'Who else is here?'

Hannelore laughed without humour. 'No one. Just Grünberg and Simons in the kitchen — they come from the labour camp at Dachau. Grünberg cooks quite well. Simons cleans. She looks as if it is beneath her to clean but she obeys, because it is comfortable here and if she does not work well she'll be replaced. The gardens are tended by old Franz from the farm, and I garden as well. Franz also chops wood and brings whatever groceries or other things we need from Munich. I have been most carefully isolated.'

'Would Grünberg or Simons betray us?'

'Probably, if it profited them. But they do what they are ordered to, and do not pry. The kitchen area doors are locked each night so they can't escape, which means we do not have to worry about them then. I expect they could escape,' Hannelore added. 'The windows are not barred. But there is nowhere here to escape to or I would have gone myself, and if Grünberg or Simons were caught they'd lose a comfortable home here.'

'You don't mind having prisoners work for you?'

'Do not worry. Neither are criminals! Simply Jewish. They are quite pleasant.'

'I meant,' said Sophie carefully, 'you don't feel it is wrong that they should be prisoners?'

Hannelore shrugged. 'Of course it is wrong. But I am a prisoner and so now are you. They must work, so why not here? I work hard, too.'

'Did you go to Dachau to hire them?'

Hannelore looked at her curiously. 'Why would I go there? They were assigned by the camp commandant or his officers, like the workers in my factories.'

Sophie was silent. How much did Hannelore know of Dachau? There had been horrifying reports from before the war, despite the positive descriptions by journalists who had been invited to review the camp. James had told her that during those visits guards played the part of inmates. Sophie suspected conditions at Dachau and the other camps were far worse now so much of Europe was close to starvation. There had also been stories from refugees of mass cremations at other camps.

But the information a prinzessin gathered would not be about prison or labour camps, but of troop movements, the progress of new armaments — rumours of extraordinary new weapons floated from both sides like smells above the hen yard. She would report on the Führer's health, perhaps, or Goering's campaigns and plans. Labour camps were not of strategic interest. Hannelore had probably never been in even her own factories except to open one, cutting a ribbon and receiving a bouquet, though Dolphie had mentioned she had established a school for workers on the estate, now closed as the war had swallowed all but the most essential labour.

Like the workers in my factories. Surely Hannelore knew people from the camps worked as slaves, not as employees, and on pain of death, for minimal rations. Or did she?

Sophie found she could not ask. Perhaps she would not until that magic time 'when the war is over'. That would be the time for Sophie Higgs, owner of so many factories, to make tactful enquiries and suggestions about the source of Hannelore's wealth.

For there was wealth at the Lodge, despite Hannelore's faded dress, her calloused hands. She had maids, when labour was desperately needed to replace the workers lost to armies, to repair the damage done by bombing. The casual warmth of a fire, the apology for a soup that nonetheless contained a substantial amount of meat, bread that was buttered, and 'even some' cheese, a rationed luxury now in France and England unless one had vast wealth and excellent contacts in the black market.

Sophie nibbled the cheese. It was extremely good, unlike Midge's attempt at home-made cheese, which looked and tasted like soap. Midge will be sorting the fat lambs now, she thought. What is not being done because I am missing? What crises at Thuringa, at Higgs, in her family? Had Rose persuaded Daniel to let her wear lipstick? She and Danny would be back at school now.

Sophie realised with sudden desperation that James might have found out about her execution. He might believe her dead. Perhaps he had even told Daniel.

Please, no, she prayed.

'Sophie?'

Sophie shook her head. 'It's nothing.' Nothing she could do. And soon, if the conspirators' plan worked, Hitler would be gone and, at the very least, she would be able to send a cable home and to Lily too. No, to Nigel — or no, Bob.

Suddenly every bone and sinew was filled with a determination to keep living. Her family did not have her now. But they *would* have her. She would make up for every moment they had lost.

I should not have done this, she thought. And then: of course I should be doing this. For soon the fighting would be done, and peace negotiations could begin.

Chapter 30

Corned Beef with Cabbage

Per person:
1 heaped teaspoon cornflour
1 slice of Higgs's Corned Beef
½ cup milk
½ chopped onion
1 bay leaf
1 whole clove
A little grated nutmeg
Salt to taste
2 cups finely chopped cabbage

Corned beef is the perfect war-time meal, so savoury that only a little is needed for each meal. Mix the cornflour with a little of the milk. Reserve. Now simmer with milk, onion, bay leaf and clove till the onion is soft. Add the nutmeg and salt. Do not oversalt as the beef will be too salty. Simmer the cabbage in as little water as possible, with the lid on. It is important that the cabbage be finely chopped, or it may resemble a wet dishrag. Drain thoroughly when soft.

Place the pile of cabbage on the plate, top with the slice of corned beef, then cover it all with the white sauce. Dust with nutmeg. Serve with potatoes baked in their jackets.

Delectable Dishes with Corned Beef, a leaflet from Higgs,
the Corned Beef Kings, 1943

ROSE

She wore a grey suit, one of Mum's that had hardly needed altering, and a neat grey hat with a tiny feather pinned to one side of her hair, which had been newly cut and permed. Mum would not have allowed the perm, nor the lipstick and powder, but they made her look older. Not all that much older, but every little helped as the old man said when he spat into the sea ...

Rose stared at the tiles in the ladies' lavatory and tried to banish nausea. Yesterday it had seemed clear that the best tactic was to wait till all the board members were seated, and the sales director and transport manager too, then walk calmly into the boardroom and take Mum's position at the table. Today her preferred tactic was to run out of the building and keep running.

Lucky Danny, back at Thuringa where cattle did not argue with the human who had decided to be their manager. He was currently organising a cull of elderly bulls and cows — it had been two years since anyone had time to actually assess the stock — and choosing which of last year's calves would replace them.

She stood and pulled the chain, though it did not need pulling. But someone might be listening. She walked to the basins, washed her hands, checked her hair and lipstick and, handbag under her arm, made her way steadily out the door and down the corridor, then opened the door to the boardroom.

The chair at the head of the table was already filled by Mr Grigson, the sales manager. The meeting had begun, even though she had notified all the members she would be attending.

What would Mum do? What would Aunt Lily do? Rose smiled blindingly. 'Mr Grigson, how kind of you to step in and take my place. I'm so sorry I'm late.'

The men at the table stood, because that was what polite men did when a woman entered a room. Rose took advantage of the momentarily empty seat to slide into it, leaving Mr Grigson no choice but to find one further down the table. Rose picked up the first paper on the table. 'Ah, the agenda. A slight change, I'm afraid. The first item is obviously confirming my position as chairman of the board.'

Someone gave a small chuckle, quickly hushed.

'My dear Miss Vaile,' said Mr Grigson kindly. 'The position of chairman is voted on by the board.'

Rose's voice was equally kind. 'And the board is appointed by the shareholders. I think you will find that I hold proxies for the entire shareholding of what is still, of course, a family company. Naturally you are all free to resign and have Manpower assign you to a factory job or the armed forces, but I truly hope you won't. With my mother away and my father ill,' a euphemism she and Danny had adopted, and yet also perfectly true, 'Higgs is going to depend on all your experience and wisdom, and Australia and the Empire depend on Higgs's Corned Beef. I will depend on you, too.' She extended her smile around the table.

'Your mother couldn't have made that speech better.' The voice was approving, not ironic.

'Thank you, Mr Pinkerton.' He was one of the last board members who remembered her grandfather, she knew, and now in his seventies — he had put off retirement till the war ended or he did, he'd told Mum.

'I still think —' began Mr Grigson.

'I believe the best course of action here is to move as swiftly as possible to the second item on the agenda, the loss of shipping to Japanese submarines. The situation is becoming critical.'

The table nodded at Mr Pinkerton's words. The general public was not supposed to know how many cargo ships had been sunk that year alone. Nor, in fact, did Rose know the full number, only the number of lost ships in firms Higgs had contracts with, but even that much information meant she knew the total must be a very large number indeed, enough to cause panic if broadcast. But, given that most of Australia was linked only by tracks, not roads, with even insufficient rail stock for military transport, the only way to transport vital equipment, food and supplies was by ship, in waters increasingly controlled by the Japanese.

'I propose we unanimously elect Miss Vaile to the position of chairman,' said Mr Pinkerton. 'A seconder? Thank you. Any objections? Congratulations, Miss Vaile. Now, to the question of shipping.'

'Retired ferries,' said Rose.

The entire table stared at her.

'I have made enquiries at Cockatoo Island. It seems that the ferries are seaworthy for short voyages, as long as they can seek a port if the weather turns. Now if you will look at page two, I have outlined the ports available between Melbourne and Townsville. I think we need to stop all shipping on the Townsville to Darwin route and convince the authorities that if the armed forces that far north want bully beef, they must accept shipment to Townsville, and arrange the transport to Darwin by rail from there. If you look further down page two you will see the capacity of the ferries currently available ...'

She lifted her eyes for long enough to see Mr Pinkerton's approving nod. The other men had obediently turned to page two — excellent, experienced men who would not bother about trivialities when they had a logistics problem to consider.

She could almost feel her mother smile at her as well.

Chapter 31

Humanity's default state is 'let's forget anything uncomfortable to remember'. This is not always bad, for otherwise the weight might be too heavy for us to bear. But in every generation there must be those who say: remember.

Sophie Higgs-Vaile-Greenman, Dowager Countess of Shillings, a lecture published by the University of Queensland, 1968

FEBRUARY 1943

SOPHIE

Dolphie did not say goodbye to her before he left with Fräulein Kunster, presumably so that the housekeeper did not suspect a newcomer at the lodge.

Sophie spent the next weeks peacefully, in Hannelore's bed, while Hannelore slept on the truckle where a maid would have slept a generation earlier, when a woman of quality was allowed neither privacy nor the effort of retrieving her chamber pot from under the bed.

It seemed the kitchen's discipline was informal enough with Fräulein Kunster gone for no one to notice Hannelore's forays for Sophie's food, or perhaps the two maids just thought Hannelore's appetite had improved. More likely, Sophie thought, they were careful not to query anything that might put their comfort here at risk.

The food was good, even if the ingredients were local. Grünberg was, indeed, an excellent cook. Poached carp, whose muddy flesh was disguised by a sharp bilberry sauce; Dampfnudeln, a sweet, steamed yeast roll cooked in a pot with milk, soft and white on top and crunchy at the base, served both with a sauce for a main course or with custard for dessert, or by themselves for a mid-morning snack; broths of dried mushrooms and fresh beetroot; potato cakes fried in lavish butter; cabbage stuffed with Weisswurst; a sweet and sour 'head cheese', more savoury than the brawn of England and Australia, served with sauerkraut; honey cakes; and an apple cake that was only slightly gritty, from the pale brown beet sugar processed at the farm.

Sophie ate. After the second day of exhaustion her appetite suddenly raged like a tiger's. Perhaps Hannelore, too, had ordered more succulent food than potato soup to tempt her, using the removal of her 'housekeeper' as an excuse for culinary extravagance. Sophie's breakfast plate held rye bread with a pat of butter, or sometimes vast soft pretzels, with sweet mustard that surely must have been stored since before the war; slices of the farm cheese, always Weisswurst and sometimes other kinds of sausage too, boiled and thinly sliced and never with the inevitable Australian tomato sauce.

And Hannelore worked, as she had said. Sophie watched her through the window, carefully hiding her shape behind the curtains. Hannelore wheeled barrows of potatoes and more barrows of what looked like compost or manure, and probably was, for other fertilisers would be almost impossible to find, Sophie imagined. Sometimes the barrow contained a hay rake or potato fork, and on those days Hannelore was particularly tired at night.

Now and then she saw the women who must be Simons and Grünberg, picking herbs perhaps, lugging baskets of potatoes, beets or turnips or the vast hard cabbages that seemed to be the only kind grown here. They wore faded dresses covered by white aprons, or even more-faded coats, woollen stockings and wooden pattens, with silk scarves on their heads that Hannelore must have lent or given them, always with the yellow Star of David that proclaimed them Jewish prisoners vivid below their collars.

Twice the two women simply sat for a short while by the lake, watching the far-off swans — any remaining wild bird in Germany had learned by now to stay out of the reach of hunters' traps or guns. It seemed, as Hannelore said, that the two servants lived as well as anyone in Germany, except for imprisonment, terror and probably anguish for family, friends and what had been their country.

Mostly, however, Sophie read a little — Hannelore had a large collection of English classics — and dozed, unable to sleep deeply either day or night, with no position that did not bring pain that must be relieved by moving each half-hour. But the sulpha drugs, the food, the rest, the lotions, were working.

'Pain' had now become 'it hurts', unless breasts, toes or vertebrae were touched. By the third day at the Lodge she could haul herself out of bed and onto the chamber pot; by the fourth wash herself and totter carefully about the room, bent like a crone and dressed in garments that fitted surprisingly well and were far too big to be Hannelore's.

'Whose are they?' she asked on her seventh night at the Lodge.

'Amelia's. Dolphie's wife,' said Hannelore shortly, looking down as she turned the frayed collar of a coat.

'What was she like?'

'Blonde, big boned like you. Do all colonials grow so large?'

'No.' Sophie refused to change the subject. 'Did you like her?'

'Yes. Because I tried hard to like her,' Hannelore admitted. 'She thought being a countess was important, and all she saw in me was "princess". She had always known much money and thought clothes important instead of simply pleasurable. She became mesmerised by the Führer just as I lost faith in him.' Hannelore placed another stitch. 'Tell me more of kangaroos.'

'They hop about a lot and eat the grass that cows might eat. And sometimes they lean back and scratch their chests like this.' Sophie demonstrated, ignoring the leap of pain. 'And in spring the males box each other to see who will mate and lead the mob. I saw two big bucks fight for two days and two nights once, until they were so exhausted that finally both hopped away two paces, fell down and slept. And the biggest female immediately mated with a much smaller male. One day you will see kangaroos.'

'One day,' said Hannelore.

It was as if the war had vanished. Each evening they talked, but not of plots or labour camps or even of Sophie's weeks in England or Paris. She spoke of Daniel, described his clinic, the new school at Bald Hill, the first time Rose had fallen for a boy and stayed smitten till she met him the next holidays and found out he hated dogs and that she had loved a make-believe that was not him; Danny's attempt at steer riding; of Midge, fruitcake and laughter and New Year by the river, holding up signs that said *More pudding, please*, or *Pass the beer, mate*, to Harry, who had lost his hearing in the Great War. The signs caused even more hilarity and were added to each year. Harry even made his own: *Turn the gramophone down, I can't hear you*, which had somehow seemed hilarious.

Hannelore spoke as she never had before, of her own childhood: the loneliness of having a mother who appeared at the isolated family castle only 'to refresh' every six months or so, the company of Dolphie, not much older than her, who had been orphaned early, and so brought up in the cold castle far from Berlin that the Russians had taken in the last war 'and were welcome to. But they were not welcome to my land,' said Hannelore.

The Lodge did not even seem to be under a flight path to Munich or other cities. The curtains were drawn at night so the light didn't attract the attention of British bombers, but that was the only precaution taken.

And they waited.

The Lodge did not have a wireless any more — Dolphie had been determined that his niece be removed even from knowledge of current politics — but there was a wireless at the farm. Surely Franz would come running up if news that the plot — successful or not — had been announced.

But there was nothing.

'He said a few weeks,' said Sophie into the silence one evening.

'He didn't give me a time,' said Hannelore. Neither ever mentioned the words plot, kill or Hitler.

'Perhaps there has to be an opportunity ...' Sophie winced as she moved incautiously.

'I'll get the cordial,' said Hannelore, putting aside her darning. It was bitter, herbal, but also strongly alcoholic. It helped the pain, but that might have been the alcohol.

And then they talked of other things.

～❀～

Dolphie arrived seven weeks later, driving without headlights, as they sat quietly after dinner. At the sound of an engine Sophie glanced at Hannelore. 'Please not into the trunk,' she said. She could not bear it. But of course she would bear it, to get home. She had just lifted her legs off the bed when the horn hooted a short tune.

'Dolphie,' said Hannelore in relief.

She slipped into the corridor. Sophie heard muffled words and then 'Have you eaten?' and his gruff reply. Their footsteps came straight along the corridor to Hannelore's room. Dolphie shut the door, then pulled the bolt. He looked more tired than Sophie had ever seen him, even after a sleepless night — or more — on the battlefield in the last war.

'We failed,' he said simply. He fell into an armchair and held his hands up to the stove. 'I drove myself here. I must be back in Munich by the morning for a meeting.' He shrugged. 'You are so tactfully not asking what happened, but there is no reason not to tell you now.'

'Every reason,' snapped Sophie. 'If we are captured we can betray you and you cannot try again.'

He raised an eyebrow. 'Will you?'

'No.'

'I did not think you would. I have read your Paris records. As for Hannelore — even for her uncle she will not speak of Lorrimer or Lily. Just now I find I do not care.' He turned back to the stove. 'It is as if the spirit of evil protects him. He was to have been surrounded by tanks and arrested if possible, or shot if not, during his visit to the Ukraine. He cancels it. He was to be shot on the way from the airport at Smolensk, but the SS guard about him makes any shot impossible. A group of officers will shoot him at lunch, with the knowledge of Field Marshal von Kluge, but at the last minute Kluge forbids it, in case it provokes civil war between the SS and the army. And finally a simple plan, surely a foolproof plan — a ... person in a position of trust ... asked one of Hitler's aides to carry two bottles of Cointreau back to Berlin as a gift to a friend. The bottles were rigged with explosives and a thirty-minute fuse. The man took them. The plane should have exploded in the air.

'And then we heard the plane had landed safely. Two bombs in two bottles, but neither exploded.'

'But the bombs?' asked Sophie urgently. 'If they were discovered —'

'Exactly. Another ... friend ... exchanged the bombs for two bottles of brandy. Both fuses were defective and had iced up in the plane. And so we tried again. No defective fuse this time. All checked and correct. A volunteer carried the bomb on his person while the Führer toured an exhibition of Soviet flags and captured weapons in Berlin. The bomb had a ten-minute fuse. The volunteer lit the fuse as soon as Hitler arrived, staying next to him at all times.'

Dolphie's smile was as bitter as the cordial. 'Despite all attempts to delay him the Führer galloped around the display like a colt in a paddock and was gone within seven minutes. The ... friend ... ran to the bathroom and removed the fuse with seconds to spare.'

'And now?' demanded Sophie.

'No one seems to suspect us. We will try again. And again. But it will not be soon. I must go to Austria — there has been trouble there, and ... the others ... are unlikely to be close to the Führer either for a while, for a variety of reasons. We must wait till one of us can get near him without suspicion, and that is not as easy these days, for Hitler sees few people, trusts even fewer, believes even shadows are trying to kill him and moves quickly when in public. I think perhaps he hears the whispers at night of the billions who wish him dead.'

'Will you help me get to Switzerland then?' asked Sophie quietly.

'No.'

'You said you would.'

'After he's gone. After you have helped us negotiate. Until then, you stay.'

'Dolphie, please! My family will think I am dead. Could you at least send word?'

'Of course not. You think there are no spies within your intelligence service either? Once you are known to be alive half the Gestapo will be wondering how and why and where you might be, and that can only lead them here.'

'But I can't stay here!'

'You have no choice. I brought you identity papers. They are in the car with some supplies for you.'

Sophie gazed at him. He met her eyes, his own adamant.

'Who am I now?' she asked at last.

'Frau Müller. Your home in Munich was bombed, your family killed, but you are originally from Alsace-Lorraine, which will account for your accent. Your identity won't stand up to scrutiny,' he shrugged, 'but if it comes to scrutiny, we are dead anyway.'

'How am I supposed to know Hannelore?'

'Not an old friend — too many people would expect to have met you. Perhaps you met on a committee for some good cause? As to how you came to be here — I brought you here, tonight, from Munich, as company for my niece, and because I knew Hannelore would wish to offer a friend refuge.'

He stood. 'I must go — I am due at a meeting tonight. I have some boxes in the car for you — I will get the women to fetch them. There are two hams and coffee and Bierwurst and some French cheese and chocolates, as well as flour and sugar.' He bent and kissed Hannelore, bowed to Sophie and was gone.

Chapter 32

One day, not in my lifetime I expect, but possibly yours, there may be institutions that study 'constructive peace' and other ways of solving the tragedies of the abuse of power, racism and other discriminations. I do not believe — I cannot believe — that force is the best solution. We must accept, however, that when too many people fail to see evil or injustice, or fail to cure these illnesses of the soul and of society, then force may be the only solution left to us.

A lecture by Sophie Greenman, published 1982

'I can't stay.'

'You must. Dolphie is right. There is no choice.'

'There is and he knows it. We could both leave. If Dolphie only wants me as a negotiator I could do that in England or, for that matter, wait in Australia and fly to England again, or even come to Germany when it is safe. He wants me as a hostage as well as a negotiator. Negotiate or we will show the world the Countess of Shillings, and the world will see the English do not care about their own people.'

Hannelore was silent.

Sophie tried to think what to say. She could plead, but if Hannelore knew a way to escape she'd have already taken it herself. There was still the possibility of putting a message in a newspaper, but Hannelore was the only one of them who could go to Munich — the Comtesse de Brabant had an excuse for not being a native German speaker, but Sophie doubted she could pass as Frau Müller yet, except in the briefest of encounters. She would need to find out where the newspaper office was. She would need money.

'Hannelore, will you help me? Please? If I can place an advertisement in a certain newspaper there is a chance James can arrange to get me to Switzerland.'

Hannelore stared. 'How?'

'I have no idea. I was sent with as little information as possible. Could you go to Munich for me?'

'You don't think he will have us watched?' asked Hannelore quietly.

'Dolphie?'

'Of course. I may have lost my wardress but there will be others — Franz and his wife and daughters-in-law at the farm, and others in town. They will not have been told I am a traitor, of course. Merely that Dolphie wants to know where I go and who I see. This is the world of Nazis, where the son informs on his father and neighbours on each other. And he is quite right not to trust me. We know each other well, Dolphie and I. If I put an advertisement in a newspaper, he will know. He will know who responds to it, too.'

'But Dolphie is now on our side.'

'No,' said Hannelore. 'Do not ever think Dolphie is not loyal to Germany. The closer Germany is to victory, the more power we will have at the negotiating table.'

'And you?'

'I want peace. I do not care any more who struts around and thinks they've won.' Hannelore gazed at the shut curtains, which hid the moon and all the stars. 'My world was so large when you and I first met. I planned to advise nations, marry for national security and help mankind. But now?' She smiled. 'My life is "how many seed potatoes must we keep to have a crop this summer?" It is "What room shall Sophie have tonight now she does not have to share mine?"'

'I'm sorry,' said Sophie softly. 'My life grew wider after I left Shillings that first time. My life is waiting at home for me, too. But I have two children and a husband and ... Lily ... too, who will think that I am dead ...'

Suddenly grief overcame her. She had let herself believe Dolphie and his co-conspirators would be successful. Even if she'd had to stay in Germany for months until the post-Hitler regime was stabilised, those she loved would know she was alive, that next Christmas she would be with them.

How much had Danny grown in the past six months? She was missing that subtle transition as Rose changed from girl to woman. She had not even asked Dolphie what was happening in Australia; nor had he offered either of them information on the progress of the war. Perhaps Australia was too unimportant for a Gestapo colonel to take an interest in, beyond its production of corned beef and wheat and wool, its iron ore and shipping, but surely he must know how Germany's Japanese allies were faring in the war in the Pacific.

She could do nothing. Know nothing.

She opened her eyes and found Hannelore smiling at her strangely. 'I still have two pigeons,' she said softly.

'I don't understand.'

'Pigeons cannot fly all the way to England but they can reach Holland, which is where these ones came from. Pigeons will always return home. And they can carry messages.'

Sophie stared at her with dawning hope.

'Very small messages that might be transmitted in code to England. A few words only.'

But that would be enough. Enough to give hope to Daniel, to Rose and Danny if they had been told she was not in Townsville. Hope to Nigel. Sophie grasped her hand and began to cry.

Chapter 33

Delicious and Economical Chocolate Oat Cakes

Make your rations go further with CARRYMAN'S Cocoa!
¼ cup margarine
2 cups self-raising flour
1 cup rolled oats
¼ cup sugar
Pinch salt
1½ ounces CARRYMAN'S Cocoa powder
Milk or water
A little extra sugar

Rub the margarine into the flour. Add the rolled oats, sugar, pinch of salt and cocoa powder. Add a little milk or water to moisten and stick the mixture together. Roll into balls and press down until very thin with the back of a fork. Bake in a moderate oven for about 15 minutes until golden brown. Take from the oven. Sprinkle with sugar while still hot.

Ethel Carryman, July 1943

ETHEL

If paperwork could feed a nation, then Britain would be fat. Ethel Carryman gazed at the files toppling out of her in-tray and the single file in her out-tray and sighed. She took out a brown paper bag, crumpled with much use, and extracted her lunch —

a Marmite and lettuce sandwich and a vacuum flask of cocoa. It was three o'clock.

She had hoped to eat in the park, avoiding the choice of snook or shepherd's pie in the canteen. Even, perhaps, snare a few minutes of sunshine, if clouds, fog and smog coincidentally cleared at exactly the same moment. But there were the new propaganda posters' designs to choose — and she knew that choosing actually meant wording a cogent summary of why her preferred poster would work and the others wouldn't for the man who was nominally her superior to present at the afternoon's meeting, as well as a few words in praise of the new slogan, whatever it might be, for the minister to amuse the House with tomorrow.

After that …

'Ah, Miss Carryman.'

Ethel looked up. It was not the minister, but the minister's even more influential secretary. Ministers came and went but their male secretaries went on until they were knighted and retired with excellent pensions to be the nominal heads of charities. Though, as Ethel had long discovered, true power resided in the hands of the secretary's secretary, the woman who had gone to the right school with the secretary's sisters, was discreet, intelligent, did not drink a bottle of claret each lunchtime with 'Chummy' and 'Boopers', and who was the one who chose which files, letters and phone messages arrived on the secretary's desk. Ethel was the secretarial exception, given the job for her experience, not her connections.

'How can I help you, sir?'

'I've just been lunching with Lorrimer. He asked me if you'd mind popping around for tea this afternoon, about fourish. There's someone he'd like you to meet.'

The other rule of the public service was that personal was political, and vice versa. James had no reason to summon her for work, nor any right to use his position to get her to visit him. Ethel had refused his invitations for two years. The only reason she could think of him calling for her now was if he had news of Sophie, but he could tell her that by phone, or, more likely, give the task of telling her to Bob, who would come and tell her quietly in person, and not summon her from the Ministry.

'I have quite a lot on, sir. The new campaign?'

'Oh, rubbish. That can wait till tomorrow.'

Which in fact it could. People needed calories and vitamins, not propaganda slogans.

'Off you pop. Enjoy your tea.' He looked vaguely amused. Most people did look amused at the thought of Ethel, a little over six feet and broad in the shoulder, not to mention the hips, with the small and dapper James Lorrimer.

She gathered her handbag, gas mask and brown paper bag. At least tea with James would mean a decent tuck in. People like him had homes in the country where the ancient retainers, too old for active service, grew a plenitude of vegetables; they had glasshouses, or friends with glasshouses, and even retired gamekeepers who might still send a hare or partridge down to London.

The paperboys gave way to her as she strode down the street. She'd lost weight, like most of England under rationing, but she hadn't lost size: tall as a barber's pole and shoulders like a Hereford bull. But since Violette had taken her in hand six years back, creating semi-medieval dresses in which even Ethel had to admit she looked magnificent, she had finally not just accepted the shape of her body, but chosen to like it. Violette had been right — it was a good figure, just half as big again as everyone else's.

Violette had also made her two dresses suitable for an office, with a jacket for each. Ethel had a dressmaker copy them in other fabrics, a bit narrower to fit austerity fashion, and shorter too — she'd always had good legs.

The line at the bus stop was so long that she had to wait for the third bus before she could get on and, even then, there were no spare seats so she had to stand. She was glad of two solid legs to stand on and enough bulk not to fall over when others bumped her as the bus swayed.

They had to detour around bomb damage twice — the V2s seemed almost constant now — and stopped once at a roadblock to let some big wig pass in a black car with flags, the kind of car James might have sent for her if she had lifted the phone and told him she was coming.

The bus arrived at the stop at last. Ethel manoeuvred around women lugging string bags bulging with cabbage and extremely small white packages that might be precious cheese or meat or a single well-cradled egg, made her way down the steps, coughed twice at the mixture of bus fumes and fog, walked around the corner and up the marble stairs of James's town house.

The door opened before she pulled the bell. Harrison must have been told to watch out for her. Harrison was seventy if he was a day and probably inserted a broomstick under his uniform each morning to keep his bearing erect.

He opened the library door for her. 'Miss Carryman, sir.'

James stood by the fire. Ethel told herself she did not at all wish she had stopped at home to change into the Violette creation James had once said made her look like a Valkyrie about to carry lucky warriors to Valhalla. He'd called her from the office, so an office suit was what he was getting. She also repressed a desire to tell him to sit down, have a decent tea and then a nap. He looked … older. Faded in some way, though his suit was as immaculate as ever. He eyed her with strange wariness.

'Ethel, so good of you to come. I would like you to meet Miss Nichols. I'm sorry to call you from work, but Miss Nichols has to leave London this afternoon. Miss Nichols, this is the friend I spoke of, Miss Carryman. Ethel, please do sit down.'

'Yes, please. A pleasure to meet you, Miss Nichols.' She looked at the girl curiously as she sat in the chair opposite. Slender, dark-haired, early twenties perhaps, and with a look that said she was coping splendidly, which meant that she had something major to cope with. Not in uniform, which Ethel would have expected with determined eyes like that.

Miss Nichols bent to the teapot. 'Tea, Miss Carryman? It may be a little strong.' She and James already had a cup, weak and black.

'Can't be too strong for me. I haven't had a proper cuppa since rationing.' She helped herself to a cucumber sandwich — definitely a product of James's hothouse — then a slice of game pie and then two more slices. James's plate held the crumbs of an oat cake. The girl's plate did not show signs that she had eaten food at all. Ethel had begun on the fruitcake before she broke the silence.

'Both of you look like you need a decent feed. Tuck in.'

Miss Nichols gave a polite smile. 'Thank you, but I'm not —'

'Eat,' ordered Ethel. 'You'll feel better with a lining to your stomach.'

'I am quite —'

'Eat.'

Miss Nichols hesitated, then reached for a sandwich. She nibbled it, looked surprised, then took the largest slice of fruitcake. Ethel put another slice of game pie on her own plate, then offered the plate to James.

A gentleman could not refuse. James Lorrimer could not refuse. He knew she knew it. He gave her the smallest of smiles, accepted the plate, took a fork and began to eat.

'Well?' prompted Ethel at last. 'You didn't ask me here to eat game pie, though I'm grateful for it.'

'I asked Miss Nichols if she would mind repeating her account of ... some events ... to you. She kindly agreed. I should make it clear that while she does not work for the organisation I am part of, she was given clearance to speak to me.'

Ethel raised an eyebrow. Was Miss Nichols MI5? Or SOE? But there were dozens of smaller operations. None of them were associated with the Ministry of Food, but there was always gossip between the 'Chummys' and 'Boopers' of officialdom, nor were they always careful not to be overheard.

Harrison quietly brought in a plate of hot toast — not buttered: James would not have his farm's produce allocated to butter his toast. Instead the toast was spread with what Ethel decided was a clever mix of stewed apple, to give the required butter-like moistness, and fish paste to add flavour. She would pass the idea on, though the idiots who approved the Ministry's recipes seemed to want nothing more adventurous than covering boiled peas with the paper the butter had been wrapped in, to give the eyes what the palate would not receive. The Women's Institute though ... this might be a good recipe for them.

Harrison retreated, closing the door, after a faint nod from James that meant they were now not to be interrupted.

'I ... I'm not sure how much to say ...' began Miss Nichols.

'Everything except surnames, places and dates. Miss Carryman can be trusted completely.'

I wouldn't be too sure of that, matey, thought Ethel, deciding on another sandwich. A few more and she could give the sausage and mash she'd been going to eat tonight to the kiddies and their mum and gran — a family she'd taken in as refugees when Poland fell.

Miss Nichols's face looked calm, but her fingers trembled on her cake fork till she consciously stilled them. 'Very well, sir. It was not ... not long ago and abroad. I was to replace ... I'll call her May. May was acting as liaison with a resistance group and we were to, well, that doesn't matter, because we didn't do it.'

She cast a quick glance up at James, still impassive in front of the fire. 'May was due to ... to leave ... the next day, after she'd seen me settled. We were packed into the back of a lorry — German. I was trying to remember how to ... how to use the equipment we would need ... when I heard someone outside yell "Juden raus!" May peered out, then shouted at our driver. "Halten Sie!" Our driver was pretending to be German, of course.'

Ethel glanced at James. This was top-secret stuff and none of her business, neither personal nor professional. But she could not interrupt Miss Nichols now.

'The lorry we were in stopped, and May told the driver to reverse. I peered out as we backed up, then stopped. We were outside an orphanage. Every door and window was shut, every curtain pulled, and out the front was a lorry, pretty much like ours, with a group of children in the back, a few more clambering inside and two cars.'

She glanced at Ethel. 'I don't know if you are aware, but some orphanages in France have been sheltering Jewish children when their parents are deported to labour camps. The Germans have begun to search each orphanage, inspecting the children, their papers.'

Ethel nodded. She had not known, but was not surprised.

Miss Nichols looked at — through — the wall, seeing the memory. 'The next thing I knew May had her pistol out. She shot the lorry driver in the head.'

Miss Nichols's voice was carefully factual now, as if describing the anatomy of a wasp. 'He fell out. Some of the children screamed at the sound of the shot, but they couldn't see what was happening, not from the back of the truck. May yelled to me, "Come on!" She scrambled out. I followed her. May gestured to the children's lorry and told me, "Get in and drive!" Then to the others still in our lorry, "Drive on!"'

She stopped, as if for breath or words.

'Continue,' said James.

'Yes, sir. I clambered into the driver's seat just as May shot another of the Germans. The engine was running. Our lorry accelerated down the road. I had to turn the children's vehicle around to follow it, so I saw May pick up the second man's machine gun. I could hear it fire as I drove down the road.'

'You escaped with the children?' asked Ethel quietly.

'Yes. There were nineteen of them. We heard later that May had killed five soldiers and wounded seven others. There was no pursuit.'

'And the children?'

'Are safe. As safe as any child is just now. They've been separated, each one taken to another area, far enough away so no one will recognise them, to farms mostly. Farming communities tend to be more tightly knit and of course children can be useful, too, especially when they are needed for the harvest or planting and so can't go to school. So many children are orphaned now, or their mothers need to work so they are sent to aunts or cousins. A new child is not remarkable. Dark hair is cut short and bleached blonde. I ... I think they will be safe.'

'And May?'

'She had been shot when I last saw her, in the rear-vision mirror,' said Miss Nichols too calmly. 'But she was still firing. I don't know if she died there, but we were told she died before she could be questioned. I think ... I hope ... she died before they could take her away.' Her hand still trembled as she reached for the teapot, poured half a cup, stewed now, then used both hands to lift it. She sipped, not looking at either James or Ethel.

'Thank you,' said James quietly. 'I know it isn't an easy story for you to tell.'

'On the contrary, sir. I would tell it as many times as I am able, if it weren't classified and might endanger others. May saved nineteen children. I wish every one of them could know her name and tell their children, too.'

'One day, perhaps,' said James. 'I have arranged for a car, Miss Nichols. I hope you enjoy your leave.'

She met his eyes for the first time. 'I'm going to my aunt's. She lives by the beach. I'd like to swim for days, just swim and wash everything I've seen and done away, but of course the beach is all landmines and barbed wire now. So I'll sit with the seagulls and pretend.'

Miss Nichols stood. Ethel stood too and offered her hand. 'Thank you, Miss Nichols. And ...' Ethel Carryman did not usually fumble for words. 'Good luck.' It seemed the most inadequate statement she had ever made.

'Thank you.'

Ethel waited till the young woman had left the room. 'I know why you wanted me to hear that,' she said quietly. 'Five men and a woman dead to save the lives of nineteen children, because you and I and that young woman know it's not a labour camp they were being sent to but the gas chambers. You want me to say that what May did was right, that killing six to save nineteen is justified.'

'No,' said James. His voice twisted. 'I wanted you to hear it because May's real name was June Anne Lorrimer, and she was my niece. Until her death she was my only living relative, which is why I was permitted to know how she died, and why. And you are one of the few people I care about who I can tell about her death.'

'James.' She touched his arm gently. And suddenly he was crying, sobbing on her shoulder as she held him and muttered words she vaguely remembered her mother, lost when Ethel was ten, using to comfort her. 'There, there, love. You let yourself cry now. I'm here ...'

The air-raid siren shrieked, disturbing two pigeons perched on the windowsill that had ignored the human drama inside.

'Cellar,' said Ethel. 'Come on, love.'

'No.' James rubbed his eyes. 'Can't let the servants see me like this.'

'I'm not giving up my life just so you can look like a stuffed shirt till your final breath, and that might be soon if we don't get a move on. Come on, or I'll sling you over my shoulder.'

'Priest's hole,' said James shortly. He pressed the edge of the mantelpiece, then pulled at a section of panelling. It opened to a narrow door, showing even narrower steps. 'There's another cellar down here. It's no secret — it's where I usually go.' He wiped his eyes, then blew his nose efficiently and picked up his briefcase. 'Come on.'

Of course James Lorrimer would have a priest's hole, just as he had hothouses and partridges and quail. The Carrymans probably had more money than the Lorrimers — the remaining Lorrimer — but they did not have a priest's hole, nor hothouses nor game birds.

Ethel grabbed her handbag, piled the last of the edibles onto a plate and ran down the stairs. A moment later he followed her.

The room below was small, but set up with textbook perfection: an immaculate single bed with pillow, sheets and quilts; a wooden keg plus two sturdy canteens that almost certainly held water; a cupboard she'd take short odds on holding packaged water biscuits, powdered milk, cocoa and other long-lived comestibles; two covered buckets, one for a toilet and one for washing; three torches, spare batteries and enamel plates, mugs and a dozen books on a shelf; a metal chest with a red cross on it; a table with notepaper, pens, two bottles of ink and blotting paper; and under the bed what looked like four small paintings, wrapped in blankets, and a compact storage box. A single chair sat neatly at the table.

'You have the bed —' began James. He stopped and listened. Ethel could hear engines now. Ours or theirs?

The world collapsed.

Chapter 34

Humans have been selectively breeding for thousands of years.
No, my dears, I don't mean dogs, or even camels, but people.
Marriages are arranged directly, or indirectly, as most young
people choose partners of whom their family circle approves.
Romeo and Juliet's fate is a tragedy because it is rare, not
common. All in all, I think we have been more successful breeding
dogs, though I, too, am one of those who 'arranges' — or at
least suggests — acquaintances that could result in productive
alliances. The most obvious pairings, however, are not all the
most successful ...

Miss Lily, 1938

The room was dark, her mouth and eyes filled with dust, but Ethel was whole and nothing hurt. 'James?'

'Here.' A hand reached for hers. 'Are you injured?'

'No. You?' She tried to breathe as shallowly as she could till the dust settled.

'No. That one hit the house,' he added. 'Or next door, perhaps.'

'I'm sorry,' she said: inadequate again.

'So am I. But the servants will be safe — the wine cellar is two levels down. They can go up to the country place till I find a flat; it will have to be a hotel for a while, with housing the way it is. Harrison could do with some country air. Luckily I sent everything I truly value out of London in thirty-nine ...'

He was turning efficiency into a wall to protect him from what must be the almost unbearable loss of the home he had shared with his wife, dead now forty years, the library where he had spun webs that crossed the world and brought countries together, however briefly.

Ethel wiped more grit from her eyes. Her hair felt like it was thick with plaster. But at least the air felt breathable again. 'I'd offer you my spare room, but I share the house with a Polish family. The grandma is a right good cook, but I doubt you'd want to share a bathroom with five kiddies.'

'I'd manage.'

'But would they be able to keep their legs crossed for half an hour while your valet shaves you?'

'I shave myself. Three minutes. As you may see tomorrow morning — I have a feeling it may be daylight before we get out again. The air-raid wardens know the cellars are good here,' he added. 'If there's no fire they'll see to others tonight first.' A torch flicked on. He passed her another. Their beams speared up the stairwell, now blocked by what looked like half the fireplace.

Fire, thought Ethel.

'I threw a bucket of sand on the library fire as we left the room. The servants will have done the same to the kitchen fire. We only have those two burning these days.'

No drawing-room fire, she thought. No servants' hall fire either. Cold beds and ...

Beds. Or rather, one bed. She sat on it, turned off her torch to save the battery, then reached for her handbag by the light of his, and pulled out her Thermos. 'Hot cocoa,' she said. 'Just what we need for shock.'

She took two mugs from the shelf — the cellar certainly was sturdy, for crockery had not even fallen — filled them, handed one to him and took the other for herself. For possibly the first time in her life she had no wish for fruitcake.

'James, about your niece — I wish I could remake the world or take the pain for you.'

'Do you think her heroic or a murderess?' His low voice held all the emotion now that he had not expressed earlier.

She examined her words carefully before she put them together. 'She's a heroine, right enough. A glorious girl: and you'll hang her portrait above the mantelpiece after the war and tell everyone who sees it what she did.'

'But would you have made that choice?'

She answered right away. For this was not just an instance of one extraordinary young woman, but the entire basis of Ethel's life and faith. 'Yes, if I'd had the courage and the skill and the quickness of wit to do it. And I'd have spent the rest of my life trying to think of what else I might have done to save those children, without killing others for their sakes. I might think my whole life and not find a way, but I'd still try. And they would never be just the enemy neither, nor their families nor the lives they might have had.'

'They were killing children!'

'They were transporting children. And, yes, at the end of that the children would die, but that does not mean that every one of those men might not have regretted what he did, or even done his best not to let it happen. Did the soldiers maybe manage to leave one or two kiddies behind? Warn the orphanage so even more might have escaped the night before? Were they doing their best that day or their worst, or just muddling on in a war they couldn't help? Would one of those men repent one day, and make restitution their whole lives? We'll never know. But it doesn't change the fact that June gave her life for nineteen children, and made sure all her comrades got safely away as well. And mayhap, if she'd lived, she might have thought of those she killed just as I'd have done.'

'You think I don't? Remember all I've killed, or had a part in killing?'

'No,' she said. 'I don't think that. I never did. I just think those in power need to spend a bit more time working out other ways to stop men like Mr Hitler.'

'When you think of one, do let me know,' he said drily.

'Well, I've got one to begin with. We teach people to grow consciences. A conscience needs to be sown and fed and watered, and to have people around with consciences for it to grow. If we do that then there'll be no beggars, or Jewish people or Gypsies locked up in camps, nor anybody shot either, because we'll see everyone as a person who has a value like our own.' Ethel paused, then added, 'I reckon your June knew that. She gave her life for nineteen children because she couldn't pass them by.'

They sat in silence for a while or, rather, the opposite of silence, for masonry still fell in trickles or unexpected crashes above them. But no noises from the street came through the thick stone walls and, to Ethel's relief, no sound of explosions from escaping gas nor the smell of smoke.

'I think we're safe enough, for now. I'd offer you my pyjamas,' he said at last, 'but I doubt they'd fit.'

'I'm sure they wouldn't. I'll make do with my petticoat.'

More non-silence.

James stood, brushed off more dust, then wiped his face with his handkerchief — a clean one, Ethel noticed. The man must have several about his person. He hesitated, then sat within touching distance next to her. 'Do you remember our last meal together?'

'In 1939. You were called away halfway through the salmon. I stayed to eat the saddle of mutton and the crepes you'd ordered, in case you came back, but you didn't, and the next day war was declared.'

'I was going to ask you to marry me.'

She stared. 'Are you sure?'

'That isn't the kind of thing one forgets,' he said drily. 'I had the ring in my pocket, in case you said yes.'

'Well, that was blooming extravagant. What if I'd said no?'

'It was my great-grandmother's. My grandmother and mother wore it too.'

But not his wife, she realised, for his mother had still been alive when she died. He must have had the ring doubled in size to fit her own finger.

'I meant, were you still going to ask me? We'd argued all through the soup, remember.'

'I remember very clearly. You called me a murderer.'

'I did not. I said those who cause people to be killed are as responsible for their deaths as those who carry out the act. War doesn't create peace. Look at this one — it's son and daughter of the Great War.'

'But war can be a plaster holding things together long enough to find a lasting peace. We failed to do that in 1918 — we betrayed the terms of the ceasefire, agreed to that 'peace treaty' the French insisted on, made things a thousand times worse. But there was no avoiding this war by 1939 — it was fight or be conquered.'

He looked at her, waiting for argument, but she did not speak. So he filled the silence again. 'There comes a time when you need to fight. But never think I haven't given most of my life to finding other solutions. Once a shot is fired, you've lost, no matter who is the eventual victor.' He looked at the floor, not her. 'I apologise for making a speech.'

'I like people to speak their minds.' Ethel considered. 'I won't disagree with most of it, either. All, of it, mebbe — but only mebbe. I'd need to think on it.'

'I spent twenty years trying to stop this war,' he said quietly, 'and a decade failing to prevent the last. War is the last resort. I must save my country and just now that means winning the war, and to do so means killing or decommissioning as many of the enemy as efficiently as we can while losing as few of our own as possible. And every night when I try to sleep I know that I am condemning the innocent as well as the guilty. But doing nothing would be worse.'

'I understand,' she said slowly. 'I found myself an easy billet in both wars, didn't I? Feeding people. Needed to be done, no question. Left others to make the hard decisions.'

He smiled. 'I don't think what you've done in either war has been easy.'

'Hard on the feet, but easy on the conscience.'

'I do love you, Ethel. Will you marry me?'

She stared at him. 'First time we meet in near three and a half years and you propose! Sure you didn't get a bang on the head on the way down?'

'Well, you might refuse to see me for another three and a half years,' James said reasonably. 'I need to take whatever chance I have. Look on the bright side — we might take a direct hit tonight and you'd only have to be engaged to me for a few hours.'

'I'd make you a laughing stock,' she told him bluntly.

'Because fools giggled at a girl of your height when you were sixteen? Today you are statuesque and move with dignity.'

'Because I'm Carryman's Cocoa, and you're game pie.'

'I think that distinction is fading fast. Nor does the world's opinion matter to either of us. I once assumed I needed to marry a hostess, a woman who would complement and support my career. Instead we both of us have achieved enough to continue with whatever we choose to do.'

'James Lorrimer could marry the bearded lady from the circus and get away with it?' She tried to turn the proposal into a joke.

'Possibly. I admit I rather hope you don't grow a beard, but I'd still love you if you did. It was love at first sight, I think, or at least by the end of the afternoon,' he added. 'Though it took me a while to recognise it.'

'There's many I love, but don't want to marry. James, I've never been interested in the, you know, marital stuff. I'd disappoint you.'

'It's not one of my preoccupations either. You don't find it repugnant?'

She shook her head. 'Just never felt the urge.' She flushed. 'Well, once or twice.'

'A handsome sport's master?'

'You,' she told him shortly.

'Ethel, there is so much I'm trying not to say. I don't want to say I need you, that I have lost my family and now my home and, even worse, that I am frightened I may lose my conscience. You could give me all of those.'

'And fill your house with refugee families or doctors evading a warrant for handing out contraception or conscientious objectors? I'll probably even take over Carryman's Cocoa after the war — George won't want it, and I'm beginning to think I'd be of more use organising food supplies for Britain outside the Ministry. I'd keep my own name for that.'

'And I might vanish for six months to America, or Bermuda. I'm not asking you to share my whole life. No one can. I'd expect your days to stay as full as mine. But you're right, this war will not end with peace but with more plasters, and, as I get swept up in whatever chaos follows, you will be the still centre of the spinning hurricane where reality and conscience waits.'

He reached into his pocket. 'Damn.' The small box was dented. He opened it with effort. 'Thank God.'

The ring inside — dull gold, a square-cut emerald, with a diamond on each side — was undamaged. 'I used one of your gloves to get the size right.' He put the ring on the table, still in its box, making no attempt to offer it to her. She knew him well enough to know he was not trying to sway her with its brilliance. She could afford her own emeralds, if she had ever wanted them. A contraception clinic, a public library, a dozen new latrines in the slums had always been far more desirable.

Nor was he asking from loneliness. He had not been lonely in September 1939 when he'd first planned to ask her: then he'd still had his aunt, who died of influenza in '41; his brother, killed in an air raid the previous February; his niece. He'd had Lily, too, and if he wanted sex when he had time for it and a hostess for his dinner parties, he had the choice of debutantes from the Ton, a new crop every year, and Lily to give him a list of suitable ones he might look over.

She looked at his hands, clenched to stop them shaking. She knew there was only one answer she could give.

Chapter 35

Sauce Eglantine

Pick your rosehips when they turn deep winter red and start to shrivel. Some varieties are larger and sweeter than others, but the size and redness are not necessarily a guide to sweetness and flavour. Briars, which are small, hard and orange, make an excellent Sauce Eglantine.

Boil 6 cups of rosehips in as little water as possible. Press through a sieve or mouli. The seeds may be fed to hens. Add 1 cup white sugar and the juice of 3 lemons. If neither is available the sauce is still savoury. Simmer till thick. Serve with roast mutton or any fried food, or with potatoes baked in their jackets.

A family recipe of the Prinzessin Hannelore

SOPHIE

Her new bedroom looked down upon the lake, across to mountains veined with snow and trees brightening with green leaf tips. It felt strange to suddenly have the freedom to walk where she wished about the Lodge, though movement was still painful.

But the pain no longer frightened her. It was easing and there had been no infection. The scars would fade, even if the memory did not. There was no need to hide the need to hobble, to wince as she bent over. The background Dolphie had chosen for her allowed for injuries, and even her lack of possessions.

Breakfast was served with ceremony again, even if it was Hannelore who carried their tray to the breakfast room, chilly without its stove lit, but brightened with a mural of deer leaping across the ceiling, and the view of the lake again, clad in wind ruffles and sunlight, out the window.

'Real coffee?' Sophie inhaled the scent. They still spoke German, for Simons or Grünberg might overhear, or someone from the farm who had come up to the Lodge. It was also necessary for Sophie to improve her fluency.

'Dolphie brought white sugar, too, enough to make jellies this summer.'

In France they said that most of the harvest was sent to Germany — that Germans lived fat and lazy on French cheese and forced labour. Sophie suspected that most food went to the armies, as it must in any country in this war.

'Does Dolphie come here often?'

'He used to. It hurt him badly, when he discovered my treachery.'

'But he forgave you?'

Hannelore smiled. 'Dolphie does not forgive. But he loves me. What other family do he and I have to love?' She put down her empty coffee cup. 'Come, Simons will clear the table. You need to choose more clothes.'

'Dolphie won't mind my wearing Amelia's things?'

Hannelore looked amused. 'Why else keep them, except to be used? Though I only stored the best — her taste was not good. Darling Sophie, so bourgeois with your new clothes. My court dress in England was made from the fabric my grandmother had worn and the furs were my mother's, altered for the new fashion. I still wear my grandmother's chemises — good silk lasts for generations.'

'Not her underpants?' replied Sophie facetiously.

'My grandmother did not wear underpants — they were a scandalous new fashion. I believe mine were the first in our family. Miss Lily dictated that underpants were advisable for any new woman who wished an active lifestyle where more than an ankle might be seen. Sophie, you have not spoken of Miss Lily since you have been here. There is something I must tell you.'

Sophie sipped her coffee, looking at her enquiringly.

'I went to see her at Shillings, a few months before war was declared, the day before I returned to Germany. I wanted to tell her that my help against the fascists was not merely because I felt guilty at Nigel's death, though that had made me see Hitler and his henchmen for what they truly were. Sophie ...'

Sophie put down her coffee cup.

'Miss Lily did not expect me. I found her in the orchard, gathering late apples, the sunlight on her face, her arms bare. I saw Nigel, Sophie.' Hannelore smiled. 'A second later I saw Miss Lily once again. But she knew what she had revealed. We talked a little after that. She allowed me to say sorry for all that I had caused, and all that she had lost, too. She told me you were happy with your Daniel, but ... but I took your husband, Sophie. I destroyed Nigel, even if I did not kill anyone.'

Sophie sat wordless. Impossible to say that Lily was now living as Bob — she of all people knew what one might scream if tortured. If they had known the right questions to ask, if they had known how much information she had, and kept on torturing her, day after day instead of giving up so soon, she might have poured out answers. She could not burden Hannelore with another secret to hide. And yet ...

'I am happy with Daniel,' she said at last. 'Or I would be, if I could be with him now. And the years Lily lived with us as my sister-in-law were some of the happiest I have known. The children don't know yet. We'll wait till they are older.' And when the war was over, and Nigel could decide whether 'Aunt Lily' might return.

'How is Miss Lily? Please?'

Sophie hesitated. 'She was reported missing after the fall of France.'

Hannelore gave a small cry. 'Not Miss Lily! But why keep it secret?' She shook her head as she answered her own question.

'We are Miss Lily's lovely ladies, all across Europe and America. It is the one thing that links us all. Lorrimer is correct to keep her death secret.'

'She may be still alive,' said Sophie hurriedly. 'So many have been lost in the confusion of the Occupation. I ... I can't believe that she is gone.' Which was true, too.

'There are many families who will only be able to count their losses when the war ends. We can pray it will be soon.' Hannelore stood. 'Come. Let us choose a wardrobe for you.'

꩜

She slid into the pattern of Hannelore's days. She could not dig potato beds, but she could weed if she sat on a sack to ease her feet and back. To her surprise, although Hannelore dined separately, she spent hours in the kitchen with Grünberg, making Käsespätzle, egg noodles, together, a task much easier with two, or three when Sophie joined them, clumsy at first but soon able to fill the noodles almost as well as the others, to be served with a cheese sauce, fried onions and chives.

Neither Grünberg nor Simons commented on her short hair, nor her sudden appearance. Sophie suspected they knew she had been up in the bedroom. But in war there were secrets, and a wise person did not ask, especially when the alternative to the Lodge was Dachau.

The three women made pretzels together, scented with caraway seeds; and potato dumplings, a difficult dish of raw and cooked mashed potatoes with nothing else to bind them; and they chopped cabbage and early apples for sauerkraut, most of the ingredients grown at the farm or at the Lodge itself with its orchards and hothouses.

Hannelore and Grünberg discussed what should be saved in the store cupboard, how the precious sugar might be used. It was, perhaps, the same ease Hannelore had once had with servants and now felt without thought around the two women from Dachau.

To Sophie's even greater surprise Grünberg seemed to regard Hannelore ... not as a friend exactly, but with ease and friendliness. She accepted Sophie with matter-of-fact sympathy.

She had perhaps once been a large woman, not fat, probably, but broad and tall in her faded dress with its prominent yellow Star of David. Now she was hunched from past harsh treatment — starvation or even torture, Sophie supposed, like her own but for a longer period, until Grünberg had been transferred here. Except for luxuries like coffee and chocolates, she and Simons ate the same food as Sophie and Hannelore. Sophie could see how neither woman would want to jeopardise her position at the Lodge.

'Were you a cook?' she asked idly one day, as she tied the small bunches of herbs that Grünberg dried and smoked over the fireplace.

'I was an industrial chemist.'

Sophie blinked in surprise. 'Does that make you a better cook?'

Grünberg smiled. Most of her teeth were missing. 'Better. If you know the temperature at which egg white coagulates you are more confident with baking soufflés. But I mostly cook the dishes my grandmother taught me. She grew herbs, like the ones here, and had an orchard.'

'A farm?'

'A summer lodge.' Grünberg hesitated. 'Frau Müller, I worked for a year in Alsace-Lorraine. I also studied in London for three years to get my doctorate. Your accent ...'

'Ah,' said Sophie.

'I want to tell you I will say nothing. Simons and I know that the prinzessin has been guilty of some disloyalty.' Her mouth quirked. 'The enemy of my enemy is not necessarily my friend, but nor would I betray them. Simons though ...'

'She cannot be a Nazi!' The other woman was resentfully scrubbing somewhere, as she did most mornings, to be followed by the continual task of fetching wood and feeding the stoves, and cleaning out their ashes and the dust that left on furniture.

'No. Simons was a musician, a cellist, though after chilblains and now years of scrubbing I do not think she will be able to play professionally again. She also has a family and will do — or say — whatever might be needed to try to keep them safe.'

'Don't you have a family?'

'Not now,' said Grünberg, and said no more.

Chapter 36

CARRYMAN'S
Cocoa Chocolate Beetroot Fairy Cakes

Very rich and chocolatey!
⅓ cup CARRYMAN'S Cocoa
⅓ cup buttermilk or soured milk
1¾ cups self-raising flour
2 large or 4 small beetroot, cooked and peeled, and either puréed or grated
1 cup brown sugar, well pressed down (optional, and hardly needed with the sweetness of the beetroot)
2 eggs (optional: the beetroot will help bind the cake and keep it moist)
⅓ cup butter, or another ⅓ cup buttermilk or soured milk

Heat oven to medium before you begin mixing, or your fairy cakes may not rise well. Heat the cocoa in the buttermilk till almost at the boil. Remove from the heat and cool. Mix in the other ingredients gently. Place in greased patty pans. Bake for about 12 minutes or till they bounce back when you press the tops lightly. Don't overbake. The cooking time will vary according to the size of the fairy cakes — large ones will take longer to cook.

From **Delicious Recipes from CARRYMAN'S Cocoa**,
1942 edition

JAMES

London smelled of smog and dust and the faint reek of explosives, even here, so far from the East End where the damage had been the worst. James kept his office window shut, but the smog crept like a yellow cat, always waiting to sneak inside.

He closed the file of the latest intelligence report on Auschwitz, and sat there, gazing into dust-hazed air, wishing he could wipe away the images the words had conjured. Impossible, once you had read them. All countries he'd known were capable of atrocities, including his own. People chose not to see, and when it was over, conveniently did not remember. But this ...

He thanked God he had Ethel back in his life now. Ethel was convinced humanity was good, even if life twisted individuals or even nations into evil; that empathy could be taught, and society guided into kindness. After a few hours of Ethel's practicality as she dished out stew for him and the Polish family, James could almost believe that it was true.

A brief knock on his office door. His secretary entered, a man of what James regarded as impeccable breeding — in other words, one with no hint of the aristocracy or old school tie. James had recruited him as a scholarship boy from Oxford.

'Mr Lorrimer, Leo Marks's girls have translated a coded message from Holland, or rather Germany via the pigeon post. I thought you would wish to see it immediately.' He held it out.

Three words and two letters. *SafeLodgePlotsSH*

James kept his voice emotionless. 'Thank you. Yes, you were right to bring it at once.'

The sensible young man merely nodded and immediately left the room.

James stared at the words again, in case somehow he had misread them, misunderstood. But it was clear. Sophie was alive and at the Lodge. She and Hannelore were safe and either plotting, or knew of further plots against the Führer.

Thank goodness he hadn't notified Daniel when his agents in Paris had been unable to find any trace of Sophie at Fresnes or elsewhere. He had almost been certain she'd been executed, but until he was sure he could not tell her family that.

And now? He could let them know she was alive. No more than that.

So much.

He had to make a phone call first. He lifted the receiver and asked for the number. Less than a minute later — Lorrimer's calls had almost the highest priority in Britain — the phone rang. He lifted the receiver. 'Bob? She's safe. She's with our mutual friend, where they once met before. They both are safe.'

Chapter 37

Some of the most notable heroes in our history have been women.
But nevertheless, girls should preferably exercise the virtues of
patience, persistence and resignation. They are destined to tend
to the running of the household … It is in love that our future
mothers will find the strength to practise those virtues which best
befit their sex and their condition.

Paraphrase of a Vichy Government textbook,
urging the Nazi values of motherhood housewifery
and a minimum of education

JULY–DECEMBER 1943

SOPHIE

Spring had been beautiful. Was it wrong to clasp moments of happiness and let them warm you, simply because bare branches suddenly wove bright leaves, because viburnums scented the garden and even her bedroom, when she opened her window to shake the winter's dust from the carpet by her bed? Wild tulips, irises and tiny jonquils bloomed in explosions of colour, while the meadows across the lake were the lilac of crocus flowers.

It was in spring that Hannelore had first taken Sophie into the forest, both of them, Sophie thought, looking ridiculously Germanic in dirndls and shawls, but the wide skirts were useful to carry beech or fir or hazelnut shoots uncrushed, which would be added later to soups and stews. Soon it seemed there were leaves that needed harvesting everywhere, though Sophie found it hard to see them, even though they were there in abundance.

Hannelore laughed. 'You need to learn to see what is in front of you. I did this every year as a child.'

'Even a prinzessin?'

'Especially a prinzessin. How can one rule an estate if one does not know it? See — Frauenmantel.' She handed a leaf to Sophie.

Sophie tasted it — pleasant enough, if faintly bitter. It would be eaten fresh, and dried, too, to store for winter.

She recognised Löwenzahn or dandelion at least. Dandelion it seemed, was especially precious, its root baked like parsnips if picked at the correct time, the young leaves sweet, the flowers made into a cordial. Bärlauch or bear leek was vaguely familiar as the wild garlic of Britain, its leaves to be rooted out of pasture because when cows ate it, it tainted the milk. Sorrel, stinging nettles and clover she knew too, but not that they could be so valued as salads or vegetables, or that the growing abundance of Giersch could be used like parsley. There was blood root, too, that Hannelore said gave a colour and new fragrance to schnapps.

'Hannelore, when will Dolphie come?'

Hannelore bent down with gloved hands to pick young nettle tops. 'When he can. When it is safe to do so.'

'But why doesn't he write?'

Hannelore straightened. 'Because I am his beloved niece, his only relative, but no longer keep house for him, am no longer on his arm at official functions. All this will have been noted. Perhaps he has acquired another mistress to wear on his arm, who I might have objected to, or we quarrelled, if I suspected he no longer had sufficient fervour for our leader. All this makes me safer, if his loyalty is suspected. It makes you safer too.'

'But don't you miss him?'

'Like a knife has twisted in my heart. As you must feel, when you think your family in Australia, of Miss Lily, in England.' She bent to her harvesting.

Sophie did not ask again.

There had been no letter, no visit, no news of turmoil after the Führer's death. Now in midsummer the Lodge's own gardens were also ready for harvest. Sour cherries, to be blended with potatoes and fermented with some of their precious sugar for a cordial that was so powerful Sophie choked on the first sip. But alcohol was the best of pain relievers, and all the more valuable in war-time for that.

Redcurrants needed no sugar for their jelly to set, though it did not last well without it. Grünberg made a redcurrant tart with a meringue top, blackcurrant pancakes, elderberry syrup, jellies and preserves of raspberries, prickly blackberries and even more vicious gooseberries that tore Sophie's hands no matter how carefully she picked around their thorns. But nothing in a war year could be wasted.

White asparagus season, and Grünberg and the silent Simons feasted on steamed asparagus too, sometimes even with sauce Hollandaise, or with a sauce of pounded walnuts that Grünberg concocted. Asparagus could be dried for winter soups, and though they did that, too, it was a pity to waste the summer succulence. They ate the strawberries fresh, too, the tiny wild ones with their intense taste — it could take Sophie and Hannelore a morning to fill a tub — and later in summer the large ones cultivated in the hothouse that also grew cucumbers, tomatoes and pumpkins.

And always, always, there were potatoes, beetroot, cabbages, cabbages, cabbages, carrots, onions, turnips and more cabbages, the mainstays of their diet, though Grünberg did miracles even with these: garlic-scented cakes of grated potatoes, herb-flavoured potato dumplings, cabbage sautéed with caraway or sweetened with apples, flour and potato noodles that needed a rich cheese covering but instead were dotted with more herbs and a little of the fresh cheese made at the farm. Roast beetroot soup, a cream made somehow from almonds, cabbage rolls filled with minced rabbit, carp stuffed with its liver and more carp and herbs. The kitchen smelled of smoke-cured herbs like wild thyme, and of fermenting sauerkraut. Franz brought them fresh-caught trout, or bream, which Grünberg served with berry sauces.

And Dolphie did not appear. But there must be a 'next' plot, and if that failed another plot, and another. Any day now the negotiations that would end the war must start.

The Lodge still had no radio. Those at the farm were evidently following Dolphie's orders from his last visit to tell the prinzessin nothing. Australia might be filled with Japanese or with Americans, or even Martians, for all Sophie knew.

All she knew for certain was that the war was not over, for old Franz was suddenly called up, though he was over sixty, and then there was no cheese or milk or butter, for all the cows were confiscated for meat for the army, and his wife and daughters-in-law ordered to move to Munich for factory work. But Franz made a chicken coop at the Lodge before he left, and moved the hens, young chickens and the rooster there, so they had eggs, and even sometimes an old hen or young unnecessary rooster to eat.

Hannelore knew how to trap a rabbit, how to fish for trout in the stream on the Lodge grounds, or net carp as they floated above the muddy bottom of the lake. Sophie suspected that Grünberg also knew how to fish, but neither she nor Simons was allowed past the vegetable gardens.

Every day, every hour, she and Hannelore listened for the sound of Dolphie's car, coming to announce that at last Adolf Hitler could no longer plan to rule the world. Sometimes they thought they heard him coming, but each time it was a far-off plane, or what might have been tanks rolling along the distant road to Munich. But they never spoke of the engine sounds they heard, or even met each other's eyes. Hope was hard to bear, and the only affliction, perhaps, that was easiest borne alone.

Sophie would have liked to rage at him. Even news that there was no news would be better than endless waiting, and if he visited, even for a day, he could tell them of how things were in Australia, England, the world. Dolphie's complete absence at least told them three things: no plot had yet succeeded; another plot was planned; and that Dolphie had still not been arrested.

Twice that year a box arrived, accompanied each time by sacks of flour, but no note at all. Both times the boxes held more coffee, crumbly brown beet sugar, a vast hard yellow cheese, and long-keeping sausage. The second box, miraculously, was delivered with a giant haunch of what Hannelore calmly said was horse meat, which Sophie had never eaten, even in France. But Grünberg marinated it with vinegar and spices to make Sauerbraten, and the household feasted on it for a week, before returning to Hasenpfeffer, a rabbit stew marinated in wine and vinegar braised with onions and wine from the Lodge's cellar, thickened with the rabbit's blood and served with potatoes and cabbage, and more potatoes and cabbage, and cabbage and potatoes, or potatoes with some precious eggs.

She and Hannelore lugged sacks of potatoes down to the cellar; more sacks of giant steel-hard German cabbage. They stored apples in tubs of bran, and eggs too, and dried grapes and plums and cherries in the hot attic, and plaited strings of onions to hang on the kitchen walls.

The hard work was good. Physical exhaustion meant she slept. The need to grow food, preserve food, cook food or the four of them would starve kept each day occupied so fully that she was startled to see weeks go by, then months.

She imagined Rose and Danny at school, tried not to think of the day they turned seventeen, and she was not there to celebrate it, nor to calculate the probable date of Danny's last examination next year, for that was when he and his friends would volunteer together late that afternoon, with thousands of other schoolboys suddenly turned soldier.

She pictured Daniel at the Bald Hill Clinic, and at Sunday lunch with Midge and Harry, roast mutton with mint sauce, gravy and baked pumpkin. Bob would be mucking out the Shillings pigs again, and James and Ethel and even Violette going about their jobs. She forced herself to imagine them all going on as before because the alternatives were unthinkable, and she was helpless to do anything except dig up more potatoes, or pick slugs from the cabbages to feed to the hens.

She tried to visualise Lily, too. Sometimes, confused with weariness and pain, for her back still pained her deeply and possibly always would, she imagined that Lily truly was just missing in occupied France, and so would come to free them both, in a car to drive them to where a guide would take them across the mountains into Switzerland. She had only to glance up from the potato bed and Lily would be strolling gracefully from the dapples, autumn leaves fluttering red and gold about her feet.

They all ate together in the kitchen now, and even sewed there in the evenings, for without Franz the only firewood was what Hannelore and Sophie could gather, which must be kept to cook with. The trees of Germany were grudging with their supply of firewood, compared to gum trees that obligingly dropped limbs every summer. They mostly burned prunings from the garden, pear, cherry, plum or apple wood, a scent that sent Sophie back to Shillings and tears onto her sewing — as she and Simons and Grünberg made themselves new undergarments from the silken petticoats of Hannelore's mother's aunt.

Christmas — only known because Hannelore marked each day on the calendar. Sophie would have spent it with the quilt over her head, crying for helplessness, for homesickness and guilt, for she had left all she loved and achieved nothing, except a cellar full of vegetables and an attic that smelled of lavender and fruit.

Hannelore, however, had insisted that gifts be exchanged, clothes foraged from the attic and secretly chosen for each other. Sophie had sensibly found dresses that could be altered for Grünberg and Simons, and discovered an embroidered warm cap for Hannelore.

Hannelore had other plans. When the four of them sat down for Christmas dinner in a kitchen warmed by cooking, Sophie wore a ball gown complete with crinoline, her hair crimped with old curling irons Hannelore had found in the attics. Simons shone in a 1920s silver cocktail sheath and Grünberg was suddenly slimly glamorous in a Chanel silk walking dress, which unlike Sophie's crinoline allowed her to reach the stove. Hannelore twisted her hair into a froth of curls above a pre-war Violette, a slim dark blue silk skirt whose pleats erupted into panels of turquoise, mauve and purple when she walked, a dagger thrust as Sophie realised Hannelore knew nothing of Violette's betrayal.

Where was Violette now? Was her 'famille' still safe?

A third package had arrived the day before, delivered in an old cart by an even older driver, who seemed to be deaf, for he failed to hear any of their questions. But the package meant that Dolphie was still able to send them Christmas Weisswurst, which they gently simmered so its casing didn't break and served with mustard, and gingerbread, and even a slab of chocolate meticulously divided into four, to be kept for some other time of celebration or desperation.

Instead they ate wild mushroom soup made from chanterelles Hannelore had shown Sophie how to forage, and a red pudding of preserved raspberries thickened with cornflour, a recipe from Hannelore's lost northern estates, and poppy-seed strudel.

And Sophie tried to laugh and praise the food and not count the days that Dolphie had not come, nor any secret word from England.

How long did it take a pigeon to fly to Holland?

Chapter 38

A War-time French Omelette with One Egg and No Butter or Cream

3 mushrooms
1 clove garlic, crushed
1 onion, finely chopped
1 tomato, peeled, seeds removed and chopped
Thyme or tarragon, ½ teaspoon leaves only
1 egg
1 eggshell of water
1 teaspoon parsley, chopped finely
A little olive oil, lard or bacon fat if available

This omelette, without butter and with a single egg only, must be made in a most different method from an ordinary omelette.

Place the mushrooms, chopped, in a pan on low heat until the juices begin to flow. Add the garlic and onion, sauté on low heat till soft. Add a little water if it is too dry, but the mushroom liquid should be sufficient. Do not add the tomato till the onions are soft or they may harden. A blackened onion is bitter. Add the tomato and half the thyme or tarragon, again on a low heat, till the juices flow. Now quickly beat the egg well with the water. Make a hole in the centre of the vegetables and pour in the egg. Shake the pan thoroughly so the egg sets in ripples like the sea. You must not stop shaking the pan or the omelette will harden. When almost set (it will continue to cook out of the pan) slide the omelette from the pan, and then surround with the vegetables and scatter on the remaining herbs.

A little grated cheese on the egg while it is cooking improves this dish. So does a large amount of butter at the beginning. But like so much of life, if done carefully and well it is delicious even without such luxuries.

JANUARY 1944

VIOLETTE

At first she thought the noise was a rat scratching inside the wall. She rose softly from her breakfast table, leaving the chicory coffee — even the black market could not obtain true coffee these days — and the two small slices of not quite bread that were her breakfast, and placed her ear to the wall.

A sobbing, almost like a pigeon, but not quite. She ran her fingers along the wall. There were no invisible joins, nor any panelling, nor even a mantelpiece that might hide a false door.

The adjoining room was a salon for customers. It did have a fireplace, but on the opposite wall. Violette peered inside the room, found it empty, then sat back at her delicate breakfast table. The table might have been priceless, but it also had a series of small notches underneath, one for each successful operation. There were seven more since Aunt Sophie ...

... She did not want to finish that thought, she decided. She had done what she could, what she must. One day, perhaps, Aunt Sophie would understand, but not for many years, for if Sophie knew the truth about who had wished to betray her it might hurt her far more than what Aunt Sophie must believe now.

And Aunt Sophie *must* be alive. Aunt Sophie, of all the people Violette knew, would not allow herself to be dead.

The sob behind the wall came again. Violette pulled the bell decisively.

'Mademoiselle?'

'Fetch me Madame Thomas, s'il vous plaît, Gisette.'

'Oui, mademoiselle.'

Madame Thomas had been the concierge of this building when it had only been a storehouse. The marble façade, the stairs most grand, the plastering and wallpaper, the secret cellars made carefully moisture-proof to store the fabrics, were all a creation of Violette, with Thuringa money.

Madame Thomas had been most efficient with the builders, so Violette had kept her on. She lived in a room off the entrance, not to greet clients, of course, for Madame Thomas had a girth most extraordinary, with ankles like a draught horse. Her bulk had not diminished despite the vicious austerity that starved French citizens but kept the German soldiers on leave drunk and fat — though even they, Violette admitted, lacked avoirdupois these days.

Madame Thomas took deliveries and called the watchman or the police if there were noises at night. Or possibly, Violette thought, sometimes she did not.

'Ah, Madame, good morning.'

Madame's hair was the colour of walnut casings, darker on the first Sunday of each month, but her eyebrows were so white they had almost vanished. 'Good morning, Mademoiselle Violette.'

'There is someone inside my wall, Madame. Possibly a child.'

Madame stilled and listened. 'I hear nothing, Mademoiselle Violette.'

'The noise has ceased. Will you bring the person to me, please?'

Madame Thomas said nothing. She did not move, either. Violette sighed. 'I am not a fool, Madame. This building was renovated when all with sense knew war would come, and you were here to oversee it, including my more private preparations, and perhaps you shared preparations of your own with the builders. You, I think, are not a fool either.'

'Perhaps not, mademoiselle,' said Madame cautiously.

'So, there is one question only I wish to know. Do the others of my staff know why, just possibly, there may be a child in my wall?'

Madame considered. 'Most of them, mademoiselle. Forgive me if I do not give the names.'

'Because a colonel of the Gestapo calls on me sometimes?'

'Because you made two phone calls, mademoiselle.' Madame's voice was matter-of-fact. 'One to him, and one to the police.'

This was Paris, of course, where nothing was secret, especially her own phone lines. But after Sophie left there had been too little time for Violette to find a public phone.

'Have there been similar phone calls since those two, Madame?'

'Non,' said Madame.

'Then, perhaps, you have two choices. You can believe I am a person who easily makes calls like that, to help the Boche. Or you can trust I had a reason, a most good reason, for those calls and let me help you now.' Violette smiled. 'Enfin, it is not a choice at all. If I am good friends with the Gestapo I just make another call this morning and you are all questioned, and the walls searched as well. And perhaps the cellars and other areas where large rooms might have been made slightly smaller seven years ago and secret places prepared. My mystery would be solved.'

'You would lose Maison Violette,' said Madame baldly. 'As you say, you have the rooms of your own, and it is not people stored there. And, mademoiselle, what is your maison without the cutters, the embroiderers, the fitters —'

'Nothing except my genius and reputation,' said Violette. 'Paris has little genius, but these days it has many fitters and cutters and models who are most eager for employment. But, in truth, madame, you may trust me. Those two phone calls apart, have I given any person here a reason not to?'

Madame gazed at her shrewdly for a time. At last she said, 'I will fetch the child. He was told to stay below, but it is dark there, and we have few candles, and there is a skylight above the wall here. You will be kind to him?'

She, Violette, was not kind. Generous, sometimes, but not kind. But she had seen kindness, learned it with Aunt Sophie and Aunt Lily. She could manage an approximation now. 'I will be kind. How did he get there?'

No hesitation now. 'A vegetable cart comes to the markets once a week. Under the cart there is a space, this wide and perhaps this big.' Madame Thomas gestured. 'Two men can hide there. This morning it was one man and a child.'

'And why the child?'

'His parents were killed,' said Madame evenly. 'The boy saw them killed. He also saw the men and women who shot some of the soldiers who killed his parents, before he ran and hid, just as his parents had told him to if soldiers came. The Boche know his name. They would like to question him. So now he must have another name and live in another place.'

Violette considered. 'Do men sometimes stay in my walls too?'

'More often women, mademoiselle.'

'For how long?'

A shrug. 'Till we can find a safer place to take them to.'

'Bon.' Violette decided. 'From now on I want the cart to deliver to us onions every week, at least a sackful, and chicken or rabbit, as many as can be obtained, or other meat. Do not worry — I will pay enough to make it possible for them to find the meat and also to pay the bribe to any flic who interferes for, of course, the cart does something illegal. A simple illegality to hide the other. But the people who stay here must be fed properly, Madame. Their appearance, perhaps, must be changed. I am most good at that, you must agree.'

'You are, mademoiselle.'

'But first, the boy. And please bring whatever you think he would like. Hot chocolate, perhaps.' She had a small supply, kept strictly for herself, but she was not sobbing inside a wall. Though she had sobbed, as a child, and hidden herself too, and been so very hungry for food and for much more.

Madame made what might have been a curtsey had her body possessed any bendability whatsoever.

The boy arrived holding Madame's hand. He was six perhaps, Violette estimated, but small for his age. Perhaps living with his parents' constant fear and tension had stopped him growing.

Violette had wiped the noses of many six-year-olds in her time at the orphanage. His pants and jersey were both far too large for him. So his clothes had been identifiable, Violette deduced. His hair had also recently been cut close to his head, so the skin of his scalp was pale. The boy wiped his nose thoroughly on his arm.

'Non,' said Violette firmly. 'A handkerchief, s'il vous plaît.'

'I do not have one.' The absence of expression from voice and face showed that he was trying not to think of all the other things he no longer had: a home, a family.

Violette held out her own. 'Now you have a handkerchief.'

He looked at the violet linen and lace with revulsion, but at least it was an expression: something had dragged him back from the nothingness into which so many children in these times retreated. 'That is a girl's handkerchief.'

'Here.' Madame Thomas fished out a square of unadorned linen, cleaned but with an accumulation of possibly two generations of stains.

The boy took it and wiped his nose again. 'I am not crying,' he stated. Violette was glad to see he raised his chin a little at that statement. This boy had courage.

'I did not say you were. Please sit down. You too, Madame.'

The chair of the king called Louis creaked under Madame, but held. The boy wriggled back on his seat, his legs dangling. Gisette arrived. Her tray held two cups of chicory coffee, a cup of hot chocolate, whipped most properly as the sisters had taught Violette to do and she had taught the cook, a plate of thinly sliced bread and a bowl of potato soup. The boy reached for the soup.

'First we say grace,' said Violette. It had been years since she had said grace, but Grandmère and the sisters had never omitted it. Probably the boy's parents said it too.

'Why?'

'To thank God.'

'Why?'

Why indeed, when the boy has seen his parents killed, and who knew what else, and his future was so uncertain?

'Because God does not do the bad things. Humans do.' The reply was automatic, but once she examined it, Violette found that strangely, she believed it. Violette had not, in fact, thought of God since she had left the orphanage. Nor was this the time to examine how she felt about Him now, though a small seed of curiosity bloomed within her.

She muttered grace quickly, Madame Thomas joining her. The boy muttered with them, so he knew the words. That familiarity at least might comfort him.

'Now you may eat. Try the hot chocolate first,' she tempted.

He sipped it, wrinkled his nose. 'I don't like it.'

'But it is chocolate!'

He shrugged and reached for the soup, dipping the bread into it.

Violette took the chocolate herself, then caught Madame's eye. She handed the cup to her. Madame smiled and began to sip. Violet took her 'coffee'.

'What is your name?'

'*She* said,' the boy pointed to Madame Thomas, 'to say my name is Tomas.'

'It is a good name. Tomas, I am sorry you are sad. But I promise you, sad times pass and there can be happy ones. I was sad too, when I was young.'

'Did your ... did people die?'

'Yes, people died.'

'My maman told me that soldiers of the resistance must die sometimes so that other people can live.'

Violette found it impossible to swallow. She put her cup down. 'That is most true. We call those people brave, and martyrs, and we do not forget them, even if for a while we must not say their names.'

'Were ... you lonely?' the boy asked in a small voice.

'Yes, I was lonely. I was scared too. I cried many, many nights. But slowly life became good and happy, and now you see I am not lonely at all.' Or not so much, she thought. 'That will happen for you, Tomas.'

'I do not think it can,' he said.

'And I am very sure it will, because I will make it happen. And when I say things will happen they do, do they not, Madame Thomas?'

'Always,' said Madame Thomas.

The boy did not look convinced, but more of the blankness left his face.

'So, Tomas, would you like to live on a farm, or by the sea, or in a town or village?'

'I do not have to go back into the dark?'

'No,' said Violette firmly.

The boy looked around the room. Evidently he approved, or perhaps did not have the strength to imagine yet another new environment. 'Can I live in here?'

Violette considered it briefly. But a boy would be too visible and the Gestapo knew she had no family in France, so she could not pretend he was a nephew or even a cousin. Perhaps, if he was not happy elsewhere, he might become Madame Thomas's nephew, but if she was with the resistance and identified, the boy might be taken as well.

'No, mon petit, I'm sorry. I would have liked you to stay. But you might have to hide in the walls and I think you are better in the sunlight.'

'With a dog?'

'You have a dog?' A dog could be identified too. She closed her eyes briefly. She could not unite this boy with his dog. It was too great a risk.

'He is dead,' said the boy flatly.

Bon. This made logistics easier, even if dealing with emotions harder. Did the Boche kill the dog, or old age, or hunger, or the thousand mishaps a dog might have in war-time? Violette did not ask. 'Where would you like to live, perhaps with a new dog?'

'By the sea,' he said promptly.

'Do you know the sea?'

'Yes. I have been there twice!'

Violette looked at Madame Thomas. 'A house by the sea then. One that has a room a boy would like, and where a dog who sleeps by a bed will be welcome, too. Do you think that can be found?'

'Yes, Mademoiselle Violette. But these days,' Madame shrugged, 'even with ration cards it can be hard to find enough extra food for a boy and a dog to eat, and expensive.'

'Money is no problem, and where money is no problem, food can be obtained. I will pay this household each month and, if Tomas is happy, I will pay double after three months. You have papers for him?'

'They can be arranged. Money would help with that, too,' said Madame Thomas drily.

'It usually does. Bien. We will discuss these things tonight, after the clients have left. Madame, if Tomas slept here in my room till this new home can be found, and you stayed with him, and Gisette brought meals to you, are there any in Maison Violette you think who might ... make a phone call?'

'None,' said Madame proudly.

A resistance cell, effectively, and with connections to other groups in the resistance. And she had not noticed! She, Violette, with the marks beneath her table, had not even seen what was happening in her own maison. She had picked her staff most carefully and not just for their skills. Of course, the people she had made her new family must have contact with the resistance, and perhaps have done much more.

And now she could join them. She had money and most excellent hiding places, and other knowledge that might be most useful, too.

Violette stood. 'I have an appointment with Madame Caron in ten minutes.' Who had a face like an eagle's and hips like an eel's and whose ensemble required most careful tailoring and many pleats about the waist.

'Call Gisette for whatever you need, Madame.' She made eye contact with Madame Thomas. 'We will discuss many things later.' Tomas would need clothes that fitted him, to begin with, and then more to fit in with whatever household he would go to. And if he did not like them, pouff! they would try another and another, till Tomas found one where he might have a happy home, and a dog …

Violette bent down to him. 'I have a secret,' she whispered.

'What, mademoiselle?' Tomas looked nervous. This boy had lived with too many secrets, Violette realised. She must not add more than needed to keep him safe.

'I like *The Adventures of Tintin*. I have all the comic books in the chest by the bed.'

'I like them too, mademoiselle,' he admitted.

'Bon. You and Madame Thomas can read them while I work.' He and Madame Thomas would also have a selection of the black-market fare her guests expected — aided by their gifts of butter and sugar to her — the madeleines, the tiny apple tarts with buttery pastry, the macarons, the puits d'amour with their rich vanilla cream, the orange puffs would be brought to this room, too, as well as a substantial déjeuner, for Violette had been a child who peered into pâtisseries, wishing to try just one of the glazed and glowing pastries displayed inside.

She left the boy burrowing into the chest, almost looking happy.

I should feel excitement, she thought, as she walked most beautifully down her perfect stairs, smiling 'Bonjour, Mesdames' at two less favoured customers, who were excited to glimpse her.

Instead she felt as if fate had laughed at her, for the last two years, to let her think she need tread so cautiously to protect those of her house. She would still be cautious, of course, and still protect them — the freedom to use the whole maison would be most useful to the resistance, and her other skills even more so. For Violette could take a young man and make him a woman most sophisticated, or an old man and make him a revered grandmère. A dark-haired woman would become blonde, with high heels to give her a different walk, make-up to produce a different face … and clothes! So few realised the power of clothes to change someone entirely.

There would be more marks under the table once owned by a king, and those must still stay secret. But now there would be other work, with her family, all of them together.

To her surprise she felt tears upon her cheeks. Truly, she was not alone.

Chapter 39

Higgs's Corned Beef Fritters

2 ounces self-raising flour
1 egg (fresh or dried)
Dash of milk
Pinch of thyme
2 teaspoons grated onion
6 ounces Higgs's corned beef, finely flaked
A little dripping, or margarine or cooking oil

Mix flour, egg and milk, then add thyme, onion and corned beef.
Form tablespoons of mixture into small flat patties. Fry on each
side in the dripping or margarine or oil till crisp. Set aside on a
plate. Add 1 tablespoon flour to the pan and brown, then add a
cup of cold water slowly, mixing all the time till rich and thick to
make a gravy. Serve with mashed potatoes and carrots or a grilled
tomato topped with a sprig of parsley.

Delectable Dishes with Corned Beef, a leaflet from Higgs,
the Corned Beef Kings, 1944

FEBRUARY 1944

ROSE

Rose leaned on the rail and watched the waves slapping the side
of the cargo ship, as ineffectual as clapping hands might be to
halt the war. The wind spat salt into her face. She let it take her
hair, pulling it from its neat curls, and probably weathering her

skin into wrinkles by the time she turned forty. She smiled for a moment at the memory of Mum insisting on hats and nightly applications of face cream. 'I still do the night cream, Mum,' she said softly, knowing the wind would hide her words. 'I even brush my hair a hundred strokes each side. And soften my elbows with squeezed lemon halves, just like Aunt Lily showed me.'

She missed Mum like an ache, and Aunt Lily too. Letters came irregularly, so sometimes there'd be months with nothing, then six letters from Aunt Lily and two typed ones from Mum that she might even have dictated to a shorthand typist between meetings, mostly talking about the weather or the new shoes that could have heels and a rosette added to turn them from an office shoe into an evening one, which meant that whatever Mum was doing in England was so hush-hush she had to be careful not to give any clue about it.

When Pa's 'holiday' showed no sign of ending by February last year she and Danny had had a long conference with Aunt Midge and Dr Patrick, who had turned out to be a total brick, patient with Pa and a regular visitor to Thuringa. Simply talking about Pa's and Mum's absence and the loss of school friends somehow helped.

All of Bald Hill knew about Pa now. It seemed that the older generation had not only once known their father as 'John', but had liked the strange persona, which Dr Patrick said was probably close to the way Pa managed his life now. The locals were strangely accepting of Pa's need to live away from house walls and other people. Dr Patrick had explained that Mum and Pa would undoubtedly have told her and Danny about Pa's history, possibly when they left school, for too many people knew of it for it to be kept a secret.

But no one locally except for her and Danny and Pa, Dr Patrick and Aunt Midge knew Mum was in England, not overseeing Higgs's operations in northern Australia. Friends even asked them sometimes to forward letters to her in Queensland, accepting that as Mum was moving from property to property, factory to factory, she had no permanent address.

The question for their February meeting was 'How much should we tell Mum?' About Pa's illness, about Danny's taking over Thuringa, or Rose's successful negotiations with the board?

The decision was surprisingly easy to make. Mum's work must be desperately important or she'd not have left them so suddenly, and for so long. It was probable she might not even be able to come back, even if her work made it possible. This was war, and you shouldered the burdens as best you could.

Nor could Aunt Lily be told. She had all the management of the Shillings estate and farms to cope with. Aunt Lily might also tell Mum, giving her extra worry with nothing she could do about it. But it was strangely good to know that she, Rose, was doing vital war work now, just as they were. And doing it well, too.

A threatened strike at the Brisbane factory had been easily solved. Like many such strikes it had not been about money at all, but the new foreman who had taken over when the man formerly holding that position was called up. Old Jonesie had thought he would be safe in the part-time Militia reserve, which was not supposed to serve outside Australia, but New Guinea had been designated 'Australian territory' and old Jonesie was up there now, bayonet in hand and being shot at.

The new foreman was a younger man, with a limp from childhood polio that had kept him from the armed forces — and sensitive about it. He'd thought that the way to manage a factory now mostly staffed by women was to strut about like a rooster while they obeyed his calls.

That could have been tolerated — every woman in these war years was used to men who thought they knew better, or who knew they didn't and had to prove otherwise. But the foreman's new demand that toilet breaks be limited to five minutes was totally unreasonable. A bloke could dash off and 'point Percy at the porcelain' and be back at the conveyor belt in five minutes. A woman experiencing her monthlies needed to find a cubicle, shut the door, remove her overalls, unpin her pad, place it in a bag for later disposal, tie on the new one back and front, adjust her waterproof pants, then check there was no stain on the back of her skirt or overalls.

The problem had been solved with a quick vote by the workers. They'd elected one of the older women to replace the rooster — she had five kids, fourteen grandkids and infinite experience in managing them all, as well as understanding the exigencies of corned beef and conveyor belts. The young man was shifted sideways into accounting — he was obviously better with numbers than people and his prospects for promotion were higher there as well.

The new forewoman would get the full wage, too, not the half pay or less expected when a woman took 'a man's role'. Mum had enforced the rule of equal pay for equal work ever since she'd taken control after Grandpa's death — one reason Higgs Industries had been able to double production so quickly at the beginning of the war, and get the government contracts. When their competitors were struggling with lack of labour, Higgs employees were urging their sisters, mothers and aunts to work at a factory with not just good pay but excellent working conditions, before Manpower called them up to far less accommodating jobs.

It felt wonderful to have solved what could have been a major problem so swiftly, leaving everyone happy. Two years ago I was pulling on my gym slip at school and those ridiculous bloomers Old Dottie insists on, Rose thought, as a spray of seagulls hovered over the stern, hoping for rubbish, then let the wind veer them back towards the shore.

She had no regrets at all about leaving school, no wish to attend university, no need to gain qualifications. When Mum returned after the war — and there finally seemed to be an 'after the war' in sight now — she would surely agree that Rose should remain on the board, as at least deputy chairman. She and Mum should work together well — Mum had implemented some of her ideas even when she'd been small and, when she hadn't, she'd given explanations that made sense. It would be good to finally work together. It had early been decided that, subject to her and Danny's continued agreement, Rose would inherit control of

Higgs while he'd have Thuringa as well as the Shillings estates from his father. Daddy had left Rose some jewellery and shares, too, she rather thought, and even some of Shillings's land that was not entailed, though none of it mattered while her primary focus needed to be Higgs's colossal operations.

Life was — good, she decided. Yes, she was worried about Mum, but Mum had survived one war already, and probably a lot more, too. Pa was ... Rose shook her head. Pa seemed oddly happy, but every time she sat with him by the tree, drinking river peppermint tea or some bitter brew from wattle sap, she'd felt anguish lurking under the calm.

Aunt Midge had told her more about that time of Pa's life now. Aunt Midge said that Pa had recovered when he met Mum, which meant that when Mum returned — it was most definitely *when*, even if Rose had to remind herself ten times a day that *if* was not an option — Pa would get better again.

Meanwhile Danny had everything in hand at Thuringa, with Aunt Midge's help, tactfully advising how many steers to sell that month, just as Mr Pinkerton occasionally telephoned her with a suggestion or an observation he carefully did not voice when others might hear.

Danny was happy, even if guilt troubled him that he could not join in with his friends' plans to enlist. She had guessed that he'd hated the thought of joining the army. He had endured school as something that must be gone through to return to his beloved Thuringa. Thuringa seemed to love him, too. Last year's calving was up; he'd put down four trenches of silage in case of a dry winter and employed almost every teenager in Bald Hill last holidays to help stack hay.

The stockmen admired him, the land girls obeyed him — and that Rita kept giving him the glad eye, which he never seemed to notice — and Mrs Taylor thought the 'Earl of Thuringa' should have a red carpet rolled out before him over every dusty paddock, and hunted out every spare strawberry in the district and probably sacrificed her own sugar ration, too, so 'their lordship' could have his favourite jam.

And her? She'd been born for Higgs's Corned Beef, trained since she was a child for it. No life could be better.

But she would still take two days in Sydney before returning to Thuringa and the small hill of paperwork that would have grown in her absence. A holiday, the first two days she'd spent just on pleasure since Pa had left for his tree. She'd needed far less time than expected in Brisbane and this ship's captain had offered her passage down to Sydney, a two-day journey instead of waiting for a week at least for a permit to be put on the waiting list for a seat — or standing room — on the train service used almost exclusively to transport service personnel to and from northern Australia.

Officially, she was on the ship to ensure that the shipment of corned beef was safely unloaded in Sydney then loaded again for England without waiting on a pallet in the sun for twelve hours. Corned beef was hardy enough to have been an army staple for centuries, but if the cans were subjected to too much heat, moisture, even cold if shipped via the Southern Ocean to escape the Japanese submarines patrolling the rest of Australia's coastline, the cans could swell and burst so the entire shipment and all those vital calories needed to keep England fighting would be lost.

But even this was a holiday: blue waves and dappled clouds, the blue haze of gum trees far off on the shore. She had seen a pod of whales the day before. War was a holiday for whales, she supposed. These days men and ships hunted each other and left them alone.

From what she had been able to gather through her Higgs contacts, attacks by Japanese bombers and submarines were now focused on Darwin and the north of Australia, and the Coral Sea, as the United States followed up its victory at the naval Battle of Midway the year before last. The peril of the last few years along this coast had dwindled.

She turned her back to the waves. This ship should be as safe as any place on the east coast. What seventeen-year-old would not enjoy being the only woman present till the crew met 'Rosie the Riveters' on the Sydney waterfront? Her mother had left a whole drawerful of lipsticks in many shades, as well as face powder, as had darling old Aunt Lily. Easily enough to see one girl through the next few years. Her poinsettia-flowered dress — a delightful change from school uniform and business suit or farm moleskins — fluttered at her knees.

'Lady Rose?' The first mate was perhaps twenty-five, tanned and what the girls at school would call 'a dish'.

She grinned at him. 'I usually answer to Miss Higgs-Vaile, but plain Rose will do today.'

He returned the grin. She liked the way his eyes crinkled. 'You could never be plain. I hope you recognise my enormous bravery.'

Rose raised an eyebrow. 'On a cargo ship doing the Brisbane to Sydney run? I think the risk level has retreated in the past few months.'

'Talking to an aristocrat whose family owns half of Australia.'

She laughed. 'Nothing like that.'

'Your brother's an earl.'

'And I'm just a girl. I mean a woman.'

He returned the grin again, his eyes slowly travelling from her toes to her eyes. 'Very much so.'

She was used to flattery: at every school dance, from the brothers of friends at birthday parties, on picnics, from young men who thought marriage to the Higgs heir was a shortcut to becoming a managing director or a lounge lizard for life. But this was flirtation.

She liked it.

'You don't live in Sydney, do you?'

The Sydney mansion had been rented out for the duration to help with the housing shortage. 'What would you say if I told you I'm taking the train back to the family property as soon as we reach Sydney?'

He put his hand on his heart. 'I'd call it tragic.'

Should she give him Aunt Lily's long sideways and totally irresistible glance? Definitely, Rose decided. 'Maybe I'll stay a few nights at the Wentworth.' She'd already had a secretary send a telegram to book a suite.

'To put on your dancing slippers? Or for business meetings?'

'Shhh.' Rose pretended to check in all directions. 'I am actually planning to get my hair done, shop for a new dress with six months' worth of coupons, and just possibly new shoes, too.' Access to her mother's business wardrobe meant she had had no shortage of suitable garments, but she was in desperate need of some more unsuitable ones. The hotel would also give her the luxury of reading in bed as late as she liked and sleeping in then ordering room service breakfast.

'But you do have dancing slippers?'

'I do.'

'With you?'

'Of course.' Or at least, in the shops to which the hotel concierge would undoubtedly guide her that afternoon.

'A night's dancing in Sydney then? I've got a twenty-four-hour leave pass,' he added. 'The old girl has to go to Cockatoo Island to get her hull scraped.' He met her eyes and there was something there beyond flirtation. 'I reckon you must still be under twenty-one, despite the work you're doing.'

'A few years under,' she admitted.

'So we'll find a place with an orchestra and no alcohol. Sometimes they have a dance at the Anzac Buffet after their concerts.'

He was serious. And suddenly so was she. She had known enough sycophants and fortune hunters to suspect this man was asking her out despite her brother the earl and the Higgs factories and not because of them; nor was he challenged by her business reputation, the slightly terrifying Higgs-Vaile girl with good legs, a sweet smile and a mind like a samurai sword.

This man had faced danger these past three years as great as any soldier in New Guinea, but without even a glamorous uniform to compensate him. He deserved — they both deserved — an evening of frivolity. She also wanted to know more about him, much more. She liked his eyes, his hands, his smell of soap and salt and something on his hair ...

'The Anzac Buffet sounds good,' she said slowly. Some of her school friends' mothers volunteered there.

'Your parents won't object if you stay in Sydney?'

She could not tell him that her mother was doing something top secret in England, and that her father was living in a tree back at Thuringa. She changed the subject quickly. 'What will you do after the war?'

'Build boats, not sail them.' The answer came immediately. 'Racing yachts — not for me, for others. I'm interested in the engineering side. Some of the local craft I've seen up north have given me ideas for new hull designs. There are new materials to try, too.'

'Like aluminium? But aluminium corrodes in seawater, though it's light and useful in superstructures.' Rose shook her head. 'And aluminium–magnesium alloys are expensive.'

He looked at her with even more interest. 'It might be possible to reduce the amount of magnesium — maybe even have an alloy with something like silica. How do you know so much about aluminium and ships?'

'Corned beef gets shipped in cans.' Rose grinned. 'If you can design an aluminium ship it won't need as much fuel and wouldn't attract magnetic detonators on sea mines. An aluminium can would not just be lighter but cheaper than steel and the coating needed so it doesn't spill the contents. And imagine the market if we could sell soft drinks in cans — soft drinks are far too corrosive for steel, except if they have very heavy coatings.'

'I don't think I need ask what you intend doing after the war then.'

Rose grinned again. 'I might be taking a couple of days hookey but I love the business. I'm like my grandfather — he saw canning as a way of getting good food to ordinary people before it spoiled. Higgs cans other foods too, though most of our production now is for the armed forces. But there are going to be so many opportunities after the war.' She was making a speech, she realised, but he didn't seem to mind. In fact he seemed fascinated.

'Imagine a whole grocery shop filled with cans,' she continued. 'Housewives could just take the cans they wanted off the shelf, without asking for them over the counter. No more cutting and weighing, no spoilage in the heat, or far less anyway. All a working woman need do to get her family's dinner would be open a can of Irish stew and then a can of peaches and a can of cream.' She laughed, glancing at the spray, the deep blue sea and sky. 'The one good thing about this war is that it's spared me all the years I might have spent studying Latin and piano lessons at school, and given me the work I love, instead.'

He raised an eyebrow. 'Which makes you ...?'

She flushed. 'Seventeen.' She put up her chin. 'But if I can run a board meeting I can go dancing with you.'

'At seventeen? Better make it only with me. You're safe with me.' He was joking but he was also serious.

'You could take me to the zoo, pat me on the head and buy me an ice cream if you'd rather.'

'Dancing, definitely. Can you jitterbug?'

'No.'

He grinned. 'You'll be able to after a night out with me. But after that you'd better introduce me to your parents, in case they worry.'

How could she tell him that neither parent was able to inspect him? Though Aunt Midge had a keen eye for men, as well as sheep.

'Come to Thuringa then next time you have leave — it only takes a day or so from Sydney. I'll take you to meet Aunt Midge. She was one of the first women judges at the Royal Easter Show. There's not much gets past Aunt Midge.'

'Not your parents then?'

He didn't miss much. 'My mother's doing war work. My father's had a breakdown. Shell shock from the last war. Pa lives in a hollow tree on the property,' she added baldly.

He didn't laugh, or even look incredulous. 'You poor kid,' he said quietly.

'I'm fine. I manage Higgs Industries, and Danny — he's my twin — manages Thuringa.'

'The earl?'

'I wouldn't call him that when you first meet him,' she said drily. 'He had a bit too much teasing at school.' Danny was also worried about what would be expected of him after the war at Shillings, though, hopefully, Aunt Lily would stay in command there.

'What do *your* parents do?' Rose decided to move the conversation along.

'Dad died when I was five years old — gassed in the last war. Mum taught sewing at various tech colleges to keep the wolf from the door, but she's managing a woollens factory now.'

'She sounds admirable.'

'She is.' He met her eyes. 'I learned very young not to underestimate a woman, Miss Higgs-Vaile.'

'My name is Rose.'

He smiled. 'If I told you why I thought that was the perfect name for you I'd be guilty of Sentimental Twaddle Aboard a Merchant Navy Vessel. It can wait till Sydney.' He glanced at his watch. 'I'd better go. I'll see you at dinner at the captain's table, Lady Rose Vaile. Ask him about the time —'

She did not hear the noise, but remembered it. The next sound she heard was his voice again. 'Rose? Rose! Breathe, damn it!'

She breathed, spluttered, wondered why she was flying, sleeping, drowning, realised she was doing none of those, but being pulled expertly through waves and debris, held under the chin with an expertise of which Miss Morrison, the games mistress, would have thoroughly approved.

'I'm breathing,' she managed. She tried to turn, to swim herself, but one arm would not work and the light faded into pain when she tried to move it.

A man yelled nearby, 'Get the girly! Have you got her yet? Have you got her?'

'She's safe here. Hold on, we've nearly reached you.'

Of course I'm safe, she thought vaguely. He said he wanted to meet her parents. He'd always look after her. But why were they in the ocean?

Something bumped against them. It looked like part of the deck they'd been standing on.

'Well done, man! Pass her up here. Lads, we've got the girly!'

Light returned as hands dragged her from the ocean, hurting her arm even more.

'Here she is. Have you got hold of her?'

'Aye, we have her!' called someone else.

'Thank God,' said the familiar voice, somewhere in the water, and then was silent, though she listened, kept listening as she lay panting in the bottom of the dinghy.

Men helped her to sit up. Seven of them shared the dinghy, one with half his face burned away, who sat hunched yet somehow conscious, not even screaming. Blood spread everywhere, but the wrong colour blood, mixed with oil and seawater. She found her arm was bleeding too, her face as well perhaps, though that might be water dropping from her hair.

But she could breathe and sit. The bleeding wasn't very much and stopped entirely when she pressed it. She glanced around, looking for her companion, but couldn't see him. Yet he must be here, because she'd heard his voice as she was hoisted up to safety.

Where was he?

She gazed about her desperately. Bodies. Fragments of bodies. Two men alive, at least, one clutching a floating table. Cans of corned beef, ruptured. She suppressed a hysterical giggle, imagining ordering the men to pick them up.

And then she saw him, clinging to the side of the dinghy, one of three men swimming, but using the boat to help them stay afloat. She managed to say, 'Help him up ...' and saw him shake his head.

'No room. We're only two miles off shore. We'll make it, love.'

And someone must have heard the explosion or perhaps there had been time to send an SOS. When she saw the shape emerge in front of them, the water parting as it rose, she thought it might have come to their rescue, then realised, dazedly, that no, this must be the submarine that had torpedoed their ship.

The hatch opened. Even then she thought the sailors would offer help, till she saw the machine guns in their hands. This time she did hear the noise, was sure she could see the lash of bullets even before she felt the pain, felt the blackness take her once again, refused to let it, and looked down.

His face gazed up at her from the water, his eyes meeting hers even as blood trickled from his mouth. All she could see was blood.

She didn't know his name.

Chapter 40

Parsley, Sage, Rosemary and Thyme Stuffing
for a Shoulder of Lamb

Combine:
1 cup stale breadcrumbs
1 tablespoon fresh thyme
2 sage leaves, chopped
1 chopped onion, sautéed till transparent in 3 tablespoons of butter
  or dripping
1 egg
1 tablespoon fresh parsley, chopped
1 teaspoon fresh rosemary, chopped
Juice of a lemon

*Mix. Cut a long, deep slice next to the bone of a shoulder of
lamb or mutton (mutton or 'two tooth' makes a better roast as it
has more flavour). Insert the stuffing. Roast the lamb very, very
slowly on low heat for at least four hours, with potatoes, pumpkin,
parsnips and carrots around it for the last two hours.*

  *The pumpkin is necessary as its charred remnants will add
sweetness and flavour to the gravy.*

  Bald Hill Progress Association Cookbook, 1944 edition:
  a shilling a copy, all funds for the war effort

DANNY

He was helping old Carmichael choose the steers destined for the
factory when the phone call came. Mrs Taylor trudged across

the paddock, wiping dust and sweat from her forehead, as well as a small halo of flies. 'Long distance, from Sydney, He wished Mrs Taylor would stop calling him Master Danny. Master Danny, a woman. Said they'd call back.'

He wondered who it was. Mrs Taylor would have recognised Mum's voice if by some miracle she'd returned, or Rose's of course. It was probably something to do with Higgs Industries. Rose would take care of it. He was hopeless at all that stuff.

'I can manage the rest of them, Danny boy.' Carmichael had a son in the Middle East, another missing last heard of in Malaya. His youngest had embarked for New Guinea two months back.

Danny nodded. He fell into step with Mrs Taylor, over tussocks, skirting cowpats. 'Got a nice stuffed shoulder of mutton in the oven for your dinner,' she said chattily. 'You can take the rest of it over to your dad to eat tomorrow. A good stuffed shoulder is even better cold than hot. There's a jar of green tomato pickle, too, and I made apple turnovers for him as well.'

'Thank you, Mrs Taylor.'

'We all do our bit,' said Mrs Taylor. 'Do you mind if I serve dinner early? It's CWA tonight and —'

'Please, just leave it in the oven. I can dish it out.' He smiled at her. 'And do the washing up.'

'You're a love. I'll make the gravy before I go and drop your dad's off to him on the way into town.' The car had been converted to a wood burner now, which meant less reliance on precious petrol coupons — even the farm's generous allowance was strained these days.

'Thank you.' He never knew what to say to Pa. That calm smiling presence seemed to think it was his job to reassure Danny, not the other way around, despite Pa's illness. He'd show him the shape of a sapling leaf, or urge him to hear the song of the stars in their vast traverse across the night. He'd never address the real problem, just smile and say, 'Just a few more days, mate.' It was even more disconcerting to find that sometimes, sitting with Pa, for a few seconds it was almost as if the universe was an orchestra, and he could hear its symphony, and that often he did walk back to the homestead calmer and more confident, even if still desperately worried about his parents.

Today he'd walk over to Pa's after dinner, and they'd sit together in the dusk, the gum leaves turning purple, the land growing new colours, as if the sun leached out all the subtleties by day. The shadow land, when the moon rose in an almost blue sky, the day birds were singing their final melodies and owls and crickets were just beginning theirs. They would talk of those, because Danny could not find the words that were truly needed, the ones that would bring Pa home.

He opened the gate that led from the house paddock to the garden, finding himself smiling, glad once again that school, cadets and the spectre of the Militia were behind him. You could never talk of things like dusk to other young men, much less sit in the darkness and watch the moon and know the stars went on forever, undisturbed by battles here on earth. But he felt no guilt now, because he had shown that his presence here really had made a difference to Thuringa's war effort.

The house was blessedly cool, and even more blessedly fly free once he'd brushed off the hundred or so clinging to his shirt before entering the hall from the back verandah, leaving his boots by the door, too. He sat by the phone, waiting for the operator to call back. At last it jangled.

'Yes, Danny Higgs-Vaile speaking. No, I'm sorry, neither of my parents is available. No, I don't have a contact phone number for either of them. They will be away for some time. Who is speaking, please? May I help you?'

He listened to the tinny voice that seemed much further away than Sydney. Another reality entirely. He managed to ask a question, then another. At last he said, 'Please say I'll be there. Yes, I understand entirely. I won't be able to reach Sydney till tomorrow morning, but I'll be there as soon as I can.'

'Do you want another three minutes?' asked the Sydney operator.

The tin voice denied any such wish. But Danny held the receiver for minutes after the phone fell silent.

He knew two things: his life had vanished. And he could not stand it.

Could not cope with any of it: Mum vanished, Pa living in a tree and Rose ...

Rose dying, dead perhaps before he could get there, even if he drove all night. But he had to at least tell Pa before he left, for surely a man should see his dying daughter, if he could make Pa understand he had to leave the river and its long slow silence and come to Sydney.

'Daughter'. Danny could not think of 'Rose'. He dared not think of his sister's body broken. What was she doing on a ship anyway? he thought angrily. She should never have been on a ship!

It had always been the two of them. Perhaps it was the twin thing, but he thought it was more likely that their closeness was from being so different and each taking up a separate share of the world's space, and their parents' lives. Even at five years old, playing in the sandpit, Rose had been delivering freight cars to her sandcastles.

He had to stand up. He had to pack a bag for himself, and one for Rose, and one for Pa, too, in case Pa somehow swam into the present and agreed to come. He must ask Mrs Taylor for a hamper and tell her that her trip into town must be curtailed and the news about Rose. Rose hurt, Rose in pain, Rose dying ...

He could not stand it.

'Mr Higgs-Vaile?'

He looked up. For a moment he could not see her face, just the gold light behind her, then it was Annie, moving quietly on socked feet towards him, her boots — and flies — left on the verandah, too. She never called him Lord Danny, either seriously or mockingly. Her face had nothing but quiet sympathy as she said, 'I'm sorry. I didn't mean to overhear. I just came in for the bathroom ...'

Suddenly he sank onto the floor. A sob erupted, then another.

'Danny!' She kneeled beside him.

'It's Rose. She's hurt. Dying. And Mum has gone and Dad is in a tree and I can't do this alone! None of it. I'm no good at it. It's all too much and —'

'Shhh, love, shhh. You're doing a splendid job. Everyone admires how you've taken charge. Shhh now, it will be all right ...' Her arms were round him. He leaned on her, breathed in the perfume of fresh sweat, shampoo, and girl and a small hint of horse. He cried, cried for it all, held her tightly to keep her close ...

He sat back at last. 'I'm sorry.'

'Don't be. We all need someone, sometimes. I'm glad it was me.'

Why had he never really noticed her before, just Rita and her staring breasts? Perhaps because Rita talked so much that Annie couldn't.

'I need to send a telegram to my mother and Aunt Lily. And ... and ... tell my father about Rose.'

'Would you like me to come with you?'

'To see Pa? Or to Sydney?'

'Either or both. I've got my driver's licence, and I know the roads.'

'Are you sure?' Because he didn't want to do the long drive alone, or even alone with Pa, if he could persuade him to come, and Aunt Midge was an hour away and might be another hour's ride beyond the homestead, and he didn't have hours to spare, and Dr Patrick would be needed at the clinic. 'If Pa agrees to come he ... he might change his mind halfway. It might be ... difficult.'

'I'm going to be a doctor. Difficult will be my job. I can stay with my grandma in Sydney,' she added.

She held out her hand. He took it. He was no longer alone.

Chapter 41

Pumpkin Fruitcake

(Can be made without eggs, butter or sugar.)

¼ cup butter (optional)

1 cup brown sugar (optional)

2 eggs (optional)

1 cup mashed pumpkin

2 teaspoons vanilla essence (optional) or 2 tablespoons finely grated
orange zest

2 cups sultanas, or mixed fruit

2 cups self-raising flour

Grease and flour a large cake tin.

Cream butter and sugar; add eggs one by one; then pumpkin,
vanilla and fruit, then the flour.

The mixture should be quite moist, but if it seems too dry
(which it may be if the pumpkin is dryish) then add a little milk or
water or orange juice.

Pour the mix into the tin; bake in a medium oven for one hour
or till it's brown on top and a skewer comes out clean.

This cake is rich, moist, a wonderful deep golden colour and
very, very good. Smaller cakes can also be made in old tin cans if
you do not have a cake tin. Cut out the top and bottom of the can
and rest it on a tray to make removing the cake easier and reduce
the cooking time. The cake should spring back if you press it with
your fingers.

Bald Hill *Progress Association Cookbook*, 1944 edition,
contributed by Mrs Harry Harrison (Midge)

Daniel pulled the damper from the ashes, expertly dusted it and broke off a crust, just as a man called John had once done. It steamed gently. He felt strangely close to the man named John at times like this. He was not John, of course, but Daniel Greenman, here for a holiday, which had been exactly the right thing to do. Just a few more days of hearing the soft rustle of red gum bark in the breeze, and he would be able to face ...

... the things he had no need to remember here.

He dipped the hunk of damper into the billy of stew, made from a mutton chop Midge had given him that morning on her way in to the CWA cake stall, along with potatoes and carrots from their garden. He'd picked the native spinach himself. The best possible lunch ...

He looked up at the sound of a car. Danny emerged. Daniel looked at him with concern. His son seemed distressed. He had seemed so much happier lately. Mostly the two of them just sat together, gazing at the clouds or a wombat mooching out in the twilight. Danny always seemed more ... settled ... after they had watched together for a time.

Daniel watched as the son held the door open for a girl with soft-looking brown hair and a cotton frock over bare brown legs. He felt he had met her, but would need to delve into the darkness of memory to find where. In a few days perhaps.

Danny stepped towards him. 'Pa?' His voice had more uncertainty than Daniel had ever heard. The girl took his hand.

Daniel smiled at his son reassuringly. 'Would you like some stew? Or damper? It's fresh made.' He pulled off hunks for each of them.

The girl took it, nibbled. 'It's very good,' she said gently.

'Pa,' said the young man again, and there was a note of anguish now, as if he had no words. Daniel knew what it was like to be in torment that words could not express. The girl quickly put a hand on Danny's arm.

'Dr Greenman,' she said. Daniel lost his smile at the use of his name. He could be 'Pa' but Dr Greenman was still impossible, because that ...

... it simply couldn't be.

But the girl was still speaking. 'Rose has been badly hurt. She's possibly dying. She's in hospital in Sydney. She needs her father. Danny shouldn't be alone either. Please, will you come with us?'

Daniel sat very still. He had managed to keep John at bay, here in the tree dapples. He did not know if he could manage it in the clangs and yells of Sydney. Even the smell of a hospital ... He had become a psychiatrist because that did not involve blood. But war had demanded surgeons ... sawn-off bone, the pile of limbs with flies buzzing, always flies, the constant scream of men and guns ...

Rose. Dying! Danny.

He could not be Dr Greenman. But he was 'Pa'. If his children needed him he could do anything. Would do anything, even if he was not sure how.

He should say something. Do something. But all he could think of was, 'I'll put out the fire. Here.' He handed the girl the damper. 'There's golden syrup in that tin. Sweet things are good for shock. Good with damper too. You both better have some before we go.' It was not enough, not the right words at all. But that was why he was here, because he could no longer manage what was proper, except in the vast simplicity of the bush.

He quickly covered the coals with soil and turned. His son was standing there, crying. Daniel took a step towards him. It felt right. He took another. He reached for Danny, and held him close. He felt his son's warmth, his pain, his strength. When had Danny grown so tall?

For a moment Danny didn't move.

Then suddenly his arms were round his father, too, and Daniel realised that his own eyes held tears, too. He was Dr Daniel Greenman, whose shoulders could carry pain again, his own and others'. He would always be Dr Greenman now, not just because his son and daughter needed him, but because they were part of him, and so he could be strong.

Chapter 42

What is love? An exchange of obligations? Or the highest form of empathy, where you care more for another than you do for yourself. Once you love, you become more capable of love. It is one of the most contagious of emotions, running between families and friends and those who love the world, but so much less recognised than the other contagious emotions of fear, resentment and hate.

Miss Lily, 1938

ROSE

It hurt.

She did not know what hurt. Possibly it was easier to work out what did not hurt. Possibly it was best not to think at all.

She could remember water. She remembered a man, an incredible man, but she did not know his name. A man who had been shot in front of her, there in the water, his blood staining the water, a man whose eyes held hers, despite his pain, as if willing her to live. And so she had lived.

But she couldn't see that man now. She had been scared then, but she was not scared now. Water was gentle, and pain was not. When she tried to open her eyes the light was too bright. When her eyes were closed she could see a soft silver light and that was best of all. If she just let the water carry her, there would be no pain at all ...

'My name is Paul, sir.'

She knew the voice. For the first time she reached for thought. It was *that* voice and now she had a name and he was not in the water, and neither was he dead.

She managed to open her eyes for a fraction of a second, and saw him sitting by her bed, in striped pyjamas, one leg in plaster, a bandage across his chest and over his shoulder, a pad strapped to the side of his neck. Their eyes met.

The light still hurt, but she could feel him close. She didn't want the water to take her now.

'Sir, her eyes just opened. Only briefly, but I'm sure they did. Nurse, would you mind fetching her brother? No, I am not going anywhere till Miss Higgs-Vaile is conscious. Rose? Rose, can you hear me?'

Footsteps. Rose didn't need to listen to footsteps. The sea washed back again, the tide carrying her out towards the sun, leaving the crash of life and waves behind. Another voice, a nurse's.

'... you should really follow doctor's orders and —'

'I am not under your command, nor his, nor anyone's except my captain's and he's not here. Miss Higgs-Vaile is my fiancée and I have every right to be here.'

'And I am her father.' A new voice. It held love, and protectiveness too.

Rose opened her eyes, and he was there, truly with her, and not on holiday in any way. 'Pa?' she whispered.

'Yes, darling. Pa's here.'

'Pa,' she said again, then tried the name. 'Paul?'

'Here, love. Danny will be back in a moment.' Paul took her hand. She managed to squeeze his fingers, felt her father take her other hand.

She could sleep now, she decided. And definitely not float away. Because when she woke they would be here, both of them, and Danny too. Her brother and her father and ... and ...

Paul.

Chapter 43

Bavarian Pretzels

1 teaspoon dry yeast or 1 cup dough from yesterday's baking
⅓ cup warm water
A pinch of salt
4½ cups flour
2 tablespoons bicarbonate of soda
More water

Heat oven to a medium temperature.

*Dissolve yeast in ⅛ cup warm water. Stir in remaining warm
water, salt and flour, and leave for an hour or till it bubbles, or
mix the flour and water with yesterday's dough. Knead the dough
until smooth and elastic, then leave to rise under a damp towel in
a warm place till it doubles in size. Remove a cup of dough for
tomorrow's baking.*

*Half fill a pan with water, and add the bicarbonate of soda.
Simmer.*

*Cut the dough into ten pieces. Roll each into a long snake
shape with your fingers, with the middle a little thicker. Pick up
the ends and bend them to the middle till they look like rabbit ears,
then pull the ends back to make a loop. This sounds impossible,
but if you have a picture of a pretzel in front of you, you will see
how it should go. Otherwise make whatever shape you like. Leave
to rise in a warm place till doubled in size. Place pretzels one at
a time in the water, leave for 20 seconds, then push each pretzel
under the water. Use a slotted spoon to remove the pretzel and place
it on a greased baking tray. Make a slit in the thickest part of the
pretzel and scatter on coarse salt. Repeat till all are done. Bake for*

15 to 20 minutes till the pretzels are gold to dark brown on top.
Eat with sweet mustard.

JULY 1944

SOPHIE

July roses, such luxurious abundance, planted in the '20s when Hannelore's factories had made her wealthy once again, with Dolphie's new wife's inheritance to play with as well. A glory of roses, even though they had not been pruned since the beginning of the war, whites and pinks and reds, a scent that followed Sophie around the gardens. The hothouse cucumbers were ready and the strawberries. Her second summer of German strawberries, raspberries ...

It would be winter in Australia. The river would have that strange not-quite-brown of cold water. There'd be quilts on the beds and a fire at night in the library, Rose and Danny in their winter uniforms, their last year at school.

Where would life take her children from here? Where were the Australian armies fighting now? Was Danny still destined for New Guinea jungles, trying to stop the unstoppable march of Japanese forces? Would Rose join the Red Cross, or even the army too? Sophie had worried all their lives, with vague motherly concern: would they break a shoulder riding a bicycle, a horse, be bitten by a snake on a picnic, be snagged by a sunken branch while swimming in the river? Polio, measles, chickenpox, whooping cough, tuberculosis, quinsy, the memory of the bullies who'd claimed they smelled corned beef in her brief time at school as they walked hand in hand through Bald Hill Central's gates, then later took the train together to their respective boarding schools.

There'd been no bullies, or Rose and Danny had faced them down, and anyway corned beef was quite respectable now, especially coupled with their titles, which they bore so lightly that those who might have mocked them never tried it more than once.

They'd whooped, and had the measles and the other common childhood ailments, from nits to ringworm, but only needing plates of mashed banana sprinkled with brown sugar, or grated apple and a glass of lemonade, coupled with a few new books to read. She had never imagined this greatest torment of any parenthood: a time when there was nothing she could do ...

She peered out of the glasshouse at the first sound of an engine, the basket of raspberries in her hand. At first she thought the noise was just another distant aircraft, for it had been so long since she had heard a car. The black vehicle rumbled up the driveway and parked around the back, near the servants' courtyard, not out the front, so it was only when she ran to meet it that she knew for certain it was Dolphie.

Hannelore emerged. Grünberg and Simons peered from the kitchen windows.

'Dolphie?' began Hannelore, as he opened the driver's door and stepped out, boots gleaming. He almost seemed to glow in the afternoon sunlight. He gazed around, as if drinking in the garden's beauty, then smiled and kissed Hannelore's forehead. 'It is over,' he said simply.

The sun danced, the birds became an orchestra. Even the air turned gold. The war was over! Or nearly so. Finally, incredibly. 'Hitler is dead?' Sophie managed.

Dolphie turned to her, still with that serene smile. 'No. The plot failed. The bomb exploded but he survived. I am associated with the plotters. They know us, now.' Dolphie looked at Hannelore, then Sophie, then back to Hannelore. 'We have all been given a choice,' he added calmly. 'To be arrested and executed, or take our own lives. I chose the latter.'

Sophie stared at him in horror, and a burning anguish, for him, herself and for the world. 'Dolphie! It ... it can't be true.'

'Of course it can be true,' said Hannelore gently. 'So many have tried to kill the Führer, for nearly twenty years. Liebe Sophie, I'm sorry your hopes were carried by a three-legged horse. But any plot had only a slim chance. You did not realise?'

Sophie shook her head numbly. She had assumed ... James had told her ... Bob had told her ... not, they had not said a plot would succeed. They had spoken of a chance, 'any slim chance'. She was the one who had dreamed that war could end so easily, with the death of just one man.

'The condemned man ate a good lunch, and dinner too. I have until midnight. In return for dying neatly and with no publicity they have agreed my family will not be harmed, nor my possessions confiscated.' Dolphie shrugged. 'It would be embarrassing to have too many prominent officers like Field Marshal Rommel on trial or executed as enemies of the Reich.'

Sophie stood motionless, still trying to absorb this new view of the world. Field Marshal Rommel, the famous 'Desert Fox', and Germany's greatest hero, had been one of the plotters too? The rebellion then had reached the highest possible level of German military — and had still failed.

Dolphie moved towards the kitchen door. Hannelore laid her hand on his arm. 'We have a choice. Escape.'

'To where?'

'To Switzerland. If we leave now ...'

He looked at her patiently. 'The roads from the Lodge will be watched.'

'We can row across the lake.'

He gestured. Sophie saw a flash that might be binoculars. 'This is the new Germany, my niece. One does not even meet death without informers checking all is as the Führer wants. Besides, when Germany loses the war — and I think we will certainly lose it now — I will be a war criminal, executed by the victors, or, at the least, imprisoned all my life.' He smiled. 'Hanneleine, my darling, come inside.'

Sophie had never heard him use the diminutive before. Here was a man who knew he had only hours of life, and he would drink each second in.

He had till midnight. Whatever would happen to her and Hannelore after that — and without Dolphie's oversight they might just possibly escape — this time must be for him. She suddenly wished she was wearing silk, not the old cotton dress perfect for weeding the onions. Her hands smelled of onions too. They must dress for dinner tonight ...

Yet Hitler was alive, would stay alive most probably, till the war's end. Dolphie must spare them some seconds to prepare. 'Dolphie,' she said urgently. 'What is happening? Please? We hear nothing!'

'Germany is slowly losing. Quite slowly, so with the Führer gone we still might have negotiated good terms. But now?' Dolphie shrugged. 'It will be up to the victors to dispose of us again. I hope the English, Russians and Americans have more sense than to let France overrule them this time, so revenge does not lead us to yet another false peace and then to yet another war. But it is almost a relief to know I will not be there to fight for justice.'

'Australia?' Sophie asked tightly.

'Ah, your country is still facing our brave non-Aryan allies, the Japanese, who are starving, and who dare not tell their generals they are losing, and the generals dare not tell their emperor. I think the Japanese will fight till the second-last man. Once there is no one to inform on the last man, he may surrender too. The Americans have taken over Australia now, instead. It is a most convenient base for their Pacific war, which you and they are winning. The Japanese are losing far more slowly than we are, because there is much territory for the Allies to reconquer and many islands before they reach Japan, and then the fighting will be savage as the Japanese battle for their homeland. But your country is safe.'

But not for those who fight, she thought. And not for those who wait and those who mourn. Please, let the pigeon have arrived ...

'Whose army will reach here first?' asked Hannelore tightly.

At first Sophie didn't understand, then she remembered. The Russians had raped and killed civilians in revenge at the end of the last war. Hannelore had been tortured. Now they might both be in the path of the Soviet forces.

'I don't know.' For the first time Dolphie spoke seriously. 'Nor do I know when. We need to make you a hiding place, down in the cellars, to be safe from bombs or mortar fire, too. The cellars will be looted, but if we pull shelves across the door to the smaller wine cellar and pile sacks against the wall where the shelves once stood, you and the servants should be safe for days, even weeks, if you stock it well. You must put your jewellery down there too, your identity papers, any small things of value.'

'I've been thinking the same thing,' said Hannelore quietly. 'But I didn't ...'

You didn't want to prepare to lose a war, for that would betray your uncle's hopes, thought Sophie. But now we have no choice.

'We will do it now,' Dolphie announced, as cheerily as if he planned a skiing trip, 'and then we will choose the best of wines for lunch, and dinner. Tell the kitchen! Kill the fatted calf!'

Hannelore managed a laugh. 'We do not have a calf. But there are young roosters, and we have champagne.'

'Young roosters for an old rooster who has fallen from his perch. Perfect, my Hanneleine. But not the decadent French wine. We need schnapps! There are still two bottles in the cellar. Sophie knows nothing about schnapps. We must teach her!'

He put his arm about Hannelore's shoulders as they walked towards the house.

Sophie looked at the man talking with such gaiety as he and Hannelore crossed the courtyard. He might have helped her get a message to her loved ones, and he had not. He could have helped her escape, and Hannelore too, and he had not. It was too late for him to help her now. For a moment she felt like beating her fists against his back.

But she was here, not ashes in a French field. Dolphie had saved her, and she was sure it had not just been because her presence might be useful. Despite it all Sophie could not hate him, this man whose gentle hands had cared for her with more compassion than necessary. She did not know what she felt for him just now, but it was not hate.

Her friend still had this one day with her uncle. She followed them inside.

Luncheon was perfect, Miss Lily perfect, with two graduates to guide it and an ex-chemist in the kitchen to furnish the table, and two roosters sacrificed. One would become a coq au vin for dinner — decadent French Bordeaux, it seemed, could be used for that, even though it was not the elderly rooster required for true flavour — the elderly roosters had been eaten long ago.

There had been little time to create a perfect luncheon, but Grünberg had done wonders: a mushroom consommé, truite au bleu, a quick fricassee of rooster breast, leaving the tougher parts and bones to simmer for tonight, a red fruit pudding with blackcurrants and redcurrants, raspberries, strawberries and cherries cooked quickly in juice, with a little cornflour to thicken it, the almond cream to replace the dairy the farm no longer supplied. The schnapps was ...

Sophie sipped the clear liquid cautiously. Its sharpness seemed to heat her entire body, then suddenly she tasted them, smelled them, from plum blossom to heavy ripe fruit. 'You are right. It's quite magic!'

'Naturally. It is the soil and sunlight of my country! Now taste this, and feel the difference.'

'Cherry?'

Dolphie poured himself more from the first bottle. 'A little softer than the plum, but less fruit scent. The last liquid to be distilled has the most fruit flavour, but it is milky and too low in alcohol to keep. Here, try the plum again.'

The schnapps was heady, the lunch rich in laughter and memories, as Sophie learned more about Hannelore and her uncle than she ever had: two children escaping from Nanny and her birch stick to gaze at the parents they seldom met, much less ever played with; the first time Hannelore curtseyed in a long frock to her father, as a four-year-old, and tripped, and Nanny's stick emerged again for a beating as soon as they were back in the nursery, and somehow in the telling and with the schnapps, it was truly hilarious.

It was the schnapps, possibly, that lowered her defences far enough to ask a question she had puzzled about for over twenty years and would never know the answer to unless she asked it now. 'Dolphie, when we met, back in the last war.'

'You mean when you shot me, liebe Sophie?' he asked cheerfully.

'Yes. Were you going to stop chlorine gas being used? Or were you there to observe its effects?'

'Both.' He looked at her steadily. 'The latter was my official purpose.'

'Dolphie gave me the co-ordinates and date to give to you to pass on to Miss Lily, so your soldiers might be protected from its horror,' said Hannelore soberly. 'Did you ever doubt?'

'Yes,' said Sophie as Dolphie said wryly, 'Obviously.'

'And I'm sorry I doubted,' Sophie added.

He poured himself more schnapps. 'Don't be. I think that day was the last of my innocence, thinking that people of goodwill on either side might work together to stop a war, or even its worst punishments. Too many people are in love with war for wars to end. Too many love the riches they may make, too many crave adventure and, even when they see its pain and loss, they do not walk away. When one person feels pain, they crave to make others feel their pain as well. Why does war continue now, despite its horrors? Because men keep on fighting.'

For a moment Sophie could smell the mud and blood, the stench of rotting flesh and faeces mixed with disinfectant, the never-forgotten smell of the last war's trenches. I have been at war for five years, she thought, and yet I have seen no fighting. The only bullets I have seen were fired at me.

But had she, too, subconsciously longed for adventure when she stepped into George's plane so unquestioningly? It had been easy to say that love and duty had carried her across the world, and yet she had left both of those behind her.

I will never leave again, she promised fate. Just take me home, and keep all who I love safe, and I will be fulfilled.

'The last war showed us what happens to those who lose,' said Hannelore, bringing her back to the present.

'And yet you worked for Britain,' said Sophie.

'No. I gave information that might defeat the Nazis and save my country. When Germany loses this war the Nazis will be swept away.' Hannelore looked at Sophie earnestly. 'Liebe Sophie, there was good in the Party once, and good people joined it, too. People who cared about the poor, who labour in the factories, the children who were starving — so much was good.'

'It was always evil,' said Sophie flatly. 'The nonsense of a master race, the anti-Semitism, a philosophy that says kill or imprison all who disagree with you.'

'Sophie,' said Hannelore gently. 'This is our only day.' She looked at Dolphie. 'What shall we do?'

'I wish a last waltz with Sophie. May I have that?'

Sophie managed to smile at him. 'Of course! I will be seventeen again, in the most ravishing white silk dress, and you the most handsome, charming man I have ever met.'

'And while we dance we can believe we have our whole lives ahead of us. Put a record on the gramophone and we will dance. But not alone — Hanneleine, call a woman from the kitchen and dance with her. I want to see you dance!'

They danced. It was strange to feel a man's hand in hers again, his other decorously on her back. Last time she and Dolphie had danced it was moonlight and love, and the dance had been a prelude to what might have been a shared lifetime.

Now it was an ending, yet Hannelore laughed as Grünberg whirled her around the room. A chemist could also be a most excellent dancer indeed, almost as good as a German count. At the end Grünberg bowed and her face seemed to glow with unaccustomed pleasure, too. 'I must attend to dinner, if you wish to eat.'

'Of course we wish to eat!' Hannelore looked flushed, and happy, and possibly only Sophie saw the tremble of her fingers.

'I will go down to the cellar and find the best, the very best champagne, too. I want it even if it is decadent. Dolphie, will you come with me?'

Dolphie glanced at his watch, an unwelcome reminder of the passing of the day, then picked up the bottle of plum schnapps, still with a half-inch of liquid. 'No. I will go out to the lake and drink a toast to my swans, and tell them they have been most clever not to have been eaten. And then Sophie will put on a silk dress, perhaps, and we will dance again?'

He stepped towards Sophie and gave her a chaste kiss on the forehead. 'You will care for Hannelore,' he said quietly, as Grünberg slipped back to the kitchen and Hannelore followed her down the corridor towards the cellar door. 'Not just now, but after the war, too?'

'I will. But her service to England will protect her, too.'

'Make sure she lives till then.' He lifted her hand, kissed it, clicking his heels formally. 'I have loved you,' he said casually. 'I loved Miss Sophie Higgs, I loved the Countess of Shillings, and I love Mrs Daniel Greenman. I have loved what might have been, as well.'

He smiled at her, still with a strange radiance that had not come from alcohol, though perhaps the schnapps had added to it. 'I do not expect you to say that you love me. You have become most rich in love, my Sophie, since our first dance before the war. So many people love you. I have only truly had Hannelore. She loves us both, like the brother and the sister she always longed for.'

'I love her, too. Dolphie ...' She had never quite known what she felt for him, much less what to say now. Then suddenly she did. 'I have loved you, too, always. But never all of you, except in the might have been, and so I could not marry you. I loved Nigel totally and fully. I love Daniel deeply and absolutely and long for him each hour. But you have always lingered in my mind and heart, and with love, too.'

She lifted his hand, and kissed it. 'There. I repay your perfect German manners with Australian vulgarity. Dolphie, Hannelore is my sister. We lost each other, for a while, but we shall not lose each other again.'

'That is good. And now I will lift my eyes up to the hills and ignore the flash of binoculars and simply see the beauty. If I must die I am glad it is midsummer, when my land is clothed in green and the plums are ripening, and others will make schnapps from them when finally peace is come. But I will have my own peace now. I wonder if the swans will sing for me?'

He smiled at her again, still drinking in every moment of the day. Sophie blew a kiss to him as she left the room to change and felt no betrayal of Daniel, for this was a few seconds and a love of a very different kind, mixed with so much that was not love at all.

She had reached the top of the stairs before she realised what Dolphie meant by hoping that the swans would sing. Swansong! How could she have been so stupid? She ran down and out the door, then heard the shot and knew it was too late.

There would be no last dinner, and no tears either. Dolphie had last seen his beloved niece laughing. His final moment had been with the land he loved. Perhaps no woman could compete with her.

And there he was, slumped on the grass, the hole in his forehead surprisingly neat, with only the smallest trickles of blood. For a strange moment Sophie imagined she saw the land reach up to cradle him. The image vanished. She began to run towards his body, then stopped as another black car drove over the rise, followed by a second and a third.

Had the watchers been waiting for the shot? She remembered Dolphie checking his watch. Of course he had not been given till midnight — how inconvenient to collect a body at midnight. She was suddenly sure he had been given until three pm.

And he had lived it perfectly.

She slipped back into the kitchen as soldiers hauled Dolphie's body to the second car. Hannelore had not reappeared. Down in the cellars she would not have heard the shot, would still be searching for the best of wines. She would not even know the cars had come.

Grünberg and Simons stared at her, then turned as a man strolled into the kitchen from the hall, in his fifties perhaps, and smiling. He wore civilian clothes of excellent cut; one arm was in a silk scarf sling, and a cut across his forehead was healing. He inspected the two women with the Stars of David on their dresses, then glanced at Sophie, in her good but faded dress. 'I am Herr Stauffen. Where is the prinzessin?'

Grünberg said nothing. Sophie suddenly realised the woman's instincts were better than her own. This man did not intend to let Hannelore live here in peace. Possibly he did not intend her to live at all. But first he would want information from her — Dolphie's friends, associates, everything she knew.

Sophie edged towards the back door. If she could yell in fright or defiance near the cellar steps Hannelore could slip behind the shelves, hide till ...

'She is in the cellar,' said Simons. 'The prinzessin and her uncle talked often. You will find she knows a lot.'

Herr Stauffen looked at Simons with interest. 'Did you hear what they said?'

'No,' said Simons. 'They made sure that no one did.'

'Interesting. And who is she?' He pointed to Sophie, but spoke to Simons.

'She is the cook,' said Grünberg.

Herr Stauffen's gaze did not move from Simons. Simons hesitated then said, 'Yes. She is the cook. From Munich, but her home was bombed, so she came here.'

'She is an excellent cook,' said Grünberg.

'Good. Then she will cook for me. I need a place to recuperate.' He looked back down the corridor. 'Kommen!'

Four soldiers appeared, army privates. 'You.' He pointed to two of the men. 'The prinzessin is in the cellars. Make sure the entrance is blocked and the house and gardens checked in case there is another exit. Do not let her escape.' Herr Stauffen gestured to Grünberg and Simons. Two soldiers grabbed them by the arms. Neither resisted as they were led away. Neither looked back at Sophie.

I must live, she thought. She could not fight this man, these soldiers or, rather, she could try, but she would not win. If she lived, her family would have a mother and wife again. If she lived and Hannelore lived, she might help her friend survive. But only if she lived ...

'There is coq au vin for dinner,' she said hurriedly, curtseying and carefully not meeting Herr Stauffen's eyes, thanking God for the year and a half of practice that had so improved her accent. 'There is gooseberry pudding and fresh noodles and salad from the hothouse.'

'You are lucky there is coq au vin,' he said. 'It smells most excellent. If it had not ...' He shrugged. 'There are many cooks.' He strolled away, back through the house that was now his.

Sophie sat, her legs no longer her own, and listened to her life change again.

Chapter 44

Eggless, Butterless, Sugarless Teacake

½ cup currants
Fresh orange juice
1 cup self-raising flour
½ cup buttermilk
3 cups grated apple

Soak the currants overnight in the orange juice till plump. Drain and mix with the other ingredients gently. Bake in a moderate oven for about half an hour till firm on top. Eat while warm, for the cake grows stale and crumbles quickly. A little butter spread on each slice will be more effective than adding butter to the cake mixture.

If butter, eggs, sugar or lard is available, cream 4 tablespoons butter or lard with 6 tablespoons brown sugar then mix in 2 eggs to add to the other ingredients.

Bald Hill Progress Association Cookbook, 1944 edition,
contributed by Mrs Harry Harrison (Midge)

JULY 1944

DANNY

He was filthy — one of the poddy calves had the squits and he was covered in it. He was just about to head up to the house to wash before dinner — he and Annie were going to the Friday night dance in Bald Hill once he cleaned himself up — when he saw Rose slowly making her way towards him through the frost-browned thistles. He watched her with happiness and relief; sun-touched from the months of recuperation at home, though she'd mostly either been on the phone or dictating to Miss Murphy, who even had to bring her shorthand notebook to the breakfast table to keep up with her employer as she regathered the threads of her empire. But much of the dictating had been done with her feet up on the verandah. Rose had even managed to attend the last two board meetings in Sydney, and had insisted the board come to the hospital for a meeting there before she left. She hardly needed the walking stick now, except on rough ground like this.

He grinned at her as she drew closer. 'Felt like a break from balance sheets?'

'I need to talk to you,' she said stiffly. 'In private.'

'Don't get too close. I'm pretty stinky. What's up?'

'I'm pregnant.'

He stopped, a cloud of bushflies hovering around him. 'You can't be!' She'd only lost the last plaster cast two months ago, a week before Paul was recalled back to his ship.

'Well, I am.' She hesitated. 'It was only once. His final leave.'

Possibly, all across the war-torn world, women were confessing, 'It was his final leave.'

He calculated. Thanks to Aunt Lily and his parents, he was extremely well educated about women's bodies, theoretically at least. 'Seven weeks. You don't think you might just be late? You've been through a lot.'

'I'm sure. I was sick yesterday and this morning.'

Suddenly he felt overwhelming joy. A baby! Like calving season but a million times better, new life filling up the war cracks in the world. 'It's all right, isn't it? You and Paul are engaged.' The matter seemed to have been decided even before Rose was able to sit up in bed. As soon as Paul had come down to Thuringa to finish his own recuperation she had appeared with an endless smile, and an engagement ring.

Rose was too young, of course, and Pa almost certainly wouldn't have given his permission till he'd known Paul much longer, though he and the sailor had spent a lot of time talking. Paul had even joined Pa on his nightly walks along the wombat tracks into the bush, or along the river, and had proved a crossword fiend at breakfast, just like Pa. But there had seemed to be an understanding that while Rose's and Paul's lives were now bound together, there'd be no wedding until that vague destination, 'when the war was over'.

'Have you told Paul yet?'

'How? Send a telegram to the ship? *Am pregnant stop please inform me of when you next have a 24 hour pass in Sydney stop will get married then.* I can't have a baby, Danny!'

'Why not?'

'Give up everything I've worked for? Just like the girls at school who planned to announce their engagement on their twenty-first birthday, but I'll only be eighteen. My life over at eighteen.'

'Mum's life wasn't over.'

'No? She was away from Higgs for years when we were born. She left just about everything to the Slithersoles to manage. I can't afford to be away from work for years! The war will be over, and the men will come back, and women like me will all lose their jobs. Once a man takes over as chairman I'm done for — I'd lose all support if I was seen as doing a man out of his job.'

'Unless Mum comes back. *When* she comes back, I mean.' The two years since he'd seen his mother, incredibly full years, had begun to seem like half his life. Mum had not even contacted them when Rose had nearly died. She seemed to have vanished. Even Aunt Lily's letters gave no hint about where she might be, much less a message from her, though Aunt Lily did still use phrases like '*when your mother returns.*'

'Mum will never have seen what I can do!'

'You're not planning ...' He knew there were places in Sydney, even in war-time, perhaps especially in war-time.

'No, of course not.' She put a protective hand on her belly; he thought she didn't even know she'd done it. 'I ... I just don't want to be a housewife. I could keep working while I'm pregnant of course, lots of women do. But I can't lug a baby or a toddler to the factories or board meetings, even with a nanny. A baby needs a settled life. A home.'

And suddenly it was obvious. 'She has a home. Here. Or he has a home. You may have to settle for a boy, you know.'

'I couldn't leave her — or him — here with a nanny either. Paul couldn't be here either.'

'But I would be,' he said eagerly. 'I'd love a baby!'

'You and Annie would take a baby?' she asked incredulously. 'You hardly know her!'

I've spent more time with Annie than you have with Paul, he thought, amused. 'No, just me. Maybe me and Annie will be together one day, but she wants to do medicine, and that's six years, at least. But I can look after a baby. I'd love to look after a baby! There'd be a nanny for feeds and stuff, but I'd be there morning and lunchtime and evening.' He grinned. 'The baby can watch us drenching the cattle. It's never too soon to learn the art of getting drench down a cow.'

'But Paul and I —'

'Will be the parents. But who says a kid can only have two parents? I'll be like Aunt Lily was for us. She was as close as any parent.' And might again be after the war, he thought, for then he could take over responsibility for Shillings too, or help with its management at least, leaving Aunt Lily free to return to Thuringa.

Her letters were still written weekly, or even more frequently, even if they sometimes arrived half-a-dozen at a time, her elegant handwriting on the familiar cream parchment, still with the same scent — she must have put a stock aside before the war. Danny found he relied on their quiet advice more and more.

'Paul wants to design boats after the war. We might move away.' But he could see a breath of hope on his sister's face.

'He can design them here. You don't need to be near the sea to design ships. He's got the river, hasn't he? You can have a house near the sea too. But you'll live at Thuringa. Build a house up on the hill, where little Danielle can run from home to home.'

'I am not calling my baby Danielle.'

He grinned. 'That's negotiable. But living here isn't. Rose darling, it can work. Pa will give his permission for you to get married now, and you and Paul are head over heels. Have a quiet wedding on Paul's next leave in Sydney —'

'People will still count the months.'

'People who count don't count. Work from Thuringa while you recover from having the baby, just like you've done the past few months.'

'I could make Higgs head office at the Bald Hill factory,' said Rose slowly. 'It's what Mum should have done years ago. There's no reason it has to be in Sydney.' She looked at him, suddenly imploring. 'Paul will be safe, won't he?'

'He'll be safe. You probably know better than me that our ships are getting through now.' He gave her his grin again. It was hard to stop grinning. A year ago Mum and Pa were gone, in their different ways, and Aunt Lily and even Rose, most of the time. But now the house would be full of family again, a family growing bigger, a deeply happy family. 'I bet Paul will be tickled pink that he doesn't have to wait years to marry you. You and he can have Grandpa's old suite till you build a house or do up one of the cottages. Pa's going to love having a baby in the house. He and I can do up the old nursery in our spare time.'

'What spare time?'

'We'll make time. I'll even hire the nanny for you. You just manage Higgs and breed.'

'You make it sound like I'm one of your cows. I don't suppose you can hire someone to actually give birth, can you?'

'Sorry. That bit you're going to have to do yourself.'

'It'll be interesting,' she said philosophically. Her face softened. 'I do like babies. Just ...'

He put his arms around her, calf squits and all, and hugged her, felt her fit perfectly in his arms, as they had fitted together all their lives. A twin thing, maybe. Of course the proper brotherly thing to do would have been to be shocked, and to promise to take a shotgun to Paul if he wouldn't marry his sister. But they had never been that kind of family.

Something Aunt Lily had said came back to him, as clearly as if he could hear her voice. 'There are so many kinds of love. Never waste a single one, simply because it might not be conventional.'

'We're going to have a baby!' he yelled, throwing his hat in the air, and failing, as he always did, to catch it. But catching it was not the point.

'Well, don't tell the world yet. Not till Paul and I are married.' But Rose was grinning too, exactly the same grin as he'd seen in the mirror for nearly eighteen years.

A baby to love, to see grow, years before he might have his own children. Maybe Paul and Rose would have more, too. A mob of kids, steps and stairs, his kids and her kids all standing by the stock rail in their boots and hats. A family, not quite a normal one, but as Aunt Lily said, normal was overrated, as long as there was love.

Thank you, dear Aunt Lily, he thought.

Chapter 45

Cabbage Soup
Serves 200.

Take 12 cabbages, 24 potatoes, 24 turnips. Chop and boil in water till needed.

SEPTEMBER 1944

HANNELORE

Hannelore had heard of the camp, of course. Dachau was where the enemies of the Reich were sent, the communists, the writers who did not extol the party, the movie producers who snickered they would not make propaganda when they'd had too much schnapps. She had seen graffiti way back, in 1935 perhaps: *Lieber Herr Gott, mach mich stumm, Das ich nicht nach Dachau gehe.* Dear God, please make me silent, so I do not go to Dachau. She knew that the rebellious from the conquered territories were sent here, and Jews as well.

She even knew, vaguely, for one did not concern oneself with matters of business, that the labour for her own factories was supplied by the prisoners of Dachau. And why not? It was a labour camp and factories needed labour. Dachau was one of the first of the labour camps, the model on which the other camps were based. Dolphie had told her that.

Dolphie had not told her this.

The bus took her from the prison, where finally her interrogators accepted she knew nothing of Dolphie's plans, except that they existed. Yes, yes, he had planned to kill the Führer, not just one plot but at least three times. No, she knew nothing more because he would not tell her, he kept her imprisoned at the Lodge so she could tell no one. 'Ask the people who had worked the farm if you do not believe me. My uncle would not even let me walk beyond the farm gates or the forest nearest the farm. The Führer himself will tell you how I have always supported the party. I could not inform the SS that my uncle was a traitor. I lived at his mercy.'

She felt Dolphie smile at her at that.

The prison was bad. A single room; a straw mattress for a bed; filth caked on the walls and a bucket for sanitation; cabbage soup twice a day and some substance that might be bread. But they did not torture her. They even left her with her clothes and jewellery.

She heard the word 'prinzessin' whispered as she was marched to interrogation and back again. No one even thought to ask the one question that would have condemned her: did you support your uncle's plan?

She would have answered honestly. Death was likely, either way. This way she'd die with pride.

They did not ask. Perhaps they knew the answer. More likely they did not care. They only wanted men's names, collaborators, army generals or colonels. When it was obvious she could not have known them, isolated in a lodge by a lake, they had no use for her. Or rather, it seemed, another use: to go to Dachau, the labour camp, to do the kind of work Nazis believed even women were good for. She was marched in a line of women to a bus already crowded with other women, most in rags, so thin their rags seemed thick against their flesh. They crammed together, four to a seat instead of two.

The women did not talk. Nor did the guards, except to bark out orders.

The bus drove out of the prison gates, along the road. Hannelore gazed out, because if this was her last glimpse of beauty she must see it: poplar trees, already clothed for autumn, as yellow as the Star of David, then a pile of bodies, untidy as if they had just been thrown together and then another.

And then an end to beauty.

Dachau. A smell of ashes and burned meat and the overpowering stench of people. Concrete walls, topped with barbed wire; a gate, with the words *Arbeit macht frei*. Gun towers, a mud-glazed ditch, more barbed wire, a glimpse of skeletal figures in faded stripes or dull grey clothes before she and the others were led into a room, crowded with many others, where she must strip off every garment, every possession, her ring, her wristwatch, and stand naked among naked strangers.

Were Simons and Grünberg already here? Grünberg had managed to speak to her briefly as they'd been led from the Lodge to separate cars. Simons had betrayed her, either from hatred, or perhaps hoping it might win some concession for her family, even their lives. Sophie, it seemed, would stay as cook. Sophie might survive. Dear God, I have little to live for now, but please let Sophie live.

The crowd about her moved and she moved too, one naked organism. More orders, yelled, as if they had lost their hearing with their clothes. Hands, a razor, her hair shaved or half tugged out. She felt blood drip onto her face. Her pubic hair, the hair under her arms. The women became one again and moved into another room. Disinfected. Bathed ... A pile of rags. Like the others, she grabbed the first that she could find, glad she was small and smaller still now, and any rag would fit. The rags here had red tags, not yellow.

Outside, to line up once again in a large square. She could see huts, and staring men and skeletons that had once been men and yet still walked and stared. The huts had words inscribed upon the roofs: *There is one road to freedom. Its milestones are Obedience, Diligence, Honesty, Orderliness, Cleanliness, Sobriety, Truthfulness, Self-Sacrifice and Love of the Fatherland.*

I do not agree, she thought. Miss Lily would not agree. There are so many roads ...

She must not have heard the order at first, for the voice had the irritation of repetition.

'The Prinzessin von Arnenberg! Komm her!'

She stepped forwards.

A man in a captain's uniform smiled at her. He seemed genuinely amused. 'You look like you could work.'

Work makes you free? She answered, 'Yes, mein Herr. I can work.'

'Good. We have the perfect job for you.'

Another line. Women, like her, in rags, like her, who still had strength, like her, because their starvation had lasted weeks or months, not years.

Another bus. This time she recognised the road. This time, she knew, when she arrived at the factory, there would be no small girl in a dirndl skirt and hair ribbons out front to curtsey with a bunch of flowers, no workers lined up to bow, no one ushering her to an office for coffee and cream cake.

The bus pulled up at the side entrance of what had been her factory. The women filed out, not just because they were ordered but because it was all that they could do. Still in single file, to the door, then separated by men she vaguely knew as foremen. If any recognised her, they made no sign. Each prisoner was taken to a different bench, one to each, like others where thin women in dresses of no colour but well-made caps that hid their hair, worked with wires and machinery.

She stood at the bench she was assigned to, but somehow couldn't hear when the woman next to her explained what work she had to do. The horror held her and made her deaf, her fingers numb. She looked at the bench but did not see.

This all was hers.

'Hannelore.' The sound of her name woke her. She looked, and saw Grünberg, taking the place of the woman who'd been by her side. Grünberg had never used her name before.

'Hannelore, you must work. The first mistake will get you a beating. At the second they will take you out and probably kill you. No one who is taken out is seen again. Do you understand?'

'Yes, Grünberg.'

'My name is Judith. Use it, if I am to show you how to live.'

Still she could not move.

'Move your hands!' hissed Judith. 'If I cannot teach you they may kill me too.'

Hannelore's hands began to move.

—⟋⟍◎

Their job was to attach the wires in detonators. The women did not know if the detonators were for bombs or other weapons. They only knew that red wires must go to red, and green to green, and black to black, twisting and attaching while other women soldered, a job that women did not do, yet did do here.

They worked when it was light, for power was scarce now. They stopped when it was too dark to be accurate and were led out, into the shadow land, into huts that had grown behind the factory since Hannelore had last been here. Perhaps they had always been here and she had not seen. There had been much she had not seen.

They slept on tiered bunks, three women to each bunk. Judith shared hers the first night, guiding her in the dimness; battling through a sudden throng of women, as if they had become rats, scrabbling at two large pots. Judith emerged with two pannikins of cabbage soup and two slices of not-quite bread.

'Eat,' she ordered.

'Why should I bother?'

'I will show you tomorrow, if you eat.'

Judith gave the same order the next morning, after they had lined up in the dark for two hours to be counted, though the counting took only ten minutes.

'Eat.'

It was cabbage soup again, with shreds of turnip and potato.

They lined up on the factory benches. Judith spoke almost without breath, not looking at Hannelore. 'If the wire is broken, the detonator fails. If the detonator fails, everything it is in fails. The fourth wire is the one to break, just under all the others. Not every time — if all the detonators fail they will know it's sabotage. One in twenty. Count them, to be sure.'

'Do the other women know this?' They were the first words she had spoken.

'Those of us who have been here the longest. Who still live.'

'But if the guards are told we do this —'

'Those who speak to the guards do not live,' whispered Judith calmly. 'No, we do not kill them. But somehow a traitor does not reach the food pots.'

'Truly?'

'I do not know,' admitted Judith. 'Only what was said. No woman has spoken privately to a guard since I have been here.'

A guard passed, inspected. Hannelore's hands stayed busy.

'Simons?' she whispered, after he had gone.

'I do not know.'

She should tell this woman that the factory belonged to her; that the soft bed she had slept in at the Lodge came from the money from this factory, and others like it; her gardens; the hothouses where cucumbers and strawberries grew even in the war; the life that had allowed her the luxury of collecting information for the enemy, feeling of value for it, came from factories like this.

She could not say the words. But when her fingers touched the twentieth bunch of wires, she twisted the correct one until she broke it.

Chapter 46

War-time Christmas Cake

4 ounces margarine
3 ounces soft brown sugar
2 reconstituted dried eggs (or 2 fresh)
3 tablespoons golden syrup or treacle
8 ounces plain flour
pinch salt
½ teaspoon bicarbonate of soda
1 teaspoon ground cinnamon
1 teaspoon mixed spice
1 pound dried mixed fruit
3 tablespoons cold, strained tea

Line an 8-inch cake tin with greaseproof or parchment paper.
Preheat oven to 300°F.

Cream the margarine and sugar. Gradually add the beaten eggs, then the syrup or treacle. Sift the dry ingredients together and add to the creamed mixture. Mix in the fruit and tea. Spoon the mixture into the prepared cake tin and make a hollow in the top so that the cake will be flat once cooked.

Bake for 2 to 2½ hours or until the top is firm and the sides are pulling away from the tin. Cool in the tin. When cool place in an airtight container.

The British Ministry of Food, 1944

BOB AND NIGEL

The plane touched down upon the snowdrifts Bob had carefully painted two days before, and rolled its thirty yards. The propellers slowly stilled, though the pilot kept the engine running. Bob gave George a semi-salute as the door opened. Greenie ducked out first, her hair freshly blonde, wearing a rose-coloured coat trimmed with rabbit fur and what looked to be US army PX nylon stockings, followed by Jones in a trench coat, soft hat and carrying a valise.

The plane began to turn to take off again, and suddenly there was no reason to play Bob. Nigel was conscious of the four moth holes in his woollen jumper, the worn knees of his moleskins, the necessary sartorial adjuncts to his character. Only his scarf was perfect: a Christmas present from Rose that he could not bear to leave unworn. The three of them hurried to the end of the field before speaking as the aircraft taxied, then rose again into a sky pregnant with another storm.

Greenie inspected him briefly, then gave him a fierce hug. 'Love the moustache.'

Jones's inspection was longer, and he did not try to hide his concern. 'You're looking thin.' He grasped Nigel's hands and squeezed them, let them drop, a demonstration of affection that would not have been too out of place in any of the roles they'd played before, including that of Miss Lily and her butler.

'You and Mrs Goodenough would have me stuffed like a Christmas turkey,' he evaded. In truth pain had consumed his appetite. He lived on weak green tea and toast, topped with bramble jelly, crabapple jelly, redcurrant jelly, all the fruit fragrances Mrs Goodenough tried to tempt him with.

He did not think the tumour had returned. This pain was different, more likely emanating from scar tissue that had been slowly increasing over the past few years, aches even from the injuries both external and internal he'd received as a young man on the North West Frontier. And simply pain, as if his body was worn in too many places, and no movement or position of rest was comfortable. 'Hereward has made up your old apartment at the Hall already.'

'Can we pop into the cottage for a cup of tea first?' asked Jones casually.

'Of course,' said Nigel, slightly surprised. Mrs Goodenough had prepared a feast for them to eat at the cottage tonight: pheasant in cider, Jones's favourite. He had already mentioned it when Jones rang to say when they were arriving.

'I don't suppose Mrs Goodenough has made cherry cake?' asked Greenie.

'Cherry cake and your favourite gingernut biscuits too,' said Nigel, who had given his month's sugar ration for them.

They began to walk. 'Is she well?' asked Greenie.

'President of the Women's Institute. She gives thrifty cookery lessons on Wednesday evenings at the Vicarage if you're interested.'

'I'll pass,' said Greenie. She gazed at the snow-capped branches, the bare ivy fingers that clung to the stone walls. 'It's good to be back,' she said quietly. 'I don't ever want to go away again.' She glanced at Nigel. 'I've grown tired of it all. Tired of intrigue, and being alert every second, every day. I just want peace.' She looked around and added quietly. 'I want to be home.'

'Don't we all,' said Jones.

Nigel nodded. He led the way into the cottage kitchen, its only warm room. Hereward had placed three small armchairs opposite the stove the year before, with a low ornate table from the Hall that Lily had brought back from Japan so many decades earlier. Nigel even slept here sometimes; the chairs were comfortable, and when one dozed off after the late news there seemed little point waking fully to go upstairs into the cold and empty bedroom with no Sophie.

They'd had less than a decade of marriage, but he still woke each morning, reaching out before he opened his eyes, hoping she might be there. But there was good reason to think she was alive and safe, according to James's sources, even if Count von Hoffenhausen had lost his life as a result of that disastrous attack on Hitler, and Hannelore too had been removed from the Lodge. The count, like many of his conspirators, had bargained for the lives of his family, which meant that wherever she was Hannelore was — possibly — still alive, and had taken Sophie with her.

James's contacts had also ascertained that there were only two servants at the Lodge serving a Herr Stauffen, a Gestapo operative: a manservant, Schmidt, and a cook, Frau Müller, who had cooked for the prinzessin before. Frau Müller might be Sophie, who, just possibly, had learned to cook in her time in Germany. Nigel had never known her to spend time at the stove. It was more likely that she and Hannelore had been forced to move elsewhere.

James had tried to rescue them twice in the past year, once with a lorry driver, amenable to bribes, illegally transporting confiscated art to Switzerland. The confiscation was not illegal — Nazi high officials could take what they liked from non-people — but sending it to Switzerland showed a lack of confidence in the Führer and must be done secretly.

Not secretly enough, as it happened. Instead of dispatching cargo to Switzerland the art's new owner took a journey himself to the Russian front. The art — and Sophie and Hannelore — remained in Germany.

James had also heard of a plane taking an agent to Germany — a Jewish German who knew this was a suicide mission, but felt his life well spent on it, and the authorities were prepared to risk plane and pilot to get him there.

For a few days it seemed possible that the plane might land in the lane between the fields near the Lodge — Nigel had photographs of it and the area was remote enough for a plane to land and take off. But it seemed it was not near enough to the agent's target. That plan, too, was abandoned.

There had been no plan since.

Nigel had plotted, of course. He had spent his entire adult life plotting, in whatever guise he had been in. He'd run through his lists of contacts, even potential contacts, for someone who might just be able to take Sophie ... where? For though he knew women who would offer her shelter, none could get her to Spain or Switzerland, and she had probably been safer staying at the Lodge than with someone who knew she must be hidden. But Hannelore would take care of her, he told himself, at breakfast, as he moved the wooden sheep, or when he woke and heard the cuckoo call at five am.

He blinked to find Jones regarding him carefully. He quickly moved the kettle from the side of the stove to the hotplate and warmed the teapot, while Greenie cut slices of the cake. She took a bite and grinned. 'Ah, that's better. I know I'm really home now. I'm looking forward to our own bed in the Hall, too, even if we do need to come down here for Mrs Goodenough's cooking.'

He didn't ask if they wanted to live in this cottage. He had given it to them purely for security, in case his cousin had inherited Shillings. The Hall had been their home for most of their lives, in one role or another. Perhaps, now, they could finally be themselves.

He tried to find a topic of conversation. Once they would automatically have summarised what they had found in Palestine — if that was indeed where they had been. But this time they had been working directly for James. Nigel did not need to know their mission, and so he neither asked nor was told. Even asking how the weather had been, that most conventional of conversation starters, might elicit enough information for him to deduce their location.

At last he said, 'I'm glad you're back. You'll be a good addition to the teaching staff.' It would be undoubtedly less arduous than the work they'd been doing, and considerably safer. He hoped that they would stay here now. Jones was five years older than him, Greenie two years younger.

Jones rubbed his hands. 'At last, I get my hands on the young ladies.'

'You'll keep your hands to yourself,' said Greenie, who rarely had. But she and Jones seemed more at ease with each other than

343

they had ever been, though there was still no wedding ring on Greenie's finger.

'Is there news of Violette?' Nigel asked abruptly. He hadn't been going to ask, but the question was too heavy to hover unsaid.

'James said she has been working with a resistance unit, not one associated with Britain. Perhaps she found ...' Greenie stopped.

Some patriotism at last? Guilt, at betraying Sophie? Or, more likely, Nigel thought, Violette had decided to buy insurance, for collaborators were vanishing all over France with the liberation. He glanced at Violette's parents as he put the tea leaves in the pot and poured in water. Jones and Greenie had not seen their daughter since December 1940, he calculated, though James could surely arrange for them to get to Paris now ...

'Violette is busy. There is so much to do now Paris is free again. Fashion will be a large part of their recovery,' said Greenie.

And there are so many conversations you do not wish to have with your daughter, thought Nigel. Violette would never seem like the long-mourned baby stolen from Greenie, nor had Greenie ever shown any wish to have other children. Jones had loved fatherhood, but even he ...

He did not finish the thought. Jones and Greenie had also loved Sophie. They loved their country, too. Violette had betrayed both and, by doing that, had betrayed her parents. And yet he still couldn't bring himself to believe she had done so purely from self-interest. Even if the Gestapo had threatened her, her business or those who worked there, surely she could have given Sophie a warning.

Perhaps she had. He would not know till Sophie returned. And Sophie must return, would return, surely by Easter or even sooner ...

Jones gazed out at the snow-dappled laneway. 'I'd forgotten how much I love this place. The smell of winter! I've eaten enough dust to last the rest of my life.'

'There'll be snowdrops soon,' said Greenie dreamily. 'And apple blossom and Mrs Goodenough's apple pie. And my sewing machine had better still be up in the attic or I'll have sharp words with someone.'

Nigel glanced at Jones, then at Greenie. There was something still unsaid. They had not come to the cottage merely to rejoice in being home. Greenie poured the tea, waited till he had sipped its fragrance, still redolent of those years in Japan. 'Bob —' safest to use the code name even now '— James has a request for you. He's had a letter from Daniel.'

'What did it say?' He felt no tug of fear. Danny had sent a cable to Shillings after Rose's accident; and another when, miraculously, it seemed she'd recover. Rose herself had written to Lily about her sudden war-time wedding, happily admitting she was pregnant. If there had been bad news he'd have heard it directly from Thuringa or from Midge Harrison.

'It's been an eventful year for them, with hard things as well as good. Daniel asked James if he could arrange another Christmas phone call.' He swallowed then added, 'With the twins' Aunt Lily.'

Nigel sat silent. He was surprised it had taken so long to ask for a phone call. There had been that first aborted call, after all, even if ordinary people could not telephone across the world in war-time. They must have hoped for a call when Rose was hospitalised, or for her wedding.

It was a simple request. Simple for him to perform, and also impossible. He ... Lily ... had only ever been one person at a time. To be Lily he would need to dress as Lily, *be* Lily. And Lily was not here. Her letters were still postmarked Switzerland. But if Lily never returned from France, how could she speak to Rose and Danny on the phone from Shillings this Christmas? Completely impossible.

Yet these were his children. Children he longed to speak to, whose voices he yearned to hear once again. Children who had also been rocked to sleep by their Aunt Lily, had bedtime poems read to them and games of cricket played with them. But they were not children now. Rose was expecting a child, managing a major company. Danny had taken on the vast Thuringa holdings.

He had never even heard their adult voices, never heard the young man who might have been his son-in-law. He still wrote weekly letters signed *with all my love, Aunt Lily* to each of them. But a letter and a voice were not the same.

'A phone call would present a problem,' he said, keeping his voice calm.

Which fooled neither Jones nor Greenie.

Jones reached over and took his hand. 'It's becoming time to decide,' he said quietly. 'France is still chaotic, but people will expect to be told soon if Lily has survived or not.'

'Lily can't survive. We discussed this before you left. There's no guarantee the secret can be kept after my death, or even if I'm suddenly incapacitated and rushed to hospital. The scandal for Danny and Rose, the legal complications, the effect on James's network ...' James's network, he thought, not mine. Only Lily had a role to play there.

'Lily could move to Australia,' said Greenie softly. 'I'm sure when Sophie returns ...'

He moved to the window and looked out. He wanted to yell in anguish, 'What if Sophie doesn't return? Do I tell Rose and Danny who I am, give them no option but to take me in, despite the new lives they have made?' Because of course Rose and Danny would do just that, especially in their grief for their mother. Or would they blame Lily for that, and be right to do so?

And this was his home. Shillings, its moss-covered stone walls, the soft blue skies of England. He had perched on the red soil of Thuringa like a seagull blown off course, happy for a while, but knowing that instinct eventually would tug him here. Jones and Greenie had been his family for forty years, even Mrs Goodenough and Hereward.

'Nigel, darling.' It was a measure of Greenie's distress that she used that name. She put her arms around him. 'It doesn't have to be all or nothing. You could be Lily part of the year, just like you used to be, at Thuringa, and come back home as Bob the rest of the time.'

Couldn't she feel it? His body was too painful to haul back and forth across the world. Too weary to continue long as Bob the handyman, either. The Hall might remain requisitioned long after the war. The village had changed, and would change even more. What life would there be for Bob Green, retired handyman?

'No need for any final decision just yet.' Jones kissed his cheek, then took Greenie's hand. 'Come on, darling, we need to settle in if we're going to get back here in time for dinner. Will I tell James to organise the phone call? He could say you're ill, if you don't want to do it.' His look said that the excuse wouldn't be far from the truth.

'Tell him to book the call.' Because no matter what complications had to be sorted out later, he would hear his children's voices, their echo of Sophie's tones, their Christmas laughter. Bob Green could not.

'Would you like us here for it?' asked Greenie gently.

'No. No, I think I would like to be alone for the call. But thank you.'

'Okay, I'll let James know. We'll see you at dinner.' Jones grinned. 'I heard a rumour that your cellar still has champagne.'

'Ice-cold champagne,' said Greenie dreamily. 'I know you two will not dress for dinner, but I am going to.'

Nigel glanced at Jones. 'Okay? Have you been mixing with Americans?'

Jones laughed. 'No. A most erudite archaeologist who learned his English when studying in New York. Hilarious story, actually. I'll tell you over dinner.'

He smiled, managed to keep smiling as his friends, his closest family, left the room, till the front door was closed and he could sit with pain. Only some of it was physical.

After nearly three years of almost total silence, the church bells would ring for Christmas. But not just yet. Dawn still hid behind the snowy hills as Lily waited for the phone to ring. It would be late Christmas Day at Thuringa. She had chosen to wear the yellow silk she had worn for Christmas 1939, before her disappearance. A gold chiffon scarf at her throat, the blonde wig, silk stockings — a guilty luxury, for so many women deserved to have worn them in the past few years instead of them staying hidden in the trunk in the attic. Her nails were subtly manicured.

And no moustache. Bob Green could fake a small one, till his own grew again — not the luxuriant whiskers he had shaved off an hour before, but enough to make it look as though Bob Green was just trying a new style for Christmas.

Lily could not exist with a moustache.

The phone rang. 'James Lorrimer? I have a call for you from Australia.' The operator had a slight French accent, which could make her either a French woman living in England, or a woman in France speaking English. James had arranged a replacement for this morning, using Christmas as an excuse. This way the local operator would not recognise Lily's voice and announce to the village she was home, nor would her replacement tell the other operators where her exchange was located. The Bald Hill operator undoubtedly would be listening in to the call, too, and possibly other operators across the world, which was why this call was booked in James's name, not Lily's — and James had the authority for a war-time call across the world.

'Aunt Lily? Merry Christmas!'

'Rose.' And suddenly Lily couldn't say another word.

'Aunt Lily? I thought you would be pleased!'

'I am. My darling Rose. I simply cannot speak. Talk to me, please. Tell me everything. Your young man ...'

'He's here, so I can't say anything rude about him. Say hello, Paul.'

A deep voice, a good one: 'Merry Christmas, Miss Vaile.'

'Merry Christmas to you, Paul.' And I know you saved my daughter's life but if you ever hurt her I will hunt you like a rat. 'I can't tell you how overjoyed I am about the baby. You've entirely recovered now?'

'Well, I think my career as an international gymnast might be over, or a ballet dancer too, but I'm not doing too badly. And Rose is ... is beautiful. Here she is again.'

'Aunt Lily? What will you do for Christmas? Did you get our presents? I'm sorry my knitting is still wobbly. I'm arranging to have samples from every one of our factories shipped to Shillings this year now things are a bit easier. You can feast on canned pineapple, dried fruit and corned beef! Oh, and the pearls are glorious! Thank you! And the book ...' She laughed softly. 'Will be most useful.' A quick aside to Paul. 'I'll tell you about the book later, darling.'

Sophie's book of Japanese woodcuts, which Lily had asked Daniel to wrap for Rose and give to her privately. Thank goodness Daniel was not a prude, but then if he had been Sophie would not have married him. Rose would indeed find the woodcuts useful. Lily had sent a similar book to Danny four years earlier, in case it was necessary to counteract the smut he might be told at school by other boys who might never have learned love could come with fun and laughter.

'You're doing well? And the baby? No morning sickness?'

'Only for a few weeks. I'm eating like a horse. Oh, I wish you were here and could feel her move. I swear she dances whenever I put a record on the gramophone. I'd better give you to Danny now. Here he is.'

'Aunt Lily? Merry Christmas! Is it snowing? Mum told us it snowed for her first visit to Shillings. It's ninety-four degrees here. You could cook an egg on the chook shed roof. I mean you really can. Annie, she's a friend of mine, tried it.'

Lily began to cry then, though she hoped her smile crossed the Date Line, and not her tears. Danny's voice was a man's now, and not a boy's. She would never hear his boy's tones again. And nor would Sophie.

'Aunt Lily, you don't know ... I mean, what Mum is doing ...' So much could not be said over the phone, not with operators listening.

Lily made her voice light. 'I expect she'll be home as soon as all the war crises come to an end. Though it looks like your Pacific War will go on a little longer even than ours.'

'You really think it will be soon?'

'As soon as possible.'

The boy ... no, the young man, was not asking if, but when. And that was what was answered too.

'Here's Pa, just for a minute.'

Daniel's voice wishing him Merry Christmas, then the two young voices side by side. 'Merry Christmas, Aunt Lily. We love you!'

'I love you, too, my darlings! I miss you so much!'

'You'll have to visit as soon as the war is over —' began Danny.

'I am sorry, your twelve minutes is up.' The Bald Hill operator did sound sorry, so had most definitely been listening in. Even James Lorrimer could only commandeer twelve minutes on Christmas Day.

'I love you!' Lily called again, hearing the echo of their voices as they spoke a final time before the phone link was cut. 'Love you, Aunt Lily. Love you!'

The phone was silent, but Lily held it a long time before she placed the receiver down.

Mrs Goodenough was coming to Christmas lunch, too, and Hereward, and Jones and Greenie of course. For five minutes only Lily considered meeting them like this. But of course people might call in, it being Christmas, the vicar perhaps, a new incumbent, invalided out after Dunkirk, a man who had never met Miss Lily but would undoubtedly realise who the woman in Bob Green's house must be.

And yet Miss Lily sat there, her hands unmoving in her lap. Bob Green had thought he had made an irrevocable choice, three years ago. But Bob Green was no relation to the children. How could she live with no right or cause to visit them, to hold her grandchild in her arms?

Sophie, Lily thought. I can't decide this until I can talk with Sophie, confess the past, see what she feels about the future, because looking at her face I'll know. Somehow from that first day Lily had always been able to see Sophie's feelings, no matter how much she might hide them from others, even from herself.

Lily smiled, remembering. Such a prickly young woman, ridiculously overdressed and over-jewelled, but Lily had seen the vulnerability too.

Perhaps she should never have permitted this call, though it had given her more joy than anything in the past three years. But it was a reminder just how much Bob Green had lost. Was it possible to bear the loss of children, grandchildren, and Lily too?

Miss Lily, stood, with a swan-like grace Bob Green could never manage, and walked upstairs to change.

Chapter 47

Midge Harrison's Tomato Jam

*Tomatoes grow well in a war and drought and make
wonderful jam.*

2 pounds tomatoes
Grated zest of three lemons
12 peach leaves
1 pound sugar or as little as half a cup

*Boil all except the sugar till soft and mushy; add whatever sugar
can be spared and stir till dissolved. Boil till thick and a little sets in
cold water — about half an hour. Bottle and seal.*

*This is like a very dark honey, quite unlike tomato. It's good on
bread or crumpets; also good with leftover cold meat or hot roasts.*

FEBRUARY 1945

SOPHIE

She had been invisible, and if she stayed that way, she might be
safe.

Sophie kneaded rye flour, ground pumpkin seeds and caraway,
added them to the bread dough and then a handful of the starter
kept covered in the bowl near the fire. She kneaded the loaf
again, then left it to rise as much as a loaf with so little true flour
could do. She checked the haunch of venison slowly stewing
in its marinade of wine vinegar, with sprigs of thyme, juniper
berries and bay leaves. There should be other spices, but she
could not remember them, and Herr Stauffen had never noticed

their absence, and nor had his guests. At first she had salivated as she cooked, imagining eating the meals to come. Now she found she could manipulate ingredients as if they were the chemicals in Grünberg's old laboratory.

Hunger was a constant companion, sometimes merely muttering, at other times taking over so her entire body shook. She was not permitted food of her own and so she ate the scraps from the plates, which she assumed was what Herr Stauffen expected. No 'Frau Stauffen' had arrived, and no close friend or mistress stayed at the Lodge either. Guests came occasionally and guests left; the same guests rarely came again. This was a man who liked his solitude, or disliked his fellow man. His wounds had soon healed, but he still only left the Lodge two days a week, when a car and driver arrived to take him to what was presumably Munich headquarters.

He slept in the room Hannelore had occupied. The manservant Schmidt lived in Sophie's room, but that was probably just coincidence, as that bed had been made up when they moved in. Schmidt must have assumed that the clothes belonged to a friend of Hannelore's. Neither he nor his employer had asked why there had been three servants, but only two servants' rooms occupied. Perhaps they thought two women shared one room. More likely they had never bothered to look. Schmidt spoke little and seemed to have even less curiosity, which was probably why he had been hired.

Sophie slept in Grünberg's chamber by the kitchen, which was small, but the bed was comfortable and the quilts enough for warmth, especially as the kitchen stove let a little heat into the room too. She dressed in Grünberg's clothes, quickly unpicking the Star of David from the older clothes, though there was no Star on the ones Hannelore had given her in the past year, when there was no one but herself and Grünberg and Simons to see.

Every time she dressed she wondered where Grünberg was, and Simons, and Hannelore. For a while she had been able to pretend it was possible that the Nazis might keep their word, that Hannelore would be questioned, possibly for months, but eventually returned. Hope ebbed slowly. She did not know when she finally accepted that the next car, or the next, would not bring Hannelore. She did know that she had never felt as alone.

Schmidt did not speak as Sophie served his scanty meals in the kitchen, hoping he would leave his crusts, a little of the meat on the bones of his stew, the potato peel, or some of the acorn coffee which was all even Herr Stauffen could obtain these days. But Schmidt too grew thinner as the year wore on. Sophie never met his eyes: friendship and enmity were equally dangerous. Best Schmidt never saw her fully. She was just the channel for food delivery.

Once a week a woman came to scrub and change the sheets and take away the washing. A silent woman, or rather one who knew it was safer not to speak in the house of an official of the Gestapo. Sophie took care not to speak to her, too.

Twice a week skeletal men in rags adorned with the big yellow Star of David clambered from the back of a lorry, and dug or planted potatoes, carrots, turnips, cabbages, while guards watched to make sure starving men did not gnaw raw ones. They tended the greenhouse and brought the produce to the kitchen too, and the guards counted every spear of asparagus, every tomato.

She wondered if whoever had been left at the farm had been arrested too, as possibly complicit with their landlord. There was no way for her to know, for she was forbidden to leave the house, except to go to the small courtyard to hang up her own washing, or the tea towels, or a shirt Herr Stauffen needed urgently. She was glad she knew how to wash and how to iron — she had learned that art a war ago, in Belgium and in France. It seemed she had not forgotten.

The Lodge was little changed; some more artwork arrived in a covered truck — a collection of statues that had no theme, a female nude, a much-clothed peasant woman, a man holding a sheaf of wheat, some modern paintings, some ancient-looking, works that had been gathered for their value, she assumed, not chosen, as she and the Lodge had been gathered.

One other new item. The Lodge now had a wireless, and a crystal set too. She crept out when Schmidt was upstairs preparing Herr Stauffen's room or straightening his clothes. She listened at the door.

Germany, the wireless declared, was triumphant, but slowly half-heard words became a pattern. England was still the enemy, so England still survived. Americans were dogs and so must be fighting. Our 'gallant allies' were still forging south, which meant the Japanese had not reached Australia, for when you reached Australia there was no further south to go. Unless the Japanese were on the mainland and battling their way down the country — hideous thought — but, if so, no towns were ever mentioned: no victorious parades in Brisbane, no mention of Sydney shipyards taken.

It took Sophie minutes to realise that the faint crackling sound through the door that came from the crystal set was speaking English. Herr Stauffen, it seemed, listened to the BBC, whether as part of his employment or not she did not know. The BBC stuttered victories as well. Of course it did. But sometimes it spoke of 'D-Day' landings, of Normandy, a Paris free and celebrating, the Netherlands, specific dates and places that must be the truth. Mustn't they?

She only had to stay alive.

Hannelore had given her this chance, and Grünberg, and even Simons and perhaps the people remaining at the farm who had not said 'Frau Müller is a friend of the prinzessin' but agreed she was the cook.

She only had to live and she'd see Daniel, Rose and Danny. Thuringa and its gum trees and the scent of hot air and cattle dung, mountains that rode blue on the deeper blue of the horizon and were never white with snow. Live and she'd see Nigel and even maybe Lily. Oh, to see Lily once again.

Daniel occupied her dreams, and Rose and Danny too, usually as children much younger than they had been when she'd seen them last, and younger still than they would be now. Sometimes Dolphie loomed there too, as she had seen him on that last hard day, but those were nightmares, night horses, to be sent galloping back into the dark, just like the flashes of her tortures that for some reason came to haunt her now, as they had not when Hannelore shared the Lodge.

But Lily never came in dreams, nor Nigel, though sometimes she saw him in the distance, but could never reach him to see whether he was dressed as himself or Bob. But one day soon the war was going to end. If she was ever to see Lily's smile again, or Nigel's, she had to live.

She simply had to live.

Herr Stauffen seemed content with her work. While he stayed content, and she remained invisible, she was probably secure. But she did not need Dolphie's warning to remember what had happened in invasions both at the beginning and at the end of the last war, and in its aftermath; she had known women who had survived and who had not.

Defeat was rarely simply, never safe. She might belong to the empire that won the war. She was now in the land that would lose it. The invaders might come in a disciplined convoy, or be let loose to loot and kill. The retreating troops would likely have no discipline at all.

Neither Schmidt nor Herr Stauffen knew about the hidden portion of the cellar. Hannelore had not had warning enough to get there. Deep in the night, quietly, Sophie lit a precious candle and took down supplies, a little at a time, that would not be noticed, pulling the shelves back as silently as possible, just enough to take her burdens through. Empty schnapps bottles filled with water. Blankets from Simons's bed. Some of Simons's clothes, which did not fit her, that she tore into strips that might be used as bandages or menstrual pads, though hunger had made the last unnecessary. A spare dress. A bucket for waste.

She did not dare take food from the larder, but she dried crusts in the wood stove at night and added them, one by precious one, into the canister below. It would be enough for a week, perhaps, but she could come out to forage, with a refuge to retreat to.

Time passed. She ate her scraps, or dried and stored them; she made the bread; she feasted on other scraps, torn from the scratchings from the wireless and crystal set as she listened at the door. She was missing, from life and from all else, missing like Miss Lily. In some strange way it gave her pleasure that she and Lily were joined like this now.

She could survive. She could pray that those she loved survived too. And that was all.

Chapter 48

To Re-use Tea Leaves

*Always dry tea leaves after they have been used to brew a pot of
tea. If you leave them to stew in the dregs, the next pot of tea you
use them for will taste stewed, too. Well-dried tea leaves may be
used three or even four times, though the fourth time let the tea sit
for five minutes, not two, before you pour.*

Advice to housewives, 1945

15 APRIL 1945

NIGEL AND BOB

James brought a small box of tea down from London, as he
always did these days. This time he must have called in at the
Hall, for he brought Jones too, still in the overalls in which he and
Greenie taught the women who passed through Shillings what
was still discreetly called 'self-defence' rather than 'how to render
your enemy swiftly unconscious when he finds you photographing
secrets'.

Nigel forced his hands to calmness as he made the tea and put
out the eggless, butterless apple teacake that Mrs Goodenough
had brought him yesterday, but which he hadn't yet touched. If
James had brought Jones there must be news that James thought
should not be borne alone.

He poured the tea, falling accidentally into Lily's grace with
the teapot. He had been doing that more often recently, but it
didn't matter. His role at Shillings as the odd-job man was too

entrenched now for strangers to notice a gesture slightly too delicate for a Bob.

'Well?' He smiled at James, aware it was Lily's smile, warm and deeply discerning, but no longer caring about that, either. 'You have news of Sophie?'

James carefully helped himself to cake, then picked up the cake fork that a Bob would not have placed on the table. 'Not exactly. The Lodge is too remote for surveillance. We still know nothing of Sophie's and Hannelore's movements after Count von Hoffenhausen's death. But MI5 has put together a group that have gone to Germany in advance of the US and Soviet armies to try to locate our agents and bring them back to England before they can fall into Soviet hands. We have officers assigned to the front-line US units too. MI5 have agreed to add Sophie's and Hannelore's names to the list of those agents.'

'I see.' Every day Nigel carefully moved the coloured pins on the map of Germany that showed the Allies moving closer to the Lodge. Now Sophie would not be lost in the confusion of retreating and advancing armies. 'How long?'

'I can't tell. They might find her and fly her back in a week, or several weeks. It might take months. Germany is in chaos, with two armies advancing and one retreating and breaking up.'

A week! Nigel ignored the longer estimates. Sophie might be here in a week!

Suddenly the persistent pain that drained his energy didn't matter. Mrs Goodenough must use the last of the cherries she had kept preserved in syrup for just this day, and the almonds up in the attic. He'd kept apple prunings in the shed especially for the fires.

Sophie was coming home. And with her warmth, and choices, and perhaps a life ...

He glanced at Jones, who sat expressionlessly. Nigel knew exactly what that lack of expression meant. Jones had already known that the rescue party had been sent. Jones was glad for him, but ...

There always had been a 'but' about Sophie for Jones and Greenie. They and Sophie were friends, but never could share

Sophie and Lily-Nigel's closeness. The three they had been for so long had never truly become four.

James put down his cake fork. 'There is something else.'

Jones's expression became slightly wary. He obviously had not known there was more.

'The Ministry may not be leaving Shillings quite as soon as we supposed.'

Jones frowned. 'But surely, with the war in Europe nearly over, there's no need to continue this kind of training.'

'There are other enemies.'

'The Soviets,' said Jones.

'Exactly. The agents we have in place now, the ones whose covers are still good, may be even more valuable. The next few years of inevitable confusion in Europe may also be our best chance to infiltrate other areas.'

'The agreement was for the duration of the war,' said Jones sharply.

'I'm sorry.' James looked at Nigel, not Jones. 'This isn't my choice. But England is stretched to breaking point, if not quite at starvation. We can't waste time and money on a new facility when there is already one set up. The Soviet armies are advancing quickly —'

'In other words, you are creating a new war as you end the old one,' said Nigel sharply.

'On the contrary, we're trying to stop a new war breaking out, trying to keep the balance —'

'That didn't work for the Great War, or this one either. Why do you think it will work now? Don't you think it might be time to change tactics?'

'My wife had told me exactly the same thing. Unfortunately she can't offer a specific strategy. Can you?' James spoke more sharply than Nigel had ever heard.

'I want nothing to do with this. I have been fighting wars, or trying to prevent wars, since I was eighteen. Whatever you are planning will not involve me.'

James carefully sipped his tea. 'Of course. Many of the staff will have to change, of course.'

Staff, thought Nigel coldly. Six years ago the Hall was my home, and the network was Miss Lily's.

Jones raised his eyebrows expressively.

'You and Miss Green will be most welcome to stay in your present positions,' said James quickly. 'The estate and this cottage, of course, aren't included in the arrangement, though security checks may still be necessary for newcomers.'

'Such as my son, the Earl of Shillings? Will he be allowed to visit his estate? Or is he earl of "an arrangement"?' Nigel kept his voice calm.

'Of course there's no need for any security check on your family,' said James calmly. Because they have already been done, and regularly renewed, thought Nigel, as James added, 'This won't last forever, just a few more years. The Hall may even be vacated by the time Danny reaches his majority.'

James stood. 'Again, I'm sorry. I argued against this, but my area no longer has autonomy. I'll tell you as soon as there's news of Sophie, of course.'

Nigel noted that James did not promise news of all Lily's other friends, who might now be part of this no longer autonomous network.

'Mr Jones, may I drop you back at the Hall?'

'Thank you, I'll walk.' Jones's face was carefully blank again. 'I assume you have no objection to my sharing this information with Miss Green.'

'Of course not. This concerns her too.' James looked at Nigel helplessly. 'Bob — my old friend, I am so sorry. I can only guess what this means to you.'

Only my life, he thought. All I have ever achieved. He thought of the photo of Sophie and the children upstairs, the new photo of Rose and her most beautiful Lily-Anne. Perhaps not all he had achieved. And Sophie would be back soon. Perhaps a new life was still possible.

He shivered at the thought that it might not.

The front door closed, sending a draught into the kitchen. Jones reached across the table and took his hand, his eyes warm with concern. 'Are you all right?'

'No,' said Nigel. He managed to smile. 'But then I haven't been since 1939. Will you take James's offer? It *was* an offer — I suspect there will be far more profound changes than he would admit in front of me.'

'Probably not. I'll have to talk to Greenie. Will there be enough rabbit in the pot tonight if we come up for dinner?'

'Always. I think we might find a bottle in the cellar, too.'

'I'll ask Hereward to snaffle one of the cheeses in the larder. George brought back a nice haul from his last trip to Normandy. He's asked for leave, by the way — I gather his destination is Paris, and Violette. I still think he should be told about her betrayal of Sophie.'

Nigel glanced at him quickly. Greenie was convinced that was why Violette still had not contacted her parents now Paris was free, though both Jones and Greenie had written to her. Neither, however, had mentioned Sophie, which was probably the best course with George, too.

'Violette must be the one to tell him. She knows her reasons. We do not.' Nigel spoke in Lily's voice, so was not surprised when Jones said, 'Lily, what do ...?' He broke off when he realised he had used the name, then began again. 'If Lily should return,' he said carefully, 'James might find that her friends are loyal to her, and not to whatever department has taken over her network.'

'I know. But I am too tired for networks now. I only want friends.' Nigel stood. 'I'd better feed the rabbits.' He had bought a Flemish Giant rabbit doe in kit two years earlier. Shillings was well supplied with rabbit meat now. He had given up most of his other jobs on the estate. England was safe, and Bob Green could let his aching body rest. And perhaps, when Sophie returned, Nigel Vaile's aching heart could rest too.

'You're sure you don't want me to stay? I could phone the Hall and ask them to give Greenie a message to meet us here.'

'I'll probably have a doze.' He glimpsed Jones's pain at the dismissal and realised he should not have pretended to his friend. Pretence had become a habit, and the long parting from Greenie and Jones hadn't helped. 'I'm sorry. I need some time to work out what I feel. We'll talk at dinner.'

'You're not alone any more,' said Jones softly.

Nigel touched his arm gently. 'I know.'

But when Jones shut the front door and the draught blew once again through the kitchen, he felt more desolate than ever in his life.

Chapter 49

To Stiffen Linen

Grate six potatoes and soak in just enough clean water to cover them overnight. Strain the liquid through muslin, then add three cups of water. Mix well then dip the linen into the liquid at once, or the starch may discolour. Remove, but do not wring out, and hang in a well-aired but shaded spot so that the sunlight does not fade the cloth. Other garments can be dipped in the remaining water, but watch for any that are not colour fast. If the dye begins to run the garment may look slightly patchy or discoloured. Iron linen while still damp, then iron again when fully dry. If this is not possible, spray water lightly, iron, and then iron again when dry.

Advice passed down in the Green family to its daughters

15 APRIL 1945

JONES

Jones opened the door of their room and watched the woman who had been known to most people for the last five years as his wife, although Greenie had refused to marry him many times, the last shortly after the daughter he had not known they shared was restored to them. Jones had not asked her again.

She sat in an armchair by the window, embroidering the bodice of a dress she had made from an old silk gown found up in the attics, to give to Violette when they were finally reunited. The garment seemed an odd gift for one of Paris's most celebrated couturiers, but Greenie and Violette's relationship had always had an element of competition, including in their genius for dress design. Greenie's skill had been kept for Lily, Sophie and herself. Violette had thrust hers into the world's most fashion-conscious city.

Jones loved his daughter, but it was difficult to find a context for that love when his daughter had made it clear long before the war that she saw no role for parents in her life.

This dress, perhaps, was a way for Greenie to say, 'See, your talent comes from me,' as well as to show Violette a mother who had put in over a hundred hours of close needlework to create it.

Violette would accept the dress, of course. She would even exclaim at its beauty, try it on and say that she adored it. Lily had trained Violette well in the arts of showing gratitude. But Jones feared that after that the dress would be thrust into the back of a cupboard.

Greenie smiled as she sewed. Her face was gentle while she did this sort of work, but rarely otherwise, especially not when armed with pistol or stiletto. Jones still did not like to remember what that knife had done to the man who had poisoned the well in Palestine, killing those children before the adults realised they must leave the village ...

Greenie looked up. The smile vanished, but her look stayed soft as it usually was when she spoke of Lily-Nigel. 'You've told him?'

'Yes. We're going up there for dinner.'

'Good. He's been alone too much. I'd never have left him if I'd known how long we'd be away. How is he?'

'Terrified they will find evidence of Sophie's death, but I'm not sure he even knows how scared he is. You know how he is.'

Greenie nodded. She did indeed know how he was. She and Jones had both loved Lily-Nigel longer and possibly more fully than they had loved each other. In his role as occasional butler, Jones had often heard Miss Lily instruct her students on the many kinds of love. He sometimes thought that the three of them had shared them all, with the exception of Eros, shared only between him and Greenie, although ...

'I think he's scared of what will happen if Sophie is found alive, too.' Greenie interrupted his thoughts. 'She's never been told the truth, not really, despite all they've shared. Or maybe because of it,' she added reflectively. 'There are the children to consider, too. Sophie will almost certainly tell them about Lily and Nigel when she returns, if she returns, rather than waiting.'

'They'll be kind,' said Jones. 'They're their parents' children after all, and brought up by a kind stepfather.'

'It's not kindness that's needed. It's acceptance. Can Rose and Danny accept the truth?'

'Can Sophie?' He sat in the chair next to her. 'It's been hard sharing with Sophie, hasn't it? It was just the three of us for so long.' It was the first time either of them had ever expressed that aloud.

'I like Sophie,' said Greenie. 'I always have. But, darling, we didn't share with Sophie. We had the crumbs that fell from Sophie's table. No, I'm not bitter, truly — those were still good years. But after the war it can finally be just the three of us again, living here.'

'You know it can't be, love,' said Jones softly. 'Too much has changed, will change.' He told her of James's other revelation. 'What do you think?' he asked at last.

'No, no, and no. This instructor business was all very well as a stop-gap till the war ended. But we've always worked by ourselves, for ourselves. I'm too old for another enemy, another war on the horizon. It's not as though we need the money.'

No, money was not an issue. Nigel had taken care of that decades earlier. 'It would mean we could stay here.' Jones gestured to the suite that had become their home. 'The cottage would be a bit cramped for the three of us.'

Greenie grinned at him. 'I was born in a cottage, but I'm bloody well not going to die in one. We'll build ourselves a great mansion on the estate, the kind that looks like it's been there five hundred years, for you, me and dear Uncle Bob, and maybe Mrs Goodenough too, with a dozen kitchen maids.'

Jones laughed at her enthusiasm. 'You'll have a lady's maid instead of being one?'

'I'm not having a stranger rooting round in my knicker drawer. No servants living in. We'll fill the house with all the Shillings treasures, and I'll have a great big sunny sewing room, and you and Bob can fill the cellar with the best of the Bordeaux. There can even be a drawing room for Lily, with a lock on the door that only we have the keys to, and parchment-covered walls and an apple-wood fire — the Ministry can go jump if they expect to keep getting the produce from the estate. What do you think?'

'Hereward might want to come too.'

'Every mansion needs a butler.' Greenie met his eyes. 'I'm not leaving here, darling. The Hall perhaps, but not Shillings. But we'll live here on our terms, and damn them all.'

'You won't be bored?'

She considered. 'Strangely, no. I feel as though I've finally come home, the home that it should have been. Not another of the Green daughters going into service with the Vailes.' She gave an impish grin. 'Darling, don't you realise the fun we can have, you and me and Lily? I could even take her place now and then, as we did in Berlin, and really confuse people.' She met his eyes. 'I want a home that's mine, and yours and Lily's, of course. Maybe I'll even plant a rose garden. But mostly I don't ever want to take orders again. I've been a lady's maid for the whole bloody British empire, giving it a nip and a tuck here or a polish there. No more.'

For a moment Jones could almost see it. A house rising from Shillings stone. The present airstrip would be perfect; nor had the Ministry acquired that land when they took over the Hall, but assumed that the resources of the estate would be available, just as they had been in the decades Lily had wrought her network here.

A house — or mansion — with no lovely ladies, no intelligence agents, entirely private, where Lily would be cherished and protected. Surely James owed her that. Her country owed her ...

No, Lily had given freely to her country and not for recompense. James was correct: the war had almost broken England. The next years of peace would be harsher and hungrier even than the war. Despite the obvious anger today, Lily would never compromise a crumb that might help the endeavours at the Hall. When it came to it, the Ministry would almost certainly requisition the airstrip, and forbid any new work locally that might compromise security. And Jones suspected Greenie already knew it.

He watched her gaze out the window, at the gardens that should be spring-like but were still mud and dull rhododendron leaves, as if the sun could not return to England until peace was declared.

'This is what Sophie could never share,' she said at last. 'Oh, Sophie loves Shillings, but her bones aren't made from its soil, its soul. Her ancestors never walked these lanes, generations of them, even before there were lanes, perhaps.'

Jones found Greenie was looking at him now and not the gardens. 'Give me your hand,' she ordered.

'Why?'

'Because as you said, things will change. For once in your life, can you obey orders without question?' She took his hand in hers. Again Jones was struck by how much she resembled Lily, though Greenie's hands were smaller, and Jones had never been quite sure of her original hair colour.

'My dear Mr Jones,' said Greenie formally. 'Will you do me the honour of marrying me?'

He stared. 'What, now?'

'You are supposed to clasp me in your arms and say, "My life's dream come true at last."'

He lifted her hand, and kissed it. 'My life's dream come true at last. But why now?'

'Because now we are no longer working for James there may come a time when we need to prove we have the right to manage each other's affairs, and because I love you.'

'Thank you for adding that,' he said drily.

'Idiot. You know I always have.'

And while you still have a roving eye, you no longer wish the rest of you to follow it, thought Jones, but had the sense — at last — not to say it aloud. And this plan, at least, was possible, a blossom growing from the rubble of their former lives.

'I want a big wedding,' said Greenie dreamily. 'After the war is over and we can plan it properly. All my family, and Violette of course. She'd have to come to her parents' wedding.'

Cunning, thought Jones, staying tactful.

'Violette can make my wedding dress. She'll like that. We'll fill the church with flowers. At least no one has rationed those. Mrs Goodenough will perform her usual miracles no matter what the shortages ...'

'What about all those who have assumed we are married already?'

Greenie shrugged. 'Nothing they can do, as after that we *will* be married.' She met his eyes. 'And Bob will walk up the aisle with me and stand with us while we say our vows.'

And stay silent, thought Jones, for that is the one bond between the three of us that no matter what can never be.

'It sounds perfect,' he said, and kissed her again.

Chapter 50

*Stupidity is not a matter of intelligence. I have known
people content with simple lives who were wise, and educated
men and women whose every decision was foolish. Stupidity
is eyes that refuse to see, hearts that fail to feel for others.
We must teach wisdom to the young, for once a person has
accepted stupidity, they may not risk admitting the failure of
their lives by choosing to see what they have previously refused to
acknowledge.*

Miss Lily, 1937

16 APRIL 1945

SOPHIE

The crystal set had muttered news of Allied troops advancing
into Germany. But that news was spoken in English, for those
who spoke English to believe. The German news on the wireless
each night and morning still spoke of German victories, of new
weapons unleashed.

So she was not prepared for the lorry that arrived without
warning one afternoon — the soldiers who loaded statues,
paintings, both new and Hannelore's, the bottles from the wine
cellar, the jars of carefully made preserves — everything, it
seemed, that would fit in one medium-sized truck and one black
car, leaving enough room for Herr Stauffen and Schmidt too.

Freedom was nearly here. She only had to live.

She watched the black car drive away from the hall where
once she'd waltzed with Dolphie, then hurried to the kitchen as

the soldiers fastened ropes around the looted statues in the lorry. It seemed she had been forgotten. Good.

The obvious food had been taken. She clambered up on a chair to gather the strings of dried mushrooms, nettles, herbs ...

A grey-uniformed soldier appeared.

'Frau Müller?'

So I am not invisible, she thought. 'Ja, ich bin —' she began. Then she saw his pistol.

She leaped the moment he pressed the trigger, so the shot went wide. She jumped towards him, which he had not expected, so his second shot missed as well. Nor did he expect a small, starved tiger cat to attack him with fingernails for claws, strings of dried mushrooms looped around his neck so that when he pushed her off and struggled up he found that his own force had strangled him. The more he moved, the tighter the noose grew.

She wondered vaguely if she would ever get to tell the commander that a string of dried mushrooms could be as lethal as a chiffon scarf.

She clambered to her feet, and looked down as his frantic hands clutched at his throat, his face red, his eyes bulging, breath gasping. She saw the moment that consciousness ebbed.

Should she kill him? No need, nor probably time. She simply ran to the cellar door, navigated the steps without a betraying light — she knew every movement needed by heart now — ran silently across the floor and grabbed the shelves to move them back, then stumbled, almost falling, as something stabbed her hand.

For a moment she thought someone had followed her, shot an arrow, perhaps, though why a German soldier would have an arrow ... She felt her hand carefully. A large sliver of glass protruded, a bottle obviously broken by the looters. She pulled it quickly, before she had time to anticipate the pain, felt blood flow, ignored it, touched the shelves carefully this time, found more glass then moved her grip.

The shelves shifted the few inches it took to slip through, then pull them back again. Just in time, for she heard boots above.

She did not dare light her precious matches, or the even more precious single candle, in case a chink of light showed through. She gathered her skirt together and pressed it against the wound on her hand, her left one, and felt it grow wet with blood.

She waited, as the sounds continued. And finally, she closed her eyes.

~❦~

She woke an unknown amount of time later. She felt oddly light, from loss of blood most probably. The padding had dropped from her wound. She touched it gently with the fingers of her other hand and found it still moist but no longer bleeding profusely.

The Lodge was quiet, though outside a thrush sang, liquid notes that danced through trees. They had not found her then.

She did not want to waste matches and candle. She felt around with her right hand, orienting herself, found the mound of bandages she'd made, deeply glad she had made them. She wished she had brandy or some other disinfectant for her cut, for the bottles down here were crusted with dust, and even bat or rat droppings. The best she could manage was a pad of cloth, tied securely, and then her hand fastened above her breast to help slow any bleeding and to stop her automatically trying to use it.

Water now. She drank nearly a whole bottle, slowly, for she must replace the blood she'd lost. She had no appetite, but nibbled at crusts of bread, knowing she needed food, and then she drank again, for she hadn't needed to use the bucket, which meant she was still dehydrated.

Simply survive, and she would see Daniel, Rose and Danny, the waving gum branches against Thuringa's vivid sky. Simply live, and she would see Lily ...

She closed her eyes again.

The cellar was hot when she woke. It took her minutes, days, months, for time had lost its meaning now, to realise she was hot, and not the cellar. Her hand throbbed, swollen to the wrist.

She tried to think, but all she found was fog. She knew she had to drink …

She drank. She tried to eat, and vomited, retching over and over till even the water left her. She crawled over to the blankets and lay down, cradling a bottle of water, which she would drink soon … soon … soon …

When she woke again she found she must have woken before, as the bottle was half empty. The fog had deepened, making it impossible to move except to pull over some more water. She drank again, vaguely pleased with herself, for she was safe. Finally, totally, absolutely safe, here curled in the darkness, underground, carefully making no sound.

No one would ever find her.

Chapter 51

Potato Cakes

For every cup of grated potato add 1 dessertspoon chopped parsley,
2 chopped cloves garlic, 1 dessertspoon chopped onion, 1 egg,
1 tablespoon plain flour. Mix well. Drop spoonsful on a hot pan
with plenty of olive oil or butter. Cook till brown on one side then
turn.

If the cake sticks, the pan wasn't hot enough or clean enough.
If the potatoes are very liquidy, you may need to add a little more
flour.

28 APRIL 1945

HANNELORE

Hannelore woke in darkness, then realised there was light coming through the cracks in the wall. It was not just dawn, but fully light, although the hut had not been unlocked yet, nor the order given for the pre-dawn roll call.

The women had heard thunder all week, thunder which was not a storm but guns. Planes had criss-crossed the late snow clouds above the factory, though anyone who did more than briefly glance out the window was beaten.

Hannelore could hear the same not-thunder now, as well as the closer sound of unfamiliar engines. And something else. A flicker, a crackling, almost too soft to hear. And the smell of burning wood.

The other women were mostly asleep, exhaustion biting deep, or lying still in the luxury of a longer time to rest.

'Wake up!' Hannelore scrambled up and gazed around in the hut's dim light. She could see the smoke now, a trickle like morning fog at the furthest corner of the hut. She screamed and tugged Judith awake next to her, then the thin form of Fräulein Schneider on the other side. She slid off the bunk, taking the single blanket with her. 'Fire! Quickly! Grab your blankets. We must get out.'

Already one wall was blackening. 'Come!' she yelled. She hauled Judith off the bed too, wrapped the blanket over both of them. 'No, don't bother with the door!'

The door and its heavy bolt was certainly the strongest part of this building. They would all be burned to death before they managed to push it down. The weakest point was where it was burning, but every woman here was skeletally weak as well.

'Follow me,' she commanded, as a prinzessin used to barking orders and, miraculously, the women did, holding their blankets and each other, linking arms, copying her as she and Judith placed their blanketed backs to the blackening wall and pushed backwards.

Nothing moved. The roof above them was alight now. Hannelore could feel the heat, like a sun fallen from the sky. She pushed again. The wall quivered, but did not give way. Any second now the roof would come down on them.

Judith yelled, 'Eins, zwei, drei ...'

Thirty women pushed together. The wood moved, collapsing, and the women fell too, wood burning around them. Women screamed, beating the flames from their ragged dresses.

'Roll!' shouted Judith, and the women rolled onto the snow-covered ground, spring snow they had cursed a few weeks ago, welcome now. Men ran towards them. The women scrambled to their feet, even those who had been burned. They ran behind their building, behind the flames of every other building, in what must be a vain attempt to hide from the running men. Their own hut must have been the last to be set alight.

The women kept on running, stumbling, straggling, helping each other, now towards the forest behind the factory, expecting the guards to shoot them every second. But no shots came. Ammunition was in short supply. Their guards must have relied on the fire to kill them all, had not dreamed they might need to arm themselves to kill weak female escapees.

And, finally, the women stopped running, still thirty of them, every woman who had been in the hut. Snow blew through the trees in scattered flakes. The trees above them stood bare, their branches dappled with snow or hung with icicles. Thirty women, all starving, with blackened faces or skin burned red raw, shivering and partly fried, still grasped blankets, their feet in their rough pattens or bound with rags blue even though they had tried to avoid the patches of snow.

Instinctively the women moved together, seeking the same warmth as when they slept together, which was not just physical warmth but the knowledge that another person lived and breathed beside them, a person who had broken every twentieth wire.

'They burned them alive,' said Judith finally. 'All except us. Burned them so they could not testify what they had done to us.' She looked at the others. 'You know what this means?'

That we did not burn but still may freeze to death in the next few hours? thought Hannelore.

'The Nazis are gone. Kaput. We are free.'

'Perhaps not yet,' said Hannelore cautiously.

'We will be soon. But we cannot stay here. There is only one place where we can find shelter, perhaps even food.'

Judith meant the factory. It is not safe, thought Hannelore, brushing a damp snowflake from her face, but safer than staying here and turning into ice. And perhaps the guards had already fled now the enemy were coming closer.

'I will go first,' said Hannelore. She looked at the other women. 'If you hear me scream, run further into the forest. If I do not come back try to find some other shelter.'

'Who would take us in? We will all go,' said Judith.

One person should spy out the land. I have been a spy for years, Hannelore wanted to say. Let me do my job again. I owe you all this, and far, far more. But she did not want to be alone and nor did she want to give more orders.

The women crept among the trees, women in rags blackened by the breath of flame, arms, legs or faces raw with heat. Snow fell in shivers from the branches as they passed. Leaves crackled underfoot. They paused at the final line of trees before the factory. The flames from the huts had died down now, a shimmer of smoke and coals. Hannelore tried not to think of how many had died there.

The factory itself was unburned.

Judith walked forwards, grabbed a singed piece of wood from the smouldering wreckage, then banged it on the ground till the burned part fell away, leaving a wooden spike at one end. Other women did the same.

The trucks had gone. The cars had gone. The women crept around the factory, women limping, women supporting those who could no longer walk by themselves, women wielding the best weapons they could scavenge. They stopped, as voices came from the window of the guards' room just in front of them. The voices of two men, perhaps three.

'Go in the front door,' Judith whispered to Hannelore and Fräulein Schneider. 'Make a sudden noise, then duck down behind the benches.'

'What will you ...?' Hannelore stopped as Judith nodded at the window.

There was a garden along the factory wall, or a plot that was a garden in summer, bordered by a rough stone wall. Two of the women hefted the largest rocks. Others wrapped blankets around their hands.

One in every twenty wires sabotaged, carefully planned by women. Now the women planned again.

Hannelore took Fräulein Schneider's skeletal hand. The two of them crept around to the front door. It stood open. Hannelore walked inside that way for the first time since the child had curtseyed and given her flowers.

She and Fräulein Schneider stepped quietly, quickly gazing around the empty room, then Hannelore deliberately scraped a metal box along one of the benches. She and Fräulein Schneider ducked behind the bench. The men's conversation in the office paused. Someone muttered a query.

Glass broke as two rocks crashed through the office windows. More glass splintered. Hannelore imagined blanket-wrapped hands pushing the rest of the glass away, the women helping each other up to the window, clambering inside, their sticks in their hands.

Men shouted. A pistol barked, a single shot. Then men screamed.

Judith emerged from the office, her hands red with blood. For a moment Hannelore thought she had been hurt, then saw she was smiling. 'Hannelore, come! There is bread and cheese in here,' called Judith. 'And *sausage*.'

The power had been turned off or blown up or possibly it was just a blown fuse. It did not matter. The women did not even bother to drag away the bodies of the three guards who for whatever reason had not left with the others. They laid Frau Fischer, who had been shot in the shoulder, in a corner and tended her, all the while chewing bread, very slowly, for Grünberg warned them that their bodies were too unused to food to absorb too much, too soon. They ate cheese slowly, too, waited, then ate more bread, then shared out the sausage into thirty equal tiny pieces.

And then they sat upon the floor, for six chairs were not enough for thirty women and none of them would sit above the others. With the door shut it was warmer, even if crowded.

Their faces were still black and red and their hands bloody, from the guards or from Frau Fisher or from their own burns or cuts from branches as they'd run through the trees, their dresses torn, hanging from their shoulders or showing bare burned legs. They leaned against the walls, against the guards' bodies, against the table legs, exhausted but not sleeping now, not while there was still food. They waited to make sure their bodies had accepted nourishment then ate again, carefully but steadily, using both hands, for they had all learned how precious a crust was, how easily it might be snatched away.

Shots outside. The women flinched, but kept on eating. Were they Russians or Americans or English? If they were Russians they might still be killed, raped, in revenge for the Russian women and children and troops who had been slaughtered in the past few years. But where could thirty women hide now?

Booted footsteps. A voice yelled in an appalling accent, 'Komm hier raus!'

Come out here. Not likely, thought Hannelore, chewing cheese.

The door opened cautiously. Men peered in. American uniforms, Hannelore thought with deep relief, but it was not reason enough to put down the slice of bread in her one hand, the cheese in the other. Judith nibbled sausage next to her.

Hannelore could see the men's horror, and their disgust too, at the wild-haired bloody women gnawing at their bread. But then she saw the moment they recognised the uniforms, saw the yellow badge for Jews, the red for traitors to the party, the purple for the Poles. Disgust turned to sympathy and a kind of incredulous horror.

'Er, Gutes Frauen, Sind Sie, um ...' The man was obviously trying to find the word for prisoners.

'We are prisoners,' said Hannelore in English, through a mouthful of bread. She nodded to the bodies. 'Those were some of our guards.' She closed her eyes for a second and added, 'You will find the rest of us have been killed in the burned huts behind the factory. Please treat the bodies with respect. Some of us are injured, one badly. We need medical help, if that is possible or, if not, clean bandages, disinfectant.'

The soldier stared at her. He yelled something about a medic to the men outside, and waited.

Another man appeared, an officer in an English uniform, not American. He stared at the women, then said, in English, 'I am looking for the Prinzessin von Arnenberg.' He added six more names that Hannelore didn't recognise, and then 'Sophie Higgs-Vaile-Greenman'.

'Why do you want them?' demanded Judith, from the floor.

'Orders from England,' said the man briefly.

Judith carefully did not look at Hannelore, but her posture said, 'Do you trust these men, or not?'

James, thought Hannelore. The pigeon had reached its destination. And now the English are looking for all their lost sheep, their secret agents. She rose, her back as straight as she had been taught it must be since she was a year old, as gracefully as Miss Lily had shown them. I am a swan, she thought, and almost laughed, the bread still in one hand, the cheese in the other. But she tucked the chewed food neatly into the spaces under her tongue as she said quietly, 'I am the prinzessin.'

'You know the password?'

Password? James would never use such a term, nor Miss Lily. But there had been a signal phrase she had memorised for identification. 'The swans are on the lake,' she said, remembering the crumpets with honey, the warmth of Miss Lily's voice and the drawing room.

The officer stared at her. Hannelore bent and helped Judith stand. 'This is my friend, Judith Grünberg. Wherever you are taking me, we go together.'

'Our orders are to take you to your home until transport to England can be arranged, your, er, highness?' said the American. He had been ordered to find a princess, but not instructed how to address her. 'A palace by the lake.'

Why would she want to go to England? Nothing she knew could be of value to the English now. But there were far more urgent matters. 'It is a hunting lodge, not a palace, but it is by a lake. Is it still there? It … it is possible that another person on your list may be there, Sophie Higgs-Vaile-Greenman, though she may be known as Frau Müller.' Sophie, she thought. Please let Sophie be there, be safe.

'We haven't searched that area yet.'

Hannelore looked around. The other women stared up at her, still eating.

'Do you have a lorry?' she asked the officer.

'We have a car, your, er, highness.'

'We need a lorry, please, or several cars, to take us all to the Lodge as soon as it can be arranged. For all of us. I can direct you there. Unless there is another safe place you know where we can all go.'

The officer shut his eyes for a second. He opened them and then said, 'No. I know of no safe place for you all yet. There are still parties of German soldiers roaming the forest. The other places ... No, they are not ... safe.'

'Then we will wait here for the lorry,' said Hannelore calmly, as the medic arrived with his kit bag, then sat, with Judith beside her, and ate her bread.

Chapter 52

SOPHIE

She lay on the cool kitchen floor of Thuringa. If she opened her eyes she would see the white branches sway against the drought-blue of the sky through the window. No, she was at Shillings, for she could hear Lily's voice.

'Sophie? Darling, where are you? The twins are ready for their tea.'

Sophie smiled, her eyes still shut. They would toast crumpets by the nursery fire for Rose and Danny, and by the end all four of them would be giggling, sticky, happy, and Nurse would scold, but be laughing too, for tea with Lily was always joyous, perfect, though the fire was too hot. They needed to pull the fire screen across, for she was burning, sweat running down her face. No, she was cold ...

At last heat and cold faded.

'Sophie, we need you,' said Lily gently.

Soon, she thought. I'll open my eyes and be with you soon. But I must be careful not to fall sleep, for if I fall asleep I will miss crumpets with Lily, Rose and Danny, and yes, Daniel will be there, for he knows all about Lily now. Daniel will eat crumpets too ...

'She will be there,' said Hannelore.

Hannelore was here too! They would have a feast. After tea they would see kangaroos, for Hannelore had always wanted to see sunlight and kangaroos.

Something grated nearby. Sophie ignored it. The sound did not belong to Thuringa, and they must be at Thuringa if there were kangaroos outside. She must tell Lily to stay here at Thuringa so no one would ever know, she could not quite remember what they must never know, but it didn't matter, not now, with everyone she loved so close.

'Lily,' she began, but her lips made no sound.

'Sophie!' Hannelore's voice was almost a sob. Hannelore should not cry. She must be happy, with sunlight and kangaroos. Sophie had to tell her …

An English voice said urgently. 'Find a medic! Hurry! Someone, help me get her out of here.'

'Sophie, it will be all right. Truly, all will be well,' said Hannelore's voice.

That was good. Sophie smiled, and decided she might sleep.

Chapter 53

What is worth giving your life for?

*If you have to ask that question, you may not easily find an
answer. Those who give their lives usually do so without measuring
its value against another's. They simply give, an instinct of
empathy or love and of humanity. Parents instinctively give their
lives for their children. Strangers leap into rivers to save people they
have never met. Soldiers fight for a cause, for the many. Would
humans have survived if, many, many times, lives had not been
given so the many could live?*

Miss Lily, 1939

4 MAY 1945

NIGEL

Nigel Vaile sat in bed in striped flannelette pyjamas, suitable
pyjamas for a Bob, and gazed at the pigeon roosting on his
windowsill with a strange new calmness.

This pigeon could not be the one that had brought the message
from Sophie. James had not told him where that pigeon had
flown to, but it was unlikely to be in England and even less likely
to be at Shillings, for they had no dovecote here, nor had any of
the tenants bred racing pigeons.

But the pigeon had arrived more than two years ago, on the
day James had rung to say Sophie was alive and at the Lodge.
And yesterday James had rung again. Sophie was in Germany,
alive, though ill with septicaemia, but James had organised that
new wonder drug, penicillin, and George the wonder pilot, too,

to bring her to a hospital in London. James would phone again as soon as she was there.

Sophie had been at the Lodge all this time. Now she was coming home. They could talk, at last; make decisions, at last; create whatever new life he would have in the new land of 'after the war'.

We have a granddaughter, Sophie, he thought. Her name is Lily-Anne.

Nigel lay back on his pillows, reassured by the pigeon's quiet presence, glad the cottage windows no longer had to be shrouded for the blackout each night. Somehow, as long as the pigeon had been there, he'd been able to believe Sophie would stay safe.

He'd lived mostly with his memories the last few months. Not of his parents, nor his older brother, the school where boredom was worse than the beatings that were, at least, over quickly. By the time Nigel Vaile had survived the North West Frontier and found a haven with Misako in Japan, Lily had learned to tweezer the trauma out of Nigel's life and feast only on what was good.

The triumph of the first time Nigel had bowled the vicar out at the midsummer cricket match; he'd been only fifteen and the vicar had played for Harrow and Oxford. Meeting a defiant, overdressed colonial girl with a fierce intelligence and a conscience she did not have the experience to hide. The same woman, confident now, dropping from the sky to announce she would marry him and ensure he survived his surgery. The joy when he finally knew she loved him. His wife, gazing at their newborn babies as he held them in his arms.

Nor did he have regrets. If he hunted for them, he might find some, but why waste time with that? His life stretched behind him, dappled with so much love. Yet for some reason, he could not see his future, and there must be a future now, with the Allied armies advancing to Berlin.

And soon he would hold Sophie's hand again, and feel her warmth. Mrs Goodenough would strengthen her with soups, and he would feed her memories: the day the doctor told them she was bearing twins, the Prince of Wales serenading her with his bagpipes to scare their unwanted guests away, the first day Lily had ridden through the Thuringa trees with her — with aching scars, but he did not tell her that — while Sophie explained how beauty could be dry, and tussocks and glinting eyes of quartz among hot rocks more lovely than a stretch of mossy field.

When she was stronger, they would talk, the conversation they should have had before Sophie left for Australia in 1936, or even further back.

And then he would choose, or rather, Sophie would do it, even if she didn't realise her reaction would be the catalyst for what came next. Choices were still possible, he told himself. Lily had a birth certificate, a passport and bank accounts. An Englishwoman could have survived the war in France, especially one who spoke with an impeccable French accent, who was charming, capable and had French friends. Those who knew Miss Lily also knew not to ask her questions. They would assume a war of glamorous secrecy, not one of feeding pigs. And somehow it would all work out, even if he could not see the path now.

He gazed up into the darkness. He no longer wanted secrecy. He wanted ...

What did he want? A night's sleep, with no sudden dagger's breath of pain. A cup of tea at breakfast, shared with Jones and Greenie, and perhaps Mrs Goodenough, who called in every morning now, as if to ensure he ate his toast. He wanted to hold his grandchild, with Sophie beside him. He wanted peace.

He reached for the photograph on his bedside table of Lily-Anne, the tired smiling face of the mother who was his daughter, and next to her, brown and confident, his son. If photos could fade from being gazed at, this would be blank by now. He reached for Sophie's photo too ...

A plane's engine stuttered above him. He hardly noticed it — there was no need for air-raid warnings now. But the bedside table was under the window so he saw the sky explode the moment that the engine stopped, a star that turned to metal, fragments and a giant flaming mass falling down. Another crash, and screams and flames. But even before it hit the Hall, Nigel Vaile had grabbed a blanket and was running. He flew downstairs and out the door and pounded up the lane.

The flames had spread already where the plane had crashed into the reception hall, but this part of the Hall was still undamaged. Women shouted, called, women in nightdresses, pyjamas and dressing gowns staggered out of the back door and the library French windows, then clustered in behind the Hall. There was no sign of Jones or Greenie.

Emily appeared, a cashmere dressing gown, sensible boots unlaced. 'Down to the orchard,' she instructed the growing crowd. 'You, Lucy, take the names of everyone who's here ...'

Nigel ducked behind her, through the scullery then the kitchen. No smoke here yet — the wind was blowing it away from the main part of the house. Screams rang like a siren from the butler's pantry. He flung open the door. Hereward gazed up at him, his legs pinned by a fallen shelf.

'Knew you'd come, your lordship,' panted Hereward. 'Knew you'd never let us down.'

How many years had it been since he'd been called that?

'Never, my friend.' No time to check if the legs were broken; nor did Nigel have the strength to carry him. He took the butler's remaining hand and pulled.

Hereward screamed again. The shelf didn't move. Nigel tugged again as Hereward's eyes shut in what Nigel hoped was only blessed unconsciousness. On the third try the man's body moved by perhaps an inch. Tug by tug he moved him further, till finally the shelf clattered to one side. Nigel kept dragging, trying to mute his own pain, through the kitchen, and into the scullery just as Dorothy and Emily staggered back inside. He let them each grasp one of Hereward's arms and keep dragging while he went back inside.

He swiftly gazed around the corridor. The drawing room, the dining room and the entire east wing were probably done for, but the women's bedroom wing on this side seemed still intact. He headed for the stairs up to the bedrooms as smoke billowed like a small tsunami down the hallway.

Where were Jones and Greenie? Had they got out while he was in the pantry?

Smoke drifted, gathered, choked, thicker up the stairs and on the gallery. A form emerged from it, thudding down the stairs. Jones, his arms supporting two young women, one cradling what might be a broken arm, the other's nightgown red with blood where it clung to her right leg. Greenie staggered down the stairs beside him, a familiar young woman in a fireman's lift over her shoulder: Di Lennon, that was it. Her mum lived in the cottage with the wisteria, her dad had been a footman …

'Servants' rooms are clear now. Ceiling collapsed,' Jones panted. 'No one was in the main Hall at this time of night. Greenie will check the guest rooms next. Then that's the lot, thank God.'

Nigel reached towards young Di. 'I'll take her.'

He felt his scars scream as he took the limp weight. For a moment he thought she might be dead, but then she groaned. He grabbed the banister with his free hand, to help support them both. Greenie vanished upstairs into smoke once more. Neither man wasted breath trying to stop her.

Flames licked the far end of the gallery now, but the fire was eating the Hall slowly, the wind still pushing it away from this section of the house, the thick stone walls and hard ancient timbers refusing to combust. He and Jones used the flames' flicker to find their way to the scullery with their cargo, and again found Emily and Dorothy, now with four helpers holding the ends of a blanket to use as a stretcher, ready to ferry the women outside.

'Don't go back in there, you two!' ordered Dorothy, her face black with smoke, burns on her arms and slippered feet below her nightdress. 'The roof could go at any second.'

Nigel almost smiled as he disobeyed her. Such a mouse thirty-five years ago, a sergeant major now. He and Jones took a lungful of comparatively oxygenated air, coughed almost in unison, then ran back into the kitchen, staying as close as possible to each other in the dimness.

'Greenie!' yelled Jones.

No answer. Something heavy cracked, then fell. The kitchen shuddered. Dorothy had been right. The creeping fire had become a dragon now, feasting on the wooden attic walls, and timber roof. Flames shimmered at the far end of the corridor, reaching upwards, as if trying to find their share of the feast.

'Greenie, where the bloody hell are you?' shouted Nigel, as he and Jones staggered up the staircase. But the fire's growl was louder than any voice now, as it swallowed carpets, the hangings on the walls. Suddenly he heard a cough, and a voice just above them on the staircase.

'Here,' it croaked.

'Greenie, get out now,' snapped Jones.

Greenie ignored him — of course Greenie ignored him; nor had Jones probably expected her to obey. She swayed above them, her purple pyjamas the only colour in the thickening smoke. 'Saw two of them heading the wrong way in the smoke,' she managed to pant. 'Fräulein and that Hilda woman. Always bloody late ...'

And suddenly two shapes, below them. The women must have found their own way down the stairs.

He was about to call down to them when he heard Emily yell, 'Fräulein, over here! Clear a space, everyone, we're coming through!'

'Come on.' Jones grabbed his hand, then Greenie's. Nigel's lungs hurt, or his chest hurt. Blackness gathered behind his eyes ...

Somewhere below Emily shouted, 'Green and Jones are still in there, and that handyman. I'm going to —'

Her voice vanished in chaos as the front of the Hall collapsed, the drawing room where he had first seen Sophie, the corridor where the Prince of Wales had played the bagpipes. The noise filled the world, and for a moment the updraught carried the smoke with it, so the three of them stood in almost clarity on the stairs.

There was no gallery above them now, no corridor below, only this momentary space. He had reclaimed the Hall again, or it had reclaimed him, as if after so many centuries of protecting the Vailes, the Hall still sheltered him, leaving him seconds to gather everything important, everything she loved, whispers too strong for flames.

'Miss Lily ...'

'A Mr Lorrimer to see you, Miss Lily ...'

'*Darling* Miss Lily ...'

'Ah, Miss Lily, I think the Kaiser might agree to ...'

Pain had vanished, and maybe eyesight too, but she saw it all in memory ...

'Get them out!' she heard Emily scream. Lily's lungs reached for air and found none.

'A *most* productive conversation with Mr Churchill, Miss Lily ...'

'Miss Higgs has arrived, Miss Lily ...'

'Lily?' whispered Jones. She found his arm round her. Jones's other arm held Greenie close. The three of them stood, their arms around each other, a small wall of life among the flames. Just as we have always been there for each other, thought Lily, an almost perfect moment, if only she could see Sophie one last time, Sophie and their children, and their grandchild ...

And suddenly she glimpsed them, as love stretched time and place, Sophie laughing astride a low-hung gum-tree branch, holding a baby in each arm, pretending to ride it like a horse. His daughter, older than her photo, the scar across her cheek and beautifully business suited, striding down an unfamiliar corridor, and smiling. There was Danny sitting on the stockyard rails, the drooling toddler in his arms, throwing a rusk down to a dog. Everything Lily had ever wanted, love and comradeship and duty done.

'I love you,' Lily said to them, to Jones and Greenie, their faces close to hers as they drank the last thin shards of air.

'Idiot,' whispered Greenie hoarsely, smiling at her, as Jones said, 'I love you, too.'

The roof fell.

Chapter 54

In my end is my beginning.

In my end is my beginning.

> Miss Lily as she packed away her dresses in 1940,
> quoting Queen Mary Stuart

6 MAY 1945

SOPHIE

The room did not seem like a hospital, despite the large number of tubes leading to and from various parts of her, the sheets tucked in with the precision only years of nursing training can give and the highly polished floor devoid of rugs.

But the painting opposite was almost certainly a Cézanne, one a patient could gaze at for hours and find a universe within. The scent was faded pot pourri, not the disinfectant she had smelled in the tent, and then the various rooms and spaces she'd been aware of for short and floating times, when nothing seemed quite real, including life. She was also clad in a silk nightdress, which hospitals usually did not provide, as well as a bright white bandage on her left hand, which was strapped to too many tubes to lift, assuming she had the strength to try.

This was a most exclusive hospital, perhaps, or at least an exclusive floor where patients would not be disturbed or seen by visitors clutching a handful of roses for Aunt Daphne. The only sound was the faint noise of traffic. A city ...

Big Ben chimed. Sophie counted. Ten o'clock in London then, and from the glimpse of faded blue between the curtains it was ten am not pm and this was either a rare smog-free day, or pre-Roman Britain, though the Angles, or were they the Saxons, did not have Big Ben ...

And she was alive. Lily would be with her soon, and if this was an exclusive hospital they could damn well wheel her to a phone, tubes and all, so she could speak across the world to Daniel, Rose and Danny, say that she loved them, that she was sorry, that she would never leave them, even travelling for Higgs was done ...

The door opened. 'Sophie?'

She managed to smile. 'James.' Her eyes flicked to the corridor — linoleum, slightly more hospital like — but Lily — no: Nigel; no: *Bob* — was not with him. Still discreetly at Shillings then.

'Ah, you're awake at last. How are you feeling?'

She gathered the fragments of her brain, her life, and found they still fitted in a reasonable whole. 'Almost entirely without sensation, which I assume means I'm heavily dosed with painkillers, and need them.'

'Severe emaciation, and septicaemia, which penicillin is cleaning up nicely.'

She remembered the cut, the swelling. 'Ah, the new wonder drug. What else?'

'Sophie, I'm sorry. They had to amputate two fingers.'

She said nothing, not even, 'Which two fingers?' She would find out in time, and what were two fingers compared to those she loved?

He sat by her bed in an armless chair that was and covered in blue silk, the kind of chair designed for the wide skirts of women but also suitable for a multi-tubed patient to sit in. 'No questions?'

'You know the questions.' Sophie closed her eyes. Even this exchange had tired her. She would live and home awaited her, somehow, somewhen, and Bob or even Lily would be here soon, and there'd be no need to talk for a while, for Lily had the gift of quietness, with everything necessary communicated without words.

James said, 'Hitler is dead. The Americans and Russians have taken Berlin. The war in Europe is almost over. Japan hasn't yet surrendered but the Allied forces have almost conquered Okinawa.' He hesitated. 'Over one hundred thousand civilians committed suicide on the first day of the invasion. The emperor has ordered all Japanese to suicide rather than surrender. The Japanese army is starving. It can't be long now.'

This should be of course the most important news. But her world had narrowed to the people she loved. She suspected it would never widen again to include the business of nations.

'Rose and Danny? Daniel?'

Another hesitation. 'They are all well.'

'But what aren't you telling me? I can read your voice, James,' she ordered tiredly. 'No matter how bad it is, I need to know.'

'Daniel is working again at the Bald Hill Clinic. He had a breakdown for a short while a little over two years ago, but is entirely recovered.' James paused as if wondering how much to tell her.

'Everything!' Sophie insisted fiercely. 'Has Danny gone to New Guinea? Is he all right? Please, James.'

'Danny is thriving. After Daniel's breakdown he left school to manage Thuringa. He is still managing Thuringa, and extremely well. Rose is in charge of the entire Higgs operation — you are going to find it interesting working together because I suspect she has no intention of leaving. She was injured in February last year —'

'What? How?'

'The ship she was on from Brisbane was sunk by a submarine. She has scars on her face and I gather her arms and chest too. She also has a devoted husband ...'

Sophie managed to lift her head an inch in indignation. 'What? How could Daniel allow that? She is far too young to be married!'

'... who saved her life despite his own injuries and whom she adores. She also has a baby daughter, Lily-Anne.'

'I am a grandmother?' Sophie asked incredulously, joy sweeping through her.

'Yes.'

She had never even considered she might have grandchildren so soon. A baby! The world twisted and would never be the same. 'We're grandparents,' she whispered to Lily, suddenly seeing herself and Nigel and Daniel linked in generations of descendants.

James reached into his briefcase and brought out a bundle of letters, tied with ribbon as neatly as if they were Cabinet documents. 'Your family were told you were in Europe and unable to contact them, but they kept sending letters in case you could be reached. I've kept them for you, nearly three years of them. In chronological order.'

Of course James would have the letters in chronological order. But she would read the most recent first, then slowly savour the rest. She reached for them with her one working hand, awkwardly because of the tubes, held them to her heart, trying to smell Thuringa, her children, the man she loved. But they just smelled of paper, part of the vast store of papers the war had birthed.

'Hannelore? Violette?' She still could not believe Violette had betrayed her simply for security.

'Violette has survived, and thrived,' James said drily. 'She even joined a resistance group after your betrayal, possibly to avoid the retaliation now being dealt out to collaborators. She seems to have vanished lately, but I am sure she will cope as well with peace as war.' He smiled, obviously glad to give her good news. 'Hannelore is safe at the Lodge. They have set up a temporary clinic there — Germany is in a bad way. She was offered a passage to England, but your condition had stabilised by then, and she refused. You don't remember seeing her?'

'She found me? I think I remember hearing her voice, but not much more. She wasn't ...' Sophie tried not to remember her own torture '... hurt?'

'I think she was,' James said quietly. 'But she seems well now, and strong enough to nurse inmates from Dachau. There's been a bad outbreak of typhus there, but the Lodge is in strict quarantine. Communication is still limited though. I think it will be a while before we can communicate reliably. Months, or even longer.'

She had expected that. But James had not mentioned Nigel — Bob. Nor had she asked about him, once he had omitted him from that first reassuring list.

'Tell me the rest, James.'

'Shillings Hall is gone,' he said briefly. 'A crippled RAAF bomber crashed into it a couple of days ago. The entire house burned.'

A couple of days ago. She closed her eyes. Just a few more days and she would have seen it again. The beloved old Hall, gone. She could not bear it. But of course, all over Europe, the unbearable was being borne. 'Casualties?'

'Three. They managed to evacuate everyone in the building, but it collapsed on them before they could get out.'

'They?'

'Jones and Miss Green had returned and were living in the Hall again. They and ...' For the first time Sophie saw James fumble, unable to continue, as her heart shredded. For who had died in that fire? Lily? Nigel? Bob?

Or none of them, she thought with sudden hope, grief receding to clarity. Just as Nigel had become Lily, who sometimes changed to Nigel, then Lily had become Bob, this was a perfect way for Lily-Nigel to evade post-war complications, including any expectations from James or others in intelligence. Lily could not be dead!

'He is to be buried in the family plot, but as Bob Green, with Jones and Miss Green in the plot next to him.'

Sophie nodded, trying to keep her face set in unspeakable grief. Burials meant nothing. Nigel Vaile, Earl of Shillings, was supposed to be buried in the family plot, too. The three of them would still be alive, because of course the three of them must be together. New faces, new names, new roles — they had trained for this most of their lives. Jones had been butler, batman, gentleman farm manager, and other roles she knew of but hadn't seen. She had seen Greenie become Lily for a few confusing moments, and turn from lady's maid to warrior in an instant.

Because Nigel could not be dead. Not when she had come so far. He had *promised* her. They would talk when she returned, and now she had, and somehow, somewhere …

'Daniel and your children have been told, of course, but only what will be placed in a notice in the *Times*, that Lily Vaile has died, after a long illness. I didn't want to make anything public until you'd been informed.' He hesitated. 'There will need to be a grave for her, of course, as well as for Bob, and possibly a memorial ceremony. But those decisions are for her family to make.'

'Thank you. That was … considerate.'

'You may wish to tell Rose and Danny more, of course. Their father's death was heroic, as was so much of his life.'

'Thank you,' she said again, keeping her voice calm while frantically trying to think where they might have gone, and how. A car waiting, then a fishing boat? They'd had papers for so many identities over the years. Travel was difficult now, but the world's chaos also meant it would be very easy to vanish, too.

'He left a letter for you,' said James. 'In point of fact he left many letters with me over the years, to be given in case of his death, with orders each time to destroy the one before. He wrote this one only a few weeks before he died.'

Of course he did, she thought. They must have planned this for a long time — not the tragedy at the Hall, though they'd taken advantage of that for their disappearance. Lily would want me to know as soon as possible she isn't dead, she can't be dead …

James pulled out the envelope, pre-war parchment, with Lily's sloping handwriting on its face. Sophie took it in her good hand. Her mind was clearer now, the pain medication wearing off, for her left hand throbbed slightly.

The letter was sealed, but of course James would have unsealed it, perused the contents, then sealed it again. Whatever message was in it would be discreet.

'Will I leave you to read it?'

'Yes, please.'

'Would you like me to return, after that?' He pulled a slim volume from his pocket. 'I will sit in the corridor and read, if you would like company.'

How had he known she did not want to be alone? Because even though everyone she loved was safe ... of course, *of course* Lily and Jones and Greenie were still safe ... she did not want to be left in this quite lovely room with neither friends nor family. James was so very good at knowing so many things. Why hadn't he guessed they weren't dead? 'Yes, please,' she repeated. She waited till the door shut, then slid the note from the envelope.

My Dearest Sophie,

If you are reading this then I am dead, and you have survived. Your survival, and your happiness, mean more to me than anything in my life, except perhaps our children and the grandchild whose existence is a miracle, as great as any of those you brought to my life.

You told me, long ago, that you always knew my heart truly lived at Shillings. I did not correct you. I love Shillings, and not because it is my duty to love it. But there has never been any element of duty in my love for you. It came unlooked for, a gift beyond any I had hoped for, and will be the greatest part of me until the moment of my death.

My death also means that this is my only chance to explain to you what to many may seem to have been a complex life, but to me has seemed simple, even if eventful.

I have already written to Rose and Danny, as their Aunt Lily, explaining that the letters they now have are only to be sent if I am dead. Rose and Danny may show you the letters, or not, as they choose, but I have reminded Danny that while he holds the title, he may at any time choose to renounce it. He has a right to choose to whom and what he owes a duty, but should not feel bound by an old and increasingly irrelevant title. Apart from Shillings Hall, its garden, and a few cottages, the estate is all leased to tenants. I suspect many, or even most, will wish to buy the properties after the war. Shillings is no longer isolated from the world, and its newcomers and even the children who have grown up during the war almost certainly will not want to inherit feudal rights and duties.

I do not know what condition the Hall will be in once it is no longer required by the nation, but might I suggest it be given to the National Trust, with one wing retained for family, and those like Hereward for whom the Hall has become home. As you are all so enmeshed in your Australian lives, this might suit you best. But while Danny has already inherited the title, you are his trustee for the unentailed property until he is thirty. I hope Danny is able to make any decisions slowly, in the knowledge that he, and Shillings, will change as the decades go by.

Other explanations must wait till you and Daniel decide the time is right for them, but I have sent a letter to Daniel, too, to be given to Rose and Danny when you think they are ready to know more. That letter is unsealed, so you and Daniel can read it first, but I hope you will agree with what I have chosen to tell them, and what I have not. Children deserve the truth from their parents, but they also deserve not to be burdened with what they do not need to know.

This then, is only for you.

I told you, several times, and also let you assume, that I am Lily-Nigel, that Lily was born in war on the North West Frontier, and in my time with Misako in Japan, as I gradually realised that one aspect of myself could only be expressed as a woman.

I lied.

I am Lily Vaile, and always have been, but until I met Misako I knew of no way to be myself. But I am also Earl of Shillings, with duties to my people and my land that could only be fulfilled by a man, for as Lily I have no right to Shillings, nor the ability to protect it. James might suspect this, but Jones and Greenie are the only ones who have always known. Jones and Greenie, too, never fitted the lives into which they were born. Class differences, now thankfully growing outdated, have meant that we were forced into a variety of roles, but those have always been a façade, instead of who we truly were, the three of us together.

Then you arrived. I loved you at first sight. That love changed, and grew. I realised you were a woman who might, miraculously, accept a Lily-Nigel, and after all, that is what society forced me to be, two instead of one. Lily Vaile could not marry you, just as she could not protect Shillings and its people as the Earl. I assumed, too, that you loved Nigel, for it was Nigel to whom you flew back, Nigel to whom you proposed. I stayed as Nigel Vaile, most of the time, for you. It only gradually dawned on me that your love for Lily was the deeper. Forgive me for my stupidity, for underestimating you, for taking so long to realise that at some level you intuited that Lily was all of me, and Nigel only a part.

My choice in Berlin was for myself, and for you. I did not choose to be Lily for the sake of the network I'd established. That could have been run by others, and indeed it is now.

Nigel Vaile died, and Lily Vaile lived. I thought I would finally be Lily Vaile forever, with you and Jones and Greenie, and I had come to love and admire Daniel too. Yet as time passed, I still did not trust your love enough to tell you the truth, that though the years with you as Nigel were the happiest I had known, the years with you when I was Lily were happier still.

But war meant that Nigel Vaile had to play a part again, even if his role was Bob. My deepest regret is that I didn't tell you all this openly, on the first day George Carryman delivered you to England. For the reasons you well understand, I had decided that it was now too dangerous to continue to be Lily, but we could still have had some small moments. That was cowardice, for I did not know if I could bear to become Bob again, after being Lily, even for a short while. But of course I could, and if you are reading this then I wasted our last chance to be together.

In any life there must be 'might have beens'. What might have been, if I had never attempted to continue as Nigel after the Great War? Would you have still proposed to me, if I had been Lily, knowing that Nigel was a mask I must put on sometimes for *society? There is also the greatest 'might have been' of all: life as Lily again, somehow, somewhere, if I survive the war. But not 'Miss Lily', for I do not think there is a need to train lovely ladies to wield power in the background now. You have helped lead the way for a woman to be her own person, striding out from the shadows that have kept women hidden for so long. 'Miss Lily' can truly vanish now, but some of her insights, perhaps, may live on.*

You and I are grandparents together, and I have known all earthly joy. I have loved you with every kind of love humanity has known, and sign myself, as I have always truly been,

Yours, past, present and forever,

Lily

She did not know when she had begun to sob. She stared at the paper. Lily's revelation was far smaller than her grief, for this was not a coded message. It was the final letter from the person she, too, had loved from that first moment at Shillings, a love that grew and changed and was as complex as the two people who had shared it.

Tears fell on the paper, smudging the ink. She waited, as her sobs subsided, then placed the precious letter on the sheet and wiped her eyes with her only usable hand. The grief was still almost too much to bear, but she was still a student of Miss Lily, who had shown her ladies how to grieve yet still see beauty, to cry but know happiness and love.

She, who had loved Nigel Vaile and Miss Lily, had loved them too much to see the truth behind them, the one who was both.

Could one even measure love?

Of course one could. Love was measured all the time. And yes, the most joy-filled period of her life, too, had been those years at Thuringa, with beloved Lily known to the world as her sister-in-law, Daniel beside her, children's laughter as they climbed the massive magnolia out the front, pretending it was a pirate ship or aeroplane. But there was only one love, even if it was expressed in different ways. The many faces of love, for a person with many faces.

The door opened. Sophie looked up, expecting James. But Ethel stood there, solid and reassuring and dressed in a perfectly tailored heather tweed, carrying it off with a panache Sophie had never seen in her before. She held the hand of a toddler dressed in a hand-knitted jersey and tartan skirt, the tiny girl's solid shoulders and lifted chin unmistakably those of a Carryman.

'All right to come on in?'

'Yes. Oh yes, please.'

'It's good to see you, Sophie lass,' said Ethel quietly. 'I thought this might be the time to meet little Sophie here.' She bent to the child. 'This is your wonderful Aunt Sophie.'

The child stared at the figure on the bed, unimpressed. 'Why?'

'Because she is courageous and we love her.'

The tiny Sophie shook her head. She pointed to the tubes. '*Why?*'

'Because she is sick and they help make her better.' Ethel spoke with the ease of long practice with the questions of the young.

The child accepted the answer and began to chew her finger.

'She's mine,' said Ethel, smiling again. 'And James's too.' She lifted a hand to show an antique engagement ring and a gold wedding band.

'But ... how ...?'

'Long story.' Ethel considered. 'Actually a very short one.' She grinned. 'You know what they say. Strange things happen in war. We're happy,' added Ethel Lorrimer-Carryman. 'Kiss your Aunt Sophie, darling.'

'No,' said the small Sophie.

'Just like her ma,' said Ethel proudly, and Sophie laughed. Heartbreak and joy, she thought. And a child who would surely need the wisdom of a Miss Lily, even in the new world born of this war ...

People died. Love and wisdom did not, not as long as memory continued. I will never forget you, she thought, as Ethel ushered the unwilling child closer but did not press her to kiss where she was unwilling. All you taught me, all the love. And somehow I always knew the truth of you, or rather felt it. Three faces, but a single, all-encompassing love.

Chapter 55

Few people truly see their own face in the mirror. They posture,
seeing the person they would like to be. Often we must see others
and see ourselves in them to realise who we truly are.

Miss Lily, 1938

MAY 1945

VIOLETTE

The newsreel wound to an end, but Violette stayed in her velvet
seat even as the theatre lights came on. The crowd moved silently,
crushed by the same weight that kept her in her seat, the flicker
of film that showed the inside of the Bergen-Belsen concentration
camp. Black and white, white faces, white bodies, black mud
and barbed wire. Only the beginning of the unfolding horror,
the newsreader had said.

Millions dead, millions still uncounted, killed for the crimes of
race, religion, physical defect. Killed with careless incompetence,
as well as efficient brutality.

You did not kill like that from duty. You killed because it
gave you pleasure. She had once been glancing idly through one
of Daniel's books at Thuringa, for one had to find something
to do when the land was cows and proper shops a day's drive
away, when she saw a chapter called *The Psychopath*, and read
it. It described people like those who had designed and run the
camps, camps for innocents and those courageous enough to
stand or fight against evil.

But those Violette killed had deserved to die.

Did they? Every single one? She suddenly did not know.

She did know that she had enjoyed the challenge, had felt no guilt, only triumph as the numbers rose.

Psychopath. The book had said you were born one. But she … she had been made, crafted by Grandmère. If you had been made, could you be unmade?

She did not know that either.

She rose from her seat and walked slowly up the aisle, then out into the foyer and to the street. Uniforms, American and English and Free French, women, children smiling, even an accordion player on the street corner. Dancing was permitted now, even encouraged. Maison Violette's salons would be crowded with women needing festive gowns.

She did not think she would design a dress again.

She had given her staff a month's paid leave, every one of them, for prisoners were returning and others lost must be sought, and every life rearranged. Even Madame Thomas had left for the seaside and Violette had gone with her for two weeks. Madame was Tante Thomas now for young Tomas, and the childless family who had welcomed him had Madame Thomas as an adopted aunt for life as well. Violette had even found a puppy, hungry and abandoned in a gutter, to complete the promise that Tomas should have a dog.

She should be lining up to buy food. The last year had depleted even her stores and the black marketeers'. The liberators had come, but food for civilians was still desperately short. She supposed she should feel hungry. She found that she was not.

She approached Maison Violette's front doors and stopped. A man sat on the step. He stood as she approached. Not in uniform. True to his conscience then, as she had been to hers. But his scars were new.

'George.' She did not run to him nor even offer her cheek to kiss. All she could think to say was, 'How has your war been?'

'A taxi-driver's war. I flew planes.'

She doubted it had been like that. 'The scars?'

'Shot down.'

She nodded, merely to acknowledge what he had said. She had heard of pilots of bravery and skill who nudged the German rockets from their course. Sometimes she had dreamed she'd seen George doing that. It did not matter now.

'James Lorrimer asked me to find you, though I was coming to you anyway.'

'He did not want me during the whole war, but wants me now?'

'He thought you might want to know — Sophie is safe, in England.'

She thought a brief prayer of gratitude, to match all those where she had prayed Aunt Sophie would be safe, but all she said was 'Good.' The guilt that stained her now was too great for even Sophie's death to add to, nor did Sophie's survival diminish it. 'My parents?'

'I ... I'm sorry. There was a fire at Shillings. They died together, getting people out.'

Violette imagined the scene. It seemed a fitting conclusion to their lives. She should feel grief. George seemed to be waiting for her to cry at the news, perhaps, or to produce her key to invite him inside.

'Lorrimer said I could take three weeks' leave when I found you,' he said cautiously at last. 'I wondered if we might spend them together.'

'It's been five years.'

'I haven't changed,' he said simply. 'The moon is still made of green cheese.'

'I have not changed either. That, I think, is the problem.' Violette would not tell him how she had spent the war, nor even the deaths before it that she had flung from her conscience as 'necessary' or 'deserved'. She would not burden him. Let him remember young love and think just that. 'We were too young.'

She smiled at him and shook her head. 'My most dear George. Find another love, and go with God.'

'Violette ...'

She thought George would touch her then. But he stepped back as she took out her key to unlock the front door. He had seen more in her face, perhaps, than she had wished to show. She did not want comfort, and certainly not from a man she loved but must not keep. And when she looked out of the window five minutes later, an hour later, or a day perhaps, he had gone.

Bien.

It was time for Violette to vanish too.

Chapter 56

*One of English's sillier sayings is that 'life must go on'. There are
times when a life should most definitely end. But a life's ending
may be played in many ways …*

Miss Lily, 1912

Midge Harrison's Sweet Potato Sugarless, Eggless Fruit Slice (extremely good)

1 cup finely chopped fresh pineapple, peaches, apricots or other fruit
    to hand
2 cups sultanas, or chopped dates, or a mix of both
1 large sweet potato, peeled and chopped
Fresh orange juice, water or cold tea
3 tablespoons mixed spice
4 tablespoons golden syrup
2 cups plain flour

Cover dried fruit and sweet potato with orange juice, water or cold
tea, or a mix of all of them, in a saucepan. Simmer till the sweet
potato is soft. The sultanas will now be plumper and almost twice
their size. Mix in spice and golden syrup. Cool. Gently fold in
the flour. You may need a bit more or less water, cold tea or orange
juice — depends how liquidy your fruit mix is.

    Pour into a wide baking tin greased and floured. The mixture
should only come halfway up the tin or even less — this slice
shouldn't be deep.

    Bake in a moderate oven for about 45 minutes or till the middle is
firm when you press it lightly. Cool in the tin, then cut into squares.

Keep in a sealed container in a cool place for up to a week. This will not last like a conventional dried fruitcake or biscuits, but it is moist and delicious.

JUNE 1945

HANNELORE

Midsummer and the thrush was singing, the only song perhaps in this ruined land, as Hannelore carried another basket of potatoes across what once had been a lawn.

Behind her two soldiers from the United States carried out yet another stretcher. The Lodge was a small haven for those who suffered injury and starvation at Dachau, a refuge from the illness that left even more bodies needing graves dug in frozen soil, for typhus had swept the camp again, even after liberation; nor had there been enough food or shelter for the inmates who had survived as snow froze the land and its starving people.

Of the hundred prisoners who had been billeted here, more than twenty had already died, despite vegetable soups and nursing. Here, at least, it seemed that potatoes had still been planted, cabbages in their usual orderly rows, even the greenhouses miraculously intact, but beyond the Lodge and its farm and wood, Germany starved, with so few to have planted crops to harvest and half its people injured, ill or 'displaced'. It might be years before 'plenty' returned.

Yet even the chickens had been waiting for her here, and the swans on the lake. It seemed that the Nazis had honoured their promise to Dolphie, in their own vicious way. After all, they had not killed her, only left her to die. Her home had been tended. And now she had not died, Dolphie's money and possessions were hers to claim, as was Dolphie's late wife's money, kept, it seemed, in a Swiss bank account. She also had the accumulated income from her factories, though those that had not been bombed had all been burned before or during the invasion.

Her factories. She could not bear to think of what she had never even thought to ask, all the years before the war when she had accepted their increasing profitability without asking how, or why.

Instead she hired cooks, orderlies, cleaners and nurses and fired three of them the first day, or, rather, they left, despite the guarantee of food and wages, for they would not tend Jewish patients. It was not just cities that had turned to rubble, but human hearts.

Only two of the women who had shared the factory hut and escaped with her were still here. Frau Fischer was still recovering from her wound as well as burns, ulcers and starvation. The other was Judith, cooking and nursing as Hannelore did, too, for many of those who had survived Dachau would need care for years, or some for all their lives. Neither woman had formal qualifications, but decades of experience, born of wars and tragedy. The other women had recovered enough to begin the search for their lives again.

Money helped. Money could buy help to go home; to find out if home existed; to buy another place to live, even if it was a temporary perch. With enough money you could buy food. Money could not bring back what was lost, of course, nor could it wipe away the terror and the agony. Money had also allowed her to turn the Lodge into a hospital, while the American authorities to whom she had given the rest of the property tried to find enough resources to feed and care for so many left starving, sick and dying in the camps, with a third of Europe, perhaps, having lost their homes or trying to find their way back to them.

'Ma'am?' The American soldiers had discovered that she no longer answered to 'Prinzessin'.

'Yes, Captain?'

'I just came to tell you that our men and supplies have finally caught up with us.' He nodded at the potatoes. 'I reckon you don't need to keep digging those up yourself now. The new medical staff should arrive tonight, too. But please,' he added quickly, 'we don't want to turn you out of your home.'

'That is kind of you. Thank you.'

Hannelore waited until he had left, then walked slowly to the kitchen, already under the control of uniformed men, placed the potatoes on the bench, then made her way to her old bedroom.

The trundle bed where she had slept in the first weeks Sophie had been at the Lodge was gone, needed for the patients. She had been needed for the patients, too, but no longer.

She sat upon the bed and remembered. There was, in fact, little joy in her memories, except the times with Dolphie, his loss still an almost incomprehensible pain. Hers had been a life of duty until an Australian called Sophie Higgs had made a snowman at Shillings Hall. Liebe Sophie, who she had loved, betrayed and loved. But she had loved her country and betrayed it too, not by aiding the Allies, but by failing to see her own source of wealth, the corruption at the heart of Hitler's dream.

True evil is the refusal to see or feel when others are hurt or killed. But what of those who did not even think to look? Surely their crime — her crime — was worse.

Hannelore had heard murmurs that there would be trials of war criminals for crimes against humanity. She would not be among their number. Ironically, being made a prisoner and slave worker had made her safer. The Allied authorities assumed she had spied for England, but she had really spied for Germany, to see the Nazi Party vanquished. But nonetheless she deserved to die for crimes against so many people, and crimes against herself.

She had prepared for this. Not cyanide, with its sudden pain. She would give herself a final gift, a drifting off to sleep, so she could remember happiness before she died. She had taken the sleeping tablets from the doctor's bag that afternoon, to add to the four she had left from when her burns were fresh. Physical pain was bearable. Pain of the soul was not.

She took those first tablets, and then the others, a slightly different shape, softer and flavoured with peppermint. She smiled at that. How American, to flavour medicines. As if those who craved sleep cared about the taste.

The first, the second, then the twenty-fourth. She lay down neatly, and remembered.

A music box, when she was nine.

Sledding with Dolphie, at fourteen, the air stinging their skin ...

The snowman, with Sophie. Dancing at the ball while Sophie danced with Dolphie, hoping that just perhaps there might still be peace, and Sophie would be her aunt, a sister. Sophie, promising her sunshine and kangaroos.

Sophie, who had forgiven her.

Hannelore had not even seen a kangaroo yet, but she had seen sunshine. She let her eyes shut, and felt her body drift into its warmth.

She woke, cold. This could not be heaven then, nor hell. Even purgatory would not leave her cold, and stiff too.

'So you have woken.' The voice was still expressionless. Hannelore turned. Judith watched her from the chair. 'I saw you steal the tablets. It was simple to substitute them.' She almost smiled. 'I made them from those American peppermints.'

'How did you know?'

'That you intended suicide, not sleep? Because I have seen thousands lose the will to live and I saw it in your eyes. I also know the factories were yours. I heard your uncle talk of them. But I did not tell the other women.' Judith shrugged. Her eyes were no longer sunken, but the shoulders were skeletal still. 'So. You have killed yourself, as you deserved. What now?'

'I ... I don't understand.'

'You were judge, jury and executioner. The sentence was carried out. In most jurisdictions if the condemned survives, then they are pardoned. Do you care to pardon yourself?'

'No,' said Hannelore, sitting up. Her body felt like melted marshmallow, and her brain refused to comprehend.

'Good. You should not be pardoned. Work out your sentence here on earth.'

'How? I'm not needed.'

'You have money. Use it.'

'Others can use it, to make what recompense is possible. I have prepared a trust ensuring that.' She had named James Lorrimer as her trustee, the one she trusted to carry out the compensation, and to understand why.

'You have a body and a mind, then. Use those.'

'I don't think I have the strength,' admitted Hannelore.

The woman stared at her. 'There must be something in this world you want.'

'Only to leave all this behind, every fallen leaf. I cannot stand it.'

'Nor can I, though I do not know how to escape, or even where I wish to go. But I escaped Dachau. I will escape this too,' said Judith. 'Surely there is something you have always wished for?'

'I wanted to see a kangaroo once.'

'What ...?'

'They are large animals that hop. In Australia. Across the world.'

'I know what kangaroos are. It seems a small ambition.'

Hannelore found herself smiling in memory. 'It has been the largest ambition of my life, since I was a young woman. To leave behind duty, and position. To become simply a friend, to visit another friend and see a peculiar animal for no more reason than it would be interesting, and fun.' Hannelore added softly, 'To no longer be myself.'

Judith nodded. She did not speak. She sat, while Hannelore watched midsummer leaves out the window. At last Judith said, 'I envy you. I have nothing. No family. No life. Not even a dream of kangaroos. But in the night sometimes I wake and want to fly, fly high and far to leave all I have known behind.'

'Australia is perhaps as far away as one can go.'

Judith shrugged. 'I have been asking questions about all these far countries. Australia does not like refugees, especially Jewish ones, or women. They will take single men only, men who can work.'

'You could be a visitor. Travel in comfort, not as a refugee. To see if you like kangaroos. Not with money from the factories,' added Hannelore awkwardly. 'The money my late aunt-in-law left is in a Swiss bank. It can only be claimed in person.'

'You would send me on a holiday to Australia?' asked Judith incredulously.

'Yes.'

'Will you come on this holiday too?' asked Judith quietly.

Hannelore stared at her, life dawning within her. 'If you invite me.'

More silence. Hannelore heard the thrush. Restitution, she thought. With everything I have, for my whole life. Duty, once again. Yet duty — with sunlight, with kangaroos, with Judith, perhaps even with Sophie, too — no longer seemed to crush her, but gave her wings of light.

At last Judith said, 'Hannelore, will you come to Australia with me, to see kangaroos? To see if Australia is far enough away and a place where we can build our lives?'

Hannelore closed her eyes. It was not fair, that she, who was guilty of so much, should be blessed with this. But had anyone ever glimpsed that elusive creature 'a fair life'?

'Yes,' said Hannelore.

Judith put out her hand, scarred from chilblains, crooked from digging potatoes and even harder work.

Hannelore took it, her own hand scarred by work and fire. 'We will go together,' she said.

Epilogue

I do not send you out into the world as swans, although you have their grace. Nor are you eagles, although I hope you fly as high, and see as clearly. You are not doves, either, for though doves have been called the birds of peace, so far they have been singularly unsuccessful. Perhaps you are what doves might be, if they had the strength and courage to say, 'This is wrong. Let us sit together, not in anger, but to mend the cracks in our broken world.'

Miss Lily, 1914

SPRING 1976

SOPHIE

'The kangaroo is in the rose garden again,' noted Daniel, dressed in shirt, socks and nothing else, glancing out the bedroom window as he hunted for his bow tie.

'It won't hurt the roses. It just likes grass.' Sophie lay back on the pillows, enjoying the view of her husband, though even these days it was still … indecorous … for women of her age to admit they felt desire, or act upon it.

Daniel pulled on his underpants. 'I know perfectly well that kangaroos don't eat roses. But if young Hoppy has found a way in, then either someone's left the gate open or there's a hole in the fence.'

'Annie's probably in there cutting a few more roses for the church. Yes, there she is. Pull the curtains before she sees you, for heaven's sake.'

'Hoppy's doing well, anyway,' said Daniel. 'I didn't know how mobile he'd be after a broken tail.' He peered about the bedroom floor again. 'Did you see where I put my tie?'

Sophie grinned. 'It's on the chair, under your trousers.'

'Thank you.' Daniel glanced back at her. 'Isn't it time you dressed?'

Sophie pulled up the sheet, scented with lavender from the bushes that grew around the clothesline as well as the sachets in the linen cupboard, and stretched luxuriously. 'The grandmother of the groom has no duties, except to get to the church on time.'

Her hair had been freshly permed and coloured the day before. Her dress hung waiting for her in her dressing room, a soft gold silk shift that would float about her still extremely good legs, and that had no buttons or even a zip, both of which were possible with only eight fingers, but a nuisance. Make-up would take two minutes. Make-up should enhance one's beauty, not disguise one's age, Miss Lily had said.

She glanced out the gap between the curtains, where spring's gum tips tried to taste the blueness of the sky, suddenly wistful. 'I wish Midge had lived to see this.' Today Midge's daughter Jennifer, an unexpected post-war blessing, would marry the young man whose parents had met in the days of his family's greatest desperation.

'Midge knew,' said Daniel confidently. 'Jelly was always going to marry the girl next door.'

Just as a boy who been taught to fly in his teens by Sophie's old — in both senses — friends Miss Morrison and Mrs Henderson, had inevitably become Aeroplane Jelly at school. The nickname had stuck, though in Debrett's he was still the Honourable Nigel Vaile, as he'd been known during the year he'd spent back in England, living in the cottage that had once housed Bob Green, working on the farm managed by Joe Hereward that was all that was left of the Shillings estate, the greenhouses put to growing out-of-season lettuce for sale, sheep wandering the garden and orchards and between the crumbled walls, their mellow stones still beautiful.

That year had convinced Jelly not just that his roots ran deep in the Thuringa soil, but that he was more an artist than a farmer. Jelly now painted the landscapes that bush pilots and eagles saw. But Jennifer was the daughter of two farmers and sister of another, and a farmer herself. She and Danny were already managing Thuringa together. She had also carved out her own niche as founder of the new Old Baldie Winery, already with a first prize in 'Syrah/Shiraz' at the Paris Wine Exhibition, with its distinctive 'bald' labels of hairless men, women, dogs and startled sheep, created by Jelly, his sole contribution to the vineyard that had been planted on the steeper rocky slopes of the Harrison estate.

Sophie had made her last visit to England while Jelly was working there, walking under the apple blossom as white petals sifted about her cheeks. She'd made a cherry cake for Jelly that morning — Mrs Goodenough's recipe — but not brought a slice to eat in the orchard. Memory was enough.

The first time she had seen Lily. The last time she'd kissed Nigel. There were so many last times as one grew older. That visit would be the last time with her friends in England, for she would not make the journey again.

The last tea with Emily Sevenoaks MP, MBE, just the two of them, toasting crumpets by the fire and spreading them with butter and Shillings honey in memory of their days with Miss Lily. Emily was chair of the parliamentary Security Committee. 'The committees are where true power lies, darling.'

The last cup of cocoa with Ethel, CEO of Carryman's Cocoa, patron of a network of women's refuges, the School Breakfast Programme, the Women's Health Network and a Dame of the British Empire for her 'services in feeding England'. James's family might refuse knighthoods, but as Dame Ethel had pointed out, she was still a Carryman, and after all the word 'dame' still had a pantomime quality, so he may as well enjoy the joke.

She and Sophie had shared a vast old-fashioned Sunday lunch of roast lamb and apple pie and cheese with George and his wife Linda and their children. Sophie's namesake had not been there. Sophie Carryman-Lorrimer had been a most glamorous debutante — that custom had still not quite died away — but was now working with a voluntary agency in Africa. James was also absent, called away unexpectedly to a meeting at Whitehall that morning. The post-war world had new enemies, and James Lorrimer would never consider the word 'retire'.

'He sends his apologies,' said Ethel. 'Or he would have if he'd had time.' She smiled. 'We're there for each other if needed. It's worked well, in its way.'

The last time she had looked across the wind-tossed wave caps of the English Channel ...

'Sophie.' Hannelore barely knocked as she entered. 'I knew it. Not dressed yet! Daniel, put your trousers on.'

'Teutonic efficiency,' complained Daniel. But he fastened his trousers, then waited while Hannelore arranged his bow tie.

'You wish for a housekeeper who is not efficient? There. You may put your coat on.'

'Did you know there is a kangaroo in the rose garden?'

'Where?' Hannelore pulled the curtains back again. 'Ah, Hoppy is doing most well, isn't he?'

'Mum?' Danny, Earl of Shillings, wandered in, tie in hand. 'Oh, Hanne. Can you make this wretched tie sit straight? Annie's taking more flowers over to the church. Judith is in the kitchen making a cuppa,' he added. 'And Mrs MacDonald is still trying to get into her step-ins.'

Hannelore shook her head. 'It is not good for the body to be confined.' She wore a long blue taffeta dress, loosely belted, a gift from Sophie made by a new designer Rose had found in Sydney, Carla Zampatti. 'Come, we will be late! Hoppy, time to go back to your enclosure!' She floated out.

'Like bloody Central Station,' muttered Daniel, sitting to put on his shoes. Outside in the marquee the caterers unfurled white damask tablecloths for the reception and the Bald Hill florist hung garlands of everlastings along the verandah. She'd had half-a-dozen helpers scouring the hills for enough all week.

Sophie cried, just a little, as they took their seats in the front pew. Midge's absence was a sword cut today and yet of course her old friend was here, as long as love and memory lasted, and so was Lily.

She touched the tiny lily engraved on the ring Daniel had given her, a few months after she had shown him Lily's letter on one of the long quiet shared walks through the bush, which had helped to ease her nightmares, just as they had once soothed his. Since then she had always worn the thin gold band under her wedding ring.

This was the best time of the year, after the frost whiskers on the barbed wire fences, and before the first horde of bushflies. The church was full already. Jelly was president of the Bald Hill Life Drawing Society, founder of the Bald Hill Arts Society, secretary of the Thuringa Bushfire Brigade, and part of the collective painting a mural on the changing rooms of the new swimming pool. Admittedly those organisations shared at least half their members, but it still made quite a crowd.

Jennifer was the treasurer of the Progress Association, as well as vice-president of the board of the Bald Hill Hospital that had replaced Daniel's clinic. It had taken nearly a decade for Jelly's mother to come back to Bald Hill permanently to take up a job at the hospital, while neighbours tactfully asked Danny, 'How are you and Annie going?' as they saw him at the cattle sales holding his niece's hand while cradling his own baby in his other arm, with no full-time mother for either in attendance. Thankfully after Annie began diagnosing the district's haemorrhoids, broken legs and had delivered Mrs Murphy's triplets, no one needed to ask again.

Sophie nudged her husband firmly — he was asking Annie far too loudly about the results of Mr Taylor's colonoscopy. Daniel refused to admit he was going deaf. Sophie had to signal him a dozen times a week when he made some comment about a neighbour in full hearing of everyone in the Moon Dog café.

Rose and Paul came in with Lily-Anne and Meg, and now it was Sophie on the receiving end of Daniel's lifted eyebrow. No, she, Rose and Lily-Anne would not discuss business in church, how could he possibly think she would? Though she might have a word with Lily-Anne at the reception about the new 'boil in the can' self-saucing chocolate puddings, made with only the best Carryman's Cocoa. Corned beef was possibly the smallest department of Higgs Industries now. Sophie did not miss it.

Hannelore sat behind them with Judith. She looked even more beautiful with white hair than blonde, but Judith kept hers dyed defiantly dark. Her dress was her favourite Dior, rows of stiffened silver satin with a collar like a silver cape. Higgs's Senior Industrial Chemist's one extravagance was clothes.

The music began. There had been ... earnest discussion ... about the wedding march. The groom had won finally over the wishes of his mother, grandmother and Aunt Hannelore, who hoped for something traditional. The bride's father, Harry, had not joined the argument, on the grounds that he wouldn't be able to hear it anyway. The bride had simply laughed, and declared that she was leaving all the wedding planning to her fiancé, because he liked that sort of thing, and anyway she was busy with the cattle sale. The Bald Hill organist now made dutiful strides with the version of 'Thus Spoke Zarathustra' from the film *2001: A Space Odyssey*, not because Jelly or Jennifer had even read Nietzsche's work of the same name, but because they believed that each marriage was its own strange odyssey. Sophie agreed.

And there was Jelly, in a floral shirt, white tie and green bell-bottomed trousers, his hair pulled back in a long pony-tail, with Jennifer's nephew Lachie as his best man.

The crowd craned their necks to look back as the bride appeared in a long high-waisted dress made of patches of antique silk in shades of white and cream and parchment that the groom had designed himself and the Bald Hill dressmaker had made, crowned with roses, her two bridesmaids in green lace miniskirts that matched Jelly's trousers. Harry looked wonderful in his dinner jacket next to his daughter — he and Danny and Daniel had agreed that no matter what Jelly's psychedelic *Dress: optional* invitation said, weddings demanded a dinner jacket. A final guest slipped into the church behind the bride and her father, quickly genuflecting before she took her seat, dressed in a plain skirt and blouse, her age impossible to guess. She looked familiar, yet Sophie could not place her. A lecturer from Jennifer's days at agricultural college?

Sophie cried during the ceremony, with a small sob when Jelly smiled at his bride with Lily's smile as he said 'I do', but that was happiness as well, remembering her wedding to Daniel at the Shillings Church, her marriage to Nigel there. Our grandson is getting married, she thought to Lily, to Daniel, holding tight to Daniel's hand. He passed her his handkerchief.

She cried just a little again into her oysters Rockefeller, their shells sitting on a bed of sea-blue jelly; her Coronation Chicken; her potato salad, avocado salad, jellied pineapple salad; and Bombe Alaska served on raspberry jelly and adorned with flaming eggshells at the reception — all easy to eat neatly for a grandmother whose left hand could not quite manage a steak knife, as well as being the bride's and groom's favourite dishes, to go with the three-tier wedding cake with pale green icing, adorned with roses that matched the bride's bouquet, made and decorated by the bride's gran. (Lily would have smiled at the menu as far too rich, then said softly that any meal designed with love should be enjoyed.)

More jellies were passed around to the guests as the evening progressed. Each of Jelly's mates, it seemed, had brought a jelly tonight, obviously a group joke: green jelly with small plastic cows in it, a whisky jelly, which would have sent any true Scotsman into a frenzy, an Old Baldie Moselle jelly, and undoubtedly more to come. The long table of family faced so many friends and neighbours, Higgs stalwarts, a small bevy of retired psychiatrists discussing golf and the hazards of sleep therapy, agriculture college graduates, young women brown from horse riding or dagging sheep, young men with shoulders like Hereford bulls. The rock band thudded. She wanted to put her hands over her ears or borrow a little of Harry's or Daniel's deafness.

The formal seating was breaking up. Daniel had gone to yell companionably with another member of the hospital board, as deaf as he was. Sophie slipped over to the shadows under the pergola, still dripping with late spring wisteria, and relaxed into a cushioned cane banana lounge, her feet up comfortably. Her toes pained her when she stood too long in closed-in shoes. She was no longer embarrassed by her scars — Daniel had slowly convinced her again that she was beautiful, and if she was beautiful then every part of her must be too — but despite modern informality she could not convince herself that sandals were proper for a wedding. She might even slip off her heels ...

'Sophie?'

Sophie turned. It was the woman she had glimpsed in church. Plain-faced, no make-up, grey hair trimmed close to her head. Only the crucifix on her lapel proclaimed her vocation, now that Vatican II meant she had dispensed with robes. But the simple clothes she wore separated her even more than a nun's old-fashioned garments might have from the girl Sophie had known.

'Violette! I mean Sister Margaret. I was afraid ...'

'That I would not accept your most kind ticket and invitation, once the inestimable Mr Lorrimer finally found out where I was?'

Sophie nodded. 'Please sit.' She gestured to one of the cane chairs. Impossible to call her Sister Margaret, and yet this woman was not Violette.

'I hope you do not mind my coming to the wedding. In truth, I did not know if I could face you. But I prayed for courage, and anyway, who notices another woman at a wedding?'

'I did. I'm glad you came. How is the mission in Brazil?'

'Difficult. So many good people dead, so many bad ones powerful.' A shrug: a ghost of the old Violette. 'Europe thinks war finished in 1945, but there are wars as bad or worse happening right now. We try to help.' The French accent had been replaced by what might be a hint of Spanish. 'Thank you for your letter. It was so kind. You always have been kind, Sophie.'

'No,' said Sophie. 'I was completely self-centred when I was young. I gloried in seeming to be kind, till I met Miss Lily, and learned to push down the wall of embarrassment about my corned-beef heritage and actually consider others.' She gazed at the other woman. 'It has been so long. Nearly thirty-five years.'

'Since I betrayed you to the Gestapo?'

'You had no choice,' said Sophie softly. 'Truly, Sister Margaret, as I wrote to you, I understood why you had to do it. It was a country at war. You needed to protect those who worked for you —'

'I did not betray you.'

Sophie stared at her. 'I don't understand.' The Gestapo and Dolphie had been so definite that it had been Violette who'd called.

The woman who had been Violette Jones hesitated. 'I could not tell you this before. I had to be sure ...'

'Sure of what?'

'That your maman ... that she was dead.'

'I don't understand.'

'Your mother was at the salon the day you were arrested. I did not like her, nor could she afford my prices after the Occupation when she no longer received money from Australia, but she was your mother, so I let her come and gaze at the parade of models and eat the pastries, and sometimes I would make her a dress for far less than its true cost. She recognised you that afternoon. I found her in my office, calling the police. She believed you had cut off her allowance, you see, though I tried to explain that it was not your fault. She was bitter not just about the money that afternoon, but that you had just refused to greet her. How could she understand that you could not risk a reunion? I took the receiver from her, but there was no denying what she had already told the police. All I could do was finish the call, have her shown out, and then call Kolonel von Hoffenhausen.'

'But Dolphie told me you had agreed to contact him — to betray me — in return for the safety of Maison Violette.'

'I thought it safe to agree and most unsafe to refuse him. But of course I would not have done it. I did not think I would ever even have to make the choice. Why would you come to Paris? Or to see me if you did, when Lorrimer made it so clear I was not wanted?'

The shrug once more. 'But the Kolonel had also promised me he planned to keep you safe, that he and others wanted peace with Britain. I did not know if I believed him. But he had refused to have you killed once before, so I called and told him the dress with acacia flowers had already been collected. It was the only thing I could do to help.'

'It was enough,' said Sophie slowly. 'Dolphie arranged for my escape.'

'Your mother died eight years later. A heart attack. But I only found out about her death a year ago, when I made a visit back to France.' Sister Margaret met Sophie's eyes. 'You thought I had betrayed you, but forgave me. I cried, when I saw that you had written that.'

'Sister Margaret ...' How to explain that she had loved Violette, and cared nothing for the mother who had never deserved the name? Was there even any point after so long?

Yes. Love mattered.

'Sister Margaret, I didn't even recognise my mother that afternoon. I had met her properly only once and found her empty of anything but self-absorption. I briefly glimpsed a woman who might have been her a few years later. She could only have known what I looked like from the newspaper photographs with the king, back in thirty-six.' And, ironically, her mother's allowance had even been reinstated after the war. 'I cared no more about her than any person on the street. But I loved the girl Violette, and Violette the woman too. If that woman had called the police, I knew it must have been for the very best of reasons. I wanted to explain I understood so many times.'

'But you could not find me? I had to vanish,' said Sister Margaret gently. 'Until the girl I'd been had gone. You might forgive, but I could not forgive myself.' She hesitated. 'You remember that I killed people in that war? I told myself that each deserved it, that the loss of every one of them brought us a little closer to freedom.'

She touched one of the sprays of wisteria, its scent softly honeyed in the night. 'Did it? I do not know. But finally I realised I had not cared about those I murdered. In my sight they were just unpersons, to be disposed of, just as Herr Hitler created unpersons too, and persuaded so many others to carefully not see. Once I knew that I knew Violette Jones must cease to be.'

But war is a different world and a complex one, thought Sophie. Or was it? There had been moments in history where World War II might have been prevented. There might have been more if there were more people like George and Ethel, willing to risk their lives or social ostracism, using kindness and forgiveness as tools for peace, trying to understand the enemy, not shrug them off as ... what word had Violette just used? *Unpersons*.

Daniel had once shown her a study proving that on average one person could convince fifteen others that hatred and violence were justified. Hatred was contagious. But one person could convince fifteen to be kind instead. So simple, even simplistic. Just be kind, so no one — human, dog or landscape, was an *unperson*.

At last Sophie said, 'You ... you feel you have atoned?'

'Instead, perhaps, that there is no need. The girl Violette was dangerous. Now Sister Margaret listens to her Mother Superior, and to her Sisters, too. It is easier to know what is right when surrounded with other people searching for that too. What was it that Aunt Lily said? "Do not waste your life on what you regret from yesterday, but wonder what may be done tomorrow."'

Sophie smiled. 'I don't remember Lily saying that. It sounds like her, though.'

'We were sitting at breakfast here, the two of us alone. She taught me much, not just how to eat my bread with grace, but how friendship can change a life, a world. It has been a hard time for Brazil. But we can stay strong together ... Ah, it is time for the bridal waltz. I am glad they have kept that. And a string quartet too! I have missed that in South America. But we do have music, music for the soul and music to dance to.'

'You don't miss designing dresses?'

Sister Margaret laughed. 'I design them all the time. We turn the old clothes donated to us into pretty frocks for little girls, for tired women, into shirts for boys and men. God gives us talents to use, not hide away.'

'Are you happy, Sister Margaret?'

'Yes,' said the woman who had been Violette. 'And you, my dear Sophie? The decades have brought you joy?'

Sophie considered. Yes, just sometimes there were nightmares, but Daniel comforted her, as the owls boomed and the possums growled outside, telling her that war was far away. Age brought loss, too, days when she'd think, Lily will laugh at that, or, I must tell Midge. But loss was the inevitable other side of love. As Dolphie said, so long ago, she had been so very rich in love. 'I have both joy and contentment,' she said at last. 'I was addicted to challenge for so long. The hard years in Europe cured me of that.'

'Grandma, Aunt Hanne's kangaroo has fallen into the jelly in the bathtub.'

Obviously even the Thuringa kitchen was not large enough to keep cool all the confections necessary for the wedding celebrations of a man named 'Jelly'. Was the jelly to eat, or to be mistaken for bath water? Not that it mattered ...

'Then take it out,' said Sophie mildly, as Daniel approached to lead her to the waltz.

~❦~

One could not leave a reception when one was hostess, even when one's feet ached and one was stifling yawns. So Sophie returned to her comfortable chair, where she could watch the guests. Even that would have constituted such a faux pas back in 1914, when a hostess must stay brightly smiling among the guests, despite her corset, her long gloves and half a ton of diamonds including a tiara.

But the guests were enjoying themselves, even the bride and groom, which was not always the case in the stress of weddings. Tomorrow Jelly would pilot his worryingly small plane towards France, for two weeks sampling the vintages, then Switzerland, where Jennifer could enjoy a honeymoon discussing the possibilities of crossing Simmental cattle with Herefords, and Jelly could indulge his passion for parachuting, gliding eagle-like above the Swiss valleys, which he would then paint in ways no one had imagined before. Sophie had never told her grandson that she, too, had balanced on the air. Sometimes grandmothers should discreetly minimise their adventures.

Tomorrow most of the family would drive back to Sydney, to work, to school, and, for her granddaughters, veterinary science for one, and the maths that had not been taught to women in Sophie's childhood for the other.

Sophie gazed at them, still dancing to this modern shaking, stamping music in a mob of others, all with boundless energy. They were so young, so beautiful, so confident, so determined to bring an end to racism, sexism and war. Sophie had marched with them in Vietnam moratoriums, and in the protests against the visit of the racist all-white South African Springbok football team, hoping the girls were more proud than embarrassed that their grandmother walked beside them, swan-like among the shaggy heads and jeans, impeccable in her knee-length green linen dress, straw sandals and wide-brimmed sun hat under her placard.

'Ah, my Sophie. You have found the perfect refuge.' Hannelore put her glass of Old Baldie's first attempt at champagne on the side table and took the chair next to her, sighing and putting her feet up on a stool. 'I did not know that nuns danced rock and roll, or whatever young people call their dances now. And Judith is dancing with her! You are crying, my Sophie.'

'Old age. All these splendid young women striding out into the world with no need of a man to carve their way.'

'You found your own way,' Hannelore pointed out, 'and so did I.'

'But we had Miss Lily. What would Miss Lily have thought of the world today? Young women in jeans marching in demonstrations, and old ones too, though we did not wear jeans ...'

'But the demonstrations took Australia out of the Vietnam War,' said Hannelore earnestly. 'They helped give us the new laws against discrimination because of race or sex or the colour of one's skin. I was afraid of marches at first,' she admitted. 'And Judith too. We remembered the Nuremberg rallies, the crowds screaming hatred. Yes, there was some anger on the marches — there is still much to be angry about. But the protestors wanted peace and tolerance, even if they had to yell to be heard.'

'You think Miss Lily would have been with us, carrying a banner?'

Hannelore nodded. 'She taught women how to change the world, even from the background where most women lived back then, but she gave us confidence to step out from those shadows too. The clothes, the charm, the elegance were only tools for us to use. Mostly, she taught us love.'

'And to love the whole of humankind, to build bridges instead of walls. But she would not have worn jeans.'

Hannelore considered. 'Perhaps, if the jeans were cut well. A miniskirt, certainly.'

Sophie gazed out at the dancers, so many of them her descendants, or the descendants of her friends. 'What would she say about the young women here?'

Hannelore laughed and shifted her feet more comfortably on her cushion. 'That they are strong and lovely ladies. That their lives are a banner for the right of everyone to be free and strong and lovely, too.'

But we prepared their path, thought Sophie. They think they invented it all, and that is how it should be, for pride in what they have achieved will take them further.

Yet their grandmothers and great-grandmothers and every generation of women before them were there at every major moment in history, though the books rarely record us. We were the women men did not see — or rather men did see us, then carefully did not remember what we'd done. You, who will not let a man open a door for you now, have forgotten us as well.

As Miss Lily had been deleted from any public record, except the memorial Daniel had carved for her, though Bob Green's heroism was remembered on a plaque in the Shillings village hall, as were Jones's and Greenie's. The women of SOE, those very public heroines of war, at least had their names engraved in stone: Violette Szabo, Yvonne Rudellat, Cecily Lefort, Denise Bloch, Lilian Rolfe and so many others, though the memory of women's roles in earlier wars had quickly faded; and nor had the more complex roles women had played in World War II, from breaking enemy codes to running espionage networks, yet been added to the history books. Word of mouth alone was a slippery memorial. So many, so much lost ...

'Someone should write Lily's story,' said Sophie suddenly. 'Lily's life tells so much about how we women saw ourselves change. If we don't write our stories they're forgotten. Maybe each generation will find different parts of them important. But how will they understand their past if they don't hear its voices?'

She remembered Rose's and Danny's serious faces as they absorbed the truth about their father. To her relief they had not blamed her or Daniel for not telling them earlier, nor even for the complications of their heritage. It had, it seemed, answered questions they'd not known how to ask.

Jelly's reaction decades later had simply been a grin and 'Cool!' Then he'd grown thoughtful. The result had been his three paintings in the Thuringa drawing room, based on blurred old black-and-white photos that had Lily or Bob in the background (both had tried to avoid photographers), and the tinted photo taken of Nigel and Sophie on their wedding day. Outside observers saw three faces. Those who knew saw the identical smile of love.

Sophie came back to the present to see anxiety shadowing Hannelore's expression. 'You will write your memoirs, Sophie?'

Dachau and your factories, thought Sophie. Assassinations in war-time Paris, the twisted threads of Dolphie, remembered also now with a cross Daniel had carved for him, for a man who tried to kill a monster. Ancient shadows holding daggers ...

'It would be fiction,' Sophie reassured her. 'Stories that hurt no one, but commemorate the path-makers.'

'Ah, fiction.' Hannelore smiled and lifted her glass of Old Baldie champagne, a wattle blossom floating on its surface. Behind them the kangaroo bounded towards one of the white damasked tables, perhaps hoping for more jelly. 'Miss Lily would approve.'

Author's Note

It's customary to say that a book is not based on any real person, alive or dead. On the contrary, everyone and every incident in this book is based on people who existed and on real events, either true or compilations. Some, like the horrific suicides on the day Okinawa was invaded, have been left to fade from history. I've had to keep putting notes next to the editors' queries in the margins in this book, and all the others in the Miss Lily series, saying: 'This happened.' 'This happened.' 'This happened.'

Authors are often asked where they get their ideas. My books are mostly accidents. In a wide-ranging life I have met many and varied people, from European royalty and prisoners of war to the last of the '30s swagmen. I listen to their stories, research the times and places they spoke of, remember the wisdom that they offer: a well-made wool cloak or leather lederhosen should last for generations; only royalty or women over sixty should wear diamonds before dark; always store ermine in linen bags; hang a wombat for three days before you cook it; you can pass off rat as chicken if you remove the bones. (I have not always needed or taken their advice.)

Legends of the Lost Lilies is the fifth and last of the Miss Lily series of novels. The series shows how women's views of themselves changed and widened over the twentieth century. It is also about the women men did not see, or rather, did see, but then for a multitude of reasons omitted from history.

The vast contributions of women in World War I have been reduced in the telling to the relatively small role of official army or Red Cross nurses. The congregations of women working in everything from espionage to code breaking to factory management in World War II have become a few dramatic stories of the SOE women who were sent to aid the French Resistance, movies about code breakers at Bletchley and posters of Rosie the Riveter. There is no room in this book — or these notes — to even begin to list the achievements of women in other fields and other countries, but they will be the subject of other books. Once you begin to look for women in the major events of history, you find them.

The ineptitude, negligence, stupidity and sometimes fascist sympathies of British Intelligence in World War II as portrayed in this book have been kept secret partly because that intelligence work continued into the Cold War with the Soviet Union, but also from embarrassment, until pressure from those who wanted the stories told meant that from about 2000 onwards slowly information emerged. Luckily for the Allies their enemies' intelligence services were as incompetent, and, in Germany and Japan, those who were competent either not listened to or forced into silence lest their warnings be treated as treason.

From 1942 onwards, in desperation, many small intelligence, technical and strategic groups were set up across Britain, some useful, some seriously inept, including one comprised of writers of fiction like Graham Greene, though the only reference I have found to it merely describes it producing three extremely useful ideas, among perhaps a hundred others that would have been disastrous. Information about many of those groups is either still classified, or no one bothered to keep the records. The latter is most likely. The war-time operation at Shillings is not based on any specific agency I know of, but as its agents were trained to be embedded for long periods, their roles would not be made public. We see aspects of World War II described in books, TV shows or movies, fiction or non-fiction, but all necessarily simplified. The war was complex, as was every person affected by it. We can aim to tell the truth, but 'the whole truth' is never possible, and, as Sophie says, perhaps each generation needs to take the stories it needs from the vast complexity of the past.

The many attempts to assassinate Hitler are true — there were others not mentioned in this book — as are his seemingly miraculous escapes from what were well-planned plots by men who knew explosives and how to use them. Dolphie is a composite from a time when anti-Semitism and even Eugenics — the belief that only the 'best' of humanity should breed — were common across Europe, including in Britain, and that early fascism attracted people of genuine goodwill, especially those in the military, including my great-grandfather, a man of intelligence, compassion and integrity who was certainly not anti-Semitic, although a member of Australia's National Guard. Nor was he a fascist for long.

The sub-camp of Dachau is not based on any of those that I know existed, but the work, conditions and solidarity, courage and sabotage of the women at some of those satellites have been documented. In at least one, the women even went on strike for better conditions — and won them.

The Holocaust is not one story, nor even forty-four million stories — roughly the number of people directly murdered by the Nazi regime, not counting those lost to warfare — but many more, for it must include the stories of the survivors too, and the friends and loved ones or even students and neighbours of those who died and survived, as well as the guards and the guards' families, anyone and everyone connected through the generations to those years.

The experiences at sub-camps of Dachau, or where concentration camp prisoners were assigned to factory work either during the day or as live-in workers, seems to be particularly varied, depending on who or what the prisoners were assigned to. The first workers assigned to Hannelore's (fictional) factories would have been dissidents who campaigned against the Nazi regime, or who were seen as enemies of the nation for one of many reasons at the time.

The routines of Dachau also varied as the war progressed. This book is set towards the end of its existence as a Nazi concentration camp, when there had been changes, as well as far more exceptions to routine. As the Allied forces drew closer, the German armed forces were in increasingly desperate need of as many men as possible, and the long-term rulers of the camps were scared about what might happen to them when American or Russian forces liberated the camps and sub-camps, and so attempted to kill as many of the survivors as possible, as well as destroying records and burning anything incriminating.

This is where I stop attempting to explain the research behind the books, and instead thank those who have been such a deep part of the creation of this series. I have no idea even where to begin. The prison camp survivor father of a friend when I was three years old? I remember his stories, and those of people impossible to count, from my early violin teacher, an Auschwitz survivor, to Gillian Pauli, who, as my English teacher, brought me books to help me find the answer to 'why' the Holocaust happened, to my friend Olga Horek, to whom I owe so much, not just for her own story of survival and courage, but for her lessons in how to live — and live well — after tragedy.

The Miss Lily series began, however, with the ever-wonderful Lisa Berryman, Cristina Cappelluto and Shona Martyn of HarperCollins, who encouraged me to turn the first draft of a far more explicit book into five books that focused and enlarged on that book's themes. Lisa has continued to be the brilliant and (almost) omniscient guide, critic, and co-creator of each book that has followed. Without her, this series and many others of my books, would not be written; nor, probably, would I have realised that I am still only beginning to learn my craft as a writer. Lisa never lets me write any book that is less than I am able. But, like Miss Lily, Lisa does that task so tactfully and with such charm that you hardly realise the iron hand that taps out the editorial emails. (NB Lisa's only other resemblances to Miss Lily are her grace, elegance, impeccable and generous dress sense, and her ability to enthral a room simply by walking into it.)

Kate O'Donnell has edited every book with genius and passion, questioning my ideas at times, and at least half the time convincing me. She too, won't let me get away with a sloppy chacterisation, and nor would Eve Tonelli, who has added so much to many books, rounding up the Miss Lily proofs and corrections with editorial sheep-dog tenacity and endless patience — or at least never letting impatience with illegible corrections and tardy replies show. As has Angela Marshall, who turns the dyslexic mess I send her into not just readable but historically accurate text, adding the knowledge of ships, horses, mathematics, the Georgian prison system, colonial shipping and much else, as well as the French and German languages I've mostly forgotten. (I am not sure I ever knew how to spell them.)

Without Angela's formidable help, both personal and professional, almost from the first books I wrote, my career as a writer simply wouldn't be. Back when *Rain Stones* was first published there was no 'spell check'; nor is there anyone else I know whose knowledge is as eclectic and passionate as my own, and in much the same areas, but thankfully, not quite overlapping, so Angela's widely varied expertise appears in all these books too.

Errors, of course, are mine, and there will be errors, even if no one ever finds out what they are, as so much of what must be added to make a complete story is what might have been, not what was written down, or what has still not been released from archives. This is why these books are fiction, even if all are based on real events, hidden at the time and for decades after. I don't want to write 'he said' 'she said' for real people, unless I am sure that is what they said, in exactly those circumstances, and why. Non-fiction also needs to cover times where the events might have been dangerous, but at the same time were repetitious and boring. Fiction has the freedom to be fascinating.

I hope Miss Lily would approve.

THE WAR IS OVER, BUT CAN THERE EVER TRULY BE PEACE?

BOOK 2

Australian heiress Sophie Higgs was 'a rose of no-man's land', founding hospitals across war-torn Europe during the horror that was WWI.

Now, in the 1920s, Sophie's war-time work must be erased so that the men who returned can find some kind of 'normality'.

Sophie is, however, a graduate of the mysterious Miss Lily's school of charm and intrigue, and once more she risks her own life as she attempts to save others still trapped in the turmoil and aftermath of war.

But in this new world, nothing is clear, in politics or in love. For the role of men has changed too. Torn between the love of three very different men, Sophie will face her greatest danger yet as she attempts an impossible journey across the world to save Nigel, Earl of Shillings — and her beloved Miss Lily.

In this sequel to the bestselling *Miss Lily's Lovely Ladies*, Jackie French draws us further into a compelling story that celebrates the passion and adventure of an unstoppable army of women who changed the world.

'If you've sped your way through *The Crown* and are looking for another historical drama fix to sink your teeth into, *The Lily and the Rose* is going to fast become your next obsession.'

New Idea

UNIMAGINABLE DANGER CREEPS EVER CLOSER TO MISS LILY AND HER LOVED ONES ...

BOOK 3

Amid the decadence and instability of Berlin in the 1920s, a band of women must unite to save all that is precious to them.

With her dangerous past behind her, Australian heiress Sophie Higgs lives in quiet comfort as the new Countess of Shillings, until Hannelore, Princess of Arneburg, charms the Prince of Wales. He orders Sophie, Nigel — and Miss Lily — to investigate the mysterious politician Hannelore insists is the only man who can save Europe from another devastating war.

His name is Adolf Hitler.

As unimaginable peril threatens to destroy countries and tear families apart, Sophie must face Goering's Brownshirt Nazi thugs, blackmail, and the many possible faces of love.

And then the man she once adored and thought was lost reappears, and Sophie must also confront a vengeful girl, intent on killing the woman she believes is her mother: Miss Lily.

The third book in the Miss Lily series, *The Lily in the Snow* is a story filled with secrets that also explores the strength of friendship and the changing face of women in this new Europe.

'With lots to say about women, relationships and power,
The Lily in the Snow is all you could want in a book — smart,
thought-provoking and endlessly engaging.'
Better Reading

AS THE KING OF ENGLAND WAVERS BETWEEN DUTY AND LOVE, SOPHIE MUST CHOOSE DUTY ...

BOOK 4

The year is 1936 and the new King Edward VIII wishes to marry American divorcee, and suspected German agent, Wallis Simpson. Top-secret documents that the king must read and sign are being neglected for weeks, and some are even turning up in Berlin.

And as Germany grows its military might with many thousands of new fighter planes every year, Britain and its empire are under increasing threat.

Can Miss Lily's most successful protege, Sophie Vaile, the Countess of Shillings, seduce the new king, prevent his marriage to Wallis Simpson, and turn him from fascism?

And if a man can sacrifice his life for his country, should a woman hesitate to sacrifice her honour?

Based on new correspondence found in German archives, *Lilies, Love and Lies* is a work of fiction.

Or *is it*?

In the fourth title in the Miss Lily series, Jackie French explores one of the most controversial events in history that saw the unthinkable happen when a king chose love over duty.

'If you want a different take on the story of King Edward VIII and Wallis Simpson, then this is a must read ...'

Better Reading

Jackie French AM is an award-winning writer, wombat negotiator, the 2014–2015 Australian Children's Laureate and the 2015 Senior Australian of the Year. In 2016, Jackie became a Member of the Order of Australia for her contribution to children's literature and her advocacy for youth literacy. She is regarded as one of Australia's most popular authors and writes across all genres — from picture books, history, fantasy, ecology and sci-fi to her much loved historical fiction for many different age groups. 'A book can change a child's life. A book can change the world' was the primary philosophy behind Jackie's two-year term as Laureate.

jackiefrench.com
facebook.com/authorjackiefrench